SHADOWS OF MAGIC

SARAH MCCARTHY

Cover design by James T. Egan, www.bookflydesign.com

Map illustration by Tiffany Munro.

CALEDONIA

CHAPTER 1

*I*t was Finn's sixteenth birthday, and both he and his parents were pretending it wasn't. Finn's mother avoided his eyes all morning, and just as he was leaving for school, she pressed something into his hand, closing his fingers around it and turning away. Finn looked down and saw a rough wooden carving of a crescent moon. A ward against magic.

Magic was rare, but a few months ago one of Finn's classmates had turned sixteen and become a wind mage. He'd tried to stop himself, but wherever he went he gathered all the air in the room to himself. He'd suffocated his baby brother. The town council got involved, brought him in for re-education, branded him with the crescent moon, but it didn't help, and in the end, he was grateful when they executed him.

Finn doubted the talisman would help him; it was just a superstition. Probably, most people stopped what they were doing, at least for a while, if you branded them. He doubted they cared whether it was a moon, specifically, but he tucked it into his pocket anyway.

Finn barely noticed what happened in school that day, which was a rarity for him, and when he got home for dinner, he was surprised that both his parents were there.

His father was occupied with fixing a rabbit trap, and didn't look up when he came in, but his mother turned immediately, her face tense and white, and a hand shaking. She didn't say anything, but Finn could see the question in her face. He shook his head. She relaxed visibly and smiled.

"Dinner will be ready soon, will you get Kel? I think she's out in the garden."

Finn found his six-year-old sister Kel sitting happily in the garden, completely covered in dirt. Her long, light brown hair was tangled and full of leaves and grass. She was holding a tomato up to her small nose, her usually warm brown eyes closed as she inhaled deeply. He laughed, brushed her off, and picked some of the bugs and grass out of her hair, as she told him about the tomato, and the worm that lived inside it.

When they went inside, his father had cleared the table, and together the four of them set out dishes and candles.

When they were all seated, his father spoke. "To Finn," he said, raising his wooden mug and smiling at Finn over the cluster of mismatched candles in the center of the table. He had the same black hair and bright blue eyes as Finn, but where Finn was skinny, with long arms and legs, his father had thick muscles and calloused hands.

"Yes, happy birthday, dear," his mother said, lifting her mug.

Kel was examining a beetle as it trundled across their bare pine table.

Mugs clunked heavily down as his mother. served out portions of roasted deer meat—killed by his father the day before. Finn hadn't caught anything, but not for lack of trying. He was just terrible at hunting.

There was silence as everyone except Kel chewed. Kel was

busy building a house for the beetle with her spoon and some leaves that had been left in her hair.

The deer meat took a lot of chewing, but no one commented on this.

"So," his father said at last, "Given any more thought to where you might apprentice?"

Finn's stomach constricted into a hard lump around the meat. He had given it some thought, of course, but there was no answer he liked, because every answer meant leaving school, the one thing he was good at. He had what his father called "book arms", and they didn't seem to be useful for much.

Finn mumbled something about maybe working at the tanner's.

"Well, let me know soon so I can arrange it," his father said.

WHEN HE'D EATEN ENOUGH to be polite—and to feel slightly sick—Finn excused himself to go read in his room. His stomach was now starting to burn, and Finn wished he'd eaten less, or nothing. He brought a mug of water with him, hoping that would help calm his stomach.

Finn picked up one of the books he'd borrowed from his teacher, stretched out on his bed, and tried to read. He was alone in the room, which was dark except for the light from the small oil lamp. Usually he went to the library to read. Lamp oil was expensive, and they used it only sparingly. On most nights, once the sun had gone down, the only light in the small cabin was firelight, and the only thing to do was sleep. Tonight was a special occasion, but still Finn expected that any minute now his father would see the light under the door, swoop in, and tell him to blow it out.

Only a few miles away, in the ruins of Old Cromwic,

where almost no one went anymore, lights blazed endlessly, needing no oil or cleaning. Finn hadn't been back there in a while, not since he and his best—and only—friend, Ronan had stopped talking. It was just as well because it was hard keeping his parents from finding out.

A loud giggle from Kel, still in the kitchen with their mother, distracted Finn from his thoughts. A low, answering laugh from their mother, and then the steady murmur as she went on with whatever story she was telling. He stared out the window into the darkened night for a moment. Realizing his chest was getting more and more uncomfortable, he reached for his clay mug, but it was empty.

He went back to his book, tried to focus on what he was reading, but the heat kept getting worse. Finn's whole chest was burning now, as if he'd eaten a hot coal. He'd read the same sentence at least three times now and hadn't understood a word.

Shaking himself, Finn took a deep, slow breath. That seemed to help. It was probably nothing.

Sitting up, he swung his legs over the edge of the bed and focused again on what he was reading. But now the words were swimming in front of his eyes. He blinked a few times, tried to bring them back into focus. That was when the words started to boil. The ink bubbled up off the page, rising in little tendrils of smoke.

Finn jumped to his feet, dropping the book, taking another deep breath and running his hands through his hair. His chest was filled with fire now; it burned through him, extending out into his arms, all the way to his fingertips.

Then, as quickly as it had come, the heat faded. His hands and arms cooled, then his chest, until there was only a single warm ember sitting in his stomach.

Okay. Okay. This is fine. Fine. Maybe I imagined that. Finn needed to get out of the house.

He walked out of the cabin as calmly as he could, calling over his shoulder that he was going for a walk, and leaving before his parents could ask any questions. Then he strode up the dirt track towards the village, breathing in the frigid air.

It was a clear night, and the moon was nearly full, so bright it cast silver shadows through the trees. For a few minutes, Finn walked quickly, his breath rising in great steaming clouds. His relief at no longer feeling like he was on fire was soon replaced by the realization that he was freezing, having walked out without a cloak. He was also alone in the dark woods.

Something rustled behind him, and Finn froze, standing utterly still, except for the uncontrollable shivering that had started. He clenched his jaw to keep his teeth from chattering. The sound came again. Finn didn't want to turn around, didn't want to see the bear or mountain lion or snake or whatever it was before it killed him. No. That was dumb. There wasn't anything there. He was fine. A twig cracked.

Finn spun around; for a moment, he thought he saw something, a dark shadow rising towards him. Then, a jet of flame shot up from the ground, momentarily blinding him. He stumbled backwards, in fear and in pain from the sudden heat. An intense blaze roared and crackled, and when Finn's eyes adjusted he saw a small bird, a tiny owl lying dead on the ground, its feathers burned. A small tree was also burning, the flames licking up its trunk and consuming dead leaves and branches.

Finn turned and looked all around him, but the forest was silent. No one was there. He waited, but no other sounds came.

That wasn't me. But the thought had the hollow ring of desperation to it. Slowly, filled with dread, Finn picked up a dry branch from the ground. He lifted it, held it before his eyes. An anxious heat rose from his chest, and instantly the branch caught fire. Finn dropped it, stomped it out with his boot. *No. How did this happen? I don't want this.*

Panic started to rise up, but with it came the heat that had started those two fires. Finn wasn't going to do that again. It didn't matter. Whatever was happening to him, Finn still had a choice. He wasn't a mage if he didn't use magic. But a little part of him wondered if he had done something to cause this. Had he accidentally made this happen? He'd never consciously asked for this. He hated magic. Magic had destroyed the world he loved, a place where he could have fit in, that much he knew was true. He'd read about magic, though. He'd just wanted to learn about the world before the Fall, been curious about what it was like. Had that caused this somehow? He didn't think so, but it was the only thing he could think of.

Finn was shivering again. He crouched down, wrapping his arms around his knees. It was okay. It was an accident. He hadn't meant to do magic, and now that he knew what it felt like he wouldn't do it again.

FOR A FEW WEEKS, Finn managed to mostly ignore the magic. He could feel it burning in his chest, and every time he felt angry or anxious it threatened to escape, to burn something around him. He tried to stay calm. He found that when he felt nothing the magic slumbered, still there, but only quietly so.

He did what he always did with problems, and went to the library. He scoured every book he could find for references to magic, trying to find a way to get rid of it. But there wasn't much. If there had ever been books on magic, they weren't there anymore. He found a couple mentions of copper, supposedly a strong ward against magic, like the crescent moon, and he tried carrying lumps of it around with him, but it didn't have any effect.

Finn lost weight, stopped sleeping, and started failing evaluations. Not just missing questions, but missing all the questions. This was a new experience for him. On the plus side, his fellow classmates seemed to feel that their bullying was no longer required now that he wasn't acing everything, and they stopped spitting on his work. He spent all his time either researching in the library or walking through the forest with Kel. There Finn felt a small amount of relief, letting himself get lost in Kel's world a little. It let him forget the fire that was burning inside him.

He thought about trying to find Ronan and talk to him about it, but he knew what Ronan would say, and it wouldn't help.

His parents noticed the change in him, but neither realized what had happened. Each tried to help in their own way. His mother started searching his room when he wasn't there, and his father started taking Finn into the woods with him after class and on weekends. This meant Finn had less time to study—not that he was getting much reading done anyway, what with all the focus it took to keep from vaporizing the ink.

IT HAPPENED AT DINNER. Finn had spent all day out with his father, stomping around in the forest, trampling plants, tripping over things, and murdering small animals. Finn had brushed himself as clean as he could before coming inside, but damp, gritty mud had found its way everywhere—into his hair, his ears, and even his under garments. At least the food was hot. A numb cold had stiffened his hands and his toes were icy.

The atmosphere in the room was also icy. No one spoke, they all just focused on their food. Finn assumed it had something to do with him.

"So..." he turned to his mother, trying to break the silence. "How was your day?"

She set down her wooden fork and pushed a strand of hair back from her face. Finn realized she looked tired. She forced a smile. "Fine." Her eyes darted to his father, then back down to her food.

Finn's father set his own fork down, not looking at her, or at Kel. Kel didn't notice, though; she was pushing her food around, making it into a tiny city.

"Finn, tomorrow I think we should go up to the higher elevations. Set some traps up there. What do you think?"

Finn glanced at his mother, but she was looking back down at her plate again. Why was his father ignoring his mother? Had they had a fight about him? Guilt and shame welled up in his chest. He'd been trying so hard to keep this to himself, to not let it affect them.

"I—I'm sorry I—" Finn started an apology, but then realized he didn't have a reason for it. He couldn't tell them about the magic. Maybe he could make something up about the bullying bothering him. Except the bullying had stopped now. He realized he'd stopped talking and both his father and his mother were staring at him now. Kel was humming to herself. Finn was still trying to think of what to say, could feel himself blushing now, when the fork he was holding in his hand caught fire.

His father's jaw dropped open, then his face contorted into rage, but it wasn't directed at Finn, it was directed at his mother. She paled, then turned to his father, shaking her head. "No, Alan, it's not—"

But his father shot to his feet, knocking his chair over backwards as he did so, and nearly knocking the table over, too. The beer jug tipped over and spread foaming, yeasty liquid across the table. Finn surreptitiously doused the fork in it. Kel had finally been jostled out of her obliviousness, and was staring up at their parents in fear.

"Just the one time, was it?" Finn's father yelled, his face dark with rage. He took a step towards Finn's mother, then grabbed a bookshelf instead, yanking it and tipping it over, the books and trinkets in it scattering and smashing to the ground. Finn's heart started to pound. He had never seen his father this angry before, had never even seen him raise his voice. His mother sat frozen in her chair.

"Dad?" Finn said, but that was not the right thing to say, apparently. His father turned towards him, gripped the edge of the table, and lifted it, so that the food and plates and bowls and glasses slid off, tumbling and crashing to the ground. Some of it landed in Finn's lap. Kel screamed, and their father looked at her with hatred. This shot a bolt of ice deep into Finn's heart. He didn't understand how anyone could look at Kel that way.

His father was breathing heavily, looking furiously from Kel to Finn to their mother. Then he seemed to come to a decision and took a step towards their mother, his face red with rage.

Terror gripped Finn. He had to stop this, but he didn't know how. He only had an instant to decide. That's when he lost control.

CHAPTER 2

Three days later, Kel sat on the ground, her back leaning against the rough trunk of a tree, and watched the sky through the gaps in the leaves. There were birds up there, singing to each other. And a squirrel, curled up in a cozy hole, resting an injured paw. A vine across the clearing from her was slowly choking to death the tree on which it climbed. Kel wanted to tell it to stop, that it was hurting the tree, and that if it killed the tree then the vine, too, would fall to the darkness of the forest floor. But she didn't think the vine would listen.

Her vision swam and she blinked to clear it. Her stomach was a gnawing void. She couldn't remember the last time she'd eaten, or why she was here in the forest, but she'd been told to wait. She remembered that much.

A twig snapped, and heavy footfalls reached Kel's ears. She flattened herself against the trunk of the tree, her heart pounding in her chest. The footsteps came closer, and a tall figure with dark, shining hair pushed a branch aside and stumbled into the clearing.

Finn.

Tears of relief poured from Kel's eyes and she bit her lip. She wanted to run to her brother, wrap her arms around his knees and sob, beg him never to leave her again. But something in his expression stopped her, some thought she couldn't quite remember kept her rooted to the spot. Instead, she stood up, pressing her hand against the warm bark of the tree. She straightened her small shoulders and waited.

Finn dropped the package he was carrying, and eased himself to the ground. His black hair was greasy and unkempt. He smelled like smoke, and there were thick burns on his arms. Soot was smeared across his face, and there were dark circles under his bright blue eyes.

He glanced up, saw Kel watching him, and immediately pushed himself back up, crossed the clearing, and wrapped his arms around her in a tight hug.

"Are you okay? I wasn't gone too long, was I?"

The smell of smoke was even stronger now. "It's okay, I'm okay."

He leaned back so he could look at her, and his blue eyes were full of concern. "I'm really sorry, I just had to get us some food."

She tried to smile, but tears welled up. "It's okay, Finn."

"You hungry?"

She nodded.

"Me, too. Could you get us some wood?"

She wiped the back of her hand across her face and nodded again. "Okay."

"Great, you just do that and when you get back I'll have this ready."

"Okay."

Finn gave her another tight hug, and then she turned to go.

"Stay close, okay?" he called after her.

She turned back, nodded, then hurried away.

Her relief that Finn was back mingled with a new, tense anxiety, but as she walked farther away into the trees it lessened. A ladybug landed on her shoulder, trundling through the blue wool fibers, looking for the sweet, green, wriggling, crunchy things it liked. After a while, when it didn't find any, it flitted away again.

Kel examined the ground as she walked, pushing aside leaves, looking for empty twigs. That was how she thought of them. There were some that were empty. It was okay if Finn burned those. Finn seemed to like them better, too, which was good, because Kel couldn't have brought him wood that still had... tree... in it.

When her arms were so full of sticks that she couldn't pick up any more without dropping some, she made her way back, hardly noticing as the armload of sharp, dry twigs scratched at her arms and face.

Finn sat with one knee angled up, an elbow thrown across it, and the other leg curled under him. His stare was fixed on something on the ground.

"Here, Finn!" The sticks tumbled out of her arms.

"Oh, great, thanks." He picked a few sticks from the jumble and cleared a space for them on the floor of the clearing. He glanced at Kel, who was watching him closely. He ran a hand through his dark hair.

"Um, Kel, could you go get some more? I think we'll need a lot. Maybe go get another big armload?"

"Oh, sure, okay," she said. The thought of a campfire set her heart thumping uneasily, but she wasn't sure why.

She started off, but then, after she'd gone only a short way, she realized she'd left her cloak back with Finn, and it was starting to get cold. She turned back, walking with her small, silent feet.

Finn was in the center of the clearing, crouched over the

small pile of twigs, his hand extended out over them. His face was twisted with anger and shame.

Below Finn's hand there came a hot little explosion and the twigs caught fire. Finn held his hand in the flames a moment, looking at it with contempt, then pulled it out with a cry of pain. The skin was red and smoking slightly. Kel's eyes widened. Finn looked up to see her still standing there and tried to hide his burned hand behind his leg.

"Please go get wood, Kel," Finn said, his voice strained.

"Sorry, I'm sorry..."

"Go!" Finn screamed at her.

Kel turned and ran, forgetting her cloak.

She stayed away for a long time. By then the light was growing dim under the trees, and she was stiff with cold. Above, the sky was pale blue, fading to a dark, bruised purple, and in the forest, everything was in shadow.

When Kel came back to the clearing, the fire was large and warm. The package lay open on the ground; a loaf of bread and some cheese lay on it, and a small pheasant was spitted and roasting over the flames.

Kel inched as close to the heat as she could and watched the fat run down the sides of the bird and drip, hissing, into the fire. Neither of them said anything or looked at the other for a long time.

Eventually, Kel tore her gaze from the roasting meat, her eyes darting towards Finn, and she noticed that tears were trickling down her brother's cheeks. She rushed over to him, and with her small hands she began to wipe away the tears.

"What's wrong, Finn?"

Finn placed his hand gently on Kel's head, stroked her hair.

"Nothing, Kel. I'm sorry. I'm fine. That bird's about done. You hungry?"

"I'm okay," Kel said.

"Here, start with this." He broke off a large chunk of bread and handed it to Kel. "You know what, we could even toast it." He took the bread back, speared it on a branch and held it out over the flames. It slowly warmed, the edges browning. Then Finn took some cheese, balanced it on the flattest part of the bread, held it out over the fire longer. The edges melted a little, although most of it was still solid. The bread was starting to burn, though, so Finn took the whole thing out of the fire and handed it to Kel.

"Be careful, it's hot."

Kel took the scorched bread in her hands. She picked off a little piece of it and used it to scrape up a bit of molten cheese. The bread was warm and crispy, and the cheese felt smooth and full in her mouth.

Finn sat and toasted more bread for Kel until the bird was cooked, and then he pried off pieces of burning-hot meat to give to her. Finally, when he saw that Kel was slowing down, he took a few pieces for himself.

They sat together, not talking, until Kel fell asleep. Then Finn draped a blanket over her and lay on his back, staring up into the dark until eventually he fell asleep, too.

THAT NIGHT KEL dreamt she was walking down a stone path, through the white trunks of birch trees, their bright green leaves rustling around her. Something up ahead was calling to her, but if it was a voice, she couldn't quite make out the words. She awoke feeling wistful, with a curious ache in her chest.

They walked for a few hours, then Finn told Kel to wait for him and went off alone into the forest. So Kel sat and waited again. She curled up against a tree trunk and played with bits of grass, running her fingers gently over their tops, bending but never breaking them. She waited all day, but Finn never came back.

That night Kel was cold. She could hear noises in the dark, saw the glowing eyes of the night animals watching her. A small family of mice curled up with her. They didn't give off much warmth, but Kel could feel their little hearts thrumming in their chests, and it was good to at least have the company of living things. In the morning, they were gone, and Kel was alone again.

All that day she sat completely still, but Finn didn't come back.

The next night, feeling even more alone, she hugged her knees up into her chest and cried with fear. A bear heard her. It came and sniffed her curiously, then heaved down next to her. Its fur was thick and coarse and matted and smelled like dirt and musk, but Kel leaned up against it, curled up between its large paws, and slept, dreaming of the path through the birch trees.

The next morning, Kel awoke to find Finn sitting there, with a warm fire blazing, making breakfast. Eggs and bacon and piles of fruit. Kel ate ravenously.

"I'm sorry, Kel," Finn said at last, not meeting her eyes.

"Where are we going?" She asked, too afraid to ask where he'd been.

Finn poked at the fire with a twig and didn't say anything. Kel waited for a while and then tried again.

"When are we going home?"

Finn stopped prodding the fire. He looked up, and again Kel saw tears in his red-rimmed eyes. "We can't go home, Kel. Don't you remember?"

"Why can't we go home?"

Finn stared at her expressionlessly for a moment. Then he looked away.

"I need to go away for a while, to get you some things. But I'll find you a place to stay before I go."

"Where? Where do you need to go, Finn?"

"Just… it's just for a little while. I'll be back. I promise."

Kel swallowed hard. Tears were streaming down her face, but she wiped them away, hoping Finn didn't see. If he didn't see, maybe he would stay. If Kel were only bigger, or stronger, maybe Finn would take her with him. Kel could help, wherever Finn was going and whatever it was he was doing. If Kel were just a little bigger she knew she could help. She didn't want to be alone again.

Kel didn't say any of this to Finn. She helped him pack up the parcels of food and stack them with the others he had brought. When they were ready to go, she piled as many as she could in her small arms and trailed after him.

They walked for a while, and then Finn stopped at a fallen log. The log was as thick as Kel was tall, and the middle had rotted away, making a hollow space. It was filled with dead leaves, but Finn scraped these out with his hands. Then he carried more logs over and leaned them against the opening, making a little sheltered room inside. He crawled in, calling for Kel to follow him.

Kel crawled into the dim space. The wood was damp and soft under her palms. She could feel beetles working their way through the rotten wood, chewing it up, making little tunnels.

Finn had spread the packages out against one edge and was opening them. He pulled a thick wool blanket out of one, which he spread at the back end of the log. He opened more packages. Most had food, which he stacked toward the front. Some had warm clothes, and the last had a glass ball. Inside, tiny red and yellow flames danced.

Finn took it out carefully and handed it to Kel, who took it reverently.

"Here. This will burn for a long time. Be careful with it."

Kel cupped the ball in both hands. She could feel the warmth of the fire through the glass.

"I may be gone for a little while, but I'll come back. I promise. Just stay here and wait for me. Do you promise you'll stay here?"

Kel looked up. "Where are you going?"

"It doesn't matter. I'm not sure. I'll be back."

"Will you come back with mother and father?" Kel asked.

A darkness came into Finn's face. "Stop it, Kel. You know they're dead."

Kel sucked in a breath, fighting back a sob.

Finn reached out and gently held her. "I'm sorry, Kel. I'm sorry I said that. It's okay. It'll be okay." Finn was sobbing now, too. Great, racking sobs. And this was too much. Kel couldn't take hearing her brother cry. If he was crying, the world must be ending. She struggled, tried to get free of Finn's arms, to look at his face, to make him look at her, to make him stop crying.

Finn let go of her, dropped to his knees and bowed his head to the floor, still sobbing. Kel crawled out of the log and ran. She ran and ran, into the woods, until she couldn't hear Finn's hopelessness anymore.

She sat cross-legged on the ground and waited, listening, her breath coming in great, ragged gasps, but it slowed eventually. And then she was calm, and she was just waiting again. Waiting for Finn to find her. Finn would find her. He would comfort her. Everything would be okay.

Kel waited a long time, until it started getting dark, and no one came. Finally, she decided she had to go back. Maybe Finn needed help making dinner. Finn would need wood. She would gather wood and bring it back to Finn and everything would be all right.

Kel gathered the largest armful of wood she could, and

stumbled back in the direction of the log. When she got there, all was quiet. No sobs, no crying, no anger. No Finn. The place was still and quiet. The little glass globe was there, sitting on the ground in front of the log, a note next to it. Kel dropped her wood to the ground, took the glowing ball, held it in her hands, and sat and cried next to the cold, dead twigs.

She picked up the note, read it through her tears. Finn had started teaching her to read a few months ago. She couldn't make out all the words, but she understood that Finn said he would come back soon. There was also some warning about the food. Kel looked up and saw the food bag hanging from a tree branch.

Starving, Kel took the bag down and brought it into the shelter with her. The sunlight was fading quickly under the trees, and the dark thickened, bringing with it the chill of night.

The ball was sealed, so Kel had no way to light a fire. She ate more of the food than she needed, put on all the extra clothes Finn had brought her, wrapped herself in the blanket, and curled up around the globe, staring into the flames until she fell asleep.

In the middle of the night, Kel awoke. Something was there with her. Something large and snuffling. Something that would leave her alone if she didn't bother it, but if she tried to stop it, it would hurt her.

Why would she want to stop it?

Because it was eating all her food. Kel had forgotten to hang it back up in the tree.

THAT NIGHT, Finn, having no idea where he was, lay on his back on the ground in a random place in the forest. Shame and guilt tore at him. He shouldn't have left Kel alone like that. But being around her was almost unbearable. His sister still cared about him, obviously, and Finn didn't deserve that.

Finn wanted to hide, to run away to someplace he knew he couldn't hurt anyone ever again. But he also wanted more than anything to protect Kel, to make up for what he had done. He had no idea how that was going to work. But, clearly, ignoring magic had not been the right choice. Ronan had been right about that all along. Finn wished he could go back, change what had happened, apologize to his best friend.

Finn felt the cold seeping into his body. He welcomed it, wished that he could just let himself drift off into it, the last of the heat leaving his body forever, but eventually he conjured himself a tiny fire. No. He had to live. For Kel.

As he lay there next to his small fire, his mind drifted back to before all this had happened, before he'd learned what he was.

"I'M TELLING YOU, this is one of the old wind-runners," Ronan said, his hands on his hips, surveying the device. They were standing at the top of a tower in the ruins of Old Cromwic, a place they almost always had all to themselves.

The city had been abandoned almost a hundred years ago, but water still flowed through hidden pipes, and weird, ever-burning flames still illuminated the rooms from glass sconces. It had been hewn straight from the cliffs of a craggy mountain; buildings and streets leaned out over sheer, hundred-foot drops. For thousands of years it had stood, a glorious testament to the power of magic. Until the Fall.

Magic had been dangerous even before that. Finn had read the accounts of mages who, unable to control their powers, had destroyed villages with earthquakes, or washed away fields and livestock with floods. Many were driven mad, either by what they had done, or by the magic itself.

Finn knew it was dangerous to come here, but he couldn't help himself. Here, the golden age of Caledonia had been preserved, and he could imagine the High Council, see the impossibly grand cities, the visitors from far off lands. Now the biggest accomplishment of New Cromwic was that they'd built a second story on the local tavern without collapsing the first story like usual.

They stood now on an exposed platform; a stiff wind was blowing, tossing Ronan's dark brown hair in front of his face. After several weeks, they'd finally managed to force their way through a locked door at the top of a tower and had found this device.

"Yeah, definitely one of the old wind-runners," Ronan said again.

Privately, Finn agreed. And, very privately, he wanted to see if it worked. It was beautiful, advanced, a technological marvel. It had shrunk the the kingdom to the size of a neighborhood. It had meant power, and prestige, and a world of ideas and engineering. But, of course, every part of it was built with magic. But, if that was so wrong, what was he even doing here?

"Think it still works?" Ronan asked, inevitably.

"No. Definitely not." But he hoped it did.

Ronan turned and grinned at him, then moved away, circling the old relic. It was a small boat with a bright red silk sail and yellow trim. This boat had never been intended to float on water. It was suspended from a thick cable running over their heads. This cable attached to the wall behind them and then stretched out into the distance, over the tops of the trees. It was held up by supporting towers every two hundred feet or so.

The wind-runners had been the quickest mode of transportation in Caledonia before the Fall. Propelled by magical wind, they had run along cables suspended hundreds of feet in the air and had been capable of carrying passengers between cities on opposite sides of the country in only a few days.

"I bet it works," Ronan said.

"It's over a hundred years old! We don't even know where it goes. What if the cable's broken? What if the wind's died out and we get partway out there and then get stuck a hundred feet in the air?"

"I brought rope." Ronan gestured to the coiled pile resting near the wall. It would be good quality rope, too. Made by Ronan's mother. Everyone knew that if you wanted good quality rope or thread or tailoring or tapestry, and you were fine not asking where it came from, or how she made it, you went to Ronan's mother. Most people didn't, though. So, Ronan always had good quality clothes, but cheap buttons, and nothing of leather or anything waterproof, and often not enough food, either, which was why Finn had brought extra bread today. His own mother made good bread, when she was home, which wasn't often.

"Or, even, best-case scenario, what if it does work and we end up halfway to Montvale?"

"You brought food, right?" Ronan grinned at him again. The grin made his nose, which was large and slightly off center, twist to the left.

"We have class tomorrow."

Ronan rolled his eyes. "As if that matters. You're just scared."

Finn lifted his eyebrows and gestured to the ground, at least sixty feet below them.

"You just don't like that this was all made by magic," Ronan said calmly, matter-of-fact.

"That's reasonable, too. In case you haven't noticed, these

21

are ruins we hang out in every day, Ronan. The people who built this are dead. All of them."

Ronan tugged on the supporting cable. It held firm. "It was a hundred years ago. They'd be dead anyway."

"Oh, so they all died peacefully in their sleep after long and productive lives?"

Ronan pushed experimentally on the boat. It was stuck. "No, non-mages slaughtered them."

"Only the last of them! Almost all of them had destroyed themselves before that!"

"We don't know what caused the Fall," Ronan replied calmly. He reached down and grasped a metal lever that jutted out from the floor near the boat. He bent his weight against it; it stayed stuck for a moment and then gave all at once. Ronan tumbled forward, dangerously near the edge, but caught himself in time. He stood, looking over the edge, catching his breath.

The lever had released some catch and turned the boat's sail into the wind. It billowed out smoothly, and the boat began to glide forward. Ronan was too engrossed in the view to notice that the boat was heading straight for him.

"Ronan!" Finn called out, but Ronan wasn't listening. Finn jumped forward, grabbing Ronan by the shirt and yanking him out of the way. The boat caught Ronan's shoulder and knocked him and Finn towards the edge. Finn grabbed out wildly for something to steady himself, and his hand, unfortunately, caught the edge of the boat. He clamped down and pulled back hard on Ronan, trying to keep him from going over, but the boat was pulling them forward, and in seconds they had tipped over the side.

Ronan was dangling in midair, Finn held a fistful of his shirt with one hand, and the edge of the boat with the other. He felt like his arms were ripping apart. He should have exercised more, like his father wanted, because he was definitely

22

not strong enough for this. He looked down, which was a mistake because he was just in time to watch the ground drop away from them. They were skimming over treetops now, and it looked like they were picking up speed.

Ronan screamed and looked up. He jerked his body upwards—Finn felt something pop in his arm—and scrabbled at the side of the boat, grasping the edge with both hands. Finn let go of his friend's shirt, and gripped the boat with both hands, too. He tried to pull himself up and over, but all his strength was spent. He could feel his arms shaking with fatigue, and his grip starting to loosen. Then there was searing pain as Ronan gripped him by the hair and yanked him upwards. Finn shrieked, a high-pitched sound he'd never known he was capable of, and then, suddenly, he was in the boat, collapsed on the smooth floor between seats.

Tears were streaming down his face, and he prodded his scalp gingerly to see if any of his hair was left. It was. The boat swayed beneath him, rumbling slightly as it skimmed along. Finn squeezed his eyes shut, wishing that this were a dream, or a hallucination, or just not happening. Any moment they were going to hit a broken spot in the cable and they were going to plummet to their deaths.

"Holy… Finn you should really see this."

Well, if he was going to die anyway… He pushed himself up off the floor, his muscles weak and watery and shaking, and crawled to the edge. As he moved towards Ronan, though, the boat listed to one side. Finn's stomach gave a horrible swoop of panic and he recoiled back towards to center. The boat was still leaning heavily to Ronan's side, though. Ronan was, of course, grinning insanely and leaning over the edge. He seemed to be trying to stare in every direction at once: his head whipped around as he looked straight down, then up at the sky, then forward, then back down again.

Finn moved to the opposite side to balance the boat. He didn't look down. He didn't want to know how high they were. Instead, he looked out. They were soaring along much, much faster than Finn had ever gone before. Treetops whizzed past them. They might already be miles from home.

Ronan laughed and turned to Finn. His smile faded slightly when he saw Finn's face. "You're mad."

"Yes. We're probably going to die!" Finn shouted over the roar of the wind.

Those treetops were close. Surely the designers of this boat wouldn't have wanted to pass so close to trees. What if there was wind?

Something winged the bottom of the boat as they sped past, knocking it to the side. It swung out to the right; both Ronan and Finn tumbled back to the bottom. The boat settled back to its original smooth speed, but immediately knocked into something else.

Right. Treetops. These trees hadn't been here a hundred years ago. Finn started searching frantically for any form of controls. "Ronan, the trees! We have to stop!"

"Shit." Ronan dove for the front of the boat, running his hands over the bow and yanking on any bit that stuck out, but nothing had any effect on their speed.

Finn looked up and saw exactly what he'd been afraid of looming up ahead. A stand of fir trees, directly in their path. He barely had time to register this before they were there. He dove for the bottom of the boat as they smashed into branches. The prow careened into a tree trunk, bounced off, twisting on the support cable, which groaned under the strain. Both Finn and Ronan were screaming now. The boat smashed against another tree trunk, then another, the front splintering. A branch speared through the sail, ripping it to shreds and jerking the boat backwards, yanking it to a stop.

There was a sudden calm, as the boat swung gently, still

suspended by its support cable, and held in place by the branch. Finn threw up. At least they weren't moving forward anymore. And the sail was broken, so they weren't going to speed up again. Finn took a deep breath and looked up to see if Ronan was still alive. His friend's blue eyes were wide, and there was a deep scratch across his face, which was a pale green. There was some vomit on his shirt.

"Okay." Finn said. "We're alive. Still. So far."

Ronan nodded, dazed.

The cable holding the boat groaned, and the boat slid down a few inches.

"Shit." Ronan muttered again.

"Okay. Okay. It's fine. Let's get out of the boat. Yeah?"

Ronan nodded again. Very gingerly, they found a large tree branch and climbed onto it and out of the boat. It lifted slightly as they moved off it.

For a while, they sat, catching their breath. Then they started the long, slow climb down the tree. About fifteen feet from the ground, though, they ran out of branches. From there down the trunk was smooth.

"Would be good if we had your rope right about now," Finn said.

"Yeah, well, I didn't actually mean to start the boat, Finn," Ronan snapped. "I was just messing with you."

"You're welcome for saving your life."

"You, too."

"You don't get credit for saving it if you endangered it in the first place."

"Okay, okay, you're right. Let's just figure out how to get down. Okay?"

"Fine by me."

They sat, squatting on the lowest branches, gripping the tree trunk and looking down at the ground.

"I think we can make it," Ronan said finally.

"What, jump?"

"Yeah."

"No way," Finn said. "We'll have to slide down the trunk."

"We'll get ripped to shreds if we do that."

"Better some scrapes than broken bones. Especially because we have who knows how long of a hike home."

Ronan looked down and grimaced. "Fine, you're right."

Finn wrapped his arms and legs tightly around the trunk and started to slowly inch his way down. He made it almost to the bottom before he slipped, the bark scraping his arms and legs and tearing his clothes to shreds as he slid to the ground. Ronan followed after.

Finn lay with his back on the ground. He was alive. That was a surprise. He didn't even mind the stinging cuts all over the front of his body and the insides of his legs.

Ronan limped over and extended a hand. Finn took it and Ronan pulled him to his feet.

"How far do you think it is back?" He asked.

Finn ran a hand through his hair. "I don't know, ten miles? At least."

"Yeah, that's what I thought, too. Did you bring the food?"

"I was kind of in a hurry."

"Dang."

"Yeah."

They started walking and hiked in silence for a few minutes.

Ronan finally couldn't contain himself and gave an excited hop. "I didn't even know it was possible to go that fast! Amazing, right?"

A bubble of guilty excitement rose in Finn's chest, and he smiled in spite of himself. "Yeah, I can't believe it still works. Worked."

"Yeah. Too bad about the trees."

"Yeah."

"I wonder if we can find another one."

Finn scrubbed a hand across his face. He hoped so. But also, he knew he shouldn't.

NOW, lying alone in the forest, Finn thought about that day, thought about how he'd felt about magic back then. The things it had built were astounding. Caledonia had been the most powerful kingdom in the world. But magic, from what he'd read, had destroyed as much as it had created, and corrupted those who wielded it. No, no matter how amazing the cities it had built were, Finn still wouldn't have chosen to be a mage. Mostly because of what it did to mages and the people around them, but also partly because of something he and Ronan had found on another day exploring the ruins of Old Cromwic.

THE BEAST RIPPED OPEN the next package. Kel could hear it chewing and licking, poking its nose into the furthest corners, getting all the crumbs. Kel pulled back from it, pushed herself into the smallest, narrowest part of the log. The creature ignored her.

It wasn't the only thing that had smelled the food. Another beast arrived, growling. It was bigger, and stronger, and chased off the first with a snarl and a swipe of its claws. It didn't bother using the door either. It knocked aside the logs that made up Kel's wall, and scrabbled about in what was left of the food wrappings. This one was hungrier, and meaner. It had been hungry for a long while, and it wouldn't be averse to eating Kel.

Kel had no weapons, only her little hands with their soft nails. The beast was eating the last of the crumbs, gathering its strength to finish off Kel, who would make a much better, fuller meal. Soft and full of blood.

Help me. Kel thought, not sure who she was asking.

But she could feel that her thoughts were heard. They were heard by an owl, sitting on a tree branch eating a mouse. But to the owl she sounded like just another mouse. And the owl wasn't going to risk itself to help another animal's mouse. That wasn't done.

And her words were heard by the worms, burrowing in the ground, and the beetles, and a hive of bees. But the worms couldn't help, and the beetles didn't understand, and the bees weren't interested.

Please, help me. Kel cried in her mind. The beast licked the last of the grease from a cheese wrapping. It was still hungry. It could hear Kel's cries, and it was annoyed by them.

Then, one small voice answered Kel's plea. A little animal. Young. Too small to take on the beast, barely big enough even to make a snack for it. But it had been alone, too. It had been spared, once, when an owl had found its burrow and had crunched up all his brothers and sisters. It alone had lived. And it recognized the cry of a young, helpless thing about to be eaten.

Kel pulled out the ball of fire, held it up. The light flashed off the dark, empty eyes of the beast coming towards her. It recoiled a moment from the blaze, cringing. A flash of white came streaking in from the right. Sharp little teeth nipped into the predator. It struck back, but the little animal was too quick, dodging out of the way and striking again on the other side.

The hulking shape snarled. Its eyes were accustomed to the light now, and it spun to face the little creature. That would have been the last the little animal remembered, but Kel had launched herself at the beast from behind. She didn't even have a rock to throw at it, but she balled up her small

28

fist and punched it in the side of its thick, muscular neck. It twisted and sank its teeth into her arm. Kel screamed, wriggling in pain, jerking at her arm, horrified, unable to free it from the beast's mouth. She kicked it, and it let go but immediately lunged for her throat.

A tiny whirlwind of teeth and claws and white fur intervened, biting and clawing the beast, dodging the heavy claws.

Kel attacked again, too, punching and kicking and screaming as loudly as she could. The beast gave a roar of annoyance and pain and fled.

Kel collapsed to the ground amid the ruin of her packages and began to cry. She felt a soft, warm little body lie down against her neck. It was shaking, gasping for breath. Kel sat up, cupped the little animal in her hands, and held it to her.

Thank you, she thought.

It didn't answer, but she knew it heard her.

Are you all right? Kel asked.

The animal wasn't sure. Kel ran a hand gently down its long body. Its fur was sleek and soft and white. It had a long tail and a sharp, black nose. Kel wasn't sure what it was. It was like a squirrel, but not as bushy.

"Smoke," Kel said. The animal was grey, now that Kel looked at it closely. Seeing it there next to Finn's fire globe— that weird smokeless fire—made her think of smoke.

Kel fell asleep cradling Smoke, and when she awoke in the morning the little animal was crouched on the ground in front of her face, watching her expectantly.

"Good morning," she said, smiling. The animal hopped to the side and grinned a sharp-toothed grin at her.

There was blood everywhere, and bits of fur, and the wreckage of what had briefly, for half a night, been Kel's home. The whole, awful scene was cheerfully illuminated by golden morning sunshine.

Kel wanted to leave and never come back, but this was

where Finn had told her to wait. So instead, she would clean up. She gathered up all the broken packages—not even a trace of food was left—and buried them. The logs were too big for her to lift, so she pushed them into a half circle, making as much of a barrier around the central log as she could. The blood would wash away in the next rain, hopefully.

Then she looked down at herself, realized she was covered in blood, too. Her dress was stained with it. Her arm hurt, too. There were deep puncture wounds from the animal's teeth. Vaguely, Kel supposed she should wash it, but she didn't have any soap.

She and Smoke were thirsty, though, so they made the short walk back to the last stream she and Finn had crossed. Kel pulled her dress off and immersed her arm under the ice-cold water, while Smoke lapped at the surface delicately, before leaping in all at once. He dove, twisting and wriggling and darting around before shooting happily back out again. Kel laughed, despite herself, and gently scrubbed away at her arm. The wounds opened again, bled a little, but maybe that was okay.

She plunged her bloody dress under the frigid water and scrubbed at it. Red clouds billowed out, but were quickly rinsed away by the current. She squeezed as much water out of the wool as she could, the fabric thick and sodden in her hands, and lay it out on the bank to dry.

Then she moved upstream and drank as much water as she could hold. It was cold and fresh, but then Kel started to shiver. She didn't want to put her wet, stiff dress back on, so she ran back to her camp, carrying it, and wrapped herself in her blanket. She placed the fire globe in front of her on the ground, and sat looking at it, trying to think of what to do.

She was hungry now, and she knew Smoke was, too.

Maybe Finn would come back. He had left a lot of food,

though, so it didn't seem like he planned on coming back for a while.

Kel's stomach rumbled. Maybe she could find food nearby.

She stood, wrapping the blanket more tightly around herself, and walked away from camp, into the trees. Smoke scampered up the blanket and perched on her shoulder.

She walked uncertainly, not sure what was there, or what she could eat. She stepped over a root, hitched the blanket up a little higher to keep it from dragging in the dirt. Mostly, there were just a lot of trees. Would tree bark make her sick?

In the damp hollow between two tree roots Kel found a cluster of spongy white mushrooms, but she didn't know if they were the kind you could eat, and she remembered her mother—who loved mushrooms and spent a lot of time in the forest alone, collecting them—warning her that even experienced mushroom pickers sometimes picked the wrong ones and poisoned themselves, so she left the mushrooms alone.

Smoke wanted mice to eat. Baby mice especially. Or baby birds if they could find some. Kel didn't want to think about that. Smoke could eat what he wanted, but he didn't need to bring any back for Kel.

Kel felt a moment of panic when Smoke scurried down to the ground and scampered off, but Smoke would be back. Of course he would come back. He wasn't just going to leave her. She chewed a nail, and stared off in the direction he'd gone, then shook herself and continued her search for food.

She passed more mushrooms, and a lot more trees, and some poisonous-looking red berries. Then she saw some bushes she recognized. Blueberries. It was still too early for them, though. It was spring, so it would be months before anything edible was here. Finn would be back long before they would be useful.

Kel stroked a leaf wistfully. She could feel the place inside the twig where the flower bud waited. The bud that would bloom and be pollinated and then bulge out into a berry. Kel could imagine that happening, knew that it would happen, slowly over the next few months. It was right there, the thing that would become food. She wished it would come out now, that it would somehow forget what season it was and bloom and… she felt something under her hand, a slight bulge at the base of the twig. It was the bud. She stared at it, confused and surprised. Had she done that?

She reached out to stroke it again, asking it to come out, asking it to bloom. And, to her great surprise, it did. The little bud poked out further and further, then split, blossoming out into a flower. Kel kept willing it to grow. It protested. There were no bees. It needed pollen, or its fruit would be sterile. Kel felt its loneliness that there weren't any other flowers. As soon as she'd felt that, she realized she could feel the rest of the buds, growing, pushing, blossoming into flowers, too.

Kel felt like she could ask them to make berries next. She knew, somehow, that she could ask and that they would do that. But it would make them sad. It would waste their efforts from that entire year. A whole year of preparing their children, for nothing. So Kel sat down, next to the riot of white flowers, and waited. She watched as bees came, happily surprised at the early crop of flowers. Kel didn't begrudge them their disinterest in helping her the night before.

She waited as the bees happily visited every flower, coming back and forth from their hive, bringing more of their friends with them each time. The worry in the flowers faded. Their berries would be alive, would be able to grow. Kel nudged a bee towards one of the last un-pollinated flowers. When they were all done, Kel reached out again, held one of the twigs, and asked it to grow. The petals fell away, and the base of the flower expanded, first green, then white, then swelling into a deep purple. Kel picked it and ate it. It was sweet and good and she immediately wanted another. She turned to the rest of the flowers, urged them into fullness, too.

The bushes were heavy with berries now, much larger than normal, and better, sweeter. Kel picked and ate until she was full, then she picked more to bring back with her.

"Thank you," she said to the plants as she left. They were happy. They knew she would take good care of their seeds.

On her way back to camp Kel stopped several times in open, sunny places to plant the berries. She dug little holes with a stick, then dropped a berry in and covered it up with dirt. Then she held her palm over them, and—she wasn't sure exactly how she did it—she helped them. She urged them to sprout, and to push their way up out of the ground. She helped them grow upwards until they were tall enough to reach up past shorter plants and feel the sun on their leaves.

She did this over and over until it was late afternoon and she was hungry again. Then she ate more berries. She couldn't eat blueberries forever, though, she knew. She would have to find other things to eat. But now she had something, at least. It was better than nothing. Better than being hungry.

Smoke came back as evening set in. He had blood on his face and looked full and satisfied. Kel didn't ask where he'd been.

CHAPTER 3

he next morning, Kel was faint with hunger. She went to the stream and drank a lot of water, but it just made her feel cold and empty. Then she went back to her berry bushes and filled her stomach. But their sweetness didn't appeal to her today, and her lightheadedness didn't go away. She walked through the forest, looking for more things to eat. Now she knew the seasons weren't a barrier to her, but still, Kel had never lived in the woods before. She knew what to eat from her mother's garden, but not what to eat in the woods.

She listened to the animals around her, watched what they were eating. Many of them were eating each other, or trying to. Birds were eating bugs and worms. Or other birds. The squirrels were eating the buds of flowers, and lichens, and mushrooms. She watched what they ate, and tried some, too. There were mushrooms that they all stayed away from, but others that the hungrier ones nibbled at. Kel gathered some of these and brought them back with her. She sat inside the circle of logs that was her home now, and popped one of the mushrooms into her mouth. First, she tasted dirt, then felt the spongy texture. She waited to see if something tasted poisonous, or if her tongue would tingle, or if maybe she would just keel over and die. None of those things happened. She waited more.

Smoke went off on one of his foraging expeditions. Kel ate more berries, hating the taste. It amazed her how quickly you could go from loving a food to hating it, even when it was the only thing keeping you alive.

She didn't die from the mushroom. The next morning, when she still hadn't felt any ill effects, Kel planted the rest of the mushrooms on the logs around her house, and made them grow. They popped up quickly, spreading out and expanding. They had huge, thick brown caps. And they were thirsty. Kel brought water from the stream, poured it over them, felt their relief and gratitude. Then she ate some of them. A lot of them, actually, and she felt a little bad about it. But then she helped them grow more, and planted them all over her camp, and she could feel that they were happy. They felt like the most powerful mushrooms in the world.

The next day Kel made the best discovery yet. A walnut tree. She sensed a squirrel looking for the nuts it had stored nearby, and could feel the squirrel's happy memory of the previous fall, when there had been more nuts than it could ever eat. And Kel found the tree and asked it to flower and it did. But then it resisted, because it needed another tree. Like the berry bushes, it didn't want to make dead, lifeless children. So Kel walked and walked and walked until she found another walnut tree, and she asked this one to flower, too, and it did. Then she called the bees.

The bees were tickled, pleasantly surprised again, and they went to work diligently. The trees were far apart, though, and it took longer than the berries had. Night was falling and they still weren't done, so Kel went home again, starving and disappointed. She ate more mushrooms, which also tasted horrible now.

The next morning the trees were ready, though, and she helped them explode with nuts. The squirrel she had heard yesterday, happily remembering last year's nuts, was beside itself at this unexpected bounty. Kel cracked the shells with rocks, eating as many as she could. They were crunchy and rich and filling.

Feeling renewed and energized, Kel gathered as many nuts as she could, taking one of the extra shirts Finn had brought and tying the bottom closed to make a sack. She carried them all back and planted them in a circle around her camp. Then she stood in the middle, closed her eyes, and felt them grow. Making twelve trees grow at once was hard. Harder than the mushrooms and the berry bushes had been, but she waited patiently, connecting herself to each tree one by one, and when she opened her eyes she was in the middle of a tight circle of trunks and leaves. They burst into flower. Kel smiled.

She ate more mushrooms and berries, and fell asleep before it was even dark, dreaming again of the path through the birch trees. The dream was becoming more insistent now, like it was telling her she needed to go somewhere, to find this path, and she wanted to, but she had to wait for Finn.

The next day Kel rested. She sat in the middle of her circle of trees, wrapped in her blanket. The sky was cloudy and a cool wind was blowing. Toward midmorning it began to rain and Kel retreated into her log. The rain grew heavier, and water leaked into her home, puddling up on the floor and dripping from the roof. She sat there, cold and damp and miserable, for a long time before she realized she might be able to do something about it.

Leaving the blanket in the relative dry of the log, Kel went out into the downpour. The rain drenched her, plastering her hair to her head, and sending rivers of water across her face and down the back of her neck. She wiped the water out of her eyes, walked barefoot through the mud until she found a patch of grass. She gripped a large handful of it and, with a whispered apology, yanked it out of the ground. On the way back to her log, she peeled handfuls of moss off the trees.

She arranged the whole lot on the top of the log. Sitting back inside, she closed her eyes and reached out with her mind, feeling for the plants. The moss creeped along, expanding, filling cracks in the log and happily absorbing the excess moisture. The grass spread, too, sprouting upwards and outwards, drinking in the water, and hanging down over the edges. Kel sent roots down into the log, watched them drink the water from the puddles on the floor until she was sitting in a mostly dry space. That was better.

Kel cracked a walnut open with a rock and chewed on it. Smoke came and sat on her lap, and Kel stroked his wet fur. She wished she could start a fire. Where was Finn? When would he come back?

As she sat, listening to the rain drumming on the roof and dripping into puddles outside, smelling the cold, sharp rain-smell, she thought about the animal from the first night. Her insides shrank and constricted at the memory. And there were more out there, she knew. She could feel them. And they would eat her if they found her. Her circle of trees wasn't enough, wouldn't keep them out.

She would think more about that tomorrow. For now, she was cold and tired and at least she had enough—sort of—to eat and drink. She and Smoke napped the rest of the day, listening to the rain.

The downpour had stopped by the next morning, although everything was sodden. The forest floor was covered in puddles, and every bush she brushed against doused her with water. Smoke stayed inside where it was dry while Kel went out to find something to fortify her campsite with.

She wandered through the tall trees, looking up the bare trunks at the branches high, high above. It was a dim, cloudy day, and mist from the rain drifted through the treetops and collected in depressions in the ground.

There were plenty of bushes and small grasses, but these wouldn't stop a large, hungry animal. She wished she could find something thorny, like blackberries. That would be perfect. Food and protection all in one. She listened to the thoughts of squirrels and birds, trying to overhear whether they had seen anything like that. But it was spring and most of their thoughts were about other things Kel didn't understand.

She was about to give up when she came across a thick, woody vine. She had seen others like it before, strangling the trees they climbed. She didn't like this vine, but it was sturdy, and it could protect her.

She broke off a few of the green, leafy shoots that extended out from its central trunk, and carried them back with her to her camp. She planted one in the ground between two of the walnut trees. It grew quickly, and much more easily than the trees had. It barely needed any encouragement at all, shooting up out of the ground, racing to wrap itself around the nearest tree and start strangling it. Kel let it latch on, but then directed it away again, towards the next tree in the circle. She held the shoot with her hand, guiding it along as it grew, helping it find the next tree. It tangled itself ravenously around this one, too, before Kel demanded it continue to the next one.

All afternoon Kel battled the rapacious vine, directing it to fill the spaces between the walnut trees. She wove it back and forth between them, like fencing between fence posts, higher and higher into the branches of the walnuts. The higher the vine got, and the thicker its base got, the safer Kel felt. The vine was thickening, filling all the space between the trees and hardening into a solid wall. Finally, when she was completely cocooned within this natural, fifteen-foot-high wall, she stopped. Then she realized she didn't have a way out.

Well, maybe that wasn't so bad. If she didn't have a way out then the other animals didn't have a way in, which was what she wanted, after all. She examined the wall she had made. She could probably climb it. It would be easier with a ladder, though.

She took one of the other pieces of vine she had brought back with her and planted it near the wall. Slowly, painstakingly, she directed it upwards, then turned ninety degrees so that it grew horizontally along the wall for a few feet. Then up again. Then right, making a second, horizontal step. Then up. Then left. Then up. Then right. Slowly, arduously, she directed it along, making a crude ladder. When it reached the top, she climbed it, found a small place to perch on the top of the wall. Here, she looked out.

She was high above the ground now, but still well below the canopy of the trees, and she could see a long way through the bare trunks. She sat for a while, looking, but all she saw were trees and bushes and forest. No Finn.

Unconsciously, she had been circling the vine around herself while she sat, and now there was a kind of nest around her. It was a nice little safe space to sit and look out.

She didn't want to make a ladder down the other side of her wall—what if another animal used it? Although, the kinds of animals that could use ladders weren't the kinds she was worried about. But still, Kel was alone and afraid. So, she brought a small branch up the ladder with her and balanced it between her wall and the nearest tree. Then she crawled across the branch—it tipped but she was able to balance on it —and made another vine ladder down the tree. That way, she could climb the ladder into the tree, cross the little bridge, and then pull the branch in and be safe.

Now she was an inconvenient meal. She could make her wall better tomorrow, maybe. But, for now, she was much safer than she'd been since… well, since she'd been at home. Of course, that hadn't been safe either.

CHAPTER 4

*R*onan had found it, of course. Ronan was the one drawn to magic, who spent all his free time exploring the ruins, sometimes with Finn but often alone.

Finn had been sick for several days, and he knew Ronan must have found something because he hadn't come to bring Finn any of their school work for the week. As soon as he felt well enough, Finn wrapped himself in his threadbare wool cloak and staggered up the old trail to the ruins.

Old Cromwic clung like a limpet to the side of a craggy mountain. Towers and balconies of grey stone, glittering with a coppery sheen, jutted out from the sheer side of the cliff the city had been built from. Flights of stairs ascended from the forest floor, up the face of the cliff. But the stairs were not the usual way that people had ascended into the city.

Finn found the closest platform. It was a bright bronze disk set into the ground near the base of the cliff. The circle of stone columns around it stretched fifty feet up to another platform just barely visible above. The disk was partially obscured by dirt and overgrown with moss and lichen, but he could still see swirling patterns of bright purple crystals. Finn would normally take the stairs, but his cold and the three-mile walk to the ruins had left him more out of breath than usual.

The wind lifted his dark hair as he stepped onto the platform, clenching his jaw. As soon as he stepped onto the middle of the disk, the platform gave a groan and jolted into movement. The wind rose to a whistling gale, and the whole platform lifted smoothly, slowly, giving him time to contemplate the view as he rose over the treetops, but Finn turned and instead examined the city, looking for any sign of Ronan.

The platform shuddered to a stop under an arched granite ceiling, which formed an open-sided dome over the platform. The granite had been formed by earth mages; they'd pulled it, molten, from the side of the cliff and twisted it into the spirals which formed the high-arched roof. At the peak of the ceiling was a large glowing orb of glass. There were marks around it, gouges where looters had tried to pry it from its mounting, but, as with most of the lights in the city, it was too strong and too firmly attached to be broken or stolen.

Finn walked up the street, towards their usual hangout, looking for Ronan.

He passed the pure-white statue of the woman with the noble brow and the calm expression. A circlet of gold rested on her head, and she held one hand out in front of her. From this hand, water poured into a pool below. Someone had smeared something dark across half her face. Most of it had washed away, but it had stained the stone beneath it.

"Finn!"

Finn whirled around to see Ronan coming down the street behind him, his bare feet slapping the stone.

"What happened to 'those platforms are hundred-year-old death traps'?"

Finn coughed. "They *are*. But, I'm sick. Climbing up here would probably have killed me anyway."

Ronan laughed. "Come on, I found something cool."

Finn followed Ronan through what they'd decided a while ago were the meeting chambers of the Old Cromwic high council. Here, the floors were marble—apparently too magically-protected to be chipped apart and looted—and the high ceilings were made of colored glass, glowing and undulating like the underside of storm clouds. Magical fire burned in glass sconces and chandeliers, and thick tapestries hung on the walls.

At the back of one of these rooms, empty of furniture but with little piles of leaves where rodents had made their homes in the corners, Ronan stopped in front of a huge painting. The colors were faded, but it clearly depicted a battle scene. Three fire mages locked in combat with a party of Baharran raiders. They were surrounded by twenty or thirty heavily-armed fighters, but they looked calm, confident. One of them had just hurled a fireball at a knot of fighters, another held two bright orange balls of flame, ready to attack, and the third, a woman, reached out her hands towards a wall of flame that held back another ten fighters.

Ronan had been drawn to this painting the first time they'd seen it, had stood staring at it for a long time before Finn finally dragged him off. Apparently, he'd come back to examine it some more while Finn was gone.

Ronan turned to Finn, grinned in a self-satisfied way, then gripped the edge of the painting and pulled. It swung out from the wall, revealing a smooth stone passageway behind.

Finn was impressed, despite himself, but Ronan didn't need to know that. "Where does it go?"

"Guess." Ronan slipped behind the painting and into the passageway, Finn following along behind.

"Torture chamber."

"That's morbid."

"Crypt."

"Seriously, Finn?

"Come on, does this seem like a nice, normal place to you?"

Ronan didn't answer.

The tunnel opened out into a wide stone chamber, lit around the edges by seven flames in silver sconces. In the center of the room, the smooth perfection of the chamber was broken by a large, irregular disk of copper pressed onto the floor. It had been poured crudely; there were splatters of copper on the floor, and large blue swathes of oxidation. In the center of the disk the image of a crescent moon had been pressed into the metal while it was still cooling.

There were new marks in the copper, gouges, and a hammer and chisel lay on the floor nearby.

"Uh, Ronan, what are you doing?"

"What's it look like I'm doing?" Ronan said, picking up the hammer and swinging it, and sending a crack through the metal.

"I mean, are you sure that's a good idea?"

"No." Ronan swung the hammer against the chisel again and a small piece of the cap fell away.

"I mean, someone sealed this off. Doesn't that imply it's dangerous? We don't even know what's under there."

"I know what's under there," Ronan gloated.

Finn looked up sharply.

Ronan paused in his hammering and gestured to the chamber. "Come on, isn't it obvious?"

Finn hadn't read as much about the magic of the old world as Ronan had. He preferred the works on politics, economics, and science.

"You should read more, Finn." Ronan bent and resumed

his work, chiseling into the soft copper. The cap, whatever it was hiding, was yielding quickly.

Ronan worked his way around the edges, loosening the cap and prying it upwards. Finn, not at all comforted by Ronan's assertion that he knew what was underneath, nervously collected the pieces in case he needed something to throw at whatever monster had been locked in there.

"So…" Finn ventured. "If you know what this is, does that mean you know why it's sealed?"

"Maybe." Ronan swung the hammer at the side of the cap, and the remaining piece popped off, sliding a few feet away.

There, underneath, was a pool of grey water with a pearly sheen. And suddenly Finn knew what this was, too. One of the old speaking pools, the magical devices that had allowed the leaders of the major cities to communicate instantaneously with one another.

Ronan knelt by the pool, peering down into it.

"See anything?" Finn asked.

"No."

"Maybe it only works if you're a mage."

"No. I know the non-mage assistants used it sometimes."

Ronan thrust a hand down into the water and felt around the edges. "Oh, there's more copper here, that's the problem."

He worked a few more minutes with the chisel and hammer, prying out pieces of copper. As he did, images began to flicker across the surface of the water. Ronan gave a whoop of excitement.

"It works! I told you!"

Despite himself, Finn came forward and peered, transfixed, into the water. It was real. He was looking at images from other towns, hundreds of miles away. Maybe even in the King's Table—the old capital—or the City of Mages. They were all images of rooms like this one, some in better states of repair than others. All empty, though.

"I can't believe no one uses these anymore," Ronan said.

A red light flickered, deep down below the surface of the water. Something shifted in the air of the room. It felt hot, suddenly. Finn gripped Ronan's shoulder.

"What was that?"

"Um, maybe it's burning out. I might have missed some of the copper."

A red light was coming towards them out of the depths. "I don't think that's it, Ronan." Finn took a step back and grabbed one of the chunks of copper. Ronan leaned forward, trying to see better.

A man's face approached. He looked like he had been burned. His flesh was blackened, sagging off him, and his eyes flashed a bright red. A hand reached out of the water and stretched its long, sharp, black nails towards Ronan. The nails paused, inches from Ronan's chest. A disembodied voice echoed in the chamber.

"Hmm...Not ripe, yet... soon..." It said, and Finn felt cold rush through his body. Ronan tried to pull back but couldn't move. The red eyes turned to Finn, and the hand reached out, but before it could reach him, Finn threw the piece of copper. It passed straight through the ghostly hand, but it landed with a plunk in the middle of the pool. Instantly, the image winked out, replaced by bright flashes of light, like lightning streaking through the water. A smell like a thunderstorm filled the room, and then the surface of the pool faded again to a pale grey.

Shaking, Finn immediately bent to his pile and started chucking in the rest of the copper pieces. Apparently the first one had done the trick, though. Ronan didn't even try to stop him. He sat, dazed, next to the pool, rubbing his chest.

When Finn had finished, he grabbed Ronan by the arms and lifted him up.

"Come on, let's get out of here."

Ronan didn't argue, just stumbled along, half-supported by Finn. When they made it back out into the sunshine they collapsed on a stone bench. Ronan bent forward, his elbows on his knees, taking deep breaths.

"Are you okay?" Finn asked.

"I think so."

"What was that?" Finn glanced back towards the door, to see if anything was following them.

"I have no idea."

"So, I take it that wasn't what you were expecting?"

Ronan looked up and narrowed his eyes at Finn. "Obviously."

Finn lifted his hands. "All right, all right, how was I supposed to know?"

"Sorry." Ronan said, dropping his head back down and taking another deep breath.

Finn thought back over how many times he'd heard Ronan say that, after they'd nearly died exploring something dangerous. It was a lot. At some point one of them was probably going to actually die. Or maybe Ronan would stop being so reckless. But, probably one of them was going to die. And most likely it was going to be Finn.

"Thanks, by the way," Ronan said.

"Sure."

They didn't go back to the old city for weeks. They told themselves this was because they needed to do research, to try to figure out what the thing was that they'd seen in the pool, but they found nothing, and both knew that the real reason was that they were afraid. And they both knew that, whatever it was, it was still out there, somewhere.

CHAPTER 5

*F*or the next several days Kel explored the forest, finding things that seemed edible and bringing them back to her stronghold. She ate a root she shouldn't have, and spent three days throwing it—and everything else she ate—back up. When she could keep food down again, Smoke brought her an egg, and she was so hungry, so desperate for something sustaining, that she cracked it open and sucked it down. It was gooey and runny and horrifying, but it stayed down and clearly it was something her body needed. Smoke brought her two more eggs the next day, and Kel ate those, too.

You're right, she thought grudgingly. *These are good.*

Smoke thought that was obvious. All that trying to eat plants. Ridiculous.

When Kel was feeling better, though, she continued collecting plants: roots and lichens, several types of berries, a few fruit trees. And birds came to nest in her vine wall, drawn by the absurdly plentiful nuts and berries. Smoke agreed not to eat all their eggs, just one or two at a time, and Kel, reluctantly, ate them too. She had grown emaciated since

Finn had left, but now, for the first time, she was full all the time. Except for having to eat everything raw, she was satisfied.

One day, the vine surprised her by sending forth flower buds. Kel helped urge them open, and they blossomed into sprays of hanging purple flowers. These drew bees and butterflies, and Kel found herself in a kind of walled garden paradise. She liked the flowers so much that she went into the forest looking for more, and she found some. Yellow daisies, delicate white trilliums, tiny bluebells, and she brought them back and filled her garden with them.

After that she spent most of her time sitting atop her wall, waiting for Finn. Now that she wasn't hungry, she slept soundly each night, and started to dream again. Every night she dreamed of the path through the birch trees. She wondered whether it was a real place, and wanted more and more to look for it. She didn't know how long it had been, how many days or weeks. Would the food that Finn had left her have lasted this long? Finn wouldn't have abandoned her to die here. He said he was coming back. He must be coming back. Unless something had happened to him. Should she look for him? But she would have no idea where to look, and she couldn't leave her home now. She was safe here. Safe. She wanted her brother to be safe, too. Where was he?

CHAPTER 6

*A*rcturus Flavius sat on his toilet, reading a little-known history of Baharra in the original Baharran language. His stomach clenched and strained, but he'd been there for several minutes already with no success. He was used to this, though.

His bathroom was the best in all of what had once been Caledonia, made of darkly polished wood, accented with silver and rubies. It was plumbed, too. It had to be, to be the best, but Arcturus resented this because he'd had to contract the work out to a water mage. He'd killed the mage after, of course, which was a small satisfaction, but the sound of the water trickling merrily below irked him. He sighed, turned a page, trying to distract himself, and waited.

STEALING WASN'T AS HARD as Finn had always thought it would be. He barely even felt bad about it, now. It was just one more thing necessary to survival. Like living in the woods, sleeping on the ground, and doing magic. This was

50

apparently his life now. Once you just accepted that you were a horrible person, things stopped being so bad and you could just go about trying to achieve what you needed to achieve. In this case, that meant taking care of Kel. In order to do that, though, he was going to have to find her.

Finn stopped and scratched at his beard. He'd never had a beard before, was a little surprised at how thickly it had come in. He hadn't been gone that long, had he?

Readjusting the sack of stolen goods slung over his shoulder, Finn looked around, trying to get his bearings. This part of the forest didn't look at all how he remembered. Things were... bigger. But trees didn't grow that fast, and forests didn't change that quickly. He must have made a wrong turn somewhere.

But, no, there was that old, half-rotten fir tree he'd passed. He remembered it because he'd thought about climbing it and jumping to his death. He'd stood there for several minutes, considering it. You didn't forget the tree you'd contemplated using to kill yourself. Maybe he'd been gone longer than he'd thought, then.

He'd go a little further, and if he didn't find Kel he'd just wander around aimlessly until something else looked familiar. He could always come back to this tree.

As Finn continued to walk, the forest looked less and less familiar. He passed a clump of the most enormous blueberry bushes he'd ever seen. The ground around them was covered with purple, seed-filled bird droppings, and the bushes looked like they'd already fruited, which shouldn't have happened for at least another month. Finn knew because his father had warned him about encountering bears who were after the same fruit you were. Turns out his father needn't have worried about bears.

Finn continued walking. He passed more clumps of enormous, startlingly healthy bushes, and places where plants had clearly been dug up out of the ground and taken away. Now Finn was curious, and slightly worried. Someone was here. He hoped they hadn't found Kel.

Up ahead, something strange caught his attention. Whatever it was, his eyes were having trouble making sense of it. It looked sort of like a hill, only there were clearly trees in it. It was covered with red and yellow and blue and white flowers, which stuck off in all directions, and amongst these fluttered and buzzed and scampered hundreds of birds and bees and squirrels and chipmunks.

Cautiously, Finn moved closer and saw that it was a natural wall, made with vines and... walnut trees. He stared at it, trying to comprehend what he was seeing, when a voice called out to him.

"Finn!"

Finn looked up and saw, at the top of the wall, his sister. The little kid was smiling and waving like everything was totally normal. Finn's jaw dropped open, and the sack fell off his shoulder.

"Hi, Finn! Wait there, I'm coming down!"

As Finn watched, Kel scrambled over to a branch balanced precariously between the wall and a nearby tree. For the first time, Finn noticed there was a ladder there, which Kel scurried down, then sprinted over and wrapped her arms around Finn's waist.

Finn detached her gently, then bent down and hugged her back.

"Kel! What... what is... how..."

"Are you hungry, do you want some food? Smoke just gathered more eggs."

A deep sense of unease crept up into Finn's heart. "Who's Smoke, Kel?"

Kel had already turned and was leading him back towards

the ladder, dragging him by the hand. "He saved me from the animal."

With growing trepidation, Finn allowed himself to be led up the ladder and down into the nest, bracing himself for an encounter with an evil, powerful naturalist mage who had for some reason taken an interest in his sister.

"Smoke!" Kel called. "Finn's back."

A ferret popped its head up over a log at the other side of the clearing. It narrowed its eyes at Finn. That didn't make sense. Ferrets weren't suspicious, were they?

"Smoke is… a ferret?" Finn asked.

"Oh, I guess so," Kel said.

"And… he made all this?" Finn wondered if Smoke was really a mage in disguise. He'd never heard of a mage being able to turn into an animal, but then, there was a lot he didn't know about magic.

Kel stopped, turned towards Finn, and laughed. "What? No! I did this."

He sat down on a rock. "What?"

Smoke had turned away in what seemed a lot like disgust —but ferrets didn't feel emotions—and Kel was still laughing at Finn. "Yeah, I did this."

"How?"

"I don't know. I just… help them grow… I guess."

"But… you're only six."

"So?"

"So, no one becomes a mage until they turn sixteen."

"Why?"

"Why? I don't know, that's just how it is. I've never heard of anyone ever being a mage earlier, Kel. Ever."

"Oh. Huh."

"Are you sure there hasn't been anyone else here?"

"Just me and Smoke, since you left."

There was a moment of sad silence between them. Then

Finn hugged Kel. "I'm sorry, Kel. I'm sorry I left. I had to get some stuff, but now I'm back and I'm not going anywhere."

Kel pulled her head back to look in Finn's eyes. "Promise?"

"Yeah, Kel, I promise." As Kel burrowed her head into Finn's shoulder, Finn looked around him at what his sister— or possibly a man pretending to be a ferret—had made. He'd never seen anything so beautiful, or so teeming with life. In the center stood the log that Finn had originally made into a shelter for Kel. That attempt seemed pitiful now. The log was covered in a profusion of the most enormous mushrooms Finn had ever seen, and all around it were rows and rows of vegetables, and clumps of fruit trees heavy with apples, pears, and plums. Whatever this was, it was not the evil product of corruption that he'd always thought magic was. No, this was beautiful.

FOR A FEW DAYS, Finn and Kel simply coexisted together. They woke up when the sun rose over the edges of the vine wall. They ate cold leftovers of the previous night's meal— Finn still couldn't bring himself to make fire around Kel. For most of the day, Finn would accompany Kel through the forest as she looked for plants. Kel showed Finn the blue-berry bushes he had noticed earlier, and the first walnut tree she had found. She told him about the little pieces of thought she picked up from the animals overhead.

And Finn listened, amazed at this new world that had opened inside his sister. He watched the girl, a little wary of this new person. She had all these powers, and no idea what they meant. They didn't seem dangerous at all, but Finn was cautious. He wanted to protect Kel, but it started to occur to him that maybe the best way for him to protect her would be to leave her alone in the forest again. But that seemed crazy, and Kel herself clearly didn't want that.

Seeing the way magic could be was causing Finn to rethink everything he'd ever learned about it and re-evaluate every conversation he'd ever had with Ronan. He wished he could see him again and apologize. He wished he could see Ronan's mother again, too.

ELLIE CARVER WAS young and unmarried when she had Ronan. This was the second, and less important of the two things that made her an outcast. But, being an outcast, living on the edge of the village in a ramshackle cottage, and being marked as an unrepentant mage didn't seem to bother her.

Finn had only visited their home one time—his parents had forbidden him to go there, but he and Ronan needed to pick up rope for an expedition.

As they approached the white-washed cottage with its mossy roof, the front door opened, and a man came out with a large, wrapped package under one arm. His eyes met Finn's and then darted away again, and he quickened his pace, pulling his hat lower over his brow.

Finn glanced at Ronan and saw his jaw was clenched as he stared down the man's retreating back. Ronan had never talked much about his mother, and Finn, although curious, didn't ask.

Ronan pulled the front door open without knocking and they entered the dim interior.

The only light came from a slanting, partially moss-covered window in the ceiling, but Finn could see that the large open living area was crammed with objects: bolts of cloth were stacked or leaning against walls, hammocks hung from the exposed beams of the ceiling, and large, intricate tapestries covered the walls. At the far end, near another, smaller window, a woman sat facing away from them, her long dark-brown hair hanging down her back.

"Hello, dear, I hear you've brought a guest," she said, smiling and rising as she turned towards them.

"So, you sold that thing you've been working on all week?" Ronan asked.

She pursed her lips and came towards them. She leaned in close to Finn's face, smiling and squinting slightly. "So, you're Finn Vogt, aren't you?"

Finn nodded, trying not to be rude by leaning back away from her. The half-moon tattoo of the unrepentant mage was branded into the soft skin of her face.

"Nice to meet you. I've heard a lot about you from this one." She smiled again and tousled Ronan's hair, but Ronan only frowned.

"How much did he give you for it?" Ronan asked.

She frowned and glanced at Finn. "Enough, Ronan."

Ronan closed his mouth, but his eyes were hard.

Later, after she'd given them rope, invited Finn to dinner, and sent them on their way, as they were walking the trail towards the ruins, Ronan started talking.

"What she makes is better than what anyone else could, and just because she's a mage they—" He kicked at the ground with his bare foot. "They're hypocrites."

Finn glanced at him, opened his mouth, then shut it again. There were reasons magic wasn't allowed but telling Ronan that would only make him angrier.

Ronan swatted at the air. "You think she should just stop doing magic, don't you?"

Finn scratched his neck. "I—yeah."

Ronan stopped, turned towards him, and pulled out the rope, holding it up. "Look at this! Look how much better it is! And my mom's not hurting anyone. The only problems she's ever had because of magic are from the stupid people punishing her for doing it." Ronan threw the rope on the ground. "And those same people come buy stuff from her when they think no one's looking. And they pay her barely anything." He picked up the rope again and dusted it off.

Finn didn't know what to say. It sucked, but it was how she chose to live. She was risking not only herself and Ronan, but the safety of the village as well by practicing magic. "I'm sorry, Ronan."

Ronan shrugged his shoulders and started walking again, so fast that Finn had to jog to keep up.

FINN REALIZED NOW what it must have been like for Ellie Carver. You couldn't just not do magic. She'd been like Kel, she'd made beautiful things and she'd never hurt anyone, as far as Finn knew. And she'd accepted the persecution that came with being a mage, and the ostracism. Finn's chest felt heavy and his stomach knotted. He wished he had spent more time with Ronan and his mom, and that he'd gotten to know her better, rather than avoiding her like he had, because of what she was.

LATE ONE AFTERNOON, when Kel was napping in the nest, Finn climbed up over the wall to walk and think. He walked in a straight line, away from the nest, and the further he got, the lighter the weight in his chest became. He loved Kel, and would stay and protect her, but it didn't actually seem like Kel needed his protection, and if Finn couldn't control his powers he was more of a danger to her than anything.

Finn sped up unconsciously, sweeping straight through a berry bush, trampling a flower underfoot without noticing.

Feeling a sudden surge of power, he clenched his fists, stopped, and rubbed them into his eyes. He crouched down on the forest floor, suddenly aware of the buzz of insects, the slanting rays of late afternoon sun, the soft, squelchy dampness of the moss under his leather boots. A small tree—just a seedling—off to his right burst into flame.

Finn leapt up, ran towards it, tried to beat the flames out with his bare hands, but they only rose higher. The heat buffeted him back. And then, almost as quickly as it had begun, the tree was completely consumed and the fire went out. A charred, smoking collection of twigs was all that remained.

Finn hung his head, pressing both palms to the side of his face. He couldn't control it. It kept on happening, no matter how hard he tried to hold it in. He remained there, squatting near the corpse of the tree, eyes closed against the roaring sound in his ears. That's when he heard the scream.

It was high-pitched, up ahead of him in the forest, and was followed by a heavy crash. Finn, afraid he'd lit something else on fire, launched himself up and forward, transitioning into a full-tilt sprint through the undergrowth. He ran headlong in the direction the scream had come from, scanning the forest for any sign of trouble. He only looked left and right, though, which was why he tripped over the body of the girl lying face down in the grass.

He careened forward, his legs no longer underneath him. His face smashed into a root, the rest of his body backing up behind him, all stopped by his face. His left shoulder scraped along some jagged rocks.

"Uhhnn..." he moaned, pushing himself gently up off his face and feeling around for damage. It felt like there was something embedded in his cheek, maybe a sharp stick. He pulled his hand away, which jerked his shoulder. The shoulder was also not too happy.

He was alive, though, and nothing was on fire, which was always a relief, in Finn's experience. He turned back to look at the body of the girl, but it was gone. Confused, Finn turned back, and there, standing in front of him, was the girl. Not dead, and looking kind of annoyed. She was tall, or maybe she just looked that way because she was standing over Finn with her arms crossed. Her skin was fair and freckled, her hair a startling white, curling long and loose over her shoulders. A few leaves were tangled in it. Her eyes, behind long dark lashes, were a warm, dark brown.

"What were you doing sprinting through the forest like a crazy person?"

Finn blinked. "I heard a scream. I thought someone was in trouble." He left out the part about being afraid someone was in trouble because he had lit them on fire.

"And, is it your general policy to run after people who are in trouble and then kick them in the ribs?" She arched an eyebrow.

"I wasn't trying to kick you in the ribs, I just didn't see you there!"

She laughed and kicked him in the leg. "I'm just giving you a hard time. I know you didn't see me. Unless your plan was to kick me and then cleverly leap face-first into a tree."

Finn laughed uncertainly, and, to his annoyance, felt himself blushing. A few seconds passed and Finn realized he was staring at her.

The contrast between her pale skin, unblemished except for several scrapes and bruises, and her dark eyes, framed by long dark lashes, was so striking that Finn couldn't stop staring. Until he realized she was aware he was staring and amused by it.

"Been in the woods a long time?" she asked.

"What? No. Well, a few weeks maybe. Er, you?"

She looked around her, lifted her arms up to the sky. "I've

always been in the woods," she said. Then she laughed, looked back down, and grinned at him. "Just kidding. I've been traveling about six months."

Finn felt himself grinning in response. The grin felt strange on his face, like his muscles had forgotten how. It made his beard itch. He reached up to smooth it and realized it was full of leaves. He tried to pick them out unobtrusively. "What were you doing, anyway? Why did you scream?"

"Trying to fly," she said, and winked at him. Finn's heart did a little, shivery dance. A tree caught on fire.

Finn jumped up, even though he knew there was nothing he could do. The girl stared at it, watched as the thing was quickly consumed in flames.

"Well, that's interesting," she said. "You don't have very good control of your powers at all, do you?" She laughed. Then she looked at him more closely. "So, you're a fire mage."

He looked into her eyes, surprised to see only interest. None of the fear and revulsion he expected.

She went on. "That's cool. That'd probably be my second choice."

She clenched her fists and closed her eyes. The leaves around them started to quiver; a breeze brushed through them, then picked up into a gale-force wind, pressing their clothes tight against them and tossing the girl's hair. A leaf dislodged from Finn's beard. Then, as quickly as it had come, the wind dropped away.

The girl held out her hand to Finn. "I'm Isabelle," she said.

"Finn." He took her hand, which was warm and strong. She had a quick, firm handshake.

Now that they were standing face-to-face Finn realized they were almost exactly the same height.

She leaned in towards him; Finn felt himself start to blush again, but then realized she was staring at his cheek.

"Um, I think there's something stuck in your face," she said.

"Is it bad?" he asked.

"Um, no. It's fine. No big deal. Nothing to worry about. Um... Let's go back to Eraldir. He'll get that out. Not that it's... you're going to be fine. Come on," she said, turning on her heel and striding off into the trees.

Finn had to hurry to keep up with her, and when she stopped short a few minutes later he almost ran into her again.

They had arrived at her camp. It was in a little clearing, with the ashes of a campfire in the middle, an old horse standing resolutely at one end, and two bedrolls, one of which was occupied by the sleeping form of a very old man.

He was thin, and his skin was mottled with liver spots and dark purple veins, some of which had burst and spread out into pale purple bruises. His hair was grey and unkempt, and he had a short, unevenly trimmed beard. One hand was resting on his sunken chest, the other clutched a mostly empty tea mug. He was snoring loudly.

"Eraldir!" The girl shouted.

He gave a jerk and opened his eyes. "I'm not deaf. You don't have to shout, girl," he grumbled, sitting up.

"Sorry, this is—what's your name again?"

"Finn."

"This is Finn. He tripped. Can you get the, uh... very small splinter... out of his face?"

Eraldir looked up, noticed Finn's face. "Eh," he grunted. "That's no big deal. I have a bigger piece of wood permanently stuck in my right calf."

The girl steered Finn down to a seat on the empty bedroll. She looked at Finn and rolled her eyes. "Yes. You've told me that one."

Eraldir pushed himself creakily up and went to rummage

in his pack. Undeterred by her lack of enthusiasm, he continued his story. "I was up in the Iron Mountains. Almost to the Baharran border, when I ran into a raiding party. They chased me for a good fifteen miles before I gave them the slip by—"

"Climbing up into a hollow tree and holding yourself suspended there, yes."

"Not holding myself! I would have fallen. Lucky for me a sharp bit of trunk speared itself into my calf, kept me up in there. They camped out, looking for me, at the base of that tree for two days! It's just lucky they didn't see my blood running down the inside of the tree." He chuckled.

Eraldir had found what he was looking for, a leather pouch, and came over to Finn. As he got close, Finn noticed the powerful aroma the man gave off. It was the smell of age and health problems, but also something rank and bitter.

"Finally, they gave up on finding me. They almost decided to burn the forest down looking for me. That would have smoked me out, heh, but I was too far gone to care at that point. Wouldn't have minded dying, you know." His bony fingers gripped something in Finn's face. Finn was about to protest or ask him to be careful, but he didn't have time. The man gave a great yank and Finn felt a searing hot bolt of pain. He just barely held onto consciousness. The pain abated to a sharp ache, and Eraldir pressed a poultice of damp herbs to the wound. Then he showed Finn the sliver. It was about two inches long, jagged, and covered in his blood and what looked like a bit of skin. He almost passed out again.

"Here, hold this on it." Eraldir grabbed Finn's hand and pressed it to the compress. Finn complied. It was nice to have something to do, and at least the worst part was over.

"Thanks." Finn attempted a half-smile, trying not to use the injured side of his face.

Eraldir was struggling to relight the dead fire. Finn wanted to help, but wasn't sure if he could do it accurately enough, so, he let the old man work and finally get it lit.

Eraldir grabbed a battered iron pot. He reached his hand out, and water swirled into it out of nowhere. Finn stared at the full pot in surprise.

They sat there in silence, watching as the water came to a quick boil. Then Eraldir poured some herbs into it and took it off the flames. He picked up the mug from next to his bedroll and poured some of the steaming tea into it. Then he handed the mug to Finn.

"Here, drink this. It will help keep it from getting infected."

Finn took the mug gratefully and tried to take a sip. It scalded his lips, and he quickly pulled it away.

"You'll want to wait while that cools." Eraldir eyed him from under absurdly large eyebrows.

"So," Isabelle said. "Do you live around here?"

Finn's chest locked up. "Um, no."

She ran a hand through her hair, found one of the leaves stuck there, and tossed it away. "So, you're... traveling?" She asked.

Finn looked down into the tea. There were leaves and twigs floating on the surface. He lifted it and took a tiny, experimental sip to buy himself time. It tasted horrible, and it was still too hot. Obviously.

What could he tell them? Not the truth.

Isabelle saved him from having to come up with a lie, though. "We're here looking for someone."

"Oh? Who are you looking for?"

Eraldir gave her a look. "Why don't you tell us what you're doing here first?"

Finn looked out into the forest. "I'm here with my sister. We... we were run out of our village. I'm a fire mage."

It was the right thing to say. Isabelle was nodding sympathetically. "No one understands magic anymore."

"Huh. As if you even knew a time when people understood magic." Eraldir grunted and poured himself a cup of the bitter tea. "When I was a boy, that's when people understood it."

"Eraldir was alive before the Fall," Isabelle said to Finn.

Finn's eyes widened. "You were?" He had so many questions. "What was it like?"

Eraldir's eyes lit up. "First off, none of this ignoring magic nonsense. In those days, we knew people had to be trained. Everyone—and I mean everyone—went to the Academy."

Something loosened in Finn's chest.

"This business of not training mages, expecting them to either learn on their own or just not do magic at all, is pure foolishness."

"I'm Eraldir's apprentice," Isabelle said.

"And a good thing, too," Eraldir said. "You'd have killed yourself or at least a few other people by now without me."

"That's probably true," she said to Finn.

"I'm still not convinced I'm going to be able to prevent that anyway," Eraldir said. "I'm assuming you've been out jumping out of trees while I've been napping?"

"Maybe." She grinned. "The best way to learn something is to make it necessary to learn it."

"Putting yourself in situations where you will be grievously injured if you don't succeed at something is not an accepted educational practice," Eraldir said. "I've told you before—"

"It's fine, I'm not really going to hurt myself. I'm nearly there, anyway. I'm getting much better at creating an air cushion."

Finn stared at her. She was grinning even wider now. He couldn't help but laugh.

Eraldir glowered at him. "It's not funny, boy. She's always throwing herself into things—literally— and, while yes, I'll admit, she has learned very quickly—"

Isabelle waved him off. "Anyway, Finn, have you been trained at all?"

Finn's fear and shame pushed up out of the dark cave he tried to keep it in. "No, I haven't been trained. My—our— parents didn't want us to do magic." Finn didn't mention that he himself thought magic was wrong.

She looked at him sympathetically. "My parents didn't want me doing magic either. I'm from Montvale actually."

Finn was confused. "But Montvale doesn't have mages."

"My mother is from here. The Uplands. My father is a Montvan. He was out traveling, fell in love with an exotic foreigner," she rolled her eyes, "and stayed with her in the Uplands for a while. Buttering up the parents. Then I was born and he moved us back home with him."

"What happened when they found out you were a mage?"

"Oh, well, my mother didn't think it was that big of a deal. She told me to just ignore it and it would go away." She laughed. "Well, I wasn't going to do that. So, I did all the magic I wanted, whenever I wanted. My father was more interested. He thought it could be useful. I wasn't really interested in that, either."

"Both of my parents were pretty adamant that I ignore it," Finn said quietly, meaning that he himself had been adamant that he ignore it.

"Yeah, not really possible, is it?"

"No."

She looked at him, and he felt like she could see right through him. The wriggling worm of shame in his heart squirmed, suddenly exposed to sunlight; he looked away, feeling it burrow deeper, looking for darkness.

"Yes, well, obviously, that's ridiculous," Eraldir cut in. "In my day that was unheard of. But of course, there was the Fall, and the war, and then the mage killings. A whole country falling apart will do stupid things to people."

"How did you survive? I thought all the mages from that time were dead."

Eraldir considered his tea. "I was sick. So sick they brought me home from the Academy. I missed a whole year of school. I would have died, if not for an herbalist. A naturalist mage who made a tea for me." He lifted the mug. "I was recovering, almost ready to return to school—to my friends—when it happened." He stared down at the swirling leaves.

Finn didn't know what to say. Isabelle cut in. "I've been trying to convince Eraldir that he should start a school again. For mages."

Eraldir shrugged bitterly. "I'd had one year of schooling at the Academy. I'm not much help."

"But you're better than nothing!" Isabelle said brightly.

The old man pursed his thin, papery lips and stared into his tea.

She turned to Finn. "Don't listen to him. He's actually a very good teacher. When he's not napping or telling ridiculous stories."

Eraldir shrugged again and looked off into the forest. Finn looked out into the forest, too, and realized that the light was starting to fade. Kel would probably be getting worried now, wondering if Finn had left her again. Guilt reared up and suddenly Finn felt like he had to leave immediately, in case Kel was worried. He really, really, didn't want to, though. He had so many questions.

"Thank you very much for the tea, and for getting that out of my face. I didn't realize it was getting so late, though. I need to get back to my sister. She'll be worried about me."

Isabelle smiled. "Sure, I'll walk you back?"

"No, no, that's—" Finn realized he didn't know where he

was. He hadn't been paying attention when she'd led him here. "Or, sure, actually, can you just take me back to where I ran into you?" He didn't want to take anyone back to Kel's sanctuary. He was afraid of the questions she would ask, especially because Kel was so young. Too young to be doing magic.

"Yeah, sure." Isabelle stood. "See you in a bit, Eraldir."

The old man grunted, still lost in thought.

They walked together through the darkness under the trees, Finn following behind her. Her footsteps were light and sure, her white hair waving gently behind her.

When they reached the spot where he had first tripped over her, they stopped. Finn looked at her, torn, wanting to get back to Kel, but not wanting to leave yet. Curious. Not sure if he would ever see her again.

"So, are you going to be staying here for a while?"

She smiled at him. "That depends."

"On what?"

"On if we find who we're looking for."

"Who are you looking for?"

"A naturalist mage."

A jolt of shock and fear ran through Finn. They were looking for Kel. "Why?"

"We were told there was one here, and that we should come look for him. Or her."

"Who told you that?"

"Someone Eraldir knows. He wouldn't let me meet her."

Finn digested this information.

"What will you do when you find this mage?"

She shrugged. "Invite whoever it is to join us."

Finn wanted to trust her, had no reason not to, but his first goal, his primary purpose in life now, was protecting Kel.

"It's your sister, isn't it?" Isabelle asked.

Finn was caught. "No, my sister isn't a mage. She's not anything."

"So, if I were to, say, follow you back, I wouldn't find a giant garden paradise?"

"Noo…" He stood there, rooted to the spot. Now he really couldn't go back. He would be leading her straight to Kel.

"Okay. Well, I wasn't planning on following you back anyway." She grinned. "I think Eraldir and I will be here for a while. Come by any time." She turned and walked back the way they had come, leaving Finn standing alone in the growing dark.

He waited a long time, listening for the sound of her footsteps returning, or the crack of a twig. But the forest was silent. At last, he turned to head back to Kel, taking a long, circuitous route on his way back. He doubled back so many times that he got lost and almost couldn't find his way back at all.

It was a light shining through the trees that led him back. Kel had placed the fire globe on top of the nest, and it glowed brightly through the trees. Finn carried it down with him into the fort.

"Finn!" Kel cried, running up to him and wrapping her arms around his waist. "Where were you?" Finn looked down into the little girl's worried face.

"Sorry, Kel, just out walking. I got a little lost." He knelt and wrapped Kel in a tight hug. "Thanks for putting the light up there. It helped me find my way back."

Kel hugged him back. "Smoke thought you might be lost."

It made sense that the ferret would have a low opinion of his navigating abilities. The ferret seemed to have a low opinion of him in general. If it even was a ferret.

CHAPTER 7

*A*rcturus let out a long, depressed sigh as he dropped the spleen back onto the table. It made a wet, splattery sound and some blood leaked out, running in a rivulet down the table and dripping onto the stone floor. Was he looking at the correct body? He turned around, to the mess of organs piled around the corpse on the other table. It didn't matter, because the two bodies were the same. They both had livers—although the non-mage's was hardened and diseased; he'd been a drinker, that was what killed him actually—they both had lungs and hearts and stomachs, and everything else you'd expect. Where was it?

In frustration, Arcturus pulled the mage's body open further, rummaged around in it desperately, but there was nothing. Nothing. It was the same.

Afterwards, he scrubbed the blood from his hands. The bodies were neatly tucked away into the kiln he kept for that purpose. A few hours of stoking the fires that heated it and the bodies would be reduced to ash. But Arcturus' mind was no longer on the task at hand. He hardly paid attention at all to which ring went on which finger as his mind considered the problem. There had to be a difference. There had to be something different about mages. But it couldn't be seen when they were dead, he was absolutely certain of that now. No, it must be something fragile, something that disappeared immediately upon death. Arcturus knew what he needed to try next.

~

SOMETHING WAS DIFFERENT ABOUT FINN. Kel worried what it might be. Her brother kept climbing up the wall and looking out into the forest. She was afraid he was thinking of leaving again.

Smoke thought he looked like a nervous mother bird watching for eagles.

"What are you looking at?" Kel called up to Finn.

Finn climbed down the vine ladder and came to sit next to her. Smoke wandered off to look for eggs.

"Oh, nothing." Finn smiled a forced smile. "Anything I can do to help?"

"No," Kel said. Then she cocked her head. A wistful, complaining voice drifted into Kel's thoughts.

...old for this. My aching knees... Those berries look good, we should—ow he didn't need to yank that hard. Oh well... just keep on going... one foot at a time... It's better than the alternative. I suppose. Sigh...

"What is it?" Finn asked.

"A horse," Kel said. To her surprise, Finn leapt up.

"A horse?" He clenched his fists, looked around him. "Kel, get inside the log."

"What?"

"Don't argue. Just get inside the log."

"What's wrong?"

"Nothing's wrong. Everything's fine. Probably. Just go hide and don't come out until I say it's okay."

Kel's lower lip started to quiver, but she picked herself up and ran to the log, crawling inside and wrapping herself up in the blanket at the very back. Smoke came and curled up in her pocket.

She heard Finn climb the ladder again. Then she waited.

I just want a short nap, is that too much to ask? I'm too old for this. All this walking around here and there. What's the point of it? Grass is the same everywhere.

The horse was closer now, its voice so much clearer than that of other animals. Usually Kel only got snippets of things, images or feelings, not a full running monologue.

Yes, well, I'm smarter than other animals, aren't I?

Oh, hi, I'm sorry for overhearing.

Yes, not very polite, is it? Oh, dear my aching back. Oh, thank heavens, we're stopping now.

It was getting hot and scratchy under the blanket, and Kel couldn't see the point of hiding. The horse's name was Sylvia apparently, and she was ancient and arthritic. Nothing to be afraid of. Finn must be confused.

There were two others with her, but Kel couldn't hear anything from them. That meant people.

Kel pushed off the blanket, crawled out of the log, and climbed up the wall to stand behind Finn.

Finn turned towards her angrily. "I told you to hide!" He reached out and gripped Kel's shoulder, but a voice interrupted them.

"Hello!" Kel looked over Finn's arm and saw a girl looking up at them. Next to her was an old man, seated on top of the horse.

Finn released her. "I thought you said you weren't going to follow me back?"

"Yes, well, I didn't say I would totally avoid the part of the forest where all the plants are enormous and fruiting out of season."

"We're not a threat to you, boy. We're here to help. Is that your sister?"

Finn grabbed Kel again and thrust her behind himself.

"Hi!" The girl grinned and waved at Kel. Kel struggled to get out of Finn's grip.

"Finn, it's okay, let's talk to them," Kel said.

"You don't know that, Kel."

Oh my, this grass is delicious.

"I think they're okay."

A huge gust of wind buffeted them from behind. It lifted them up and knocked them off the wall. For a sickening moment, Kel felt herself hanging in open air next to Finn, and then they were both plummeting towards the ground. They landed in a large sphere of water, which materialized between them and the ground at the last second, breaking their fall.

"Isabelle!" The old man thundered.

"I would have caught them!"

"You had about half a second before both of them were either dead or maimed!"

"They're fine! Right?" She turned to Finn and Kel, who were both lying flat on their backs on the ground, in the center of a mud puddle.

"I'm fine." Kel sat up. Smoke leapt out of her pocket, dripping wet, and scurried off furiously.

I think I'll just lie down in this lovely patch of sunshine.

Sylvia moved off and settled herself on the ground.

Finn jumped up. "You nearly—" Several trees around them burst into flames. Finn instantly cut himself off, tried to control himself.

The old man made a movement with his hand, and water

doused the blazing wood. Kel flinched, feeling the trees' cries of pain.

"You've got a temper, boy," the old man remarked.

"Thank you for putting them out, Eraldir," Finn said quietly.

They all stood there, staring at Finn. Eraldir looked at him calculatingly. "You know, I was told to come here for your sister, but I think it might be you who needs the most help."

Kel wondered what they were talking about. How did Finn know these people?

Finn looked at the ground.

"Villagers ran you off, eh?" Eraldir said.

Finn didn't look up.

"Lit something on fire you shouldn't have?"

Finn fell to his knees, hands pressed to his face. Seven more trees caught fire. Eraldir doused them immediately.

"It happens, boy. It happened even in the old days."

Finn looked up. Tears were in his eyes. "I'm sorry."

"Don't be sorry. Learn."

Finn hung his head again. Kel came over and wrapped her small arms around him. Finn extracted himself gently and stood up. "What do you want with us?"

"We want you to join us," Isabelle said. "We're starting a school."

"School's a bit of an overstatement," Eraldir said.

"I've convinced Eraldir to take on some apprentices."

Finn looked down at Kel. He put an arm around her small shoulders. "This is my sister, Kel. She's only six, but she's a mage."

Eraldir looked at Kel with interest. "That's something I've never seen before."

Kel pressed herself into Finn's leg.

"What makes you think you can help us?" Finn asked.

"I don't know if I can help you, boy," Eraldir said. "At the very least, though, I can put out what you light on fire."

Finn gave a short nod.

Kel noticed something about the old man. There was something crumbling about him. In his belly, things weren't right. Things hadn't been right for a long time, but they'd carried on, continuing to work through the years, but they weren't going to work much longer. Kel wondered if the man knew, if the girl knew. But she didn't say anything.

FINN PULLED KEL ASIDE. He held the little girl's hand and led her around the curve of the nest to where Eraldir and Isabelle couldn't see them. Then he knelt and looked into her eyes.

"We need to go with them, Kel."

Kel looked at the high vine wall next to them. Her nest. She couldn't leave it now. It was safe here.

"I don't want to go." Kel looked down at the ground, but Finn gripped her chin and lifted it so their eyes met.

"Kel, I—I have to go."

Something shook loose in Kel. The small piece of security that had been tenaciously growing back. It broke into a million pieces and Kel fell into a dark well of panic.

"No! You can't go!" She yelled it, and tears sprang up in her eyes. The leaves of the nearby plants rustled, and the birds in the trees took flight.

Startled, Finn looked up, but then turned right back to Kel. He let go of his sister's chin and held her shoulders, stooping farther down. Kel's heart was pounding, and her breath came fast. She was starting to get lightheaded.

"Hey, Kel, it's okay. It's okay." Finn wrapped his arms

around her, but Kel, instead of feeling comforted, felt only constricted, and at the same time abandoned. Finn was going to leave without her. She couldn't trust him, couldn't relax, because as soon as she did Finn would be gone.

Tears trickled down Kel's cheeks, and she fought to get out of Finn's arms.

"Kel, calm down."

"NO!" she screamed, squirming out of Finn's grasp. The nest caught fire. Kel, startled, looked at it, the flames reflected in her eyes. The smoke blew into her face and she coughed. Then she looked at her brother in terror and ran.

Horrified at what he'd done, Finn looked from Kel to the burning nest and back. "Eraldir?!" He called.

"I've got it boy," Eraldir called back.

Hearing this, Finn turned and ran after Kel. But the little girl was small and fast and knew these woods better than he did. Finn stopped to listen, heard nothing. So, he sat on a log, put his head in his hands, and took a few deep breaths.

Then he looked up again. "Kel?" he called out. No answer.

He heard footsteps and turned, hoping to see Kel, but it was Isabelle.

"Eraldir put out your fire before it got out of hand," she said.

Finn let out a sigh of relief and rubbed the back of his hand across his face, glad to find there weren't tears there. He didn't want her to see him crying.

She stood there, hands on her hips, looking at him.

"I take it your sister doesn't like us?"

"No, it's not that. I think she likes you okay. She just doesn't want to leave."

"How long have you been out here?"

How long had it been? Finn stared off into space. "A few weeks? A few months maybe?"

She lifted an eyebrow.

"Well, she'll come back on her own, right? She's not going to leave her nest forever."

Finn could see the logic in that, but he didn't want to give up. He wanted Kel to know that he wouldn't leave her. Except it wasn't true. He couldn't stay here, lighting things on fire. Eventually someone would get hurt, and it wouldn't be Finn. "I think I'm going to wait out here for a while, see if I can find her."

"Want me to blow all the leaves off the trees and bushes? Lot easier to find her if she's got nowhere to hide."

He couldn't tell if she was joking. "Um, no thanks. I'll just keep looking."

She shrugged. "All right. Suit yourself. I'm going to go find some trees to climb." And with that she ambled off.

Finn waited for a while, listening to the wind in the trees. A few times he heard large crashes, and exclamations of surprise from Isabelle, but she was a long way off and Finn knew now that Isabelle screaming probably wasn't a big deal. He wondered if she were in real danger if her scream would be different. Would he know when to actually come to her rescue? Not that she needed rescuing, nor was he really equipped to rescue her. He'd probably just light her on fire. He'd have to leave the rescuing to Eraldir.

Finn looked up to see Kel standing in front of him. There was a smear of green along one cheek, and her hands and knees were dirty. Her eyes were red-rimmed and puffy, but she looked at Finn solemnly.

Finn didn't move, didn't want to scare her away. "Kel," he whispered. "Thank you for coming back. I'm so sorry. Eraldir put out the fire, though, so everything's okay."

"I don't want to go with them."

Finn nodded. "I know, I'm sorry. You want to stay here."

"No."

"No?"

"I want to go home."

Finn's heart became a lump of metal. "I'm sorry, Kel. I'm so sorry. We can't go home."

Kel looked down. "I don't want to go with them."

Gingerly, moving very slowly, afraid he would startle her, Finn pulled Kel into a gentle hug. "I don't want to go either. I want to go home, too. But we can't. Remember? And, I can't stay here, Kel."

"Why?"

"Because I can't control my magic, Kel. I can't control it like you can. But I'm going to learn how. Eraldir is going to show me how to control it. And he might be able to teach you things, too."

"Like what?"

"I don't know. I don't even know what there is to learn, what's possible. But maybe there's more you can do, too."

"Once you learn, can we come back?"

Finn bent his forehead to lean against his sister's small head. Her hair was soft. He closed his eyes.

"I don't know, Kel. I promise that once I can control my magic we'll talk about it, though."

"We'll decide together?"

"Yeah. We'll decide together where to go. Just you and me."

Kel was quiet for a few moments.

"And Smoke?"

"Yeah. You, me, and Smoke. Mostly you and me, though. Smoke doesn't get a vote." He didn't want to find himself perpetually outvoted by a ferret.

"All right."

Finn sat up and took Kel's hand. "Yes? You'll come?"

"Okay."

Finn leaned down again. "Thank you, Kel. I'm sorry. I promise I'll work hard and learn as quickly as I can. Then we'll go where we want to go."

"Okay."

Finn led Kel back to Eraldir, who was lying on his bedroll, chewing on a piece of dried meat. Isabelle had joined him and was eating some berries.

"These are great berries, Kel," she said. Kel nodded shyly and stepped behind Finn.

"We've decided we'll go with you," Finn said. "And... thanks."

"Excellent." Eraldir clapped his bony hands together. "I'm sick of being in the woods. Hard ground to sleep on. Have to cook all your own food." He stuck a finger in his ear, dug out some ear wax and wiped it on his pants. "Lots of places to pee, though. Gotta say, that's pretty convenient. When you get as old as I am, you start to appreciate things like that. Did I tell you, Isabelle, a few months back I couldn't pee at all for about a week and a half."

"Yes, Eraldir. You did tell me that. Also, I was there." Isabelle looked like she wished she'd never experienced that in the first place, but, it having so stuck in her mind the first time, it didn't really matter how many extra times she heard it. She wasn't likely to forget.

"Yes. Toilets. No one appreciates them. Baths though, that's something you can't get in the forest."

"So, do you have anything you need to take with you?" Isabelle interjected.

"Or, hot baths anyway. When you get as old as I am you need a good hot bath. Keeps the muscles moving."

"I'll get my pack," Finn said. "Where are we going?"

"Westwend, boy. Where the mages are."

Finn stopped, halfway towards his pack. The last time he'd seen Ronan flashed before his eyes.

THAT NIGHT, a few days after his sixteenth birthday, Finn had stayed in the library studying until well after dark, trying to distract himself from what was happening inside him. It had been difficult, because if he lost focus the ink started to smoke. But he wasn't going give up. He knew what magic did to people, what it had done to their country, what it had done to his friend, and he wasn't going to give in to it. If he could ignore it long enough, he knew it would go away.

He left, turning a corner down a deserted street, and a voice spoke from behind him.

"Happy birthday."

Finn spun around to see Ronan in the shadows, leaning against the smooth stone wall, the side of his face with the half-moon tattoo illuminated by the glow of Finn's lamplight.

Finn hadn't seen Ronan in weeks. His cheeks were hollow, and there was a manic glow in his eyes. Finn could barely look at him.

"What?"

Ronan shrugged and pushed himself off the wall. "Just wondering how your birthday was."

A sick feeling of suspicion crept into Finn's stomach. "What did you do?"

Ronan's eyes widened. "Wait, really? You, too?"

"I don't know what you're talking about."

Ronan's mouth dropped open. "The great, high and mighty Finn? What kind are you?" The old gleam of excitement was back in Ronan's eyes.

"I'm not anything," Finn said.

Now Ronan was looking at him with something that

might have been pity. He looked like he was going to say something else, but Finn cut him off.

"Leave me alone, Ronan." He turned and started to walk away as quickly as he could.

"Finn, wait!" Ronan ran after him, stopping him with a hand on his shoulder.

"Hey, I'm sorry, Finn. I know you didn't want it."

Finn wouldn't meet his eye.

"Um, hey, look, I just wanted to let you know that I'm leaving."

Finn looked up. "You are?"

"Yeah. You know Westwend?"

Finn had heard of the city; it was much larger than Cromwic. Older, and higher up in the mountains.

Ronan continued. "Well, I heard there's mages living there. A bunch of them." He dug into the ground with one bare toe. "In secret, of course." He looked up at Finn. "Do you want to come?"

Finn paused, and a vision flashed across his mind's eye. The world as it had been before. Towering cities filled with thousands of people, wind-runners connecting them so you could cross the entire country in just a few days, the high council and attendant court, trade and diplomacy.

"Come on, Finn," Ronan said, and the old grin was back. "You and me, we'll rebuild the old world—not that you've got magic now, of course. Obviously."

Finn shook himself. Part of him wanted that, wanted that so badly, but everything he'd read about magic was that it was dangerous, that it destroyed the people who wielded it, that it wasn't controllable, that even the most skilled mages maimed and killed those around them. It had destroyed everything it had built, and more.

"No, Ronan. You know how I feel about…things."

Ronan's face hardened, but the anger was softened by

pity. "Well, if you change your mind." But they both knew he wouldn't.

"Bye, Ronan."

"Bye, Finn."

Ronan turned to go, and somewhere very deep down, Finn felt that he was making a terrible mistake. But he let Ronan walk away.

CHAPTER 8

*T*he woman sitting across the gilt table from Arcturus was leaning forward, playing with the stem of her crystal wineglass as she smiled, strands of dark hair framing her face artfully. Arcturus wondered how long she had spent in front of a mirror, watching herself move, getting her hair to look like that. She was saying something now, but he wasn't listening. The other things she'd said hadn't been interesting, either.

Arcturus picked up his silver fork and pushed the last of his dessert around on his plate, not even enjoying looking into her lovely blue-grey eyes anymore.

ERALDIR WAS MIDWAY through the process of mounting his horse, still espousing the virtues of various bathrooms he had known, when Finn returned with his pack.

"Is there anything you need to bring, Kel?" Finn asked. "I've got the globe in my pack, and the blanket and extra clothes."

Kel hadn't brought anything with her to the forest, except for the clothes on her back, but she didn't want to leave all the edible plants and seeds and the vines that she'd found. She wanted to bring as many of them with her as she could. And where was Smoke? She couldn't leave without Smoke.

Smoke? she thought, reaching out, but she couldn't find the little animal. She took her time gathering up nuts, seeds, and plant shoots, dawdling and delaying as much as she could, reaching out every few minutes to look for him, but the ferret never answered.

Isabelle was losing patience. "Finn, what's taking your sister so long?" A heavy wind rattled through the tree branches.

"Why don't you go practice flying if you're bored?" Finn snapped. "Who else do you know who could build a plant fortress, let alone a six-year-old? Give the kid some time."

"When I was six, I spent all my time swimming in Lake Iori," Eraldir said. "There are the most monstrously large fish in there. The magic makes them grow like crazy. One nearly swallowed me once."

Isabelle groaned and rattled a bush with a gust of wind.

Kel hated to hear them angry at each other because of her. She rubbed one hand along her forearm and looked at the ground.

Eraldir stopped in the middle of his story about the giant fish. "What's wrong, girl?"

Kel rubbed her fists in her eyes, trying to stop the tears that wanted to come.

"I don't want to leave Smoke."

"With a brother like yours you can have smoke anywhere you want. And plenty of places you don't want, girl."

"Smoke is her ferret," Finn said. He reached his arms tightly around Kel and held her head softly to his chest with his hand. He smelled like soot and pine trees. Through the rough fabric of Finn's shirt, Kel could hear his heart beating quickly and solidly. A deep, strong, thunk in her brother's chest. It comforted her.

"It's okay, Kel. No one's mad. Well, Isabelle's annoyed, but that's okay. And Smoke will come back, too. He's probably just gone and found some sun to dry off and warm up in. Right?"

Kel sniffed.

"Everything's going to be okay." Finn's voice became rougher. "I'm not going anywhere, either."

Kel buried her face farther into her brother's chest. Her tears stopped, and she pulled away to see a wet spot on Finn's shirt. She looked down and scuffed her foot in the dirt.

"Okay. I guess we can go now."

Finn patted Kel's shoulder gently. "How about we leave a message for Smoke, so he knows which way to go?"

Kel's eyes lit up and she smiled. "Okay."

"What should we leave him?"

"Um," Kel thought. "Eggs. Or, eggshells."

Kel ran to the bird nests and gathered three white eggs and a few handfuls of empty, broken eggshells. She left three whole eggs in a clear space outside the nest. Then, they left.

WALKING through the forest behind the wind and water mages, Finn felt a lightness, a looseness he hadn't felt since— well since before he'd become a mage. His muscles felt like unstrung bowstrings. The knowledge that he was safe, that the world around him was safe from him, left him almost collapsing with relief. He felt like he might fall over at any moment, but if he did he'd probably just float right back up again. Gratitude flooded him, cooling and calming, and a tiny seed of hope sprouted. As long as he stayed around the old man he wouldn't hurt anyone anymore.

He was uncertain, though, that it was the right thing for Kel, to go off with these two. He was responsible for his sister now. And Kel was something special.

Hours later, Finn was still buoyant as they walked through the hot, thick, late spring air under the trees. Isabelle had headed off into the woods alone to practice, saying she'd catch up with them soon. Behind him, Kel was meticulously placing tiny pieces of shell every few feet and stopping to look back every few minutes. It was a little weird, her attachment to that ferret.

"So, Eraldir," he ventured. "How far is Westwend?"

Eraldir nudged Sylvia with his heel to keep her from running into a tree. "Oh, not far, my boy. Ever been there?"

"No." Finn hadn't ever been out of Cromwic. He didn't want to think about his village, though. Or whatever was left of it.

"Ah, Westwend. Large town on the banks of the Green River, up in the foothills of the Iron Mountains. Near Copper Creek. The mines? Lots of mining towns up there. I don't come up here too often. My skills are more useful to farmers. Especially in the Uplands where they get droughts. But I pay a visit to Westwend every now and then, when I get some coin saved up. Sometimes there's work for me in their sluices or cleaning the streets. And, of course, I was the one who diverted the Green River in the first place."

"Diverted?" Finn asked, and then wished he hadn't. Eraldir probably would have gone on anyway, though.

"Oh yes. Split the whole thing in two. Westwend's a veritable island fortress now. Best thing for them since... well, probably just the best. They're close to the Baharran border, you know."

Finn did know. But knowing distances on a map was one thing, feeling what it was like to travel somewhere, and knowing how long it took, was another.

"So, they were being raided a lot; after the Fall, the Baharrans got wind of the trouble here pretty quick. Caught on to the fact that we weren't blasting their warriors off the face of the earth with fire mages anymore." He leaned down and elbowed Finn. "That's one thing I'll say about Baharrans. They're fast. And brutal. Though I guess that's two things. They caught me once, did I tell you that?"

"You—"

"Just after I left Westwend actually, I was captured by a raiding party. They cut off three of my toes before I escaped." He reached down, pulled off the battered leather sandal he wore, then the thick wool sock, and reached a foot out towards Finn for inspection. The smell was overpowering. Finn placed a hand over his mouth and leaned back. Eraldir's foot was indeed missing three toes. The big one and the two smallest. Of the remaining two, one was normal, but the other had an infection; the nail itself was black, and the skin around it was sickly yellow.

"Yep, I know, I know. Pretty gruesome. But, I escaped. I was worn out from all the water work, but I got my energy back and drowned them all before they got to anything important like fingers." He grinned at Finn, tried to reach his foot up to put the sock back on, but his leg wouldn't bend far enough. He lost his balance and toppled sideways. Finn grabbed him by the shoulder, catching him in time to center him gently back on the saddle. Sylvia pulled up short. "Thank you, boy, much obliged. And, here, could you just…"

He handed Finn the sock.

Finn pinched the sock delicately between two fingers. He really, really, didn't want to get anywhere near that foot, but the only alternative was waiting while Eraldir went through the twenty-minute process of climbing down from his horse, which he would need help with anyway. Then he might still need help with the sock, then he'd need more help getting back up. Gritting his teeth, Finn grasped the sock, and gently edged it over the veiny foot.

"Ah, thank you, my boy." Eraldir handed him the sandal. It had black, toe-shaped, sweat stains. Resigned, Finn took that, too, and worked it over the foot.

Eraldir kicked Sylvia with his heels, and they were off again at their plodding pace.

"Anyway, where was I?"

Luckily, at that moment, Isabelle came back.

"I see you guys are getting to know one another," she said, interrupting Eraldir's train of thought.

"Where'd you go?" Finn asked.

She scratched her head. A twig fell out of her white, wavy hair.

"I climbed to the top of the tallest tree I could find, then I made the strongest wind I could and saw how far I could get the tree to bend over."

"Do you ever fall off that way?"

"Yes. Or, sometimes the tree is springy and when I stop the wind it flips back the other way and catapults me off." She laughed. "Sometimes the tree just breaks, though."

Finn heard a small, dismayed sound from Kel's direction. Isabelle ignored it.

"What kinds of stuff can you do?" Isabelle asked.

"Light fires, basically."

"That's it? I mean, what have you tried to do with it?"

"Not everyone jumps into their magic so recklessly, Isabelle," Eraldir said. "Back in my day—"

"So, you've never experimented with your powers?" she asked, incredulous.

"I told you, my parents didn't want me to." *I didn't want me to.* He looked at the ground.

87

"And you just did what you were told?"

"Yeah, pretty much."

"Why?"

Why? He shrugged, not sure he could explain it to her, and even less sure that she would understand.

"You haven't spent enough time in Caledonia to fully understand what attitudes are like here, Isabelle," Eraldir said. "I've been trying to tell you, magic may have been unknown in Montvale, but here it's worse. It's feared. Most people don't have magic at all. And most mages are like Finn. Untrained and very dangerous. Things have calmed down a lot, but you're still not safe as a mage. All that anger and distrust is right below the surface. I mean, the number of times I've been run out of a village, a forest of pitchforks behind me..."

"People are idiots," Isabelle said.

"No, Isabelle, they are not," Eraldir said. "Never make the mistake of assuming that people who don't agree with you are stupid. They have their reasons."

"Stupid reasons," she grumbled.

"How many of your family members have died from magic?" he asked shrewdly.

She didn't answer.

"What about you, boy?" Eraldir asked. "You think it's stupid that people fear magic?"

Finn swallowed around the stone that had suddenly materialized in his throat. He shook his head.

"You think it's wrong that people don't want magic done?"

He was about to shake his head again, when he realized, to his surprise, that he didn't think magic was evil anymore.

He was dangerous, he knew he was. He didn't need any more proof of that. He hated himself more than anyone else ever could for what he had done, but what if, when his magic came, he hadn't tried to ignore it? What if he'd let himself experiment? Learn? Be a little more like Isabelle? As far as he knew, she hadn't killed anyone, despite her insane recklessness.

"Yes." He had to squeeze the words out around the stone. "I think it's wrong to keep people from doing magic."

Eraldir sat back, looked at him.

"Good."

And that was the moment when Finn realized what he wanted in life. He didn't know how he was going to do it, but he would make the world safe for mages. Safe for his sister, and everyone like her. A world that would have been safe for himself. A world where people without magic didn't hate it because they hadn't been given a reason to fear it.

Non-mages were right to be angry with him. They were right to fear him. He glanced over at Isabelle, her hair blown artfully back by a wind she was probably creating. They had a right to fear her, too. For a different reason. Finn would hurt them without meaning to, Isabelle would hurt them out of indifference or over-exuberance.

"Can't you imagine what it would be like not to have magic?" he asked her.

She gave him a scornful look. "Of course I can. I spent the first fifteen years of my life being nothing, just like you did."

"You weren't nothing then, though."

"Yes," she said bitterly. "I was."

A wave of pity surprised Finn as it rushed up through him. He wanted to know what had happened to her to make her so bitter, but Isabelle sped up to pass him, a heavy wind parting around her and buffeting Finn and Eraldir back so they couldn't follow.

The subject was dropped, and they continued in silence.

~

THAT NIGHT, Kel dreamed again of the path, but this time the leaves of the birches were bright yellow, floating down around her, flashing in the sunlight, to settle on the ground. She awoke crying.

CHAPTER 9

*M*ercifully, the man's screams had stopped. He had remained conscious for a truly vexing amount of time, screaming and screaming. Arcturus had wrapped a cloth around his head to deaden the sound, but it hadn't worked well. Now all was quiet, and Arcturus could focus on peeling back the skin.

He paused for a moment to check the man's pulse. Yes, still alive. Good. Arcturus felt a thrill of anticipation as he parted the layers of muscle and fat.

"Here, boy." Eraldir thrust a stick into Finn's open hand. The bark was peeling off the damp wood.

"What's this for?" Finn asked. It was late afternoon; Eraldir's bones had been acting up—whatever that meant, but Finn knew better than to ask for clarification—and so they'd made camp early. Isabelle had lent Finn some oil for his boots, and he had just sat down on a log a short distance from their camp to work on them when Eraldir had ambled over, picked the stick up from the ground and handed it to him.

"Ready for your first magic lesson?"

Finn dropped the boot he was holding. "Yes, of course. Yeah. Where should I—"

Eraldir grunted and pointed to the stick. "First thing, if you feel the urge to light something on fire, direct it there."

Finn looked at the stick. "Oh, okay."

Eraldir gestured to himself. "Try to avoid this general area."

Finn blushed. "Yeah, sorry."

"Don't apologize for something you haven't even done yet, boy. Although, you probably will have to later."

Finn hoped he was wrong.

Eraldir braced himself heavily on Finn's shoulders and lowered himself to sit on the ground, leaning against a tree trunk, his feet stretched out long in front of him, his legs crossed at his ankles, with their bunchy wool socks.

"Ah, that's better. Too much traveling." He scratched at his stomach. "Right, let's see you light that."

Finn, still sitting on the log, edged away from Eraldir and held the stick up in front of his face. He'd been accidentally lighting things on fire all day, but now that he wanted it to happen, of course it didn't.

Eraldir waited patiently while Finn stared at the stick.

"You're a terrible older brother."

"What?" Finn looked up, his stomach clenching.

Eraldir shrugged his bony shoulders. "It's only luck that you haven't killed your sister."

The shame, the truth of what Eraldir was saying was too deep; it hurt too terribly to be looked at, and instead, hot rage poured up, obscuring it, protecting him. "I protect her, I got her out, I got her food and clothes and who are you to—"

Finn forgot he was supposed to be aiming for the stick,

and the ground around them burst into flames. So did Eraldir's hair, and his pants, and his shirt, and the log Finn sat on, and the trees around them. The small bottle of boot oil exploded into a fireball. The heat roared up, searing Finn's face and forcing his eyes shut. He fell to the ground, wrapping his arms around his face. Finn barely had time to hit the ground, though, when, with a great *foomp* he was struck by a freezing wave of water. Everything was silent, Finn was underwater. He couldn't breathe. And then the wave had passed, and he was kneeling on the ground in a puddle, his wet wool clothes hanging off him, water streaming out of his hair and down his face, dripping off the end of his nose onto the ground.

"The stick, boy. I told you to aim for the stick."

Finn looked up to see that everything in a ten-foot radius around him was burned and blackened. Eraldir's clothes were hanging off him in blackened tatters, and his hair and eyebrows were singed. Finn looked down and noticed he was still holding the stick. It was completely unharmed. Great.

"Grab me that over there, would you?" Eraldir said, pointing to a pile of cloth Finn hadn't noticed earlier. It sat at the base of a tree about fifteen feet away.

Feeling shaken, confused, and still fighting the anger and shame, Finn went to pick it up and found that it was a set of clothes. He turned around to see Eraldir stripping off the last of his burned garments. Trying not to look, Finn handed the fresh clothes to the old man.

"Well, not bad, not bad, I'd say. You're more powerful than I thought. Good thing I overestimated. All right, boy, you can stop averting your eyes now." Finn looked back, his heart still hammering with fear. He wondered if Eraldir would see how dangerous he really was now. Would he say that Finn couldn't be taught?

Eraldir grimaced and tugged at his wool pants. "You even got my knickers, boy."

Finn sat, running his hands along his own soaked pants, trying to calm himself down. Eraldir sat back down and looked at him. "Sorry I said that, boy. I know you care about your sister. You're not a bad brother."

Finn knew what Eraldir had said before was true, though. Regardless of what he was saying now.

"Ah boy, don't look so serious. I only said that because I knew it'd hurt your feelings."

This didn't make things any clearer for Finn. But, at the very least, maybe Eraldir didn't actually hate him.

"And, don't worry about the clothes. Those were my old clothes. Totally infested with mites. I hardly ever wear them."

Finn swallowed. "Okay, so... you're telling me I lose control of my magic when I'm upset. I already know that."

"Exactly!" Eraldir leaned forward and patted Finn on the only part of him he could reach, which was his foot. "You're a quick one. It's not so much that it happens, but why, and how, that we want to know here."

"Why does it happen?"

"Well, magic in humans is an odd thing, boy."

"What do you mean, magic in humans?"

"I mean, the Ael had it first, and not like we have it. We've got a pale, fragmented, broken version."

"The Ael?" Those were only in children's stories. Immortal beings made of magic, shapeshifters that had roamed the lands for thousands of years.

Eraldir grunted. "Yes, the old ones."

"I thought those were—"

"Oh no, they're real. Not many left that haven't faded."

That had been in the stories, too. The Ael eventually faded back into the magic they were made from, or sometimes they merged with trees or rivers. In the stories, humans called them up, asked favors from them, but any favor came at a terrible price. Finn had so many questions, but they weren't quite distracting him from the doubt and fear he felt shifting inside him. Eraldir continued before he could ask anything more about the Ael.

"Look, boy, you've really got to stop it with this hating yourself thing. You're not the only one, you know."

"But I light things on fire! The worst you could do is blast water everywhere!"

Eraldir raised an eyebrow. "Oh, so you're the only one who's a danger, are you? How about you just think for a minute and ask yourself whether water might ever be a problem. How many people can breathe underwater? How many people can breathe if their lungs are filled with it, eh? For that matter, what do you think blood is made of, huh?"

As Eraldir spoke, something deeply unsettling happened in Finn's body. There was a ceasing of a motion that he hadn't even realized was there. His heart sped up but felt like it was pounding against an iron wall, as if the blood in his veins had become solid, immobile. Just when he began to panic, it stopped.

"You're not the only one who is a danger, Finn. You're not the only one who has killed."

The complete seriousness that Finn saw on Eraldir's face was discomforting.

"I don't think humans were meant to have magic, boy," Eraldir went on. "I don't know why we do. But we've got no choice in the matter, aside from killing ourselves." The solemnity slipped away, replaced by Eraldir's usual flippancy. "Now, I'm not saying you shouldn't kill yourself. That's a choice a man's got to make for himself, but learning to control it, mostly, isn't impossible. For most people."

It was weird to hear someone else describe exactly the conflict Finn had been having with himself. He'd thought he was the only one who felt that way. The only one who didn't think he would be able to control this, who had considered killing himself to protect the people he loved. Those that were left. He wondered if Eraldir had ever killed anyone, but he couldn't quite bring himself to ask.

Eraldir grunted. "Like I said, I don't think humans were meant to have magic. Somehow, we do, though, but we don't have a real way of connecting to it, to the power that feeds it. The Ael, now, they could draw on all of it, connect to it and channel it. Some of them even merged with it. For some reason, some of us can, and the closest thing we have to what they have is our emotions. It's a broken, clumsy way of connecting, and I don't know why it happens, but I do know that learning magic includes learning to control your emotions. Well, control is probably a strong word."

"So, what, I'm supposed to make myself angry whenever I want to light a fire?"

"Not angry, boy. Afraid."

Finn paused, and Eraldir continued.

"You weren't really angry back there, boy. You were afraid."

Finn considered this.

"Now, me, water seems most connected to a general feeling of ennui. I start to think about how nothing I do really matters, and how I don't really want to do anything, and up comes all the water I need. Sometimes other emotions, too. It's not a precise thing."

"Huh."

"Feelings come from thoughts, or from body movements, I've found. Working on those seems to be helpful. Or, there's other things, too," he reached over and handed Finn a blackened pine cone. Finn took it dubiously. "Maybe you find this pine cone particularly comforting. Or frightening. That could help."

Finn stared at the pine cone. He felt nothing.

Eraldir reached out and took it back. "Or not, it doesn't have to be that. Just an example." He cleared his throat loudly. "Point is, try things." He shifted his weight and grimaced. "All right, that's enough from me for today. You stay here. Practice. I need tea."

The old man heaved himself up and ambled off. Finn watched him go, feeling dazed and emotionally wrung-out. Which maybe was the point.

Now he had a concrete way forward, a skill he could practice. He wished it were something different, though. If magic had been about memorizing a bunch of incantations, or formulas, or reading the stars, or arranging rocks in a pattern, or reciting things in different languages, or knowing history, Finn would have known exactly how to go about it. This was different. It made sense, though, that learning about magic—something he was terrible at—would include learning about something else he was terrible at.

Finn ran his hands through his wet hair and closed his eyes. It was okay. He could do this. He knew he couldn't ignore magic, and now he didn't even want to anymore. He was going to learn this, and then he was going to help everyone else who was like him learn this, too.

KEL'S FIRST LESSON, later that evening after dinner, did not go as well as Finn's had. She didn't want to get close to the old man, with his disintegrating insides, so she clung to Finn's leg, burying her face in the rough fabric of his pants. Finn bent down, pried her off and held her at arm's length.

"It's okay, Kel, I'll be right here if you need anything. Eraldir is just going to teach you about magic."

Kel shook her head.

Finn tousled her hair. "Look, Eraldir's nice; he's just trying to help. He'll show you how to be even better, make bigger and better plants. Maybe you'll be able to reach out farther and you'll be able to hear Smoke."

Kel hadn't thought of that. Her powers had just been progressing on their own, and it hadn't occurred to her to wonder what else she could do. She closed her eyes and tried. *Smoke!!* She thought it as loud and as hard as she could. Then she listened closely. Still nothing.

She glanced at the old man, who was sitting by the fire, watching her. The firelight cast shadows across his face. Kel's stomach clenched at the thought of getting any closer, but maybe Finn was right. Maybe there were things she could learn.

"All right," she said.

Finn smiled. "Great. I'll be right over here if you need anything."

Kel watched Finn walk to the edge of the camp, to where Isabelle was sewing up a hole in one of her shirts. Then Kel clasped her hands together and turned to the old man.

"All right, girl, first off, can you grow plants from their dried counterparts?" He pulled out a handful of leaves and twigs.

"Um, I don't know. For some plants."

Eraldir frowned. "Just seeds, then, mostly?"

"Yeah."

He sighed, "I was afraid of that. But, let's try anyway, shall we?"

"There's a seed in there," Kel said, pointing to Eraldir's handful.

Eraldir squinted at it. "Where? Eh, I'll just take your word for it." He tossed the bundle behind him. "All right, then, let's see what you can do."

Kel walked over, found the seed where it lay in the grass,

and asked it to grow. It was dry. Thirsty. Trying to grow made it ache and hurt.

"Could you give it water?" Kel asked.

"Sure, sure I can." Eraldir sent a sprinkling over the whole area, splashing Kel. Kel didn't mind, though, because she felt the joy of the seed. She warmed to Eraldir a little.

Then she asked the seed to grow again. It sprouted happily this time, shooting up and sending out long, feathery leaves.

Eraldir clapped his hands. "Wonderful! Fresh tea tonight!"

Kel was concentrating now, though, and the plant bloomed white blossoms. Now it was lonely.

"Do you have any more seeds?" Kel asked.

Eraldir rummaged around in his satchel, found another handful of the same plant, and held it out to Kel.

Kel grew a few more around it, to keep it company, while Eraldir watched.

"Marvelous, girl. You have impressive control over your abilities."

"Can you help me reach farther?"

"What do you mean?"

"Smoke, he's too far away for me to hear him."

Eraldir's bulbous eyebrows knitted together.

"You can hear the thoughts of animals?"

Kel nodded.

Eraldir stared at Kel, who looked at the ground and scuffed her foot in the dirt.

"Hmmm..." he stared off into space for so long that Kel was afraid he had died. Then he started. "Can you hear Sylvia's thoughts?"

Kel nodded.

"What has she..." he stared at the horse, who stared off into space, her head hanging tiredly. "I suppose she complains a lot?"

Kel nodded again.

"It's probably that and grass?"

"Yeah."

"Well, that's Sylvia all right. She was given to me by an old hermit farmer lady who lived outside of the Uplands." Eraldir picked a few fronds from the plants Kel had grown and started absently chewing on the end of one. "All the way up there in the mountains by herself, with a whole herd of horses."

Kel waited politely for him to finish, but he was staring off into space, lost in thought. "Liked horses a lot better than people, I'd say. Or, a lot better than me, anyway. But, her crops were all drying up, and there were forest fires headed her way."

Kel sat down next to her plants, watching an ant crawl up the stem. "Or, brush fires rather. Not a lot of forest in the Uplands. It's mostly goats up there. And this woman's herd of horses. She must have brought them up from the plains. You don't usually get horses up there and they were always falling off cliffs. That's how I found her. Followed the horse skeletons. I was curious, just heading from one village to the next, cutting across country and suddenly there's a whole bunch of dead horses. I hadn't seen a horse in years, since the last time I'd been down on the plains. There was a lady there, who... well, you're a little too young to..." he lapsed into a contented silence. Then shook himself. "What were we doing?"

"Trying to help me reach farther."

"Right you are! I'll just lead Sylvia away, you chat with her or whatever you do, and when you can't hear her anymore you call out to stop me."

Eraldir ambled slowly away, leading Sylvia. Kel asked her how her knees were doing and then listened to the long monologue that followed. A few minutes later Eraldir came back, though.

"Bad plan. Wrong direction, girl. You go out, I'll stay here."

Sylvia was still complaining away, describing in detail every facet of her knee aches and how they felt different on different days, according to the weather and what she'd eaten for breakfast. Kel stood and walked out into the trees, listening. Sylvia was there, in the back of her mind, but other than that Kel was alone again. Like she had been before. Alone in the trees and the dark forest. She could hear wind in the treetops, and the voices of other animals drifted towards her. Images of fears and wants. She wasn't afraid, though. This time she knew all the plants around her, like old friends, and knew what she could do with each of them. There was so much to eat, so many vines to twist into walls. Large trees that could lift her high into the air at a moment's notice.

She realized she couldn't hear Sylvia anymore, so she turned and walked back. The horse's voice drifted up to her again. She walked away until it was too quiet to hear. Then she marked the place where she lost contact with a pile of stones. She walked back to camp.

Eraldir was boiling tea with the fresh leaves Kel had grown. "Well, how far did you get?"

Kel pointed. "Two minutes that way. I marked the place with stones."

"Great. Back you go then."

"What?"

"Go sit there. At the pile of stones. Listen to her. Then try to move the stones a little further away. Come back when you have a headache." He poured off some tea into his mug. "What?"

"Um, is that all?"

"Is that all, girl? What, you think I'll just give you a magic word or one of those high-knee dance moves and it'll fix everything? No, no. This is how you learn. It's slow, and it's difficult, and it takes a long time. I guess that's the same as slow. But really, I can't emphasize that enough. It's slow. And it might not even work. Maybe you just have a fixed distance." He softened. "Probably not, though. Most things can be improved upon with practice. And time. Lots of time." He waved his mug toward the woods. "Off you go now, I'll poke Sylvia every now and then so she doesn't fall asleep."

Kel shrugged and ambled off into the woods. If she didn't have to be around the old man for her lessons, so much the better.

She sat alone for several hours that evening, staring at the mossy stones and listening to Sylvia complain. She succeeded in moving a few feet farther away. At first, she was elated that she'd made progress, but then she thought about how much farther away Smoke must be. At this rate, she'd never reach him. But, it was only her first day. Maybe she'd make more progress tomorrow. She worked until she had a headache, like Eraldir said, and then returned to camp and went straight to bed. She was so tired that for the first time in a long while she didn't dream.

～

ONCE FINN HAD SUCCESSFULLY PRIED Kel off his legs and convinced her to have her first lesson with Eraldir, he went to talk to Isabelle.

"Hey, mind if I join you?"

She looked up at him, "Sure, just don't distract me. Sewing's not really my thing." She bent back over the small tear in her shirt. Finn noticed there were a lot of mended rips in her shirt. That made sense for someone who went around jumping out of trees. "Oh, hey do you have my boot oil?"

Finn winced. "Um, sorry, I…"

She pursed her lips and sighed. "You lit it on fire, didn't you?"

"Uh, yeah, kinda. I'll get you more." He wasn't totally sure where he would get oil, but it seemed like the right thing to offer.

"It's okay, I have more. I kinda figured you might."

"Thanks. Sorry."

Relieved, Finn sat, propping his elbows up on his knees and turned back to watch Eraldir and Kel. They were talking. To be more accurate, Eraldir was talking. Finn hoped it was about something relevant and useful.

"So, how did you and Eraldir meet?"

She poked herself with the needle, swore, and shook her hand. "I was in a camp for exiled mages outside Lake Iori."

"What? There's a—"

"Yeah. About fifty totally untrained mages living in a makeshift town outside the city on the shores of the lake. They won't let them in." She shook her head. "The only magical city left. The only place where magic is still the norm, still totally accepted, and they won't take anyone who's not from there."

"What were you doing there?"

She shrugged. "I'd heard my mom talking about it, and I decided to go. Obviously, I didn't know they wouldn't let me in."

"So, you ran away from home, just like that?"

She didn't look up from her sewing. "Yes."

"Did you… did you leave a note?" He finished lamely.

"I left… something." She giggled.

Not totally sure he wanted to know, Finn asked anyway. "What?"

"A mountain lion."

"What?"

"I—" She interrupted herself with a fit of giggles. Then she took a couple of deep breaths. "I—" she put her head in her hand and giggled into it for a minute. "Okay. Whew. I'm fine. I'm—" But then she was giggling again.

Finn, even though he was sort of afraid to hear what she had done, couldn't help but laugh, too. At the same time, though, he hoped this wasn't a story about a mountain lion murdering her parents. That thought reminded him of his own situation, and suddenly he didn't feel like laughing anymore. Isabelle caught something of his mood and looked up.

"Oh, no it's okay. They're fine. Everyone's fine. Probably. I just dressed it up in my clothes and left it in my room. My dad's really superstitious. He probably thought I was turned into a lion, or that I was one all along. Some kind of lion changeling." She giggled again.

"How did you even catch a lion in the first place?"

"It was an accident. I dropped a tree on it. Not a big tree. It was still breathing. I just knocked it out a little. It's happened to me plenty of times."

"What, that you've concussed a mountain lion?"

"No, that's only happened the one time. I mean, I've knocked myself out a lot."

That made sense. Also, dressing up a mountain lion and leaving it in her bedroom for her parents to find later seemed like the product of a decision-making process based on frequent head trauma.

"Anyway, it was only out for a second, but I had my mom's sleeping tonic with me, so I gave it that before it had a chance to wake up completely. After that it was out for a while."

"Why did you have that with you?"

"I thought she should be awake for once," Isabelle said tonelessly.

Finn wanted to reach out to her, wanted to put an arm around her, but he wasn't completely sure how she would take it. A punch on the arm seemed more her style. He hesitated. Then started to reach an arm slowly around her shoulders. He was halfway there when she noticed. Isabelle turned to stare at him, one eyebrow raised. He removed the arm. The tree behind her caught fire.

Finn jumped up, but Eraldir had already put it out.

"None of that now, boy!" He called across the camp.

Finn, embarrassed, turned back to thank him, then he noticed Kel was gone. He stood and walked over to Eraldir.

"Where's Kel?"

"I sent her into the woods to listen to Sylvia."

"What? You sent her off by herself? You're supposed to be teaching her!"

"I am teaching her."

Finn looked around, trying to see which direction Kel had gone in.

"She's fine, boy."

"She shouldn't—"

"Be alone? You mean she's never been alone in the woods before?"

Finn blushed and looked at the ground.

Eraldir continued. "She's safer out there than any of us are. Maybe safer out there than she is here, even." He gave Finn a look.

Finn felt like his own throat was trying to strangle him, but he managed to say. "You're right."

"Course I'm right. Do you know how old I am? I don't. But it's old. Anyway, since Kel's out there communing with my horse let's get you some more practice, too. More practice this time, less theory."

Finn swallowed and nodded.

"First off, you're going to light our campfire for us every night. And our candles. And whatever else we need to be on fire. The more purposeful fires you set, the fewer accidental immolations you will perform. Probably."

"I can do that," Finn said.

"Excellent. The next thing you've got to learn," Eraldir told him, "Is to be aware of the connection to magic within you. For this, you've got to meditate. Every day. Until you stop burning everything down." He poked Finn's leg with a stick. "So, cross your legs,"—Finn did—"put your hands on your knees, and close your eyes."

Finn closed his eyes and put his hands on his knees, hoping Isabelle wasn't watching.

"Now, focus on where the magic is coming from."

Finn easily found the fiery source of energy. It was a chaotic ball of heat in his chest. "Now what?"

"Now you just keep doing what you're doing for an hour while I take a nap."

Finn opened his eyes. "What? That's it?"

"Yep." Eraldir lay down on his bedroll, stretching his bare toes—all seven of them—towards the warmth of the fire.

"But, what's the point?"

"The point is it helps. Don't ask me how it works. I didn't say I knew everything. I just know that this helps." Eraldir closed his eyes.

Finn sighed. Apparently, this was Eraldir's teaching style. Send Kel off into the woods by herself and then make Finn sit with his eyes closed. Efficient. It wasn't like Finn had made any progress on his own, though. He might as well take the advice he was given. He closed his eyes and focused on the roiling magical heat.

What was Isabelle doing? Finn wondered what she thought of him. She probably didn't think about him, wouldn't care either way. There was something soft under all that bravado, though, something that Finn wanted to protect.

Oops. He was supposed to be focusing. He turned his attention back to the fireball. Would focusing on it make it worse? Create more fires? Now that he was afraid of creating more fires, was his fear lighting things on fire already? He opened his eyes just to check and make sure nothing was burning that shouldn't be. Nope. Just the campfire.

With his eyes open, he noticed that he was calmer. He was still aware of the magical heat within him; maybe even more aware than he usually was, but in a relaxed way. Huh. Maybe this was doing something after all.

He closed his eyes again, focused back on the source. His mind kept drifting, though, thinking about Kel and Isabelle. The image of Eraldir's horrible feet kept popping up, too. After a while, he gave up and opened his eyes.

"You're not done with your hour, yet," Eraldir said, his eyes still closed.

Finn sighed and closed his eyes again.

The hour was a struggle. His mind kept drifting away and he kept wrangling it back. Minute after endless minute. But he stuck with it. If this was what it took, this was what he was going to do. He was angry at himself for giving up, and angry at himself, too, for being so bad at it.

"All right, you're done for tonight," Eraldir said.

Finn opened his eyes. It was dark. Isabelle was asleep already, rolled up in her blanket by the fire. Kel was back, too, asleep on her blanket.

"Don't get frustrated," Eraldir said. "The point isn't what your mind is doing. The point is that you keep on trying. You're never going to not get distracted. Now, get some sleep."

Finn fell asleep quickly. The last sound he heard was the gentle shushing of the wind. Then he fell into a deep, dreamless sleep and awoke earlier than anyone else, feeling energized and refreshed.

He stood and stretched in the cool morning air. The light was still thin and grey; the sun hadn't even fully risen yet. He walked a short way away from the others and sat cross-legged on the cold ground. Then he meditated.

Eventually the others woke, too, and Finn, feeling a deep, settled calm, went to start the fire for breakfast.

ARCTURUS SIGHED, and gave a small burp as he climbed the stairs to his rooms. He was beginning to lose hope. The work was going slowly. They died so quickly after he cut them open, he'd had to get new ones for each area of the body he wanted to examine. That meant five this week, and none of them had yielded any results. As far as he could tell, there was no difference between a mage and a non-mage. None, except that they could do magic.

Arcturus let himself into his rooms, shutting and locking the heavy oak door behind him. One by one he lit the silver candlesticks. It was a chore, yes, but it was something he had always done himself. He cleaned his rooms himself, too. That way no one ever came in here but him.

The candles lit, he seated himself at his heavy oak desk and pulled out his black leather ledger. For a while he tried to occupy himself with figures, with wine orders and the price of linen, but it wasn't any good. Tonight, he couldn't think of anything else, because no matter how much he had achieved without magic, it wasn't enough.

As he always did in times when he was close to giving up hope, he pulled out the black stone box. He lifted off its coldly reflective lid and pulled out the single gold coin it contained. It was the only piece of gold he kept in his room, the only piece of gold he ever carried on his person. Gold was for people without subtlety, without taste. Arcturus preferred silver. The sign of real power.

He turned the coin over in his hand, felt the cold, smooth metal under his fingertips. He remembered when he first saw the coin, half-buried in refuse on the side of the street. It was his sixteenth birthday, and he was bruised and bleeding, stumbling along, finding a place to hide until his mother calmed down.

He hadn't been sure if he could ever go back, if she'd ever let him back into the small, run-down house where they lived. Disappointment and hurt filled him. That morning had started so well. He'd looked forward to this day for so long. His mother had been so sure, so confident. This was supposed to be the day their troubles would be over.

Arcturus had never met his father, but his mother told him he was a mage from Lake Iori, a powerful one.

Arcturus placed a hand on his stomach, remembering the ache of hunger, the yawning emptiness he'd felt then. The desperation. He'd held that coin in his hand and thought of buying something with it. He could have bought himself a meal. Or shoes. The coin felt like a birthday present, and Arcturus despised it. He was supposed to be a mage, and this is what he'd gotten instead. Arcturus had never been given anything in his life, up until then. He saw the other boys his age begging in the streets, saw his mother do it too, and worse. He saw what it did to them, saw the dead look in their eyes when they gave up and waited for someone else to help them.

Today, on the day he should have been a mage, should have finally been loved by his mother, been able to protect her and take care of her, he had instead been given a single, stupid, gold coin.

Arcturus had sat there in the street, leaning against a wall, with people stepping over him, staring at that coin, for a long time. And then he had decided.

Arcturus was never going to beg. He didn't buy anything with that coin that day, and he'd never asked for or accepted help from anyone ever again. That day he started a delivery business, running things from shops to business people for free, earning the occasional tip. From there he bought things to sell and hired other people. One by one he had acquired more and more businesses, more and more wealth and power and prestige, and always he had kept the coin as a reminder to himself of who he was. And who he'd never be.

CHAPTER 10

*T*hat evening, Kel had her next lesson. Like before, Eraldir sent her out into the woods alone to listen to Sylvia complain, and to try to move farther away.

To Kel's frustration, the distance she could go was shorter today. But, she sat, listening and slowly edging farther away.

She was sitting cross-legged in a bare patch of dirt. The sun was low in the sky and orange light slanted through the trees, illuminating the dust and pollen in the air. A mosquito buzzed near her ear; without thinking, she told it to go away.

To her surprise, the mosquito obeyed. A little tendril of curiosity crept up through Kel. She felt bad for depriving it of its meal, though, so she felt around, found a sleeping deer not far away, and offered the mosquito the location as an apology. It would be an annoyance for the deer, but only an annoyance.

A rustle of leaves caught her attention and, looking up, she saw a nest in the crook of a tree. She couldn't see inside from where she sat below it, but she could feel four tiny pulses of life inside it. As she watched, she felt something else. Something long, with slit eyes, sharp, poisonous teeth, and a gnawing hunger. It slid up the back side of the tree, where Kel couldn't see it. The scent of the eggs pulled it forward, upward.

Where were the parents? Why weren't they guarding their nest? Kel watched as the cold reptilian eyes came into view. A forked tongue flicked out of the lipless mouth. The snake, its long, thick body covered in red and white scales, undulated towards the nest.

It arrived, poked its head inside. Kel, watched, frozen.

The snake slowly unhinged its jaw, wrapping itself around the first egg, its head distorting horribly as it swallowed the egg whole. Greedily, it then went for the second egg, and the third, and the fourth. Until all that was left of the bundles of new life were four lumps in the snake's torso, waiting to be slowly digested.

Satisfied, the enormous snake slithered away. It glanced at Kel with cold, empty eyes as it passed.

Kel didn't know why this bothered her so much. She'd eaten eggs herself many times. Smoke ate eggs every day. But the nest, it had been so safe, so filled with the potential for new life. And now it was cold and empty.

Something dark swooped down to the empty nest. It cawed fiercely, furiously. Another joined it. The two crows cawed together, then they looked at Kel, their black eyes glinting with anger. Kel scooted back, inching away from them.

No, no. She thought. *It wasn't me. It was a snake.* She tried to send the image of the snake, tried to tell them it wasn't her, but they weren't listening. The first bird dove, streaking towards her with its sharp beak and talons out. It ripped into her arm first, then launched itself straight for her eyes.

Kel reacted without thinking; before it could reach her, she held up her hand, thinking of the mosquito. *Stop.*

The bird faltered, flapping its wings, but then resumed its

course, even more angrily. Kel made the command stronger this time, angry at the unfairness of the crow's attack. *Stop. Leave me alone.* She imagined it flying away, leaving for another part of the forest.

The crow screeched and hovered in midair, beating its wings up and down, and then it turned and flapped away. Its companion, still sitting in the nest, cocked its head and examined Kel with a bright black eye. Only Smoke and Sylvia had ever spoken to Kel, but now the crow clicked its sharp beak and an image of that same beak, bright with Kel's blood, came into Kel's mind. Then it pushed off the branch and winged after its companion.

Tears filled Kel's eyes as she watched the crows fly away. Their fury entered her mind, even as they diminished and she lost sight of them. No longer wanting to be alone, she wrapped her arms around herself and stumbled back towards camp, crying. She didn't notice that she was headed in the wrong direction, though, and she also didn't notice Isabelle watching her from the branches of a large beech tree.

"So, I guess you're not friends with all the woodland creatures after all," Isabelle said, jumping down and skipping over to Kel. She knelt and squinted at Kel's arm.

"Ouch. Let's get you cleaned up before Finn sees you and freaks out."

Isabelle pulled a wooden box and a handkerchief out of her pocket. She twisted the lid off and poked her finger into the clear, gooey substance inside.

"This is great for scratches," she said, scooping out a finger-full and smearing it on the largest of the cuts on Kel's arm. Kel flinched, but it felt cool, and she relaxed.

"Thank you," she said, remembering her manners.

"Sure. So, what happened?"

Kel told her about the crows.

"Stupid birds."

"I don't know why they're so mad at me. I told them I didn't take their eggs."

"Maybe they were just being dumb. Crows are the worst. They hate it when you disturb their nests. They'll follow me sometimes. Or try to."

Kel could understand why birds didn't like Isabelle, if she was always knocking over their trees and blowing them around. She was like a bird herself, though, Kel thought. Always sitting up in trees and trying to fly.

"All right, kid. There you go, all cleaned up." Isabelle stood, pocketing her jar of salve.

Kel looked back at the trees, wondering if the birds were still there. Isabelle sighed. "I'll take you back to camp."

"I'm not supposed to be back yet. I'm supposed to be practicing."

Isabelle stared at her, annoyed, for a minute. Then she sighed again.

"Fine. You keep practicing. I'll stick around and keep the birds away. I can do that and practice at the same time. Just don't distract me."

Kel shook her head. "I won't."

It took them a few minutes to find a place where she could hear Sylvia again. The crows didn't come back, but she could feel that they weren't far away. They knew Isabelle was there, and they didn't like her, but they were watching. They hadn't forgotten.

THE NEXT MORNING, Finn, as usual now, woke earlier than everyone else to meditate. If there was one thing he knew how to do, it was study.

He settled himself cross-legged on the cold ground. The

sun wasn't even fully up yet, and the air was cold and the light dim. He closed his eyes and focused.

Sometime later, he heard someone calling his name.

"Finn! Come on, let's go already!"

He opened his eyes to see that the sun was fully up. The day was bright and warm, insects buzzed around him. Three crows sat on a nearby tree branch; ordinarily, Finn wouldn't have paid much attention, but it was the way they were sitting there—all in a line, not moving, their bright eyes cocked towards him—that caught his attention. He made a mental note to ask Kel about it.

Isabelle came stomping over to him first, though, distracting him.

"Come on, Finn. We're all up and packed and have been for, like, hours now. Let's go. You can sit down again at lunch."

He looked up to see her white hair blowing around her. Her brown eyes were more amused than annoyed, though. She extended a hand; he took it and she yanked him up onto his feet.

As they walked that day, Kel was still nervous about the crows, and found herself wanting to stay close to the group. Despite her initial discomfort around Eraldir, she was finding that the old man knew a lot about plants, and was never averse to talking about them, or watering them when asked. So, rather than hang back or stop to look at bugs or plants, she walked along next to Eraldir, questioning him.

"What's this?" She asked, pointing to a tall green shoot which carried a profusion of pink flowers.

"Ahh… that's foxglove, girl."

"Can you eat it?" Kel reached out to stroke one of the flowers, then noticed a bee nestled up inside.

"Oh no, definitely not. That one's a poison in most hands. I knew an old herbalist, a traveling friend of mine. He made several different decoctions from it. We were attacked by a bear once, our fault really, on our way to the summer shell-fish festival at the Macai lands, and I got the wind knocked out of me and my arms and legs all scraped up. My chest swelled up to about twice as big as it should have been. And not because I'd spontaneously grown bear muscles after fighting off a bear. Some people think that happens you know but it's just not true. No, it was pus. I was just a big bag of pus after that. He put some of that on the scrapes and made me drink a decoction of it and a couple other herbs. Was it lavender? I forget now. No, marigold, that was. Lavender's for stress. And it just smells nice."

Lavender for stress, foxglove for pus, and marigold for scrapes, Kel thought to herself, tuning out the rest. She reached out to one of the flowers—not the one with the bee in it—and as she reached they aged into seeds. She picked the seeds, looked at them closely, and slipped them into a pocket of her dress.

THAT EVENING they were all sitting by the campfire talking and eating. Kel was quietly poking her spoon around inside her bowl, picking up one vegetable at a time and tasting it. She liked the flavors individually, liked to see how each one made her feel.

Isabelle laughed loudly at something Finn had said. Eraldir grunted. Then Kel heard the rustle of wings. She looked up and saw a black shape perched on a tree branch behind Isabelle. A second joined it. Then a third.

I really didn't take your eggs, Kel thought desperately. *It was a snake. I'm sorry.* The crows ignored her. They didn't think she'd taken their eggs anymore. *Then why are you angry?* They didn't answer her. If they attacked now, someone was going to get hurt. Probably the birds, but also maybe Finn, too. *Leave us alone!* Kel put more power behind the thought. One of the crows stumbled back, almost falling off the branch, but quickly righted itself.

It was the wrong thing to have tried. Their sharp beaks clicked and their claws dug into the branch, ripping away at its bark.

I'm sorry. Please. Kel glanced up, saw more dark shapes circling above, blocking out the stars. She could hear birds settling into the trees behind her. Rows of dark, rustling feathers, sharp beaks, and flashing eyes.

What do you want from me? She received no answer.

"What's up with you, Kel?" Isabelle asked. "You look like—"

She was cut off by the birds' attack. Hundreds of them swooped into the camp, cawing and pecking. Finn dropped his bowl and leapt to his feet.

"Aargh, damn birds!" Eraldir yelled, pulling his cloak over his face and waving his arms around wildly.

Kel covered her face with her arms. Claws tore at her skin and her hair. Heavy bird bodies smacked into her and stabbed with their sharp beaks. Five or six latched onto her arms, flapping their wings and trying to yank them from her body.

Two things happened at once. The birds burst into flame, and a cyclone of wind whipped around them. The cries of the birds turned to strangled shrieks of alarm and pain. They flapped their wings trying to get away, but the fire consumed them. The wind stoked the flames, whipping them up into a frenzy, and soon more than just the birds were on fire. Their blankets, the neighboring bushes, and the trees around them, too, lit up. Heat blasted them; Kel cried out, falling back, crawling away from the maelstrom.

Water exploded over everything. It hit the fires and burst into steam. It splashed across Kel, soaking and cooling her. Everything was dark and smelled like smoke and mud. Isabelle giggled.

Kel heard Finn call out her name.

"I'm okay, I'm here," she said, and Finn came splashing over to her. His strong arms picked her up.

"Are you hurt? Are you burned?"

Kel's heart was skipping like a hummingbird's, and she realized that yes, she was in pain. Her face and arms were seared, and she squirmed out of Finn's grasp; any pressure felt like fire on her skin.

Finn bent down to examine the burns, careful not to touch her this time.

"I'm so sorry, Kel. Does it hurt?"

It did, but not any worse than times she'd touched her mother's cast iron pan when it was still hot.

"I'm okay."

"Will someone please—very carefully- relight the camp-fire, so we can see?" Eraldir asked.

Kel's eyes had adjusted to the dark now; the moon was waxing towards full and its silvery light illuminated the mist and smoke hanging around them. A tiny flame popped up where the campfire had been. At first it wouldn't take, the wood was too wet, and it winked back out. But then another flickered into being, and the wood sizzled and dried and the flames took hold again, and warm red and yellow light filled the camp again.

Eraldir threw his burned cloak off and looked at them. "You two," he said, his words clipped, "Are not allowed to fight things at the same time anymore."

"We sure showed those birds, though," Isabelle said. She

plucked a small feather off one of the dead crows and started to tie it into her hair. She looked at Finn. "That was impressive."

Kel looked at Finn and saw that he was pale and stricken and hadn't heard Isabelle's compliment.

"If that happens again" he said, "you can drive them off."

"Sure, sure, but hey! Look on the bright side, that was some very accurate fire setting!" She punched him on the arm, then grimaced, realizing her knuckles were burned. "Eraldir, you have anything to help with burns?"

Eraldir ambled over to his pack and rummaged through it. "Course I do… you know the number of times I've been lit on fire? Probably more times than you've been not on fire. The Southland fire ceremony gives me an advantage, though. Everybody there spends three days on fire. Really makes you appreciate the rest of the year, I'll tell you that."

Isabelle turned to Finn. "Really, though, that was progress."

He looked skeptical.

"Really. I mean, there were, what, a hundred birds, and we were being attacked, and you set exactly those hundred birds on fire and nothing else. It was my fault everything got out of control, not yours." She lifted her eyebrows at him.

Hope dawned in Finn's face.

"Yep, course I'm right. Aren't I right, Eraldir?"

"Yes. You are correct. You are the one who made our camp into a terrifying fire maelstrom in order to get rid of a couple of birds. Great job." He pulled some giant spiky leaves out of his pack.

She grinned at Finn. "See?"

Eraldir slit the leaves open with a short knife, then scraped the gooey gel out from inside. He handed out spoonfuls of the stuff to each of them, with instructions to spread it on their burns.

Kel did as she was told and felt a wonderful, cooling relief.

Eraldir handed her one of the full, spiky leaves. "Aloe," he grunted.

Kel pocketed the leaf. She would try growing it later.

No one asked why the birds had attacked them in the first place. Isabelle knew, but didn't seem to think it was important to tell anyone, so Kel didn't either.

The others went about cleaning up the camp, drying things out and patching up burns in their blankets and packs, but Kel could feel more crows out in the darkness, watching them, seeing the burned bodies of their comrades, their rage increasing. She kept trying to apologize, to explain, but they weren't listening. She had committed some terrible transgression against them, but she didn't know what it was, and they refused to explain.

CHAPTER 11

The next afternoon they came to a rushing green river. It cut a rocky swath through the trees, carving out small waterfalls and canyons here and there so that they couldn't travel directly on its banks, but could always hear the roar of its waters not far off, and smell the spray from the falls as they climbed higher into the Iron Mountains.

"We're not far off now," Eraldir said. The four of them, Eraldir riding Sylvia, stood at a bend in the narrow trail they'd been following, resting and admiring the view of the river. "This is the Green River. Westwend is just north of here."

Just as he finished saying this, a small tremor shook the ground under their feet.

"What was that?" Isabelle asked, her voice shaking. Finn turned to look at her, and was surprised to see her arms wrapped around herself in a tight hug, and her eyes wide with fear.

Eraldir's brows knitted together. "Felt like an earthquake."

"Does that happen a lot here?" She asked.

Eraldir cracked a grin. "Scared?"

She dropped her arms and glared at him. "No."

Eraldir chuckled, which triggered a coughing fit. When he'd gotten his breathing back under control, he answered her question. "No, it doesn't happen often. More here in the mountains than down on the plains. And pretty much never where you're from. Last big earthquake I was in wasn't natural causes, though. It was in the Uplands, village of Penrith, about five years back. I'm guessing neither of you've heard of it. Terrible, tiny little collection of hovels. Why anyone'd want to live there I have no idea. The goat stew isn't bad, but really you can get passable goat stew anywhere. And you can get sick of anything, no matter how good it is, soon enough when you have to spend a winter snowed in under ten feet of ice in a tiny cabin with two surly mountain men, three goats, and some trained bees. Wanted to gouge my own eyes out with an icicle, I'll tell you. But, anyway, where was I? Oh yes, the earthquake. That was an earth mage who didn't know what he was. Flattened half the village. I don't think it was any particular loss, though. That's a weird place, Penrith. I stayed in an inn there once. Only stayed one night. There was something off about that innkeeper. He was some kind of mage I'd never seen before but was pretending he wasn't. Creepy place. Don't recommend it as a travel destination."

Eraldir stretched his stirruped feet out in front of him. "Well, what are you guys standing around asking me questions for, let's get going!"

Isabelle caught Finn's eye. He rolled his eyes at her and she grinned and shook her head. His heart skipped a few beats.

They walked in silence for a few minutes, Isabelle and Finn walking out ahead of Eraldir and Kel. Finn glanced at

Isabelle and noticed she was rubbing her arms nervously again.

"Don't like earthquakes?" he asked.

She narrowed her eyes at him, trying to decide whether he was making fun of her or not. She must have decided he wasn't, because she answered him.

"What's to like?"

"Nothing, I'm not saying I like them, but they don't really bother me." He paused. She looked angry. He wished he knew the right thing to say. "I mean... you seem so fearless... you're always jumping out of trees..."

She tossed her hair. "That's easy. That's something I can control. But earthquakes are just so much bigger, you know? Doesn't it just make you feel tiny? Helpless?"

Finn considered this. "Yeah, I can see what you mean. I guess I just don't think about it. But, yeah."

She glanced at him out of the corner of her eye. "Yeah. I mean, if a mountain falls on you, there's not much you can do about that."

That made sense.

"What are you afraid of?" she asked.

Killing everyone I love. That I was right before, and magic really is evil. "Um, spiders," he lied, saying the first thing that came to mind.

Isabelle gave him a piercing look, then rolled her eyes. "So, do you think there's an earth mage around here somewhere?"

"Eraldir seems to think so."

"Do *you* think so?" she asked.

"I don't know, maybe. I've never met one." That wasn't true, though. He had known one. "Have you?"

"A few. At the refugee camp at Lake Iori. But I don't think you can tell whether an earthquake was natural or magical just by what it feels like."

Another small tremor passed through the ground below them. Isabelle compressed her lips into a thin, stoic line, and her face went slightly green. Finn asked her if she needed anything, but she just shook her head, refusing to make eye contact.

Finn turned back to Eraldir. "How much farther?" he asked.

"Eh, not too sure. A few miles maybe."

It turned out to be more like fifteen miles. Apparently, distances had seemed shorter in Eraldir's younger, more spry days.

Luckily, they came across a wide dirt road cutting through the trees, which let them travel faster. It was deeply rutted from wagon wheels and switch-backed efficiently up the mountainside.

They came around a bend and suddenly there it was: Westwend. Just as Eraldir had said, it perched on the edge of a cliff. The river split in two at the far end of the city, each branch gouging a chasm along one side of it, before cascading over the sheer drop-off, so that the city was triangular, protected on two sides by the divided river and on the third by a towering cliff, over which the water plummeted.

The branches of the river had carved deep canyons, meaning that anyone wanting to attack the city would have to first climb down a cliff to the river, then ford the river, which itself was a rushing torrent, then scale the other side. Any misstep would mean being swept away by the current and shot over the cliff. It was hardly surprising that the place looked prosperous and peaceful.

"Not bad, if I do say so myself," Eraldir said, hands on his arthritic hips, surveying his work. "Course, I washed away most of the original village in the process, which they weren't too happy about. So, good work, but pitchforks in the end. Still, I've been back a few times since then and usually they don't remember me. That was about fifty years ago, I think. There's an inn here, they make the best pies I've ever had." He licked his lips.

The sun was getting low in the sky now, and it would be evening soon. Eraldir said they'd better hurry to one of the bridges, because the town guard hauled them up every night.

"These folks do take their safety seriously, not that I—" Eraldir stopped mid-sentence, which was so unlike him that both Finn and Isabelle looked up to see what had happened.

Eraldir had pulled Sylvia's reins in tightly and was sitting stiffly in his saddle, staring straight ahead. Finn followed his gaze and saw at once why he had stopped. Three dead bodies, hanging in a row from a thick tree branch alongside the road. Burlap sacks covered their heads, and their feet were bare. One was a young woman, Finn could see her long black hair poking out from under the sack. It was hard to tell with her face covered, but she looked about his age.

"Criminals?" Isabelle asked.

"Maybe." Eraldir looked up at the darkening sky. "Come on, we'd better get across the bridge before sundown."

They followed him to the sturdy wooden bridge that stretched across the chasm. A gate barred the way, manned by two guards. One stepped out to greet them, the other stayed back watchfully.

"State your name and business here."

"I am Eraldir, a traveling water mage, and these are my three apprentices, Finn, Kel, and Isabelle. We come to stay at the Flagon."

Finn got an uneasy feeling in his stomach that Eraldir shouldn't have mentioned they were mages, and he wished they'd made up some other backstory for themselves.

"You'll not find work here, mage. The folks in these parts don't tolerate that sort of stuff anymore."

"Oh, we're not looking for work, we'd just like to stay in

the inn. We can pay." Eraldir reached into a pocket and pulled out several grubby strings of coins. On each string was a different currency; most towns minted their own now. They varied widely in shape and color, but all had holes bored through the middle so they could be kept on strings; Finn recognized the small silver coins they used in Cromwic.

"Now, let's see, are you fellows the gold circles or the ovals?"

The man cleared his throat and looked over his shoulder. "The circles. With the river on them." Eraldir shoved the rest of the coins into his pocket, untied the string, and slid a few grubby gold coins off and held them out to the guard. "See, we've got plenty of money." Again, the man glanced back at his partner in the gatehouse. "Maybe you'd like to just illus-trate to your partner as well that we're capable of paying." Eraldir took off another couple of coins and handed them to the man.

The man narrowed his eyes, but he pocketed the coins. "Alrigh'. Just, listen, I mean it, don't go around doing any kind of magic. And if anyone asks, you didn't tell me you were a mage. If anyone finds out I'm the one that let you in here..."

Eraldir bowed. "Of course. No one will know. I assure you."

The man waved to his partner, who raised the portcullis for them. Eraldir, Finn, Isabelle, and Kel passed beneath it and it crashed back down behind them.

"Damnit, Gavin!" They heard one of the guards yell, "You can't just let it drop like that! I told you, let it down easy-like!"

Eraldir was now whistling a contented tune, but Finn's stomach was knotted and a large part of him wanted to run back to the gates and ask to be let out again. He didn't mind that Eraldir had bribed the man, but if these people didn't want to let mages in he'd just as soon let them have their way. He didn't turn back, though. He had decided to follow Eraldir and Isabelle and so that's what he would do. Eraldir might be crazy, but Finn knew he was already getting better at controlling his magic. If he thought he could have convinced Eraldir to leave he would have tried, but something told him the old man would not be dissuaded from a warm bed indoors and his favorite food without good reason.

Westwend was dirtier than Finn had pictured it from his father's descriptions. On returning from trips to purchase supplies and sell his animal hides, he'd described the straight-sided buildings, all reaching at least two stories, sometimes three, with their dark pine timber frames, white, lime-washed, wattle and daub clay walls, and bright red tile roofs. Those would have been so much more resistant to fire than the dry thatch roofs of Cromwic, Finn thought wistfully.

Finn's father would often mutter about Cromwic's inferiority when their tiny market didn't have the type of bowstring he wanted. Cromwic had one market, but Westwend had seven. And that was only the official markets. The streets were full of vendors with carts selling sweets, breads, fruits, fried meats, bright shawls, piles of smooth-dipped beeswax candles, bolts of linen imported from the south, and reams of cotton in every color imaginable imported from even further south. Finn was suddenly self-conscious of his rough, home-spun wool pants and his dirty linen shirt, which was also his only shirt, and had been made by his mother. He reached out a finger to touch a piece of yellow cotton fluttering in the breeze. The man behind the cart narrowed his eyes and Finn pulled his hand back.

All the things his father had described were here, but he hadn't mentioned the thick mud that churned underneath, sucking at Finn's boots as he pulled them out. He also hadn't mentioned the overpowering smells and thick smoke. With every in-breath came the smells of wood stoves, open braziers, meat cooking—or burning—on spits, baking bread, and rotting fruit. Then there were worse smells: the sweat of the passing men and women—not that Finn had any right to complain, he was probably much worse—rotten food, discarded bits of animals lying in heaps waiting for trash collectors, and occasionally the strong whiff of urine or something worse. He hoped his nose would adjust quickly, and he kept his mouth shut.

His father also hadn't mentioned the towers. In the center of this knot of humanity were three towers, over three times as tall as the wooden and clay buildings that huddled around them. Finn could see them lancing up into the sky over the tops of the red tile roofs. These towers were what was left of the Westwend from before the Fall and had been built by earth and fire mages. Finn wondered how people could live here, with those dark iron giants with their weird, ever-glowing lights, always looming over them. But people in Westwend had always been a little more tolerant of magic than the people of Finn's village had, willing to look the other way if it benefitted them.

The sun had dropped behind the horizon now, and a chill wind picked up, mercifully clearing the air. Shop-keepers were shutting doors and pulling down shades, and tired merchants pushed their carts through the thick mud, bumping over rocks, making their way home. A few glanced at them suspiciously. One man stopped what he was doing and stared, eyes narrowed, and watched them until they turned the corner. That was when Finn noticed how quiet it was. A market closing usually meant end-of-day chatter between merchants, happy to be on their way home. But as they passed through the streets there was only the clatter of shutters being closed and wares being packed into wagons. Only occasional muttering or whispers broke the quiet.

Finn glanced at Eraldir, but he seemed completely oblivious to the ominous feel of the place.

"Does something feel off to you?" Finn whispered to Isabelle as he reached back and took Kel's hand. Kel was dragging her feet, looking down at the ground.

"Yeah," Isabelle said, her usual bravado gone.

"Have you been here before?"

She shook her head, glancing up at the shuttered windows. "It feels like something happened here. Something bad."

Finn nodded. "And recently." He wondered who those bodies outside had been.

"Yeah. I hope we're not about to die because Eraldir really wants pie."

"Ah, here we are!" Eraldir interrupted them. They were standing out front of a large, two-story building. It had the same dark timber frames as those around it, but its clay walls were painted a deep blue with a decorative design of red triangles. A sign hung out front that read "Arcturus Flavius Presents: The Full Flagon." Below it was a smaller sign which read "Rooms available, inquire within."

There was a stable off to the side, manned by a slouching boy. He was about Kel's age, and, upon hearing Eraldir's greeting, he heaved himself up off the barrel he'd been sitting on and came over to help the old man off his horse.

"Take good care of Sylvia now, there's a good lad," Eraldir said, handing the boy a few coins. The boy pocketed them with a shrug and wandered off with Sylvia in tow.

"Era—" Finn tried to get the man's attention, but he was already pushing his way through the front door.

Finn gave Isabelle a look, and the three of them followed him in.

They entered a large, warm room, brightly lit by several chandeliers. The place was crowded with people sitting around large wooden tables, eating and drinking, but the talk was low and quiet. At one end, a staircase led up to second, upper level, where a group of well-dressed individuals sat around a large table. Particularly notable among them was a large man dressed in black and shining silver. His hair and beard were dark and sharp, cleanly cut. He was picking at pieces of fruit arranged in a bowl, and surveying the room. His eyes locked with Finn's and Finn looked away. He could feel the man watching him still, but didn't look back.

The main door burst open behind Finn, and in rushed a woman, mud-spattered, dressed in leather, with a sword hanging at her side. She ascended the steps and knelt in front of the man in black.

"Mr. Flavius, sir," she said.

So that was Arcturus Flavius. He looked a lot richer than your typical innkeeper. Not quite the simple man with the apron and the broom that Finn would have expected.

The woman, still kneeling, was saying something that Finn couldn't hear.

Arcturus smiled a thin smile, and stood to address the room.

"Excellent news, everyone."

The people eating, who had been watching the exchange out of the corners of their eyes, now turned in their seats to face him.

"We've just caught another one." A wave of applause broke out. Arcturus raised his hands and the noise died down. "Barkeep—a round of drinks for everyone." More clapping followed this announcement. "This is a great step forward for the security of Westwend." He lifted his glass to more applause. "Now, do remember that this is a service that I, Arcturus Flavius, am personally providing for our city. Did the mayor do anything about it? No. Did the guards do anything about it? Not until I paid them to." As he said the word 'paid,' he banged his glass down on the table and when he finished speaking he paused, letting silence fill the room. "But I am not a man to stand by while people live in fear. Not in my city. Not in Westwend." He lifted a fist and the room cheered. He gave a deep bow, and sat, to riotous applause.

Finn glanced at Isabelle to see if she might know what this was about, but she only shrugged.

Finn, Isabelle, Kel, and Eraldir made their way through the applause to the bar at the back and pulled up stools. Eraldir lifted a hand to catch the attention of the thin, nervous man behind the bar, who nodded at him and finished up with another customer before heading over.

"What can I get you?" the barkeep asked as the others pulled up stools.

"Four pies I think," Eraldir said. "What do you have tonight?"

"Lamb, kidney, of course, and venison."

"We'll have one of each, then, sir. Two of the kidney." He smiled and lifted his enormous eyebrows at Finn.

"Of course, sirs, ma'am. Anything else?"

"We'll need beer. Er, perhaps not for the young lady. What have you got for her?"

"Milk might be a good choice, sir."

Finn thought he might prefer milk, too. He didn't know for sure, but he imagined he might be more prone to lighting things on fire after a pint or two. But he didn't want to draw attention to their group, so he didn't ask. He could feel other eyes on them, too.

The bartender went away to warm their pies and get their beer, and the four of them sat in silence, listening to the talk around them. Despite the earlier applause, the atmosphere was still tense. People spoke quietly, in clipped tones, and there was no laughter. Even Eraldir felt it and was quiet for once.

They ate in a strained silence. Only the sound of Eraldir's chewing and moans of enjoyment—the pie was hot, with a flakey, buttery crust and thick steaming gravy—broke the quiet. The townspeople finished up their dinners and one by one trickled out into the street to make their way home, or stumbled up the stairs to their rooms at the inn. When Eraldir finally finished up his last bite, mopping up the last of the gravy with the last of the flaky crust, Finn let out a long breath and waved at the barkeep.

"We'd like rooms for tonight, too, do you have any available?"

The man's eyes darted across their faces. "Of course, sir. How many will you be requiring?"

Finn glanced at Isabelle. "Er, three?"

Eraldir sighed. "Everyone needs their privacy. It's fine outside, but once you get inside everyone needs their own room, and of course the old man has to pay for it."

"So, three rooms then, sir?"

Eraldir looked at Finn, "I'm assuming you don't have any money?"

Finn shook his head.

Turning back to the barkeep, Eraldir sighed and massaged his stomach with a grimace. "Yes, yes, three rooms. One for me, one for the lady, and one for the boy and his sister."

At least he hadn't used Finn's name. Finn didn't know why, there was no reason anyone here would know him, but for some reason it made him uneasy.

The man inclined his head slightly. "Very good, sir. Right this way."

He led them up the stairs and down a hall, then turned left down another hall. The place was deceptively large.

"Will you be staying just the one night, then?" the man asked as he inserted an ornate silver key in the lock of a heavy oak door.

"A few nights, probably. Taking a rest from our travels, you know."

"Very good, sir. Ma'am." He pushed the door open and handed the key to Isabelle, who took it, smiled at Finn and Eraldir, and swept into the room, shutting the door behind her with a quick wave and a "See you at breakfast!"

The man opened the door next to Isabelle's room and handed the key to Eraldir, who took it with a burp and said a perfunctory good night to Finn and Kel. The burp hit the barkeep full in the face and for one second the man's expression became one of overwhelming horror before his professionalism tamped it back down again.

"Your room's up this way, sir," the man said to Finn. He led them down another hall, past a few paintings and an arrangement of dried flowers. "Here we are." He pushed open another solid oak door and handed the key to Finn. Inside were two beds. A thin rug covered the floor. The room was dark, but there were oil lamps on the tables by the beds, and Finn saw flint and tinder. He wouldn't be needing those. Kel went in and sat on the bed.

The man was standing there politely, waiting for them to go into the room so he could leave, but Finn decided to take the opportunity to ask him a few questions.

"Um, excuse me for asking, but I've never been here before and..." He didn't know how to ask this. "Er, what I mean is. What was the speech about?"

"Arcturus Flavius has..." the man paused, searching for words. "...addressed a scourge that others in authority have long been too afraid to address."

"Arcturus; he's the one who owns this place?"

"Yes, sir."

Oh. The man's boss.

"Well, thank you. I was just curious. Um, what scourge is he addressing?"

"Why, magery of course."

In the back of Finn's mind, he'd suspected who those bodies swinging from the tree branch had been. What they'd been. But actually hearing it made it real. Solid. He tried to keep a neutral expression, then realized that maybe a more positive expression would be less suspicious.

"Oh, have there been problems with mages here?"

"Have you not heard?"

"Heard what? I—I've been traveling for a few weeks now... so I haven't..."

"Not far from here, a mage murdered his parents and burned down the whole town. Killed half the people living there. Burned them alive. Laughed as he did it." The man shuddered.

"What?" Finn thought he might faint. That's not how it happened. Half the town? I didn't laugh. His recollections of that night were vague. He remembered the fire, and the screams, remembered trying to put it out, but only making it worse. "Half the town?" His voice came out as a faint whisper.

The man nodded soberly. "Of course, no one's felt safe since then."

"Of course." Finn nodded, but his face was numb, his mind a buzz of static.

"You're quite safe here, though, sir. Just now, as you heard, Mr. Flavius captured another unregistered mage. They'll be executed straight away."

Finn felt himself go pale. He was lightheaded and dizzy.

The man watched him, his eyes narrowed in suspicion. "Well, I have duties to attend to, sir. Will you be requiring anything else?"

"No, thank you."

"Good night, then, sir."

"Good night."

The man hurried away.

Finn stood there in the hallway, watching the man's retreating back. His palms were sweating and his heart raced. Part of him wanted to grab Kel and run. Find some way out of the city immediately. The large amount of pie he'd eaten sat like a thick, heavy mass in his gut. Another, stronger part of him couldn't leave, kept bringing to mind those three bodies, swaying in the wind. Mages killed after… after what he had done. How many other cities were turning on their mages because of Finn? How many innocent people were being persecuted, murdered, because of him?

He imagined that somewhere in this inn was another mage, still alive, bound and gagged, maybe tortured, and soon to be executed. He had to do something.

He looked back into the room and saw Kel sitting there. He wanted to protect his little sister, to atone for what he had done to her, leaving her to grow up without their parents, but it hadn't only affected Kel. It was affecting every mage here. He'd made life worse, and probably shorter, for every mage in this city and maybe every mage for miles around and years to come.

He was going to fix it. Somehow.

What can you possibly do? The thought chided him. He could barely take care of his sister, let alone stop whole towns from killing mages.

But maybe Isabelle and Eraldir already had the solution. Maybe mages could learn to control their powers so that they could stop accidentally hurting non-mages. If they could do that, then non-mages would stop hating them. What they needed was a school. On the other hand, school was the only thing Finn had actually been good at, and maybe he just assumed it was the solution to everything. He suspected he was being a naïve idiot, but some, deeper part of him thought it could work.

First things first, though, he had to warn Eraldir and Isabelle.

He gave Kel a hug, told her he'd be back soon, and set off down the hall. He hadn't gone more than a few steps when the ground rumbled and shook. Finn stumbled against the wall, knocking a painting askew. The shaking stopped, and Finn righted the painting before continuing.

As he walked, he imagined what he would say, imagined their reactions. Isabelle would probably fly off the handle and go storming off to murder the innkeeper and rescue the captured mage. That's exactly what Finn wanted to do—well, at least the rescuing part—but they couldn't both do that. They'd probably end up burning the inn down. He couldn't do it alone, either. True, he'd been practicing every day and getting better at controlling his powers, and, as Isabelle had pointed out when the crows attacked, he was very accurate now, but he still lit fires on accident when he was upset.

Eraldir would be able to help. He might have a better idea how to rescue the mage, if Finn could convince him to help. At least Eraldir's powers didn't pair explosively with Finn's.

Yes, he would talk to Eraldir and Isabelle separately. First he'd talk to Eraldir, then he'd warn Isabelle about the mage hunting, then he and Eraldir would go rescue the mage. Later, once the mage was safe, they'd talk about the school. He just hoped there was enough time. The man had said the mage was going to be executed immediately. Finn quickened his stride.

He made it to the hall where Eraldir and Isabelle were staying, and was standing there trying to remember which room was Eraldir's when he heard someone coming down the hall towards him.

Finn whipped around and saw Isabelle, her face hidden behind a large pile of cakes. She hadn't heard him, and he watched her stop in front of her door, groping in her pocket for her room key. One of the cakes tumbled off the top of the stack, and Finn moved to catch it.

Isabelle yelped, jumped, and dropped the rest of the cakes, most of which landed on the floor, a few of which landed on Finn, stuck there by frosting.

Eraldir's door opened. "I'm an old man and I need—" he stopped mid-grumble and stared at them, his mouth still open. He tilted his grizzled head to the side. "Er, I'll just leave you two alone..." he said, moving back into his room and starting to shut the door.

Well, since both were already here, he might as well warn them.

"Wait," Finn said. "I need to talk to you both."

Isabelle had unlocked her door and was now gathering up her cakes. She sighed, annoyed. "Can't it wait until morning? There's an enormous bathtub in here full of hot water. Do you know how long it's been since I've had a bath?"

Finn glanced at her hair, which was greasy and full of leaves, and the thin layer of grime on her skin.

"Don't answer that!" she snapped. Another small earthquake shook the floor. Isabelle's face went white and she took a large bite of cake.

"I'm really sorry," Finn said. "We should talk about this now." He looked at Eraldir, whose brows were raised quizzically.

"Fine." Isabelle said. "Come in. You're not going to keep me from my bath though." She swept into her room, leaving the door open behind her. She dumped the cakes on the table and went through an adjoining door, closing it most of the way behind her. Finn could hear her furiously tossing clothes on the floor, and then a loud splash.

He and Eraldir looked at each other uncomfortably. They went in, closing the door behind them, and sat at the small table near the empty fireplace.

"Well?" Isabelle called from the other room. "If it's so important, what's taking you so long?"

Finn took a deep breath. "I just spoke with the barkeep. There's been... trouble... with mages here. And... well... I think those three bodies we saw... the people here are killing mages."

There was silence from the bathroom.

Eraldir sighed. "I assumed as much."

There was a loud splash, then the roar of wind. Isabelle swept out of the bathroom, dry and fully dressed, her white hair swept crazily about her head. She stomped over to the table and sat down.

"I expect you, Finn, to use your fire powers to make me another bath later."

"Sure, sorry," he said.

Eraldir cleared his throat. "I had hoped we were past all this." He placed a liver-spotted hand on the table and picked at a rough patch in the wood, his eyes clouded.

"Past Finn's ruining my bath? That literally just happened, Eraldir. I thought time was supposed to seem shorter to you when you got older."

Eraldir sighed. "No. Past the violence between mages and non-mages." He picked up one of Isabelle's cakes, looked at it, then set it down again. "Back when I was a boy, you know, it was the other way around. Mages ran everything. Those were the days. You could go from one end of the kingdom to the other in less than a week on the wind-runners. Everybody had a floating castle or a fifty-foot high fountain or a fruit orchard on top of their house. Of course, it wasn't a good time for non-mages." He passed a hand across his face. "Most of them were servants or laborers or just poor as dirt. I wish I'd... but I was only a boy then. And that was just how things were; no one thought too much about it.

"And then the Fall happened. And the wars. Almost all the mages who had any real power were dead. And people were angry. The non-mages rose up and started killing off those of us who were left. They took control of everything. That's when Lake Iori closed its borders, stopped letting anyone in who wasn't from there. There were attacks. We were under siege. There were so many of them, and they were so angry. They would have gotten us eventually, if it weren't for Eirin Morgan, a girl out of the Uplands. She stepped up and made peace. Surrendered. A lot of mages hated her for it, but she saved us.

"After that, things quieted down. Sure, you get the occasional pitchfork mob, but..." His eyes were haunted, seeing visions from the past. He shook himself. "This is not something we want to get involved in. Hopefully it's just an isolated incident, and it will die down on its own. As far as they know we're just travelers passing through. They don't need to know we're mages."

Except you told them we were at the gates, Finn thought, but didn't say anything.

"Yeah, except you told them we were," Isabelle said.

Eraldir grunted. "They won't say anything."

"I think the barkeep I just talked to suspects I'm a mage," Finn said.

The floor shook, and Isabelle took a small cake off the table and shoved the whole thing in her mouth.

"Non-mages are idiots," she said around the mouthful. "I'd like to see them try to bother me."

"This isn't our fight, Isabelle," Eraldir said.

"Of course it is!" She sprayed crumbs in his face. "They're killing mages! We're mages!"

"Shh…" Finn said, "They might be listening, and if they don't know we're mages I'd like to keep it that way."

"They have reasons for the way they feel, Isabelle," Eraldir said.

Isabelle shrugged, contemptuously. "Yeah, well, they should have thought harder before they started killing people."

"What do you propose we do?" The old man asked.

Isabelle deflated a little. "Not run and hide, that's all," she said.

Eraldir looked at Finn. "And you?"

"I think we should run and hide." Isabelle glared at him. "At least at first." Finn wondered how much time had passed. He had to end this conversation so he could talk to Eraldir alone. "Then," his heart swelled in his chest, "I think we should start a school. Like you said. Take all the mages with us, get as many as we can out of the cities. Especially this one."

"Interesting," Isabelle said. "I like it. Except for the running part. It's the non-mages who are bothering us who need to learn some decency. They need to learn that if you kill mages bad things are going to happen to you. Otherwise more people in more towns are going to think it's okay to kill us."

"What are you going to do, kill everyone?" Finn asked, annoyed.

"Maybe."

"That's a terrible idea," he said. She glowered at him. "I mean, I'm sure you could, but wouldn't it be easier to just start a school someplace else?" He turned to Eraldir. "Is there any place we can go? A place we could take mages to?"

"You mean something like Lake Iori?"

"Yeah, another Lake Iori, only a place where we can set up a school and take in all the exiled mages."

Eraldir steepled his fingers and looked up at the ceiling. He took a long, thoughtful breath, and Finn cringed inwardly. Here comes another hour-long monologue, he thought. And meanwhile there's some helpless mage trapped in a dungeon awaiting execution. Well, probably not a dungeon. Most inns didn't have dungeons. As far as he knew. He'd never actually stayed at an inn. His thoughts were interrupted by Eraldir.

"Well... I assume you don't mean existing settlements. There aren't many left that are particularly friendly to mages anyway. Only a few that even tolerate it. I thought Westwend was one of them, but apparently things have changed since I was last here. Strange. I wonder why. These things happen though, I suppose. And of course, the City of Mages itself is still a death trap... tried that myself once when I—"

"So, is there any place else?" Finn cut him off.

"Hmmm..." His eyes lit up, and he brushed back some of his wayward grey hair. "Don't know why I didn't think of this earlier! Perfect place, boy. It's got everything, and also it's not got what we don't want, which is people. I'm assuming, anyway. Haven't been there since I was a boy. My parents brought me to court on a visit. My mother was the Mage in Residence for six months when I was about five years old. The food..." Eraldir sighed and closed his eyes.

"Do you mean...?" Finn asked, excitement bubbling up in his chest.

Eraldir opened his eyes, annoyed at being jolted out of his reverie. "The King's Table. The old capital of Caledonia. When there still was a Caledonia. It was gutted after the war. I imagine it's been ransacked, probably empty by now. It's been about ninety years after all, but so far as I know there aren't any official settlements there. No one wants to live there anymore. And yet people still live in the Uplands..." he shook his head.

Isabelle was intrigued. "Is it a fortress?"

"It's *the* fortress," Finn said, "It's repelled three separate Baharran attacks and five from Montvale—no offense—but, more importantly, the high council ruled from there. I wonder if they have a... a..." Finn's eyes were going glassy, "a library..."

"Oh yes, Isabelle, he's right. You'll like it. Very high in the air. Carved out of and built on top of a mesa in the middle of the plains. Enormous tower in the middle. Very dangerous. Right up your alley. Doubt the library's still there, though."

"Huh," Isabelle said. "A mage fortress. In the old capital. It's not a bad idea."

"Yeah," Finn said. "I mean, if we don't have to fight..."

Isabelle glared at him again. "At some point, we're going to have to fight them."

"Not if we can show them we're not dangerous."

Isabelle rolled her eyes. "We are dangerous."

"I mean, to them."

"Me too."

"I mean, we can show them we aren't going to... that we'll follow laws and—"

"Why should we follow laws we don't get to make?"

"We can help make them."

She lifted her eyebrows. Finn really didn't want to be taking the time to argue this now.

"Look, maybe you're right. But, at the very least we can try to get a better handle on our powers. I'm sure there are tons of people out there like me without good control who are hurting people and making it worse. Right?"

"Maybe. That still doesn't—"

"No, of course not. But—"

Isabelle stood, pushing her chair back from the table. "All right, we'll go. Tomorrow. But you're wrong, Finn. We'll never be treated well until we make them treat us well."

She turned and swept back to the bathroom, shutting the door behind her.

Eraldir was looking at Finn. "What triggered this, I wonder?"

"Her? Isn't she always like this?"

"No, I mean the mage killings." Eraldir continued looking at Finn.

Finn looked down at the table. This wasn't the time for confessions, though. There was a mage that needed rescuing. He looked up into Eraldir's dark brown, green-flecked eyes.

"There's one more thing," Finn said softly, hoping Isabelle wouldn't hear. "There's a mage being held captive. They're going to execute them soon. I'm not sure exactly when."

Eraldir's eyes lit up. "Ah, a rescue mission, is it?" He cracked his bony knuckles, then glanced at the closed door, from behind which came the sound of splashing and wind. "Probably best we leave her to her bath." Eraldir pushed himself creakily to his feet and hobbled over to the door, motioning for Finn to follow.

"How do you know they're being kept here?" Eraldir asked.

"I don't. The barkeep just said they were captured today, and that the owner of the inn is leading the group doing the mage killings."

Eraldir stopped with his hand on the door handle. "That's not much to go on, lad."

"No, I know, but what if they are here?"

"And what if we run into the innkeeper while we're out prowling his establishment late at night? I'll tell you from experience, innkeepers don't appreciate that. And this one's a mage-hating, rabble-rousing, high-and-mighty, entitled rich man." Eraldir glanced back over his shoulder. "Whew, glad to see he's not standing behind me. Can't tell you how often that happens. I've often wondered if I've got some sort of conjuring magic set up connected to whomever I'm insulting."

"We can't just leave them to be executed, can we?"

Eraldir placed a hand gently on Finn's shoulder. "I know you want to help, but this really isn't our fight. If we get involved in this, well, it's not likely to go well for us. The best thing we can do is what you suggested. Get to the King's Table, set up a new academy for mages. Decrease the amount of accidental and harmful magic in the world. I know it's terrible, but… think of the bigger picture, Finn."

"But…"

"Look, if you knew they were here, even that would be enough, and I'd say let's go try to rescue him or her. But we don't. If they're here, they're guarded. If they're not here, there are still probably guards around. Rich man like Flavius'll have armed guards everywhere, watching the valuables and the non-valuables alike, just to throw people off and intimidate them. And just because he can." Eraldir glanced back over his shoulder again.

What Eraldir was saying made sense. They didn't even know if the mage was being kept here. They had larger plans to think of, and trying to rescue this one person would jeopardize those plans. Yes, Eraldir was completely right, but Finn was going to try to rescue the mage anyway. He had to. It was his fault they were in jeopardy in the first place. If he told Eraldir that, though, the old man would try to stop him, and, despite his frailty, Finn suspected he would succeed.

"You're right," he said, sighing and nodding. He might have overdone the sighing a little. Luckily, Eraldir didn't seem to notice.

"Don't worry, lad. Don't be too hard on yourself. There are plenty of mages to rescue. Plenty of good to do in the world yet."

Somewhere in the inn, a door thumped open. The sound of indistinct voices drifted up to them.

"We'd better get to our rooms before someone catches us, eh?" Eraldir said.

Finn nodded and hurried off towards his room.

When he heard Eraldir's door close, though, he doubled back, heading for the staircase.

CHAPTER 12

inn moved through the darkened inn as quickly and quietly as he could. His senses had never been so sharply focused, both outwardly and inwardly. He was watching the fiery ball in his chest closely; he wasn't going to give himself away by accidentally lighting something on fire. If he could help it.

He crept through the now-empty dining room, could hear low voices from a room across the hall, but he avoided those, moved instead towards the kitchens. If they had a mage captive here, where would they keep him?

The kitchens were empty, dark, and orderly. Pots and pans, spoons and knives, hung in neat rows on the walls above the large, wood-burning stoves. A pan with a towel over it smelled like it held rising bread dough. The smell of flour and yeast reminded him of his mother's kitchen, and a lump formed in his throat. He was going to make up for that, though. Somehow.

A door at the end of the kitchens opened onto a narrow set of stone stairs. That seemed promising. Not that they couldn't be holding a captive in any one of the guest rooms up above, but if Finn were keeping someone captive it just seemed like somewhere underground would be the place for that. Fewer windows to escape from.

At the bottom of the stairs, though, was only a small cellar. It was completely dark. Finn decided to risk a little light, and conjured the tiniest possible flame in the palm of his hand, holding it up and peering into the darkness around him. The room was crowded with kitchen supplies. Against the wall were bins of potatoes, carrots, beets, and other vegetables. Sacks of flour and sugar and coffee lined another wall. Disused pots and pans and an old, sooty stove were stacked in the middle. Herbs hung drying from the beams overhead. Kel would be interested in those, Finn thought.

He searched all around, but it was a dead end. The only way out was the way he had come in. Finn went back up the stairs.

Wandering the halls, he started to think that Eraldir had been right. Why would they keep their prisoner here? There was probably an actual lock-up for criminals somewhere in this city. But, Arcturus didn't strike Finn as the type of man to let other people help. He seemed like the kind of person who would be in control, in charge, and would want his prisoner to be kept on his property. Not that Finn had much to base that on, only a few observations: expensive, impeccable clothes, his presence there in the dining room, keeping an eye on things himself, but on a higher level than everyone else. Finn didn't know a lot about people, but he knew a man who liked control when he saw one.

Finn moved down the hall, very carefully trying each of the doors he came to until he found one that was locked. A locked door seemed promising to Finn, so, after pressing his ear to the wood and listening for a long time and hearing nothing, he melted the door handle and hinges and lifted the door out of the way. Behind the door was a narrow set of stone stairs, descending into the dark.

He didn't want to leave the door just leaning against the wall, it was such an obvious sign that something was wrong. If anyone noticed it they'd be sure to sound the alarm, but he had no way to reform the metal, so he settled for placing the door back in its place behind him. Then he conjured his small torch and hurried down the stairs.

The stones became damp and slippery under his feet. At the foot of the stairs he came to a long stone hall. To his right the light from his hand reflected off a huge puddle. Flooding?

Finn went left, came to another puddle, which he waded through. The water looked fresh and clean, not rancid. That meant it was either flowing in from someplace and out another, or it had only flooded very recently. They hadn't had much rain, but maybe water from the river had found its way in. Or maybe there was a captive water mage down here.

It was lucky that Finn had taken the time to stand and contemplate the puddle, because suddenly he heard voices up ahead. Immediately, he extinguished his flame. As his eyes adjusted, he realized there was light coming from around the corner.

Ever so slowly, Finn waded through the water, trying not to make so much as a ripple. Then he walked the length of the hall to where it turned another corner. He waited, listening.

"I tell you, I think I saw something," a man's voice said.

"Dammit, Reg, that's the fifth thing you've 'seen' in the last three hours. How many more rats and ghosts and gusts of wind are we going to have to investigate?"

"You're right, you're right. I was wrong before, but I'm telling you I really did see something this time. There was a light over there."

"All right, well, go check it out, then. Might as well. Not

like we've got anything better to do. She's not likely to try escaping."

Well, that sounded promising. And also bad. He looked around for someplace to hide, but there was nothing. Only smooth, empty, stone walls. He didn't have time to run back to the stairs, either. If he went too quickly the man would hear him, and if he went too slowly the man would see him. That left fighting. No, no, no. Dread thickened his throat and his heart started to pound. A heavy knot twisted itself up in his stomach. Could he fight the man? The only weapon he had was fire, but the whole point was to not hurt people. If he rescued the mage but killed two men to do it...

Finn stood, immobilized by indecision. The man was coming closer.

The footsteps stopped, just a few feet from the corner.

"Hey Reg, does it feel colder down here to you?"

"What? Yeah, obviously, dummy. We're underground. It's colder down here."

"No, no, I mean. There's... there's ice here." Finn heard him bend down. "Cripes, it's growing! Reg?"

"Run, Coop! It's the mages. They're here for her. Get the reinforcements!" Finn heard the slice of metal on scabbard as a sword was drawn.

Finn couldn't help himself. He peeked around the corner.

The two men were too distracted to notice him. Ice was indeed forming up around them. It mushroomed out of the ground, encircling them, thickening, climbing up to form heavy walls around them. Coop tried to climb over his, gripping the top with his fingers, but it was too slippery. His feet scrabbled on the slick walls, unable to find purchase. Reg hacked at it with his sword, but every dent he made was instantly filled back up again. Within seconds the walls had grown over their heads and sealed together, trapping them both in their own thick-walled ice prisons. They banged on the walls; tiny cracks formed, but the prisons held firm. The ice continued to thicken until the walls were so cloudy that Finn couldn't see inside anymore.

From the other end of the hall, Finn could hear someone coming. They were mumbling to themselves.

"Whew! I'm getting too old for this, that's for sure..."

Finn stepped out from behind the corner. "Eraldir?"

The old man looked up, noticing him for the first time. He was breathing heavily. "What are you doing here, boy?"

"What am I... what are you doing here? I thought you said it wasn't worth it, that the mage was probably somewhere else..."

"Yes, and I'm glad to see you listened to me about that."

"But..."

"Oh, I knew where they'd be keeping her. Was locked in this cell myself, a few years back. I just didn't think this needed to be a group effort. More of a solo mission, seems to me." He took a deep, gasping breath. "Plus, you keep lighting things on fire. I figured that might give us away. As you can see," he gestured to the ice prisons, which were slowly starting to melt, "I have fairly effective ways of neutralizing guards without being seen. Although, I confess this wore me out more than I was expecting." He grimaced and rubbed his stomach.

"You lied to me!"

Eraldir lifted his bushy eyebrows and rested a gnarled hand on the wall, still breathing heavily. "So, you're the only one who's allowed to lie?"

Finn opened his mouth furiously, but, finding nothing to say, shut it again.

Eraldir turned to the door. "All right, well, normally I would fill the lock with ice and break it, but truth be told I'm a bit spent. Haven't needed that particular trick in a while. So, how about you try something?"

Finn would be only too happy to melt something now. He only wished the lock were bigger. Why stop with the lock, though? Finn conjured a wall of flame, which consumed not only the lock but the whole door itself, which was also made of iron. At first the iron wouldn't melt, but Finn turned the heat up and up until the thing softened and disintegrated into a puddle of molten metal, which gave off blasts of heat so intense the stones around the door were melting, too. Eraldir and Finn both leapt back, shielding their faces. A wall of ice sprang up between them and the source of the heat, and instantly vaporized. Eraldir continued to blast ice and water at the pile of metal. The water came in spurts, and it hissed and vaporized. The hallway was quickly filling with a thick, hot mist. Finally, it was cool enough, and the metal and stone, though still warm, were at least solid.

"Dammit, boy! Totally unnecessary. All you needed to do was melt the lock off." Eraldir's hands were on his bony knees now.

Finn grinned. It felt good to be in control, to use all the energy that had built up inside him.

Eraldir wasn't grinning, though. He was looking behind Finn.

Slowly, Finn turned, feeling waves of heat coming from something behind him as he did so. Fifteen feet of the tunnel behind him, past the ice prisons—which were magically still standing—had melted into molten rock. Flames flickered over everything, and chunks of melted ceiling dripped, hissing, into the liquid floor. That wasn't the worst part, though. In the flames and shimmering heat in the tunnel were faces. Burning faces, their mouths open in silent screams of agony. Their skin was on fire, melting off them, dripping down onto bodies below. The floor was covered in the images of bodies, flickering in and out like mirages as the flames swelled and abated and swelled again. Finn recognized his parents.

Finn's first thought was to hide it, cover it up with something, anything. He had to keep Eraldir, or anyone, from seeing it. But he couldn't take it back, couldn't affect it, couldn't pull the fire back into his heart, no matter how desperately he wanted to. He waited for it to go out, hoped to see it lessening, but it didn't. The figures in the flames writhed in agony. Houses burned, people fled in terror, the fire consuming them.

"Eraldir, how did... what did I... how do I get rid of this?" He couldn't face the old man, couldn't stand to look at him. His sweaty hands clenched, his nails biting into his skin.

"You can't, boy."

"Can't I undo it somehow? Can't you put it out?"

"No boy. I can't." Eraldir said softly behind him.

At last Finn made himself turn back to look at Eraldir. The old man was bent over, his hands on his knees.

"That was the shadow," Eraldir said.

"What?" The word came out in a choked whisper.

Eraldir sighed. "I should have warned you earlier. I... I didn't think you were powerful enough for it to matter much. Most mages aren't."

A sound came from down the hall.

"Look boy, there's no time to explain. They'll likely have noticed something is wrong by now. I... left a bit of a mess on my way in. For now, you need to pull yourself together so we can get out of here."

Finn had heard the sound, too, through the thick buzzing in his head. He looked up, saw Eraldir looking at him with sadness and pity.

Finn pushed himself to his feet and nodded to Eraldir. "Let's go."

The molten metal had cooled and solidified by now, and they stepped across it easily, into the small cell. At the back, on the floor, lay a young woman about Finn's age, bound and gagged and looking at them with wide, terrified blue eyes.

She had long blond hair, which was now dirty and disheveled. Her eyes were red-rimmed from crying, and her dress, a soft yellow, was stained with grime and soaked with water.

Eraldir knelt creakily in front of her.

"Hey there, girl, don't you worry now. We're going to get you out of here."

Tears leaked out of her large eyes as Eraldir loosed her bonds and helped her to sit up. She took a few deep breaths and then started crying in earnest. Eraldir patted her on the back.

"Er, there there," Eraldir said. The girl cried harder.

Finn just stood there watching, having no idea what to do.

"Er, listen, girl, we need to get you out of here, okay?" Eraldir said.

She nodded, sniffed a little and wiped her hands across her face. Her hands left grey-green smears across her cheeks. She looked at her palms and started to cry again.

Finn took a deep breath, stepped forward, and knelt down. "What's your name?"

She looked up, her blue eyes met his and for a few seconds she just stared at him, startled. "Jesmaine. Jes."

"Hi Jes, I'm Finn." He smiled.

She sniffed again, then gave him a watery smile. "Thank you for rescuing me, Finn."

Eraldir grunted. "It was a team effort, really, although I was the one who dealt with the guards."

Jes looked at Eraldir, surprised, like she hadn't noticed him there, despite all his previous comforting, then she turned back to Finn and held out a small hand. "Could you help me up?"

Finn held out a hand and she took it, but she held it so weakly that he had to grip her hard to lift her to her feet. She wobbled and he gave her his arm to hold on to.

"Thank you," she said, smiling at him.

This was exactly what it was supposed to be like when you rescued someone, right? So why was Finn wishing she would let go of his arm and stand on her own?

"All right, all right, let's get out of here," Eraldir said. "Come on, you two."

Only then, walking out of the cell with the beautiful, fragile blonde girl on his arm, did Finn stop to wonder who it was that they were rescuing, and whether she had done anything to deserve being locked up.

He glanced down at her and found her looking up at him. She batted her eyelashes.

THEY MADE their way as quickly as they could, with Jes stumbling occasionally and needing to be helped up by Finn, back to Finn's room where they found a worried, lonely Kel, still dressed and sitting on the bed. She leapt up and came quietly with them.

They knocked on Isabelle's door several times, but no one answered. Eraldir tried the door but it was locked. With a sigh, he placed a finger directly in front of the lock. A thin spike of ice grew out of the end, wormed its way inside the keyhole. Eraldir listened intently, there were a few clicks and the door unlocked. He pulled the ice key out, breaking it off the end of his finger and tossing it aside.

Grimacing and massaging his chest, Eraldir pushed the door open. The room was dim; Finn could see the pile of cakes, greatly diminished, on the table. A great snore issued from the bed.

"Finn—the candles please?"

Finn carefully lit one candle, then another. Light slowly filled the room, and Isabelle, asleep on the bed, gave a grunt and turned over.

Eraldir approached. "Isabelle!" he whispered. She didn't respond, so he shook her by the shoulder. She punched him in the face, and he stumbled back.

Isabelle leapt out of bed, fully-dressed, white hair flying. She landed in the middle of the room in a burst of wind, but then she noticed who she'd punched.

"Oh, hey Eraldir. What's up?"

Eraldir massaged his nose gingerly, and it started to bleed. "Ow, girl, what was that for?"

Isabelle had noticed Jes, though, who was still holding Finn's arm. Her eyes narrowed. "Who's the girl?"

"This is Jes," Eraldir said trying to staunch the bleeding from his nose. "The lady was in distress, and young Finn and I rescued her. Well, it was primarily me that rescued her. Finn mostly—well, he helped somewhat."

Finn cringed.

"Why can't she talk for herself?" Isabelle said, walking to stand in front of Jes, hands on hips.

Tears welled in Jes' eyes, she opened her mouth a little, and then closed it. Isabelle arched an eyebrow.

"The lady has had a trying experience, I'm sure," Eraldir said. "Currently, however, we need to leave."

"Offended the hosts by stealing their prisoner?" Isabelle sighed. "Interrupted bath. No full night's sleep in an actual bed. This is your fault, isn't it?" She glared at Finn. "That's what you were coming to tell us, only you didn't want to tell me, just Eraldir."

"I—"

But she had already turned and started shoving things into her pack. Eraldir went next door and grabbed his pack, too, and they were ready to leave.

CHAPTER 13

They made their way down through the dark and silent halls to the dining room without incident, but there they encountered a problem. The dining room wasn't empty. It was a good thing Eraldir had insisted they go without lights, or they would have been noticed.

Clustered in the middle of the dining room, between them and the door, was a group of about twenty heavily-armed men and women. In their midst stood Arcturus Flavius, addressing the group in a low voice.

"Yes, hopefully it was the others that rescued her, but we think it may have been someone else. If it was her gang, they're long gone. If not..."

"I say we search the inn now!" a man shouted. He was immediately shushed into silence by those around him.

Finn glanced at Eraldir, jerked his head over his shoulder. Eraldir nodded, and they started to edge away. They'd find another way out. Isabelle, though, stood with clenched fists, watching the men. Finn touched her elbow, trying to get her attention, and she turned to look at him, but the light of battle was in her eyes. She cracked a knuckle.

"Come on Isabelle, let's go." Finn whispered.

"Come on, Finn. Look at them there, all waiting for a fight. We can take them. I haven't had a good fight in a while."

"Those are swords they have there, and they're probably planning to use them on us," Finn hissed.

"You go, then," she said, turning back to watch.

Finn glanced desperately back at Eraldir, who had Kel by the hand. Jes held Kel's other hand.

"I'm not just leaving you here," Finn said to Isabelle. "Come on, we have to get my sister out of here."

Finn noticed suddenly that the dining room had gone silent. How loudly had he said that? He turned to look, but the men were all focused on Arcturus, who was staring coldly at the man who had interrupted him.

"Ronald."

"Yes, sir?"

"Can you tell me who is in charge here?"

"You."

"Me?"

"Yes, you."

"You, *sir*."

"Me? I thought you said…"

"No, idiot. Me. Me, sir."

"Yes, you."

"Sir."

"Yes?"

"No. Dammit. Call me sir. That's all I'm saying."

Isabelle giggled.

"Oh, sorry."

"Sorry?"

"Sorry, sir."

"That's better."

There was a pause.

"Anyway, as I was saying… There's someone listening at the door."

"That's not what—"

But the rest of the group had understood what he meant. As a unit they turned, drew their swords, and sprinted towards Isabelle and Finn. Grinning, Isabelle sashayed forward into the room.

Finn turned back to Eraldir, "Go! Run. Take Kel." The old man gave a single nod and spun around, pulling Jes and Kel with him.

Then Finn lurched into the room after Isabelle. Her hands were open, palms up, and her white hair lifted off her shoulders. The men had stopped their charge, and stood in a large, uneasy half circle, none quite daring to get too close to her. She laughed.

Arcturus stepped forward.

"I, Arcturus Flavius, leader of the Magical Safety Commission, hereby put you both under arrest."

"For what?" Isabelle said mockingly.

"Well, in your case, darling, that would be aiding and abetting him." Arcturus gestured towards Finn.

"And what's he done?"

"Besides free a known mage, who was under arrest and awaiting execution? He's responsible for the murders of seventeen people, including his parents and the mayor of his hometown."

Surprised, Isabelle cocked an eyebrow at Finn. "Really?"

He nodded.

"Well, I'm sure they deserved it." Then she kissed him.

He had never been happier or more disturbed in his life.

She turned back to the group, "Are you sure? I mean, how do you know? Maybe we're not even mages."

The men glanced at each other, then looked to Arcturus.

He smiled, "Well, you, darling, are clearly a wind mage.

And this one's a fire mage. He was asking Billings here," Arcturus gestured to the barkeep who stood next to him, "some very suspicious questions. On top of that, your friend Eraldir—a known mage—bribed Gavin here to let you all in after explicitly telling him you were his apprentices. And then, as if that wasn't enough, Ambrose happens to know young Finn. Finn Vogt, isn't it?"

Finn's eyes widened, and Arcturus smiled a superior smile and continued.

"Ambrose lived in Cromwic himself. Can't live there anymore, of course, because Finn burned it down. Not to mention that you just asked him and he admitted it." He smiled, spreading his silver-ringed fingers wide. "So, you see, we are not some low-class rabble, or pitch-forked gang, persecuting without evidence. We are the defenders of the weak against the strong. The everyday people against those with power who abuse them."

Isabelle smiled. "I think you're scared of me."

"There, darling, you are wrong." Arcturus nodded to his men, who followed his orders immediately, leaping towards Finn and Isabelle, swords drawn, faces set in grim determination.

Isabelle laughed, and an explosion of wind drove them back. It emanated from her, blasting into them with the force of a hurricane. The building groaned and swayed around them, and Finn stood next to her, unsure of what to do. He couldn't light anything on fire without creating another conflagration of wind and flame that would burn the whole inn down and probably kill them all. So, he watched, helplessness and frustration mounting, as Isabelle drove them back.

The men leaned into the wind, gritting their teeth and advancing towards her. Suddenly the wind stopped and they fell on their faces. Isabelle chuckled. Then a great cyclone swirled up around them. Some of the men had dropped their swords when they fell, and these were picked up, slicing through the air, becoming a tornado of weaponry. One sword sliced into a woman's arm, another sunk deep into a man's torso. The air was filled with screams of terror and Isabelle's laughter.

Through another door at the other side of the room a group of soldiers burst in, hustling along three prisoners: Eraldir, Jes, and Kel. A chill ran over Finn's face and down his neck and arms to his hands, which broke out in a clammy sweat. As he watched, the men bound Kel roughly and gagged her as she tried to cry out. Finn could feel the heat of rage burning up inside him. But he couldn't do anything; the wind howled around them, ready to ignite any flame into a maelstrom of death. He had to hold it in, but he didn't think he could much longer. He had to find some way to release the pressure.

Candlesticks. There were unlit candles around the edge of the room. Finn concentrated hard on one, lit it gently. The wind immediately blew it out. He lit another. It went out. Around the room Finn went, desperately keeping his concentration, letting out a tiny bit of fire at a time, lighting candle after candle, releasing the heat that threatened to burst out of him. Anything more and they would all die. Kel would die.

Isabelle wasn't laughing anymore. She was starting to tire. Most of the swords had embedded themselves in furniture or people, and so her wind was only wind again, and the guards were fighting back. They threw objects, which she dodged, or sent hurtling back at them. She blew sand up off the floor into their eyes. But the gusts were getting weaker, and she couldn't keep up the constant tornado anymore. She was weakening, and the guards could tell. They redoubled their efforts, inching ever closer.

Finn had been so focused on the candles that he didn't notice when Arcturus made a move for Kel.

"Stop this now or the girl loses an arm." Arcturus held a long, glinting knife above Kel's arm.

Isabelle looked at Finn. Finn gave her a pleading look. The wind stopped. Isabelle crouched down, bent her head to the floor. Finn thought she had something else planned, and the soldiers must have, too. Some moved forward, lifting their weapons, and others backed away. A tremor ran through Isabelle's back and she threw up. All the men moved back.

"Good, good. Now you'll all come along quietly I'm sure. Apparently, our dungeon is too well known, so we'll have to find someplace else for you."

A woman and a man came forward, carrying ropes and gags with which they bound Finn and Isabelle. Isabelle spat the last of her vomit in the woman's face before allowing herself to be tied.

They were pushed over to join Eraldir and the others. Finn wished he could take Kel's hand, but since he couldn't, he made eye contact instead, trying to look reassuring.

Arcturus came to look them over, smiling. "The townspeople will be so happy when you are executed. You're notorious, you know," he said to Finn. "No one has felt safe since they heard what you did."

Finn looked down at the floor; he couldn't meet the man's eyes. That was what he wanted, after all; he wanted people to feel safe. Maybe he just hadn't realized it but his death might accomplish that. Isabelle kicked him in the shins. He looked up to see her eyes blazing furiously. She tried to say something around the gag, but couldn't quite get it out.

Whatever she had been trying to say was interrupted anyway by a violent tremor of the earth. This wasn't a short tremor, either. The ground shook and shook, rattling the walls. Pots and dishes slid to the edges of their shelves and crashed to the floor. Some of the men drew their swords again. Finn thought this was strange—there was no one here to fight—but he was wrong.

Floorboards in the middle of the room split apart, revealing a gaping chasm. Out of this leapt three figures. The first was a tall woman in her early thirties with dark red hair, like dried blood on a rusty sword. She stepped forward, reaching out one hand, conjuring a ball of fire which she hurled at the man closest to her. He went up in flames, screaming. She conjured another ball but the guards were already scattering. She hit a woman in the back, and the woman went up in flames, too, consumed within seconds, her screams choked off almost immediately. A wall of fire leapt up around the prisoners, and their bonds ignited, burning away painfully.

"That's two of yours, Arcturus!" the woman yelled, but Arcturus had disappeared.

The woman stopped to survey them, fire crackling around her. Her eyes were light brown, almost yellow, and she looked at them coldly, her expression a sharp contrast to the heat all around her.

"Who are these people, Jes?"

Jes was rubbing her slim wrists. "They're mages, Reina. They rescued me." Jes was looking at the floor, and Reina didn't look at her, her eyes focused instead on Eraldir, whom she had just noticed.

"Eraldir. Why am I not surprised?" she said.

"Reina Jeesh. Last I saw you, you were lighting things on fire for a gang of highway robbers over near Montvale. You still working as a weapon for hire?"

She narrowed her cold eyes. "And last I saw you, you were sitting in a boat with your back turned on a bunch of mages, floating off to your comfy island paradise. You still pretending to care about anyone but yourself?"

The walls of flame around them had started to catch the ceiling on fire. No one but Finn—always painfully aware of things burning when they shouldn't be—seemed to notice.

"Um, Eraldir? The ceiling's on fire, could you—?"

Eraldir looked up, took a deep breath, but nothing happened. "Sorry, boy, I'm a bit depleted at the moment. Used the last of it on that fancy key. Can't resist showing off for a lady, you know." He winked at Jes. "Guess we'd better go."

Reina's eyes swept over the group, and she seemed to come to a quick decision. "We can talk later. You can come with us. For now."

The walls had caught fire, too, and the heat coming off them was scorching. Finn wrapped his arms around Kel, shielding her with his body as Reina hustled them towards the crack in the floor.

Isabelle stopped at the edge of the hole, and gave Reina an appraising look. Then she jerked her head back, indicating Jes. "You know she was betraying you, right?" Isabelle said to Reina.

"What?" Fire flicked through Reina's fingertips.

"Yeah. I heard them talking; she came to warn the innkeeper about whatever you're planning."

Reina grabbed Jes by the elbow and jerked her forward. Jes resisted, staring fixedly at the ground, tears pouring out of her eyes.

Finn wondered when Isabelle had heard that. Still, now was not the time. "Did you have to tell her that now, Isabelle?" he hissed. Burning chunks of ceiling were beginning to fall.

"Is this true, Jes?" Reina shook her.

The girl only sobbed harder.

Finn still felt like the only one who cared that the building was incinerating around them. "Come on, let's get out of here"

Reina looked around, "Right." She grabbed Jes by the hair and jerked her up, pulling her over to the hole and throwing her in.

Finn gripped Kel by the hands and slowly lowered her into the pit. Unknown hands took her from him. The heat was searing Finn's back now, and he jumped in without thinking. He slammed into the ground, rolled, and picked himself up, squinting into the darkness. He found Kel's hand, pulled her into a quick hug, then looked up. Someone stood in the shadows a short way down the tunnel. Above Finn, Isabelle was still standing at the edge of the hole. He heard a huge gust of wind, and an explosion. Brightness surged above him and Isabelle jumped down, landing next to him.

"Whoa," she said. Finn noticed that a bit of her hair was on fire, and he patted it out with his hand.

The unknown man came running forward, his hands outstretched and his eyes locked on the opening, beyond which an inferno blazed. "Get out of the way," he said, not sparing them a glance.

Finn started to move out of the way, but as the man passed, his face came into the light and Finn stopped in his tracks. His jaw dropped open. It was Ronan.

The ground shook, frissons emanating from where Ronan stood, barefoot as always; his hands lifted to the opening, eyes half-closed against the blasting heat, and with a rumble the two sides of the hole reared up and slammed together, closing them in darkness.

Ronan had made it to Westwend. Finn felt a surprising rush of joy at seeing his one-time best friend. Though, Ronan also reminded him of Cromwic. The past had begun to seem like a bad dream, unreal in a way that let him almost forget what he'd done. Seeing Ronan brought that back. If he'd left when Ronan had asked him to, none of this would have happened. Of course, maybe he would just be swinging from one of the tree branches outside the town. But, still, Ronan had been right, and Finn had been wrong. Ignoring magic didn't work, and neither of them had chosen to become mages.

He'd always assumed Ronan had chosen to become a mage. He had wanted it badly enough. Finn's eye was caught by the dark tattoo on Ronan's face, and a stab of guilt of went through him.

CHAPTER 14

*R*onan brushed past Finn and Isabelle, sweeping through the dark towards Reina and the others, illuminated by a ball of guttering flame held in Reina's hand. Finn knew he should say something, stop Ronan and say 'hey, it's me,' or 'turns out you were right,' or something. But Ronan had passed so quickly that, by the time Finn got his courage up to say something, he would have had to shout it down the tunnel. So, instead, he just followed awkwardly behind.

Now they knew where the earthquakes had been coming from. Finn could feel Isabelle walking next to him, her body tense. He reached out and put a hand on her shoulder, and to his surprise she didn't jerk away.

The rest of the group was standing in a huddle around Reina, who stood over the prostrate form of Jes. The girl was still crying, and she lay in the dirt of the tunnel floor, curled into a ball.

Finn glanced at Ronan, who wasn't looking at him, but instead was focused on Jes, an unreadable expression on his face.

"Are you sure?" Finn whispered to Isabelle. "About what you heard?"

"Oh, yeah," Isabelle said casually. "That's what they said while you were trying to convince me to run away from the dining room. She came to warn them about something they're planning."

"Thank you," Jes said through her tears, still not looking up. "Thank you for rescuing me."

"I only rescued you because you're a goddamn water mage and leaving you there wouldn't hurt you at all. If I thought you'd have died in that fire I would have left you there," Reina spat.

Jes cried harder.

"I always knew you were a coward, but I had no idea how much of one." Reina kicked her in the ribs.

Finn stepped forward to intervene—Jes was so wretched and helpless—but Reina had already turned away.

"Ronan, you do something with her. We'll take her back until we decide what to do."

Ronan reached down and scooped Jes up. She wrapped her arms around his neck and pressed her face into his chest. Finn saw him gently stroke her arm with his hand.

The light in the tunnel went out.

"Dammit!" Reina said. She cursed for a few seconds, and Finn could hear her trying something, but no light came forth. So, he conjured a flame.

Reina was standing with her hands upraised, opening and closing her fingers, a look of fury and frustration on her face. She turned to look at Finn, blinked in the light.

"All right, you light our way, then." She turned down the tunnel and gestured to Isabelle. "You, come with me. I want to hear exactly what you heard."

Ronan had glanced at Finn when he'd lit the flame, his eyes drawn by the sudden burst of light; he had started to look away again when suddenly his eyes widened and his head jerked back in a quick double-take.

"Finn?" One of his arms slipped, and Jes' legs slid to the ground.

"Er, hi Ronan."

Ronan stared at Finn's face, then at the fireball held in his hand. "What are you doing here?"

"Um, I had to leave Cromwic." The words he needed to say were building up inside him.

"I heard they started killing mages. I guess they found out you were one, too?"

They definitely had found out he was a mage. "Yeah."

"Sorry."

That was what Finn should be saying, not Ronan.

The others were getting farther away from them, and Reina yelled at them to hurry up. A shadow crossed Ronan's face, and they both turned to keep up with the group, Ronan lifting Jes easily back up into his arms.

Now that they were walking side-by-side, and Ronan was no longer looking him straight in the face, it was easier to say what he needed to say.

"I'm sorry, Ronan."

The walked on in silence for a few steps, Ronan waiting for him to continue.

"I'm sorry I was such a jerk. You were right about magic. I tried to avoid it, and... I couldn't."

Ronan readjusted Jes' weight in his arms. "I get where you were coming from." But there was tension in his voice.

"You were right, though. I... I totally lost control. That disaster? That was me."

Ronan stopped and stared at him. Finn couldn't meet his eyes. Up ahead, Eraldir's bag caught fire. Eraldir swore and put it out.

Ronan glanced towards the still smoking bag, then back again, and took a deep breath. "Wow."

Finn ran a hand through his hair; it was damp with sweat. "I'm really sorry, Ronan. You were my friend, and I was a jerk to you when you became a mage." His eyes fell on the tattoo.

"Yeah, you were." But there wasn't much force behind his words.

"And even after that, you tried to help me, when I became one, too."

Ronan's mouth curled into a sad half-smile. "I felt bad for you."

"Yeah, well. I wish I'd listened to you."

They stood in silence for a moment, the others getting farther ahead of them.

"It's okay, Finn." Ronan looked away, readjusted Jes in his arms. "Let's just go."

It wasn't okay, though; Finn could tell. There was something else Ronan wasn't telling him. Or maybe he just hadn't forgiven him for how he'd reacted when Ronan had become a mage. That was understandable.

Up ahead, Reina suddenly stopped; the tunnel branched into three here, and she was peering down the leftmost path, hands on her hips. "Ronan! Get up here and remind me where this one goes."

Ronan nodded at Finn, then hurried up to join Reina.

Immediately, Isabelle appeared at Finn's side.

"Who was that?" She eyed Ronan's back appreciatively.

Finn felt a stab of jealousy. "Um, a friend. We knew each other back home."

"Hm." She watched Ronan a few more seconds, then turned and punched Finn on the arm, grinning. "Hey, good job, by the way."

"With apologizing?"

"Definitely not, if this is you trying to apologize to me.

Not sure what it'd be for, either."

"No, I apologized to him."

"Oh, what'd you do to him?"

"Long story."

She rolled her eyes. "I meant with the candles. Good job with the candles."

"Oh. Thanks." He'd forgotten about that. She was right. He'd kept complete control of his powers. He would have felt happier about that if she hadn't returned to eyeing Ronan.

Suddenly, Eraldir stopped short in front of them.

"Sylvia!" he cried, and made to turn back.

A small voice spoke up. "She's all right."

Finn and Eraldir looked down at Kel. Finn had completely forgotten she was there.

"You can hear her?" Eraldir asked.

Kel nodded. "The stable boy was out riding her. They came back and saw the fire and now they're at another stable somewhere."

Eraldir passed a hand across his forehead, and gave a great racking cough. "Well, that's a relief. Thank you, girl." Eraldir patted Kel on the shoulder. "I suppose we'll have to go find her later. And speaking of later..." Eraldir glanced forward at Reina's straight, angular back. She was a way ahead of them down the tunnel now, striding through the dark, flanked by the other two mages. Eraldir lowered his voice. "Reina and I go way back, as you may have noticed. She... well... she tends to be a bit volatile." He glanced at Isabelle. "Not that I'm saying that's a bad thing, necessarily. Just, one thing I know about Reina is that she likes to be in charge. People who don't do what she says tend to die publicly and painfully. So, for now, when she asks, we're on her side. We'll do what she says. Got it?"

"If she's so dangerous, why were you antagonizing her?" Isabelle asked.

"Oh, Reina won't kill you for antagonizing her." Eraldir waved a hand airily. "She'll kill you for not doing what she says, but antagonizing, insults, light torture, that's all just small talk for her."

"Huh," said Isabelle.

Awesome, thought Finn. Just great.

THEY WALKED FOR A LONG TIME, down through the bare tunnel, turning left or right at branches. Eventually they came to a large warren of inter connected, cave-like rooms.

It was the middle of the night, but you wouldn't have known it. The place buzzed with activity. Mages glanced up and nodded to Reina as they passed, but then went immediately back to work. Some were forming stone sconces along tunnel walls, others were following along behind, filling the sconces with flames. A group of earth mages stood in a small knot, arguing about how best to reinforce a new tunnel. Finn noticed that one of them had a stone leg, another a stone ear.

"Hold your breath," Reina called out ahead of them.

Finn had barely registered her words when suddenly he couldn't breathe. There wasn't any air in this part of the tunnel. He gasped, but his muscles weren't strong enough to suck the air back into his lungs as the vacuum pulled it out. He stumbled forwards and the air was back.

"That's happened to me before," Isabelle commented.

Finn coughed. "What was that?"

"Some wind mage being stupid."

"Can't they put the air back?"

"No, it's gone."

"Will it come back eventually?"

Isabelle shrugged. "Not as far as I know. Ask Eraldir."

Finn planned on it.

Reina led them all to a large back room. One end was

stacked with crates and barrels and coils of rope, but at the other was a large fireplace and a long, heavy wooden table. The group seated themselves around the table, except for Jes, whom Ronan brought through another door, closing it behind him as he came back out.

Reina gestured to the fireplace, and a roaring, crackling light filled it. She sighed and something in her face relaxed.

"All right, Eraldir," Reina said when they were all seated. "I want to know what you're doing here."

"I could say the same to you, Reina," Eraldir said. "But, actually what I'd rather ask is if you have any food. All this excitement has left me starving."

Finn realized he agreed, even though they'd just eaten a few hours ago.

Reina stared at Eraldir for a moment, then shrugged. "Ronan, bring us some food. And bring me a couple of bottles of my wine… and get Ambrose and Reginald."

Finn could see the tightness in Ronan's face, but his friend just nodded to Reina, and went off through another door.

Reina crossed her arms on the table in front of her and stared off into space, saying nothing, until Ronan came back in a few minutes later, carrying several bottles of wine—all of which he put in front of Reina—a few loaves of bread, and a basket of dried apples.

Ignoring the food, Reina uncorked one of the wine bottles and took a long swig straight from the neck. Finn wondered who Ambrose and Reginald were. Was it code for something?

"All right, Eraldir. You go first," she said. "Why are you here?"

Eraldir was already halfway through a loaf of bread. "Well, let's see. I was over near the lake, on my way back from traveling through the plains, but it had been a terrible season and I hadn't had any work at all for months. It must have been the same for others, too, because, when I got back, the camp—well I guess you're familiar with it—was even fuller than usual. And this girl—"

Reina clunked the wine bottle down hard on the table. "You and your stories. They get worse all the time. Start more recently."

"I was in the process of being accosted by a group of mage-killers when you popped out of the floor," Eraldir said, his face deadpan.

"Less recently."

"I was born in—"

Finn thought Reina was going to hurl the wine bottle—now mostly empty—at Eraldir's head, so he cut in. "—We've been traveling, and we came to Westwend to rest. I'm Finn, this is my sister Kel, and this is Isabelle, and we're Eraldir's apprentices."

Reina gave a bark of laughter. "Apprentices! That's rich. So, you're relying on this long-winded walking corpse to teach you?"

"We're on our way to the King's Table. We're setting up a school there."

Reina cocked an eyebrow, and took another long swig from the bottle.

"Well, that sure sounds like fun."

"Anyway, then we heard there was a mage going to be executed, so we tried to rescue…" Finn trailed off, not sure if he should continue, judging from the look on Reina's face.

Reina was gripping the wine bottle so tightly her knuckles went white. The sleeves of her shirt ended at the elbows and Finn noticed the veins on her arms stood out over thin, ropy muscles. "I can't believe that little…"

"Your turn, Reina, what are you up to?" Eraldir said, changing the subject.

He hadn't needed to, though, because just at that moment Ronan came back carrying a large glass jug of water. Inside were two very small goldfish with enormous eyes.

He set the jug in front of Reina who, completely ignoring Eraldir, leaned forward and tapped on the glass. "Hey there, Ambrose, Reginald, mommy's back."

The two fish gave no sign of being aware of her, just floated along, gently waving their fins.

"You keep goldfish?" Isabelle said, fighting back a laugh.

Reina narrowed her eyes. "You have a problem with goldfish?"

"No, just... you seem more like the piranha type. Or, like you'd have a bunch of bears in a pit and you'd feed people to them or something."

Reina's eyes were back on her fish. "Maybe you would like a bear pit. I could see that. You don't seem like you've got a lot of subtlety to you." Isabelle scoffed at this. "You don't see the nine hundred and ninety-eight other fish that I started with." She touched a rough fingertip to the smooth edge of the glass. "I pitted them against each other in groups of two. Some didn't eat each other at all. They just stayed there together, moving slower and slower until they both died. But the rest fought when they got hungry enough. And one always ate the other. I pitted the winners against each other over and over again. Ambrose and Reginald here are the last ones."

Reina lifted her wine bottle and poured some into the tank. Both fish shot up into the maroon cloud, zigzagging through it. Reina chuckled. "They have good taste in wine. Completely ignore the cheap stuff. It's good they like it, too, because I've been so busy I haven't had time to get more goldfish for them."

"So, your goldfish are cannibals?" Isabelle asked.

"Yes. The only nourishment these fish have ever had is

wine and other goldfish."

Finn could tell by Isabelle's silence that she was impressed.

No one really knew what to say after this, so for a while they all just sat there, watching Reina drink and feed wine to her fish. Finn wondered how Kel felt about this. He looked over and saw that the little girl was staring at the blood-thirsty, cannibalistic goldfish with a look of horror on her face. Finn put an arm around her and squeezed her shoulder.

Finally, Reina broke the silence. "So, you're setting up a mage school." The statement was addressed to no one in particular. "You and I have similar goals, then."

"You're making a mage school, too?" Finn asked.

"Not a school." Reina at last tore her eyes from the fish and pushed their jug aside, sloshing some water out the top as she did so. "A city."

"Whereabouts?" Eraldir asked.

"Here."

"Isn't this already a city?" Finn felt like this was a stupid question.

"Yes, but right now it's run by Arcturus Flavius and his non-magical guards. And he's been killing my mages and I won't have that. Not to mention he's costing me a lot of money."

"Been buying too much of his pie?" Eraldir asked.

Reina turned, stared at him for a moment, and then turned away again. "He's got the whole city under his thumb, got the idiot citizens paying him to run an army, then he extorts money from those of us he knows are mages. We pay him off so he won't turn us in. The man's making a fortune." Reina shook her head in admiration. "Still, I got him back today. Killed two of his toy soldiers and burned down his inn." She smiled. "He's a cunning, devious, bastard and I'm going to take away everything he cares about."

"Ah, so you're in love, then, Reina? Well, I'm happy you've found someone." Eraldir said.

Reina winked at him and took a long slug of wine. Then she turned to Ronan. "It's getting close to sunrise. You'd better get to work or it'll look suspicious."

Ronan heaved a great sigh and nodded, but didn't move. Reina turned to the others and explained. "Some of us pretend not to be mages. Ronan works as a shoemaker." She lifted a foot to display her boot, which was black, rising to her mid-calf, and laced all the way up to keep it snug to Reina's slim form. The stitches were tiny and perfect, barely visible. "That way we can get information on what's happening out there." She grinned at Ronan maliciously. "Ronan makes beautiful shoes."

Ronan glowered at this. "Yes, shoes," he said bitterly.

Finn was taken aback by this new anger in his friend. "Why don't you come with us?" he asked. Ronan looked at him thoughtfully, but before he could say anything, Reina interrupted.

"Hey, kid, you trying to poach my soldiers? Leave him alone," Reina said. "He's the best earth mage I have."

"Anyway, Finn," Ronan said, "We shouldn't have to leave. These cities are just as much ours as theirs. Westwend was built by mages originally."

"Finn doesn't like confrontation," Isabelle said to Ronan, grinning mockingly at Finn. Finn didn't like the warmth of the smile Ronan gave Isabelle, and they made eye contact longer than he thought necessary.

"What are you going to do when the non-mages fight back?" Finn asked.

"I'll light a few on fire, see how many of them decide to keep fighting," Reina said.

"Okay, so, you're going to take over the city. And they can

either just let you do that, or if they fight you'll fight back," Finn said.

"You got it."

"But you're way more powerful than they are, so you fighting them probably means they're all going to die."

"That's their choice," Ronan said simply.

"But, you know what's going to happen!" Finn said. "Doesn't that make it your choice, too?"

"Just because we're more powerful doesn't mean we have to walk on eggshells, kid," Reina said. "In fact, it means the opposite. I'm not sitting here quaking in Ronan's boots with the fear of hurting someone. I know I can hurt people, and it's their job to watch out for themselves. Not mine."

They went back and forth a few more times, and Finn felt his frustration with their callousness starting to rise. As it did, the source of his magic burned hotter. Eraldir asked Ronan something, but Finn didn't hear what it was. He was starting to lose control, and if he wasn't careful, he was going to light something on fire. He closed his eyes, took a few long, deep breaths. The fiery place in his chest was roiling and throwing off arcs of heat. He watched his frustration slowly settle down and drift apart. Then he realized Isabelle was saying his name. He opened his eyes to see her looking at him.

"What was that?" she asked.

"Just trying not to kill anyone."

"Oh. Well, good job." She gestured to the room. "No one's dead. Unless Eraldir counts for like, half a point."

Ronan was gone now, and Eraldir and Reina were arguing about something.

"You don't really agree with them, do you?" Finn asked Isabelle quietly, even though he knew the answer.

"You know I do. Non-mages are idiots, and they're letting their stupid fears get the better of them and they think they're better than us so they go around telling us what we can and can't do and murdering people if they don't agree."

"Which is exactly what Reina's doing, too, right? The non-mages are just afraid. And it makes sense that they're afraid. I mean..." he swallowed. "I've given them a reason to be afraid."

She shook her head, half smiling. "You feel way too guilty for the way you are, Finn."

Maybe she was right. But didn't he deserve to feel guilty? He'd murdered seventeen innocent people, including his parents. On accident, yes, but that didn't make it any less horrific.

Isabelle grabbed a bottle of wine, uncorked it, and took a drink.

Without looking at him, she spoke. "My mom's a fire mage, you know."

"Really?"

She nodded, still not looking at him, and took another drink.

"She doesn't think anyone knows. I don't even know if my dad knows. But I saw her once. She's not as powerful as you; she was just trying to light a candle. Lit the bed on fire. Whole thing went up in flames. She lost her mind, beating it out with her robe. After that's when she started taking the sleeping draught." Isabelle shook her head in disgust.

"Did she ever talk to you about magic?"

"No, never. I found out about it from some traveling mercenaries, in the taverns in town."

Finn tried to imagine a fourteen-year-old Isabelle, drinking in bars with mercenaries. It wasn't hard to picture.

"There's no point in being afraid of what you are," Isabelle said. "And anyone who tells you different is an idiot who's pretending the world is something it isn't and wants you to pretend, too."

178

"I just don't want to hurt anyone."

"No. You want no one to hurt anyone."

He paused. Yes, that was true. Was that so bad?

"Yeah, I guess you're right," he said. "I think these guys are going to hurt a lot of non-mages, and... I mean... yeah, they're defending themselves, but there are other options."

He'd said it more loudly than he'd intended, without noticing that Reina and Eraldir had gone quiet.

Reina had drunk the whole bottle of wine, now, and her head had been resting on the table, but she lifted it now and spoke. "You can't talk, aren't you the one that murdered your whole family?"

"How'd you..."

"Sorry, boy, I may have mentioned that," Eraldir said.

"Hey," Reina said to Isabelle. "This is my wine, so you ask before you go drinking it."

"Do you want it back?" Isabelle opened her mouth and pulled to bottle closer to her, leaning over it. "I've already thrown up once today, so there's probably not much in there but wine now."

Reina eyed her coldly. "I get the feeling that if I called your bluff I'd find out it wasn't really a bluff. I like that. That's your bottle, now. You've earned it. But. You, take another without asking, I'll cut off one of your fingers and I'll make Finn choose which one." She smiled at Finn.

Isabelle laughed and raised the bottle towards Reina before taking a drink.

"So," Reina said, suddenly business-like. "You had plans to make a mage school. You can do that here. I have mages that need schooling. The traitor's forced my hand and I'm moving forward with my plans tomorrow. I'll have control of this city within the week, so I can give you whatever resources you need."

Finn and Isabelle both looked at Eraldir, who was looking

straight at Reina. There was a long pause. "What kind of assurances do I have that you won't interfere with what I teach?"

"None. You'll teach what I want you to teach. I know my people, and I know what they need, and I know this city. But. Despite what I said earlier, I know there's no better teacher than you."

Eraldir cleared his throat, but didn't say anything.

Reina's yellow eyes were sharp, focused intently on Eraldir's face. "And you've spent time at Lake Iori, too. So, you can tell me their secrets; you can tell me what they keep behind their magical wards, why they keep the rest of us riff-raff out." He opened his mouth, but she cut him off. "Oh, I know you haven't spent much time there since your parents died. I know you can't stand to be there. I know how guilty you feel. Everyone you knew, all your friends, dead. Except for you."

Eraldir was looking down at the table now. A tear escaped the corner of his eye, and he wiped it away with a gnarled hand. Reina continued.

"You can make up for that here. Sure, you could go riding off on that ancient horse of yours, with your two murderous apprentices, looking for a fortress that may not even exist anymore. And, even if you found it, build a school that no one might ever hear of. If you live long enough to even get there, that is." She paused, and the longer the pause got, the more it felt like a threat. "Or. You could set up your school here. Tomorrow. There are mages here who've spent their whole lives hiding what they are. They're so twisted up inside they're barely able to function. You could save them."

Eraldir wiped another tear away and cleared his throat a few times. "I... I guess you're probably right. All right. Yes." He placed his hands on his bony knees and leaned on them, his shoulders hunched.

Reina lifted her wine bottle, took a swig, and clunked it down on the table. "Excellent. Let's get some sleep, then. War starts tomorrow." Her face darkened. "Just as soon as I decide what to do·about the traitor."

She extracted herself from the table, scooped up the rest of the wine bottles in one arm and the jug with the two fish in it in the other, and stalked out of the room. Over her shoulder, as she went, she said, "You'll sleep here on the floor. Stay in this room until I come get you."

"Eraldir?" Finn leaned toward the old man, who now looked frail.

Eraldir's head snapped up, his whole demeanor changed, and he grinned at them both. "What, boy?"

"Er, are you all right?"

"Well, my left arm went numb about an hour ago, I have to pee like a bear that's been trapped in a snowstorm for three days, and there's this ringing in my right ear..." He stuck his little finger in his ear and jiggled it around. After a few seconds of this he pulled it out, examined it, then wiped it on his pants.

"He means about Reina," Isabelle said. "We're not staying here, are we?"

"What? Oh, no, of course not. I told you. She's crazy." Eraldir glanced behind him, but Reina was gone.

"But..." Finn said.

"Acting, boy! You think I'd have lived this long without being able to pretend to do what a power-hungry dictator wants? The number of times that single tear bit's come in handy... That's the next thing I'll teach you. Once you stop accidentally lighting people on fire. That's probably less important, to be honest, in terms of survival, but I can tell it's important to you."

Isabelle laughed.

181

Eraldir continued. "No, no, we'll leave first thing in the morning."

"Why not now?"

"It's near sunrise already. I'm an old man and I need my sleep. I was already behind, after all that sleeping in the woods, and now this hullaballoo... Are you excited about finding your way back through a bunch of tunnels with a bloodthirsty fire mage and her army chasing us? I usually like to be well-rested for that sort of thing. Plus, my magic is depleted. No. Rest first, then escape."

He heaved himself up from the table and shambled unsteadily over to his pack.

"I'll just be over here behind these crates, sleeping. Don't wake me unless one of you is dying." He walked off, with his tea mug in one hand and his bedroll tucked under his arm. Finn watched him go, wondering if there was any part of the act that had been real. Those things Reina had said—Finn hadn't thought about that before, but it made sense. If Eraldir was the only one alive from before the Fall, that meant that everyone he had known then was dead. All his childhood friends. Finn could relate to that... though Eraldir has probably been a bit less singlehandedly responsible for the deaths of all his loved ones, unless they were talked to death.

When they were alone, Finn suddenly remembered that Isabelle had kissed him not too long ago. His heart leapt at the memory, but then crashed back down remembering how she'd looked at Ronan. He turned to look at her. Her brown eyes stared into his, and she smiled.

He had meant to ask her something, but looking at her he was quickly forgetting what it was. Something was nagging for his attention at the back of his mind, though. What was it? Kel. He turned to the seat next to him, but Kel was gone.

CHAPTER 15

*K*el enjoyed the pie they had for dinner at the inn. She picked her way around the meat, but the crust was hot and flaky, and the peas floating in the thick gravy burst with flavor.

The inn was the first building Kel had been in since... since before she had been in the woods. It felt different to her now. Decaying, empty. She missed the pulse of life everywhere around her. There was still life here, but it was like when you looked up at the stars too near a campfire. A few constellations were still visible, but the endless profusion of glittering pinpoints was gone. She was so distracted by this feeling of silence around her that she barely paid attention as they were led up to their rooms.

When they reached their room, Kel sat on the bed, which was hard and full of mites, and listened to her brother talk with the barkeep. Finn was worried about something. Kel wondered what it was, but Finn didn't come in and explain. Instead, he just ran off, leaving the door open behind him. Kel waited a while to see if he was coming back, and then, when it became clear that he wasn't, went and shut the door.

Her hands were filthy; black dirt was caked under every nail. She picked some of it out, watched it fall to the floor. But then she felt bad for the little crumbs of dirt. They were pieces of the forest, and now she had brought them here, where they would dry out and turn to useless dust, to sit in a corner or under a bed. She scooped them back up again and tucked them into a pocket.

The dirt didn't belong here, and neither did Kel. She swung her legs, kicking her feet softly against the bed. The mites ignored her. She wished that these people had never found her and Finn. She wished her brother had just stayed with her in the forest. But Finn couldn't do that. Kel knew it was true. Finn needed these people. He needed to learn about magic.

The loneliness and emptiness of the city made an aching hollow in Kel's chest. She wanted to leave, to go back to her nest, but she couldn't. She couldn't leave her brother.

Maybe she could find the forest, though. Maybe she could reach out far enough to connect back to it. She reached out with her mind, found Sylvia again. She listened only briefly, then reached out further, searching, stretching the bounds of where she could go. It felt like fabric was wrapped around her. She could push against it, but the farther she went the harder it pulled on her, and the longer she stayed the more tired she got. Eventually the stretchy fabric would overpower her and she would be flung back into herself.

At the farthest reaches of her power she could feel a dark cloud gathering, a wall of anger rising against her. She shied away from this, even as she tried to reach farther.

Time passed. Kel found herself tiring, losing focus, but she pressed on, pushed her mind farther and farther; each time she was snapped back to herself she immediately redoubled her efforts.

You're giving me a headache, Sylvia said, but she ignored her.

The door to the room was thrown open, and a wide-eyed Finn came careening in, scooping up his pack and Kel's, tucking them under an arm and grabbing Kel's hand, tugging her up off the bed, jerking her out of her practice.

"Come on, Kel, we've got to go."

"What? Why?" Kel shook her head, dazed. A slight buzzing filled her mind, making it hard to think.

"No time for that. Come on."

Without even looking at her, Finn jerked Kel forward, pulling her out of the room and banging the door closed behind them. Kel blinked in the bright torchlight of the hall, saw Eraldir and a girl with soft blond hair and a tear-streaked face.

"Who's—" But, before Kel could even get the question out, Finn was dragging her down the hallway.

The aloe leaf fell out of Kel's pocket, she tried to stop, reached out for it, but Finn, still looking ahead, yelled at her to keep going. After that Kel didn't pay attention to anything else, just struggled to keep up. Finn's hand was slippery with sweat, and burning with an unnatural heat that made Kel fearful. She wished Finn would let go of her, would let her walk more slowly.

Kel started to feel dizzy. She had spent so much effort on reaching out, straining towards the woods, that now, suddenly, the boundaries of her own mind felt loose, untethered. She was vaguely aware that they had stopped at Isabelle's room, but her head was swimming. She blinked, trying to clear it, but she blacked out, and when she became aware of herself again she found they were hurrying down the steps toward the dining room.

After that, things came in flashes. She watched Finn step out after Isabelle, his hands loose and shaking, hers white and clenched into fists. Then Kel was a bat swooping from tree to tree; she snapped her jaws shut, trapping a fly. Then she was following Eraldir down another hallway. A bolt of lightning crashed into her branches, burning her bark. She was a tree, perched alone on a rocky bluff, burning as the animals who called her home ran away.

A man in black stood next to her, held a shining knife above, threatened to cut off her arm— her branches? She was a frog, cozily encased in silty mud. Everything covered except her eyeballs, and even those were a muddy green color, she knew. She felt very clever. No bird or snake or other predator would see her here.

A woman with hair like blood, illuminated by flickering light, kicking the blonde girl, who cried and begged for mercy. A flash of birch trees.

Emptiness.

Everything was still. Kel didn't know where she was, or who she was. She was in some place, a place below all other places, and it was empty. Somewhere, her legs were moving, and her heart was beating, but here she didn't have a body.

She wasn't alone, though. There was a presence, and just outside the edges of this still place she could sense... everything. Just outside of this calm center was a world teeming with life. Curious, she moved to the boundary, contemplated it. At first she thought she was seeing herself reflected in a wall of glass, but, as she reached out to touch the wall, the shape moved, and it wasn't herself Kel was seeing, it was a man, or creature. It reached out its hand, and Kel felt a wave of love, deep and overpowering, and the boundary began to melt away.

Eraldir's voice jolted Kel back to reality, though, before the boundary was completely gone. She crashed back into awareness of her own body, with a sense of frustration and... grief. There was something there that she needed to know.

Kel realized Eraldir was worried about Sylvia, and she heard herself answering him, telling the old man where she was.

And then she blacked out again, found herself back in that still, empty place that wasn't a place. And the man was gone, but the boundary was open. Without even thinking, Kel moved across the boundary and her awareness expanded out infinitely. She might have lost her mind, but that presence was still there with her, calm, holding her safe. She could feel every worm in the soil around her, every bug and insect in the air above ground. Chickens slept in their roosts, rats nosed through garbage, cats with glowing eyes stalked the rats, and bats swooped—the echoing senses of the bats were incredible.

Her reach went infinitely far now, outside the city to owls, bears, trees, bushes, vines, snakes, past the angry wall of crows, past the shores of a great sea where there were things Kel had never seen or heard of: fish as big as cities, eels, shrimp, barnacles and clams. Great leaping monsters that could swallow Kel whole, and would, if given the chance.

It was a wild cacophony of life, and Kel could feel it all happening at once, but that calm presence kept her safe. *Who are you?* Kel asked, but she received no answer in words. Instead, she felt a love as infinite as the world.

In the midst of all this, Kel realized she could sense Smoke, eating a pigeon egg.

Smoke?

The animal lifted its head. It recognized her, had been waiting for her back at the nest.

Focusing on one piece of the vast landscape took power, more than Kel could sustain for long, and, almost as quickly as the link was established, it was gone again.

The awareness of everything went with it. Kel crashed back into herself. She was walking, guided by Finn's hand.

She took a deep breath of the damp, dirt-scented air, and expected to be pulled out of herself again at any moment, but the boundaries of her mind had solidified again somehow. She took another slow, deep breath. *What was that?*

THE WOMAN with hair like blood brought them to a room where they all sat around a table. Kel was shaken, but a deep, even pleasant, exhaustion had overtaken her. She tried to pay attention, tried to understand where they were and what was happening.

But then the woman brought out a jug with two goldfish in it, and the thoughts those goldfish had, even though they only came in flashes, were filled with violence, murderous rage, and despair. Kel had never felt these emotions in fish before. Fish usually didn't have many feelings at all, but these did, and it hurt Kel to look into their hopeless, empty eyes.

I don't belong here. Kel thought. The memory of the infinite love she'd felt called to her.

Kel turned to look up at her brother. Finn was arguing with the woman. Finn wanted to protect her, she knew. Finn loved her, but there was all this going on around them. Kel didn't know what it was, and it didn't matter to her. She didn't belong here, in this place or with these people. She belonged in the woods, with Smoke, with that great, infinite love. She was afraid of the vastness she had sensed, afraid it would destroy her, that she would forget who she was, but also intoxicated by it. She had to go there again, to experience that oneness with everything.

Even more importantly, she needed to be where she was supposed to be. This city with its subjugated animals and dead plants was like a cold, thick liquid covering her and numbing her senses.

She knew now where Smoke was, too. Back at the nest.

Kel knew she could find it. The crows were a problem, but suddenly Kel knew she could find a way to solve that, too.

Kel watched Finn gesture with his hands as he talked, his black hair had grown long and messy, it flopped into his face and he pushed it out of the way. Finn had borrowed a blade from Eraldir and shaved off the beard, but the beginnings of a new one covered his chin.

Finn would never let Kel go alone, and he would never go with her, either. Even if Kel could convince Finn to come back to the woods, she wouldn't want to. Finn needed to be here. Kel could see that.

Ever so slowly and quietly, Kel edged down the bench, away from Finn. Then, when Finn turned to talk to Isabelle, she quickly pushed herself up, grabbed her pack, and left.

Kel thought of Finn, imagined what Finn would feel when he saw Kel was gone, and a bubble of grief welled up in her chest, but the bubble popped, dissipated, and in its place was a new lightness. Freedom.

For a while Kel just wandered randomly through the tunnels, listening to the thoughts of the worms around her. They weren't very helpful. Worms didn't understand things like cities, or forest, and they didn't travel far in their lives anyway. Kel was hesitant to push her abilities past their usual limits. She didn't want to lose herself again.

But as she walked, she tried anyway, reaching out a little farther each time, until there, just at the edge of her reach, she felt it. The forest. It was too far off for her to sense any of the individual plants or animals, but there was a sense of aliveness there, much more so than in the city around her. She followed this feeling, turning left and right and eventually coming to a long tunnel with no branches.

The path ended in a hole, a vertical tunnel with a ladder sticking up out of it. There were no lights in this tunnel. The others had had torches, but this one was completely dark. Kel climbed down, her fingers gripping tightly to the splintery wood. At first, she was comforted by the worms in the dirt around her, but then the dirt became rock, and here there was nothing. No animal sounds. Down and down she went.

Kel's foot hit solid ground; she stumbled, surprised, but managed to get her footing. She felt around with her arms in the darkness, scraped her shoes along the floor, found the edges of the tunnel and began to follow it.

Every step was torturous. The floor felt smooth, but she couldn't see anything, so she lifted her feet high and set them down carefully, feeling for rocks or holes.

Her foot splashed into an icy a puddle, the water soaking into her sock, and she recoiled, but it wasn't too deep, just a few inches. She waded into it, arms held out in front of her, waving slowly back and forth, sometimes brushing against the walls. She could hear water now, too, trickling down the sides of the tunnel, dripping from the ceiling.

And then the puddles were gone, the water was gone, the air felt a little drier and warmer. Her hands bumped into a wall. And something wooden. Another ladder.

It creaked as she stepped onto it and began climbing. The sounds of the worms returned. Then ants, then rabbits. Above her Kel could sense birds, too, and trees.

Kel reached up for the next rung on the ladder and felt instead a door. She let go of the ladder with both hands, pressed her palms flat against the solid piece of wood.

Kel pushed, straining against the piece of wood. It shifted, just slightly, and Kel blinked as a blinding ray of light shot down into the darkness, stinging her eyes.

"Once more," she muttered to herself.

She strained against the door, and it shifted again. More light shot down into the darkness, illuminating the way she had come.

Kel could hear birdsong now, and her eyes had adjusted

enough that she could see through the gap. Trees. Bushes. Forest.

A shadow passed through the sunlight.

Kel was about to give one final push when a voice interrupted her.

"Why don't you let us get that for you?"

A heavy boot clunked down near the opening, and thick fingers wrapped around the edge of the wood, heaving it to the side.

Kel was again blinded by the sun, but when her eyes had adjusted, she looked up and saw a row of smiling, swarthy faces. It was the Westwend guard.

FINN STOOD UP, scraping his chair back away from the table. "Did you see where Kel went?" he asked Isabelle.

"Um, no."

Finn looked around the room helplessly, went to each of the exits and peered out as far as he could see, but Kel was nowhere to be found.

Reina had instructed them not to leave the room, and Finn didn't want to risk provoking her, but she was probably asleep by now. After all, it was late, they'd been up all night, and she had a war planned for the morning.

Finn poked his head out one of the doors, looked cautiously left and right, and was just about to step out when Isabelle interrupted him.

"Well, she's not that way," she jerked a thumb over her shoulder as she walked back in one of the doors. "It ends in a locked door. I'll try this way." She walked out of the room again.

Finn watched her go, jealous of her complete lack of fear. Annoyed at his own nervousness, he peeked his head out the door one more time and looked as far as he could in each direction. It was just the wide, empty tunnel they'd come in by.

"She's not that way either; it's locked, too." Isabelle said behind him. "There sure must be a lot for you to look at over there... I'll check this last door here."

Finn grit his teeth and stepped out into the hall. He was immediately tackled by an enormous man wielding a saber.

Luckily, the saber was dull, because it didn't cut the skin when it was pressed up against Finn's throat.

"What're you doin' out, eh?" Fishy breath wafted into Finn's face. His attacker's full body weight was now being supported by Finn's rib cage, and the air was forced from his lungs; he tried to breathe but only managed a tiny gasp.

"Answer me, eh?"

The man's eyes focused on Finn's face and they made eye contact. Finn tried desperately to convey "you're choking me" with his eyes. The man blinked.

"Oh, whoops. Sorry, there." The man rolled off him, grabbed Finn by the collar, and jerked him up. Then a rush of wind blasted into Finn's mouth and down into his chest, inflating his lungs. This was almost as uncomfortable a feeling as being crushed had been. The man must be a wind mage.

"Hey! What are you doing to him?" Isabelle said sharply from behind Finn's back.

"He was out wanderin' around. Tha's not allowed."

"He was two feet outside the door, you call that 'wandering around'?"

Finn coughed. "Sorry, we're just looking for my sister. She's missing."

"I haven't seen anybody this way since Reina posted me here."

"When did she post you here?" Isabelle asked.

The man's eyes narrowed suspiciously, and he didn't answer.

"Look, we're not trying to escape or whatever, we're just looking for my little sister," Finn said.

"Well, I'll let ye know if I see 'er, but you're not t'leave here. Reina's orders."

Isabelle stepped forward. "Oh, and you're going to stop us?"

A gust of wind emanated from Isabelle and whipped around the man, knocking the saber out of his grasp. She caught it neatly.

He stared at her, unimpressed. More wind blew through the tunnel, it swirled around the man, picking up dust from the floor as it did so and lifting the lank black hair from his meaty shoulders. Finn realized it wasn't Isabelle making the wind anymore.

The wind increased to a howling peak, lifted the giant man off the ground. He crossed his legs under him, so that he looked like a large sphere floating in midair. Finn had never seen someone so enormous look so buoyant.

Isabelle sent a few gusts at him, but they were swallowed by the wind rocketing around him. Then came two smaller tornadoes, one each for Finn and Isabelle. They were lifted gently, the wind tugging at their clothes and hair, and moved inexorably back inside the room. The wind set them down, and the door to the hall slammed shut.

"Why do you even have a saber, then?" Isabelle yelled through the door, but she looked impressed. "I bet I could do that." She tried a few experimental gusts.

"So, where's Kel, then?"

Isabelle shrugged. "Well, either Reina took her or she must have left before she posted that guard there, right? Or, maybe she was small enough that the guy didn't notice her."

She thought for a second. "Or the doors I checked weren't locked earlier."

"She wouldn't have just left without telling me. Reina must have her." But why? It didn't make any sense. Finn felt lost, suddenly. "Why would Reina take her somewhere?"

"She wouldn't. She doesn't have any reason to. I mean, even if she did have some reason to interrogate Kel, we're already her prisoners, as far as she knows. She doesn't even know she's a mage, right?"

"Maybe she wanted more information about me?"

Isabelle raised an eyebrow. "You're not that big of a deal, Finn."

"Yeah, I know, I know, but..." he trailed off. They were silent for a while, and into that silence crept doubt. Finn didn't want to even consider the idea that Kel had left on her own, couldn't imagine why she would. But that wasn't right. If he was being honest with himself, he could imagine a reason why his sister might leave. The reason they were alone together in the woods in the first place. The image of a dining room, with curtains on fire, came to his mind. Flames pouring out of windows, igniting roofs. Screams and running. Kel's small hand in his as they ran.

Finn thought, too, of how frightened Kel had looked, alone in the woods. How she'd begged Finn not to leave her. Finn wished he hadn't. Because now his sister was alone in a city of people who would kill her if they found out what she was, and Kel was so small and trusting. She wouldn't think to conceal what she was if it might help someone.

No, if he was really honest with himself, Finn knew exactly why Kel had left. Why should she follow around the big brother who murdered their parents, left her alone in the woods, dragged her off to some unknown city, and then paid so little attention to her that he didn't even notice when she left?

Finn finally looked back up and met Isabelle's eyes. There was understanding there. She didn't say anything, just watched and waited.

"Should I go after her, then?" Finn asked.

"What do you think?"

"She chose to leave."

"Yeah."

"She's so small, though. I need to protect her."

"And how has that been going so far? Real well?"

"I destroyed her home, killed her parents, left her alone in the woods. Then, when she survived all that, after she'd made herself a new safe place, I took her away from that. Brought her to a city where almost anyone might kill her."

"Yeah," Isabelle said. "And now she'll probably just go back to the woods and make herself another plant fortress, right?"

"Yeah, but…"

"She's also significantly less likely to be lit on fire if you're not around."

"Well, yeah, but…"

"But what?"

"What if she doesn't make it back to the woods?" Finn said.

"Fair point." She crossed her arms over her chest and tapped a foot thoughtfully. "She talks to Sylvia, right?"

A light dawned in Finn's heart. "Yeah, she does."

"So… ask the horse if she's okay. If she's in trouble, sprint off to her rescue. If not… let her go."

"She's six!"

"She's also the most powerful naturalist mage I've ever seen. And she's quiet. She'll probably just go curl up in a log somewhere and get befriended by some bunny rabbits."

"But, she's six years old! I can't just let her go off in the woods by herself!"

195

"If she wants to go, do you really think you can stop her?"

"I'll talk to her. I'll convince her to stay."

"You know, my parents tried to make me stay."

"You and Kel are completely different people."

"I'm just saying. She has much easier access to mountain lions than I do."

Despite himself, Finn cracked a smile. He quickly tried to cover it back up with seriousness, though. "That's not funny, Isabelle!"

She grinned. "It's a little funny."

"It's mostly terrifying and disturbing!"

She took a step towards him, smiling. "Really?"

"Yes!" She was standing close to him now, and, if he'd been brave enough, he could have reached out and touched her hair, brushed it back from her face. Finn's heart was speeding up, and he had started to forget what they were even talking about.

"You're adorable, Finn Vogt." Isabelle reached up, wrapped her arms around his neck and kissed him. For a while, Finn mostly forgot about Kel.

STRONG ARMS REACHED DOWN and lifted Kel out of the tunnel.

"What're you doing down there, kid?" The man set Kel down next to the tunnel entrance. The rest of the group crowded around the hole, peering down into it.

"Captain, it looks like a tunnel. Want me to go check it out?"

The man was watching Kel closely. "Not yet. Where does this tunnel go?"

"I don't know, I just found it." She looked down at her feet. Her mother had always known when she was lying.

"Okay, so where did you find it?"

196

Kel paused. There was no way to answer this question without talking about the mages or their hideout.

The man took Kel's chin in his hand and forced her face up. His eyes were bright green. "I can tell you're lying to me, kid. And, when people lie to me it makes me suspicious. Makes me think they've been doing something wrong. When people tell me the truth I just learn what I need to and then I let them go on their way. Or take them back to their parents, if the case warrants it. I have a son about your age, and I always know when he's lying, too."

Kel felt like someone had tied a knot in her chest. All she wanted was to get back to the forest, but, if she told this man everything, he might go after Finn.

"What's got you so worried, kid? How come you're so afraid to tell me what you're doing out here?"

"I just want to go back to the forest. Please let me go."

The man's eyes softened. "Back to the forest? Is that where your parents are? Look, I'm here to help. I'm not your enemy. Some kid pops out of a tunnel too scared to talk, I don't think it's her fault. I'm sure you didn't do anything wrong. What's your name?" Kel didn't answer, but the man let go of Kel's chin and dusted her off. "Are you hungry?"

Kel nodded.

"All right then. You know, I'm kind of hungry, too. Let's have a snack." He stood, took Kel's hand, and led her over to a fallen log. Over his shoulder, the man called out some orders. "Gavin, you run up and call for reinforcements. The rest of you, set up a perimeter around the tunnel entrance."

The man hoisted Kel up onto the log and sat down next to her, pulling some rough rye bread wrapped in wax paper out of a pocket. The bread was cut into the shape of a heart. Slightly embarrassed, he gestured to the bread. "Jack packs my lunches." He shook his head, but was smiling. "Anyway, I'm Nathaniel Jenkins. Nate, or Captain Nate around here."

He waited, but when Kel didn't say anything, he went on. "Our boy's name is William. Like I said, he's about your age. What's your name, kid?"

"Kel."

"Kel. Good name. What's your family name, Kel?"

Kel didn't answer.

"Where are your parents, Kel?"

"They're dead." Kel hadn't said it out loud yet. Somehow, not saying it out loud had let a little piece of it stay not fully true. She started to cry.

"Oh, kid, I'm sorry." Captain Nate put an arm around her and waited while she cried. At one point, he handed Kel his handkerchief.

The tears came for a while. It all came rushing up. The unspoken tension in the house, rising day by day. Then the argument at dinner. Someone threw a plate, the food sliding off it as it crashed into the wall, shattered, leaving a dark spot on the wall. And then... the world ignited.

Kel would have died, too, probably. Transfixed, too horrified to notice the heat, watching... but Finn had grabbed her hand, pulled her out of the house as it collapsed around them, sparks shooting up to the sky, flames pouring out of the windows and licking up the roof. People running towards them, screaming and shouting. More fires. More houses burning. And then they were in the woods.

The crying stopped slowly, and Kel felt lighter. She wiped her face with the handkerchief.

Nate waited a little longer, but then he went on, speaking gently. "How did they die?"

"In a fire."

Nate's big hand was on her back now, patting it softly. "Oh, man. That's terrible. How long ago did it happen?"

"A few weeks."

"And you've been on your own since then?"

"I've been with my brother."

As soon as she said it, Kel realized she shouldn't have.

"Your brother?"

Kel didn't answer.

"Where's your brother now?"

Kel still didn't answer.

"Your family name doesn't happen to be Vogt, does it?"

Kel still said nothing, but she shifted her body uncomfortably, and she heard Nate suck in a surprised breath.

"Whoa. Look. It's okay. I'm on your side. You didn't do anything wrong." He paused. "Really. You're just a kid, you can't help what he is. You're running away from him, aren't you?"

"I just want to get back to the forest."

"I don't blame you." His arm went back around Kel's shoulders and his hand gripped Kel's arm tightly, comfortingly. "Look, it's going to be okay. I'm not going to let anything bad happen to you."

Kel thought she heard sincerity in Nate's words.

"You care about your brother, don't you?" Nate said.

Kel nodded.

"So, you don't want to do anything that might hurt him."

Kel shook his head.

"Of course, kid, that makes sense."

"He won't hurt anyone. He doesn't want to hurt anyone."

"I'm sure he doesn't want to. But he did, right?"

Kel didn't answer.

"Look, kid. You've had a hard time, and I get that you're loyal to your brother. I understand that. I do. I even admire it. But your brother isn't your brother anymore."

"What do you mean?"

"I mean, look, I don't know if this is true, but what I've heard about magic is that it's the souls of the elements possessing and consuming a human being. Your brother gave himself to a fire spirit, maybe knowingly, maybe unknowingly, in exchange for power. Fire mages are usually power-hungry. They give their souls to these fire spirits who devour them from the inside. It drives them mad, and causes them to destroy everything around them, but it gives them the power they were craving."

Had Finn wanted power? Kel had never heard this idea before. Was it true? And, did that mean that she, Kel, was being eaten alive by some forest spirit? She didn't feel like she was being eaten alive.

Nate patted her on the shoulder. "I'm sorry, I know it's hard to hear. I'm sure your brother wasn't a bad guy, but it's my job to protect people. Look, we're going down that tunnel anyway, whether you tell me anything or not, but it's a heck of a lot more dangerous for us if we go in blind. If you tell me what you know I'll make a bargain with you. If it's at all possible, I will help your brother avoid execution. Now, I'm just going to ask you one simple yes or no question. All you have to do is nod or shake your head. If you do that, you can help keep a lot of people safe."

Kel did want that. She had wanted to trust her brother, though, too, but where had that gotten her? Kel realized she already felt safer with Nate than she ever had with Finn.

"All right, Kel. Here's the question. Ready?" Kel nodded. "If I send my men down through that tunnel, am I going to find a mage hideout?"

Kel looked into Nate's green eyes and nodded slowly.

"Thank you, Kel. This will help a lot of people." Nate stood up, handing Kel the rest of the rye bread, just the tip of the heart was left. "Here, how about you have the rest of this? I'll be right back. You sit right here, okay?"

Kel watched Nate get up and walk over to join one of his men who was crouched behind a tree watching the tunnel entrance. He whispered something, and gestured urgently.

Kel began to feel uneasy again. Wishing she hadn't said anything, she set the last of the bread down on the log beside her.

Nate was still distracted, and none of the other guards were watching her, so Kel turned around on the log, dropped to the ground on the other side, and started to run.

Her feet skimmed over the ground, sensing every root and branch without needing to see them. Joy rose in her, overshadowing the doubts and worries about Finn.

There was something else here, though. The crows. They sensed her, too, and as Kel ran she could feel them gathering against her, rushing to meet her. She slowed to a walk, and then stopped in a clearing, staring up at the ancient trees around her. The crows arrived in droves, like the settling of ash.

Please leave me alone. Kel thought.

The crows—all the hundreds of them watching her from their branches—were silent. Kel felt their fury, their sense of betrayal.

She tried to turn to one side, to walk through a gap in the trees. Thirty crows swooped down, pecking and scratching, until she backed up into the center of the clearing again. Then they returned to their perches.

Captain Nate was a quick and quiet runner, and Kel didn't hear when the man came up behind her. "Kid, what..." Nate's voice trailed off. Kel turned and saw him stopped at the edge of the clearing, looking back and forth between Kel and the crows. Kel realized what it must look like, her standing there with two hundred crows arranged around her, watching her. A look of fear passed over Nate's face, but he swallowed, and drew his sword.

Nate was staring at Kel like her body had sloughed away to reveal a giant, venomous snake. "You're a mage, kid?"

"Yeah, but..."

Nate lifted the sword point, held it at the ready. He licked his lips and readjusted his grip on the sword. "I thought that couldn't happen until you were sixteen."

Kel was trapped. The crows at her back and the captain in front, fear and revulsion etched across his face. Somehow, that hurt almost as bad as not being able to get back to the forest. She thought Nate liked her.

Nate continued. "I wondered why a five-year-old would want to go into the woods by herself."

"I'm six."

"What were you planning to do with those crows? Set them on me and my men before we could tell anyone about where your brother is? Well, too late, kid, I've already informed Arcturus."

"No, they're not—"

"You're coming with me. Walk over this way, real slow, and if you try anything, if one of those crows moves at me, I'll kill them and you. Got it?"

"I can't—"

"Yes or no, kid. Walk over here or I kill you now."

Kel started to walk towards the captain, desperately hoping the crows would stay still.

When Kel was about five feet away, Nate held up a hand to stop her. "All right. That's far enough. Now you walk ahead of me. Slowly. Don't look back. Don't reach for anything. Anything unexpected happens and you're dead."

Kel nodded hopelessly and, keeping her arms tight to her sides, walked back through the forest ahead of the captain.

CHAPTER 16

When Finn awoke the next morning, it was because someone tripped over him and dropped a pile of crossbows on his head. Luckily, they weren't loaded. He helped the girl pick up the weapons and then watched as she ran off.

Everywhere around him people were running here and there with piles of weaponry, food, buckets of oil, and other supplies.

Rubbing the sleep out of his eyes, Finn got dazedly to his feet and looked around for Eraldir and Isabelle. He felt a little nauseous from being up so late, but there was also a warm glow of happiness in his heart. What was that from? Oh, right. Isabelle. That quickly winked out, though, when he remembered that Kel was missing.

He found Eraldir sprawled in a corner, an empty tea mug lay on the floor next to his open hand, a small puddle of foul-smelling tea in front of it.

At first Finn wondered if Eraldir was even still alive; he couldn't see any movement, but then Eraldir snorted, dropped the mug, and rolled over. Finn called out his name a few times, but, while not dead, Eraldir was apparently sleeping too soundly to be woken.

"Here," Isabelle said, coming up behind him. She bent down, gripped Eraldir's shoulders, and heaved him up into a sitting position. "Sometimes you have to, like, get him started." She slapped Eraldir's cheeks with her palms a few times, then opened his eyelids with her fingers. The pupils dilated—further proof that he was alive—but the old man let out a long snore. "Hmm... well, this usually works... Eraldir! There's pie!"

The old man shook his head. "I don't smell pie," he said in a dreamy voice.

"No, really. There's pie in the other room. Come on, all you have to do is wake up!"

Eraldir shook his head again, and his eyes blinked open. "Oh, morning you two. Did I hear something about pie?"

"What? Pie? No." Isabelle said. "Why would there be pie?"

"I figured it was just a dream... If it doesn't smell like pie, then there's no pie, that's what I've learned." Eraldir sighed. "Well, you two, ready to escape a ruthless dictator today?" He glanced back over his shoulder, checking for Reina, but there was only the bare stone wall.

"Kel is missing," Finn said. "We need to go find Sylvia."

"Sylvia? Why? Oh, I see. Well, that's not a bad plan I suppose. Assuming she's still alive."

"What? Why would she be dead?"

Eraldir waved a hand airily. "Do you know how many of the people I know are dead? You get this old, it just seems to happen. You start to expect it."

Finn supposed that made sense, in a depressing way.

"About time you were up," Reina barked. Finn jumped. Where had she come from?

"Huh, guess there's a short time delay," Eraldir muttered. Finn had no idea what he was talking about.

"I heard you met Noe here last night," Reina said, gesturing over her shoulder to the enormous wind mage who stood behind her. "Disobey me again and I'll cut off one of your ears. Noe will be keeping you company today. He's your war nanny. Soon as I have control of the city I'll set up the training facility. 'Till then, do what Noe says, and kill as many non-mages as you can."

Without waiting for a reply, she stalked off. Finn looked around at the people hurrying through the room. Some of them were indeed missing ears or fingers. Many of them had symbols branded into their skins. These people couldn't be happy being led by someone like Reina, could they?

"Mornin'" Noe said, picking at the edge of his saber with a short fingernail. Apparently, Isabelle had given it back to him.

Finn glanced at Isabelle. Somehow, they were going to have to get away from Noe. Eraldir apparently had the same idea.

"So, Noe, where are you from?" Eraldir asked casually.

"Here."

"Ah, yes, and, er, is it a nice place to live?"

"No."

Noe's eyes flicked methodically from Eraldir to Finn to Isabelle and back to Eraldir again. He didn't break his concentration for a second, but continued watching all of them.

Isabelle tried. She batted her eyelashes and leaned on Noe's arm. He looked down at his arm in surprise, but then continued his scanning. "I was so impressed by your magic last night, could you show me how you do that?"

"No. Stop tryin' t'distract me," Noe said. "It's really obvious what ye're tryin' t'do."

"Sorry, Noe," Finn said. "We just need to go find Eraldir's horse."

"All righ', let's go."

"What?"

"Sure. I'm just s'posed to keep an eye on yeh. Didn't say I had teh keep yeh here."

"Oh, well, great. Thanks."

WITH NOE'S HELP, finding Sylvia was no problem at all. All they had to do was find a naturalist mage—whom Noe pointed out to them—and ask her if she'd heard a horse complaining recently.

"Oh, that's what that was? A horse? I wondered." The woman rolled her eyes. "Never heard an animal with an internal monologue before. I would have been interested if I hadn't been so busy trying to block it out."

"Can you hear things besides animals?" Finn asked. "Like, other naturalist mages?"

"I've got a connection to plants and animals; I'm not telepathic," she said.

"Humans are animals, right?"

She shrugged. "Not according to magic, apparently. Sorry."

"Can you talk to Sylvia?" Finn asked. If the mage could talk to Sylvia, and Sylvia could talk to Kel…

"No, sorry. I can hear things from animals, and sometimes plants, but I've never heard of a naturalist mage who could talk with animals. This horse is sure something different, though. I'll give it a shot." She closed her eyes; a line formed between her eyebrows as she frowned in concentration. Then her eyes snapped open. "Nope, sorry. I can't get through. Or she's ignoring me."

"That's all right, thanks anyway," Finn said.

The mage could tell them where Sylvia was, though, and how to get there, in exchange for the promise that they would feed the horse, groom her, and then take her as far away from Westwend as possible.

Noe led them out into the tunnels, following behind so he could keep an eye on them. As they walked, a fishy smell drifted up to Finn and he looked back to see Noe munching on some trout again.

Isabelle wrinkled her nose. "You really like trout, huh?"

"No."

"Then why do you eat it constantly?"

"Reina says tha' if I eat only trout I won' be so fat."

"What? So, you've only been eating fish? For how long?"

They'd stopped now, and the three of them were staring at Noe.

Noe looked down. "A few weeks."

Eraldir clapped him on the shoulder. "A man needs more than fish, boy. I should know."

"Yeah," Isabelle said. "That sounds miserable. And who is she to tell you what to eat? That's stupid."

Noe folded up the package of fish and put it away, still staring at his feet. He shrugged. "Wind mages are s'posed t'be small. Like you. Light."

"What? No. That's stupid," Isabelle said. "Last night, when you attacked us, both Finn and I thought you were very graceful, didn't we Finn?"

Finn wasn't sure if graceful was the right word. Buoyant, yes, and impressive. Maybe graceful. But he felt so sorry for Noe, he had to agree. "Yeah, we did."

Noe looked up. "Oh, well, thanks."

Isabelle patted him on one enormous shoulder. "Yeah. Don't listen to her. You eat whatever you damn well please. Here, want a cake?" She pulled one out of her pack.

Noe eyed it with longing.

Isabelle thrust it into one of his meaty hands. He took it gently, reverently.

"There you go, boy," Eraldir said. "Can't eat just fish. I tried the same thing myself once, with squirrels. I was trapped up in the mountains—the Iron Mountains—hiding out from a necromancer who wanted to use me in a ritual. He thought he could use me to get past the defenses at the old City of Mages. Nothing to eat but squirrels for months. I must have eaten hundreds of them. Squirrel pelts are tiny, but I sewed them all together into a new set of clothes. I'll tell you, nothing better than squirrel underwear. Downside was I turned yellow and some of my teeth fell out." He opened his mouth and pulled back his lips to show them the gaps in his teeth.

"Ah," Noe said, leaning away from Eraldir and glancing over at Finn. Finn rolled his eyes and Noe smiled.

They continued walking, and Finn could hear Noe eating the cake behind them, making small sounds of enjoyment.

After a while, Eraldir began to question him about Reina's plans.

"So, Noe, are you allowed to tell us what's happening today?"

"Yeah, sure."

"So, what's the plan?" Isabelle asked.

"Ronan, tha's the best earth mage, is liftin' up a fortress into th' middle of th' city."

Eraldir went pale, and spun around to face Noe. "What?"

"Ronan's built a fortress underground an 'e'll be liftin' it up today."

"That's cool," Isabelle said.

"No," Eraldir said. "No, it isn't. Noe, has Ronan ever done anything like this before?"

The man considered this. "Er, not tha' I can think of."

"What, Eraldir?" Finn asked. "What's wrong?"

Eraldir bit his lip. "Well, boy. You remember the trouble you had when we rescued the lady mage?"

Of course Finn remembered.

"Well… I never fully explained that." He looked around, as if suddenly remembering where they were. "There's no time now, though. We may have to… but, no, your sister. And… but… we need to stop her."

Noe placed a meaty hand on his sword hilt. "Stop who?"

"Er, no one."

Noe rolled his eyes.

"Um, never mind. Let's just go get my horse, okay?" Eraldir said.

"Not until y'tell me what yer talkin' about."

Eraldir sighed. "All right. Well, it has to do with…" He looked around, and they were all watching intently. "Well, there's no time for that whole thing, now. Of course, it won't really make sense unless I tell you the whole… but no…"

Finn could see Eraldir struggling against his need to tell the full story, with all the details. He cut in. "You said something then about the shadow?"

Eraldir looked up and blinked. "Oh, er, yes, right. The shadow. I guess it doesn't really matter where it… but… no. No, the shadow is a part of magic not fully understood. What we do know is that it's the underpart of magic, the largest part, the part that connects all the different types. For every act of magic, there is an equal amount of shadow. Usually, it collects in the mage." Eraldir's liver-spotted hand went unconsciously to his chest. "It dissipates over time. The more aware a mage is of the shadow, the more they can hold, and the more quickly it dissipates. If a mage tries something too big or too powerful, the shadow can be too much to hold, and it spills out into the world. Shadow works differently for different types of magic. The shadow of wind, water, and naturalist mages destroys that element."

Finn remembered the airless space they'd passed through in the tunnel the night before.

Eraldir's hand pressed flat to his own chest, massaging it. "I told you that I was the one who... who diverted the river around Westwend..."

They nodded.

"That was the biggest act of magic I ever performed. It... killed a lot of people. Destroyed a lot. There's a place, the place where I stood. At the north end of the city, where nothing will grow, because there's no water there anymore."

"I've seen it," Noe said quietly.

Eraldir shook himself. "Fire, earth, and thread mages are different. Usually, the shadow creates more of the element, in unwanted ways, sometimes ways that stem from the unconscious fears of the mage."

Eraldir looked at Finn solemnly. "If Ronan tries this, boy, I don't know what might happen. It might kill everyone in Westwend."

"Doesn't Reina know all this?" Finn asked.

Eraldir lifted his hands in frustration. "No, boy! Of course she doesn't. No one knows this kind of thing anymore. Mages are all untrained now. Everybody just tries things and sees what happens and it's no wonder so many people die."

"Will she listen to you if you tell her?" Isabelle asked.

"Probably not. Might as well try, of course. And even if she did listen to me I doubt she'll care. Reina doesn't mind collateral damage. Welcomes it, rather. She's gotten more and more destructive over the years and now I think she just wants to see people die."

Noe was picking at the last of the cake. A few crumbs fell to the ground. "I don' wan' people t'die."

"Then why are you working for Reina?" Isabelle asked.

Noe shrugged. "She gave me a home. When my parents found out wha' I was, they kicked me out. I was living on the streets when Reina found me. Gettin' t'be around other mages, bein' in a place where I could do magic all the time..."

"We can give you that," Finn said. "We're starting a mage school. Far away from here, away from non-mages."

"Yeah, and we'll have plenty of food, we won't tell you what to eat, and we won't threaten to cut your fingers off," Isabelle said.

Noe looked at them at them, uncertain whether he could trust them.

Finn continued. "You don't have to betray Reina. You don't have to fight her or anything. We'll just leave. You can come with us."

The same look with which Noe had contemplated the cake came into his eyes. "Okay," he said at last, then smiled.

"Great, great," Eraldir said. "Now let's hurry up and find my horse. And see if we can stop Reina killing everyone in Westwend. And then get out of here. And then pie." A small tremor shook the earth.

THEY FOUND Sylvia in the small stable, near one of the exits of the secret tunnels, that the naturalist mage had mentioned. Finn knelt in the straw in front of her, held her head, and looked into one of her rheumy eyes. "Sylvia? Can you hear Kel? Do you know where she is?"

The horse made no movements, just stared ahead dispiritedly.

"Here, lad, let me try," Eraldir said. A symphony of popping joints played itself out as he squatted down in front of the horse. "Sylvia, old girl!" He shouted this, and the horse blinked slowly. "Excellent. She's heard us." Eraldir rubbed his hands together, lost his balance, and fell over onto Finn. "Whoa there. Sorry about that lad. Don't have the balance I used to. Just prop me back on up there."

Finn struggled to get out from under the pile of dry bones that was Eraldir, averting his head as far as he could to avoid the smell. Noe rescued him by lifting Eraldir up by his arms and holding him upright.

"There we go. Thanks, lad," Eraldir said to Noe. "When I was young I had great balance. Used to walk rooftops for money until the other kids caught on that it was easy for me. Then I got an inner ear infection from a cold I caught from a pirate while we were marooned on a giant, lifeless rock out in the middle of the ocean. He and I drew lots for who would eat the other. I won, only 'cause I cheated, though, and he tried to kill me. Luckily, he was eaten by a manatee before he could gut me. Not long after that I was rescued by a passing group of travelling sea nuns. He had his revenge, though, gave me the cold that took my inner ears with him to the bottom of the sea. My balance has never been quite the same since." He sighed. "I've never liked manatees much, but I still feel I owe them a debt that must someday be repaid."

Finn's eyes were closed and he was slowly counting down from ten thousand. When Eraldir paused for breath Isabelle cut in. "Does Sylvia know where Kel is?" Finn's eyes snapped back open.

"Oh, right you are. Right you are." Eraldir turned back to the horse, whose eyes were also closed. "Sylvia!" Her eyes blinked open. "Blink if you know where Kel is!" Her eyelids fluttered. Finn couldn't tell if that was a yes or if she was just reacting to a faceful of Eraldir breath.

KEL STRAINED against the ropes that bound her to the tree, but stopped when the guard lifted his crossbow. More soldiers were arriving every minute, and Captain Nate was ignoring her now, hadn't spoken to her since ensuring she was tied securely.

Four soldiers stood around Kel, one with a crossbow pointed at her heart. Nate had given orders for her to be shot immediately if she tried anything. The soldiers didn't speak, just stared at her with contempt. Being hated was a new, and terrible, experience for Kel. She felt intensely lonely, with the men looking at her with revulsion, and the forest pulling away from her, too. The plants were still benignly present, but the crows had communicated their dislike of her to the other animals, and even the birds and squirrels were ignoring her now. She could feel the crows nearby, too, watching her with their black eyes, waiting to block her path if she tried to enter the woods. If the forest didn't want her she had nowhere to go. Tears welled in her eyes, but she blinked them back.

Suddenly, a voice interrupted her thoughts.

Girl! Oh, this is such a hassle. I'm starving and they won't leave me alone. Never a moment's peace. Never a moment's peace at all. Girl?

Sylvia?

Yes, girl. There are people here asking for you. Eraldir and those two younger, angry ones. And a giant who smells like fish.

Her heart leapt, it must be Finn! But she wanted to make sure. *Who?*

Who knows. Sigh. I'm too old for this. I should be left in a nice, sunny pasture. Not reduced to passing you messages. Please inform them that I'm not a message carrier.

Sorry Sylvia, I didn't ask them to try to talk to me.

They want to know if you've been captured.

Yes, she had been captured, and these men would hurt her unless she escaped, and, even if she did escape, the forest didn't want her anymore. She wanted so badly for Finn to come rescue her. And now here he was, he'd found a way to contact her. She knew if she told him she was in trouble he would come and try to save her.

213

Kel closed her eyes, feeling her wet lashes stick together, and swallowed around a lump in her throat.

If Finn came to rescue her he would have to fight. He would kill all these men. Or they would kill him. He might kill Nate, too, and Kel liked Nate, even though he thought she was evil now.

And then, after all that, even if Finn could rescue her, she would just be back where she'd started, following along behind Finn. Except this time he might watch her more closely and she might not be able to run away as easily.

"Well?" Finn said, placing a hand on Eraldir's shoulder. Sylvia was staring ahead, unblinking, and had been for several seconds. Then she blinked. Once. Twice. Three times. No. She wasn't captured. "What? How can she not be captured? Where is she?"

"You're puncturing my shoulder with your fingernails, boy. Ease up a bit."

Finn relaxed his grip. "But, where is she?"

"Yes or no questions only, boy."

"Fine. Is she in Westwend?"

"No."

"Is she lost?"

"No."

"Is she hurt?"

"No."

"Is she in the forest?"

"Yes."

"Does she need help?"

"No."

"Why did she leave?"

Eraldir lifted an eyebrow at that.

"Okay, okay, never mind. Is she mad at me?"

"No."

"Is she okay?"

"Yes." Well, good, at least Sylvia wasn't just saying no every time.

And then the question that meant the most. "Is she coming back?"

A pause. Then, "No."

Loss and sadness washed up through Finn. "What is she doing?!"

Eraldir sighed.

"I mean..."

Sylvia gave an annoyed snort and shut her eyes.

"Come on, Sylvia." Eraldir patted her head and scratched her behind the ears, but she remained unresponsive.

Eraldir turned and looked back at Finn. "Sorry, boy. I think that's all we're going to get out of her."

"But..."

Eraldir grabbed Finn's shoulder and started to heave himself up. Noe gripped Eraldir's arms and lifted him smoothly into a standing position.

Finn was pacing restlessly. "But... what's she doing?"

"What about that... that pointy-faced, wingless bat she had with her... what's its name... Ash?"

"Smoke?"

"Right, right. Maybe she went back for it."

Of course. That made sense. Relief washed over Finn. He had thought Kel had left because she was angry at him, but the kid just wanted her pet back. She was weirdly attached to that thing. Yeah. That was it. It wasn't, but he could almost convince himself it was.

"So, Finn, you going to let her leave?" Isabelle asked.

Finn ran a hand through his hair. "I... I don't know."

Eraldir clapped a hand on Finn's shoulder. "Well, boy, it

SARAH MCCARTHY

sounds like she's doing just fine on her own, and if she wants to leave there really isn't much you can do to force her to stay."

There was a part to this that Finn hadn't acknowledged to himself. He was relieved. Maybe Kel really would be better off alone. Finn couldn't quite convince himself of this, though. The kid was six years old. Almost seven. Either way, though, alone in the woods at seven wasn't much better.

"Finn?" Isabelle punched him lightly on the arm.

"Oh, sorry... yeah?"

Eraldir was struggling to climb up onto Sylvia. "Oof. We'd best be on our way." The ground shook and Eraldir fell off into Noe's arms. Noe tipped him back up onto the horse. "Coming, boy?"

Finn made his decision. *Goodbye, Kel,* he thought. *I'm sorry.* He nodded once. "Let's go."

CHAPTER 17

Kel wished briefly that Finn would ignore what she'd said, and come after her anyway. But he wouldn't. He didn't know where she'd gone, and probably assumed she was long gone, into the woods by now.

A tight spot in Kel's chest loosened. *Goodbye, Finn.*

She opened her eyes. The four men were crouching around her, only about five feet away, weapons trained on her and eyes riveted.

It was time to get free.

The sound of boots crunching over twigs caused Kel to turn, and she saw Captain Nate coming towards her.

The man had his hand on his sword hilt, and his eyes were locked on Kel.

"Give me a minute with the prisoner," Nate said. The man with the crossbow lowered it and rubbed his arm.

Once they were alone, Nate sat down on a log a few feet from Kel, still watching her warily.

"I've been thinking," Nate said. "If you were going to use those crows to attack us, you could have just killed me there in that clearing. They probably could have overpowered me."

Nate's green eyes pierced into Kel's, and he went on, "What were you doing with those crows, kid?"

Kel stared back at him. "Nothing. I wasn't doing anything. They won't let me back."

"Back where?"

"Into the forest."

"Why?"

"I'm not sure." With only Nate here, this was the perfect opportunity to escape. There were some bushes around that could grow fast, get in his way, and she could use the tree to lift herself into the air. She looked up to see Nate watching her, his hand resting easily on the pommel of his sword.

"So, you weren't doing magic? But, I'm right that you're a mage?"

"Yeah. I guess." How fast could he get to her with that sword?

"How long have you been one?"

"I don't know. Since a couple of weeks ago." She wished there were vines around. There might be seeds left in her pockets, but she couldn't reach them, the ropes were too tight.

"How did it happen?"

"What do you mean?" She scanned her pocket mentally, and found a single seed of the vine. She'd have to make it grow straight from her pocket.

"I mean, how did you become one? No one younger than sixteen is a mage. What happened?"

Kel shrugged. "I was alone, and I could just do stuff." She didn't know if she could be fast enough, but she was ready to try.

"So, you didn't talk to anything, meet anyone strange?"

"No." Kel looked straight into Nate's eyes as she said this, her heart speeding up, collecting herself, getting ready to escape.

"Huh." Nate interlaced his fingers and examined them; he turned to watch his men, eyes lost in thought. Now. She should go now. But she hesitated, curious about what he was going to say. "You know, I've never actually talked to a mage before." Nate took a deep breath. "When I found out you were that fire mage's brother I felt sorry for you. I thought you were just a little kid, running away from her violent and dangerous older brother..." Nate took a deep breath. "Then I saw you in that clearing and I thought you'd tricked me. That you and he were both these evil mages. I thought I'd misjudged you, that you'd lied to me. I've had some time to think, though, and now I'm more inclined towards my first impression. I'm not usually wrong about people, you know?"

All Kel's plans of imminent escape dropped out of her head in surprise. He didn't think she was evil after all. After spending all this time with Finn, Kel could understand why Nate had reacted badly when he thought he saw her doing magic.

"Will you tell me the rest of the story?" Nate asked.

Gratitude flooded Kel. It was such a relief that at least one person here didn't hate her, and she realized she wanted to tell someone about what had happened. Escape could wait a few minutes, she supposed. But only a few. She told Nate about being in the forest, and he listened silently, only nodding occasionally. Then she told him about meeting Eraldir and Isabelle, and the crows, and about coming to Westwend. As she talked, feelings of fear and loneliness welled up inside her and then passed, drifting away and leaving her feeling better than she had in weeks.

When Kel finally finished, Nate was quiet for several seconds, then he sighed. "I don't envy you at all." He sighed and rubbed his hand across his chin. "So, what happened after that? How'd you end up in the tunnels?"

Kel told Nate about Finn leaving her in the room at the

inn, returning much later with a girl in tow. Nate nodded. He'd heard about the escaped mage. When Kel got to the mage hideout, and the conversation with Reina, Nate leaned forward anxiously.

"What exactly is she planning, kid, do you know?"

Kel shook her head. "She just said she's planning on taking over the city today."

The blood drained out of Nate's face, but he didn't lose his composure. "She say anything else? Anything at all?"

Kel started to tell him about the goldfish, but Nate waved her off, asked her to describe every detail she could remember of the hideout, and the way there from the tunnel entrance. Kel didn't remember very clearly the way she had come, though, and couldn't give good directions.

"Thank you," Nate said, his sharp eyes catching and holding Kel's. "I know you feel like you're betraying your brother, but you're not. I'll do whatever I can to help him."

A lump formed in Kel's throat. "He didn't mean to do what he did. He doesn't want to hurt anyone."

Nate put a hand on her shoulder. "I believe you." Nate turned to look back at his milling soldiers. "And now, I think it's time to get you out of here." Kel agreed. But part of her wished she could stay with Nate. "Unfortunately, I've already told everyone you're a mage. Had to tell them or they would have been in danger guarding you. Not that they weren't, even knowing that. I'm sorry, kid. I let my fear get the better of me. Arcturus is on his way down here—he'll be here in a few minutes—and it's likely he'll torture you for information about your brother and then when he's done he'll kill you. Killing Finn Vogt's mage sister would be a big coup for him."

Kel's mouth got drier and her palms got sweatier. Her escape better work.

Nate noticed Kel's panic, and he held up a palm. "Hey, it's

okay. Don't worry. Like I said earlier, I'm not going to let anything happen to you."

"If you let me go, though, aren't you going to get in trouble?"

"Well, that depends. You have a plan to get away?"

Kel nodded.

"Great. Well, then. Look, I was already having some qualms about tying up a kid like that, and sometimes my men can be jumpy with their trigger fingers, especially with mages, so I tampered with the crossbow they've got aimed at you. I figured you wouldn't try anything with an arrow pointed at you anyway. It won't fire the way it is now. Will that be enough for you to get out of here on your own?"

"I think so. Thanks."

Nate patted her on the shoulder. "Sure thing. Look. I'm sorry you've had a rough time of it."

Shouts came from across the camp. Nate stood quickly. "I'd better go. Good luck with the birds, kid." He waved to the guards, who came quickly over and took up their positions around Kel. Kel smiled at them, and they shifted nervously.

FINN'S MIND raced as he hurried down the tunnel with Isabelle, Noe, and Eraldir. They had to get back to the mage hideout before Reina started her war. Eraldir would try to warn her about the shadow, while Finn would try to convince as many mages as he could to leave. He would have to be careful who he talked to, though. Try to convince someone loyal to Reina to leave and they'd go straight to her.

"Noe?" Finn asked.

"Yeah?"

"Are there any mages you know of who'd be willing to come with us?"

Noe thought for a moment. "Not s'far as I know."

Well, maybe he'd start with the people who were missing the most body parts.

~

ARCTURUS SIGHED and massaged his stomach with one be-ringed hand as he walked, escorted by guards, down to the edge of the forest. It was not his custom to walk, but the quickest route was down a steep, rocky path and, from what his men had reported, there was no time to waste. He kept his eyes on the trail as he walked, picking his way nimbly through the stones and dust. When was the last time he'd walked a dirt path? It reminded him unpleasantly of when he was a boy. Now, though, his feet were swathed in the finest leather, made by the best shoemaker in town. A man he knew to be a mage. As always, using something made by a mage made his stomach sick, but a small glow of consolation warmed his heart when he reminded himself that this was a mage who was forced to do something other than magic to survive, and, not only that, but this mage was also now forced to pay Arcturus a hefty sum each week to keep making the shoes he so despised. Yes, on the whole, these shoes made Arcturus Flavius very happy.

The guards at the edge of the woods were quiet and tense, Arcturus noted; all eyes were on a small hole in the ground.

"Where is Captain Nate?" Arcturus asked the nearest guard.

"Questioning the prisoner, sir," the man said, inclining his head deferentially.

Arcturus turned to see the young captain striding out of the forest, brushing a branch out of his way. Arcturus noticed the way the eyes of the female members of the guard followed him surreptitiously as he passed. It wasn't just that Nate was handsome, either. There was a confidence, a happy sense of being secure in one's place in the world, and it was that, more than the admiring glances, or the broad shoulders, that Arcturus envied.

"Sir," Nate said, inclining his head in a bow before straightening again.

Arcturus drew himself up just a fraction of an inch higher so that he was looking Nate straight in the eye. "Captain. Give your report."

"Early this morning my patrol happened across a hole in the ground, with a little girl trapped in it. We helped her out and questioned her. Turns out she's escaped from the mages. There's a hideout underground—the hole behind me leads to a tunnel which the kid says leads back there, although she says there are a lot of different branches of the tunnel and she's not sure which way she came. Not only that, turns out the kid is a mage herself."

Arcturus started. "What? From what you said I was assuming she was young. You mean this 'kid' is older? Sixteen?"

"No, sir. She's only six. She herself doesn't know how she ended up a mage."

"And you've seen her work magic?"

"I have."

Arcturus considered this. He'd never heard of a mage younger than sixteen. Had the mages found some way of making it happen earlier? And, the real question, the question that opened a terrible chasm of hope for him, would it work on non-mages? He shook himself from his reverie.

"Anything else, Captain?"

"Yes, sir. The kid also overheard Reina Jeesh planning something."

Ah Reina Jeesh. Beautiful, furious, and delightfully spiteful. She'd been a fun opponent. The closest thing to an actual adversary Arcturus had ever had. Extorting money from her had been the most fun of all.

"Oh? What's that?"

"She's planning an all-out war sir. The kid says she's planning on starting her attack today."

Well, Arcturus had known it would come to that eventually. Reina wouldn't have continued paying him for long, and wouldn't be satisfied just by burning down his inn. He smiled at the memory. That was a hefty blow she'd gotten in. One of his first businesses, and he admired her for it.

"Do we know anything about her plans for this 'war'?"

"No, sir, just that it could start at any moment."

Arcturus liked Nate's reserve. He could tell that just under the surface Nate was boiling with urgency, but his respect for the chain of command held him back, kept him waiting for Arcturus' order. That was what Arcturus liked most about Nate. Nate let himself be controlled.

There was something else there, though, now that Arcturus looked at his captain more closely. Nate was keeping something from him.

"Is there anything else, Captain?"

"No, sir."

Interesting.

Arcturus turned to one of his guards. "Go muster the troops. Every able-bodied man and woman armed and at the ready. Half stationed in the town square; send the other half here." He turned to say something to Nate, but on second thought turned back to the guard. "Oh, and I suppose you might as well inform the mayor. See if he wants to evacuate or something."

❧

FINN, Eraldir, Isabelle, and Noe slammed back into the throng of war preparations. Mages rushed everywhere, moving crates and boxes out of the way of what Finn could now see was the edge of a fortress. Finn spotted a mage in the corner; she was small, poorly dressed, and missing three fingers on her left hand. Maybe that would be a good place to start. He turned to ask Noe, but the man was gone.

Confused and slightly worried, Finn turned to Isabelle. "Isabelle, did you see—"

Isabelle was already walking away from him though. "I'll meet you back here in, like, ten minutes!"

Finn turned to Eraldir. The old man shrugged. "She'll probably be back, lad. I think she likes you, you know." With that, he went to find Reina, leaving Finn alone in the chaos.

He hoped Noe wasn't off betraying them to Reina.

He also hoped he didn't tip off another mage who would go betray them to Reina. He didn't have time for subtlety, though. He had to get as many as he could, right now, and then get out of here.

But the faces around him were determined, focused, haggard.

"Excuse me," Finn said, reaching his hand out towards one of the passing mages, but the mage either didn't hear him or didn't care, and just shouldered past. Finn looked back to the corner, for the seven-fingered mage, but she was gone.

So, Finn wandered against the flow of traffic, looking for someone who looked afraid. What was the facial expression for 'I'm participating in a war I'd rather not participate in?' Most of the faces around him were angry; they reminded him of Isabelle, stepping out into that dining room. Ready for a fight. No one looked particularly interested in having a leisurely and rational discussion about politics.

Powerlessness and hopelessness overwhelmed him for a moment. Then, he saw a door, and he got an idea.

It was a small side room, piled full of supplies. Inside were about ten mages that Finn could see, stacking crates.

Finn stepped in, slamming the iron door shut behind him and spot-welding it closed with a quick burst of flame. The fire caught the other mages' attention, and they stopped, still bent over their work, and turned to stare at him.

Finn cleared his throat. "All right everyone. Raise your hand if you're completely excited about going to war today."

No one raised their hands, but that could be because they were all just staring at him, bemused.

"Um, great. Okay. Well, look, I just want to give you another option. If we go to war today a bunch of people are going to die. Lots of innocent people. Mages and non-mages. And, I know that mages have been treated horribly—" He was starting to lose their attention, he could tell. They were starting to get annoyed. One was even raising his hand in a slightly ominous way. "There's another option. A new mage academy. A fortress. On the plains. No non-mages anywhere around. We're rebuilding the old country. Mages will write the laws." Now he was just saying things, anything he thought they might want to hear. "Free food, free place to live, education..."

"What are you talking about?" A man with stone teeth who was holding a crossbow and three large knives said.

"Er, I'm talking about a mage school, better than West-wend could ever be, and it's there now, all we have to do is go there."

"Why haven't I heard of it?"

"Um, it's new."

"How new?"

"Oh, um, pretty new. I'm not exactly sure."

"Get out of our way, kid," a woman with long, grizzled

grey hair and burns across her neck and arms said, pushing past him. She tugged on the door, found it stuck shut. "Dammit, kid, what did you do?"

"I welded it shut, sorry. Just, please listen?"

She narrowed her eyes. "You welded the door shut? But that's iron."

Finn brushed a hand through his hair awkwardly. "Um, yeah, I just melted part of it."

"Where? Show me."

He showed her the small, melted spot, now hardened into a thick iron blob. Her eyes widened. "Rafe, take a look at this." A grizzled man with scars on his arms came and examined the weld.

"Hmm. Impressive. You learn this at your school?"

"Er, yes." Kind of... did learning from Eraldir count? He'd be the main teacher there, anyway. Quite possibly the only teacher.

"How far away did you say it was?"

"It's on the plains, at the old King's Table... a few weeks away." He was completely guessing on that. Hopefully no one knew how far it actually was.

"What do you think, Rafe?" The man with the knives asked.

Rafe stuck his hands in his belt and leaned back, thinking. "Oh, he's lying about something, but I think the part about the school is true."

The woman dropped the burlap sack she was holding. "Well, if he's only lying about two-thirds of it it's still better than being here. You ever cut off anyone's ears, kid?"

"No." Finn was glad she hadn't asked a broader question. Like whether he'd killed anyone. Or, more appropriately to his gifts, melted anyone. At least he'd never cut off anyone's body parts. That was something.

"And who runs this school?"

"I do." There was a short silence and then someone laughed. Finn scrambled for something else to legitimate his claims. "The main teacher is Eraldir, though."

"*The* Eraldir? The last mage from before?"

"Yes."

The atmosphere in the room shifted subtly.

The man with the knives picked up two more. "Sounds good to me. Let's get out of here."

Finn looked at the mages who had been standing there, quiet, not saying anything, just observing.

"What about the rest of you? You can stay here if you want."

A few chose to stay. Finn melted his weld and opened the door, let out the mages who wanted to go, then welded it shut with the others still trapped inside. He figured there'd be an earth mage among them who could get them out, or a fire mage who could melt his weld after a while, he just couldn't run the risk of them warning Reina. It wasn't fool proof, though. Any of the mages he'd just let out might go off and warn her any minute. Assuming Noe hadn't already.

The group was clustered around him now, though, watching him expectantly.

"Er... okay, great. Let's split up, find as many people to come with us as you can, then meet me back at the main entrance in fifteen minutes. If you don't find us, try to meet up with us outside the city. We'll wait in the forest for a while after." The mages went hurrying off in all directions, melting back into the crowd around them. Now for the hard part.

Finn found Ronan sitting by himself, meditating in a small side room. He noticed that there was even more grey mixed in with his dark brown hair now.

There were a lot of things different about Ronan now. He paused there, in the doorway, looking at his friend, thinking about what it used to be like. They'd made so many plans together.

"CENTRAL BANK OWNED by the High Council," Ronan said lazily, from where he lay, stretched out on the grassy slope. His hands were behind his head and he stared up at the gathering clouds. They were dark, but the sun still shone hotly on them. It was the heat of summer, and the air was thick with the pressure of a coming storm. Below, a hundred feet down the side of the steep, rocky hill, the villagers bustled about setting up tents for Cromwic's midsummer festival.

"I agree. One currency for the entire kingdom. More efficient, and no one just making up their own. Did I tell you someone tried to pay my dad with some hexagonal copper thing?" Finn picked idly at a piece of grass.

"Yes." Ronan pushed himself up and looked at Finn. "Are we ever going to actually do any of this?"

"What do you mean?"

"You know what I mean. Are we ever going to actually do any of this, or are we just talking about it?"

Finn ran a hand through his dark hair and looked down at the villagers. "I want to, but who would listen to us?"

Ronan lifted a hand, "Who cares? We're right. Things are terrible the way they are."

"Yeah. What if we invited one representative from each town to a meeting somewhere? Got them to agree, expanded the size of the council and gave them all seats."

Ronan shook his head. "Too messy. Invite them, get a few people for the High Council, but not everyone. Invite them to court, though. We only need the richest places to agree. The rest will have to go along."

"I'd rather have everybody there willingly participating."

"Yeah, well, that's cause you're naive."

"I'm not naive."

"You think you can run a country without making anyone do anything they don't want to do?"

"No." Finn was annoyed at himself for not having a better answer. Ronan waited. "I mean, people do better work if they're invested in something."

"Yeah, but you can't get everyone to agree with you."

Finn knew that was probably true, but a large part of him wanted a world where everyone just discussed things rationally, then came to a unanimous agreement. Without any fighting.

"Finn, it's impossible to get everyone to agree. Sometimes, if you think something is wrong, you should fight. Even kill."

"And where is that going to get us? That's just going to cause wars."

"Maybe wars have to be fought."

"If you have to justify your point with war then your point clearly wasn't very good."

Ronan flopped back onto the grass and stared up at the few tiny clouds.

"And we'll need mages," Ronan said.

Now Ronan was just goading him. Finn uprooted some grass and tossed it lazily at him.

Ronan laughed.

RONAN HAD BEEN RIGHT AFTER ALL. They did need mages. But he was wrong about the rest of it.

"Ronan."

Ronan's eyes snapped open. "Hey, Finn. You guys are staying after all?"

"No, we're leaving now."

"What? But you just got here."

Finn ignored this, pressing on. "Um, look. I wanted to talk to you about something. I heard you're planning on lifting a fortress up into the city today."

Ronan's demeanor changed, his eyes narrowed. "Yeah."

"Have you ever done something that big before?"

"It's not going to be hard."

"Um, are you sure you want to do that? There might be effects that you haven't planned on."

"Seriously, Finn? Still?" Ronan pushed himself to his feet and turned away. "You're a mage and you're still trying to tell me not to use magic."

"I'm not telling you not to use it."

"Yes, you are."

"Well, maybe, just in this instance, but—"

"What happened to 'I'm sorry, Ronan, you were right'?"

"You are right—"

"Then why are you still trying to keep me from—"

"Because, if you do this, you're going to kill people! And, I know what that's like!"

Ronan stared at him, his face tense. "Yes, you do. Stop putting that on me. I've never killed anyone, unlike you."

Hurt flared up in Finn. "It was an accident. And you're going to kill people today. You know that, don't you?"

Ronan curled his lip. "I have better control than you do, Finn. I'm only going to kill people who kill mages. I'm not going to kill people who are trying to protect me."

"What are you talking about?"

"You know, I felt sorry for you. It was so obvious you were a mage and trying not to be. I felt bad for you."

"I know. You were right."

"Yes! You should have listened to me!" Ronan stepped

towards Finn, and Finn was surprised to see tears in Ronan's eyes.

"Ronan, what's wrong?"

"I asked her to watch you. Not that she could have done anything."

"Who?"

"My mother."

Finn's heart stopped, and he felt his face and arms go numb. "What?"

"Yeah, you killed her, too. Burned her alive just like your parents and everyone else who got in your way."

"Oh, god, Ronan." There was nothing Finn could say. "I'm so sorry." The impact of what he'd done hit him again.

"Yeah, well, you don't get to lecture me on safety. You are not the expert on magic here."

"I just don't want you to make the same mistake I did."

"I'm not."

"But, you're going to—"

"Shut up, Finn. I have to go."

If Ronan went, if he walked out that door and lifted Reina's fortress into the middle of Westwend, there would be no going back. They would kill hundreds of non-mages. They'd take the city, probably, but all the non-mages in the country would be up in arms. There'd be slaughter. First of mages, then more non-mages, then more mages. It wouldn't end.

Finn stepped between Ronan and the door. He didn't know what he was planning. He wasn't going to fight Ronan, not really.

"You don't have to do this."

"I want to."

"Come with us instead. We'll rebuild the government. Like we talked about. Stay here and you're just a slave to Reina."

This got a glimmer of a reaction from Ronan, and Finn pressed harder. "She'll control you, it's almost as bad as the non-mages, right? Come with us and you can lead with me. We're going to the King's Table, Ronan."

Ronan hesitated.

CHAPTER 18

*K*el waited as Nate walked away. She didn't want to make her escape too soon after talking with the captain, didn't want to bring suspicion down on the man. She'd wait two minutes, and then go. Kel closed her eyes, counting to herself, and leaned her head back against the rough bark of the tree.

Kel's mind slipped and suddenly she was a bird, a hawk, wheeling through the sky. Her right talon was sore, and she flexed it. Smaller birds darted out of her way, flitted into the trees at her approach. The world was sharp and clear below her. Every detail, each individual leaf standing out in stark relief, even from so far away. A warm updraft caught her and lifted her even higher.

Kel wrenched her eyes open and shook her head to clear it. She wasn't sure how much time had passed, maybe only a few seconds. She looked around, saw Nate talking with someone, a man dressed in black and silver. They looked her way. It was time to go.

She took a look at the man with the crossbow. Hopefully Nate had been careful when he disabled the bow. If that

234

thing still worked, Kel wouldn't get far. She wished the animals would help her. She needed someone to distract the guards for a few seconds. An idea popped into her head suddenly; she could force them. The crows had obeyed when she'd sent them away. She could feel the crows around her, watching from the trees. Could she command all of them at once?

Something told her that she could. But she'd be forcing them to risk their lives for her. Some of them would most likely die, and she would have sacrificed them to save herself. She wouldn't do that. Suddenly, in a flash of insight, she realized what the crows were angry about. It wasn't the eggs at all, at least not after the first few moments. It was about control. She'd forced them away.

Nate and the man in black were coming towards her now. The man in black had a nasty, hungry look in his eyes. She took a deep breath, and smiled at the guard, who narrowed his eyes. Then the plants around them exploded into movement. Vines shot up, wrapped around the guards' legs, bushes swelled between Kel and the men, blocking their view, and the tree to which Kel was tied gave a groaning creak and stretched itself up towards the sky, heaving Kel into the air with it. This was not a tree used to growing from its base. It was a hemlock, which normally grew from its top, but it obliged Kel's request, stretching up and up as far as it could. And it was only a request; she wasn't going to force anything, ever again.

Kel shot up, fifteen feet in the air in only a few seconds. The trunk was expanding, too, and the ropes were tightening across Kel's chest. Vines coiled around the ropes, pulling them away from her. One by one the ropes snapped. One of the loose ends caught Kel across the arm, leaving a stinging red welt. As the ropes holding her broke, Kel reached for the vines, clinging to them to keep herself from falling. Her arms and legs were stiff and slow after being immobile for so long, but she held on. The crows watched from nearby trees, their eyes glittering.

Shouts from below, and a crossbow bolt zinged past her head. Better get farther up into the canopy. Kel looked frantically back and forth, searching for another tree. A towering cedar loomed nearby, too far to jump, but only about ten feet away. Another bolt zipped past Kel, ruffling her hair and narrowly missing her face this time. A crow clicked its beak, waiting for her to order it to fly at the men shooting at her. But Kel didn't even bother to ask it for help.

A vine shot out for the cedar tree, finding purchase, wrapping around its trunk and quickly expanding into a narrow bridge. Kel sprinted for the tree, a bolt clipped her right arm and she leaned to the left to dodge it, but she leaned too far and lost her balance. Windmilling her arms, she struggled to stay on the vine bridge, still running for the other tree. She almost made it, almost righted herself, but she felt herself tip over that subtle edge, that place of no return, and slowly, so slowly, she tumbled off the vine.

She smashed through a tree branch; it broke under her weight, scraping her as she fell, but the next branch was thicker. It broke, too; she crashed through it, but managed to grab it as she fell through. Her left hand got only leaves, these broke away, but her right got actual branch, held on tight. The branch groaned and sagged, she was only about ten feet above the ground now. Pain shot through her leg. Kel looked down and was horrified to see an arrow sticking out of her calf. She closed her eyes, expecting another arrow through her heart at any second.

Kel reached out frantically into the plants around her. The tree she hung from swayed its branches, shooting up as quickly as it could, its bark splitting with the effort. Kel could feel the tree cry out in pain. Vines engulfed the shooters below. There were so many now, twenty or thirty. The bushes and the vines wrapped around them, blocking their vision so they couldn't see her.

Her magic was not usually a quick magic. Plants are slow, they grow slowly, calmly, thoughtfully, and that was how Kel was, too. Slow, thoughtful, not used to quick action, or fighting, or fleeing. She was asking too much of them, she knew. Kel begged for an animal to help, for the watching crows to lift her up, carry her away, but the crows ignored her request, sensing her desperation, daring her to try to force them to help. And the plants, too, were hurting now.

Kel heaved herself up onto the branch, crawled along it towards the trunk of the cedar tree. Tears coursed down her face, her arms burned from scratches, and the bolt still sticking out of her leg caught on a branch, jerking her leg muscle, sending nauseous waves of pain through her.

She found the trunk; without stopping to think she tore the bolt out of her leg, ripping skin and muscle as she did so, but she needed it out, couldn't stand to have this foreign object sticking out of her. Blood flowed thickly down her leg. Desperately, Kel looked around her. There were branches above her, thick enough to hide her. The men below couldn't see her through the bushes, but they were firing indiscriminately now. Bolts whipped through the air around her, not aimed but fired so thickly that it might not matter.

Ignoring the blood coursing down her leg, Kel climbed grimly up the tree, pulling herself higher and higher, branch by branch, until the sounds of the men and the bolts faded away. Still higher she went, as the trunk of the cedar narrowed and the branches she clung to became more and more tenuous.

She'd picked the right tree. It towered over most of those around it, sticking far above the canopy. When there were no more branches large enough to bear Kel's weight she stopped, gasping, wrapped an arm around the narrow trunk, and leaned against it. For a while she closed her eyes, feeling the wind, feeling the sway of the trunk as it bent in the breeze, hearing the rustle of branches around her.

The rustling became louder, and she opened her eyes to see a legion of crows gathered around her. Hundreds of them, they lined every branch nearby. Her body tensed, expecting an attack, but it never came. The crows only sat watching her.

One of them dug its beak into its wing, and tugged out a feather. It swooped closer, landing on the branch in front of her, holding the feather in its beak. She reached out an arm, sticky with sap and shaky from climbing, and took the feather. The crow ducked its head, eyed her with one bright eye, and then took flight. The others rose after it in a dark, swirling cloud, heading off over the treetops, and dispersing into the wind.

She closed her eyes again and collapsed back against the tree in relief, clutching the feather tightly. She understood, now. The crows had been angry about their eggs, but not for long; they'd attacked her mostly to have someone to blame. It was what she'd done after that had made them so furious. She'd made them do something they didn't want to do. They knew she was capable of controlling them, they hated her for it, and if and when she tried to, they'd fight with everything they had.

Eventually she opened her eyes again and looked down at her leg. It was still bleeding, the wound looked ragged and dirty, and blood was dripping out of her. She felt faint just looking at it, but pulled off her shirt and pressed it to the ragged, bloody edges. Taking some deep breaths to calm herself, she tried to think. How much time did she have? Would they try to climb the tree after her? She didn't think they could. The trunk was smooth for the first twenty feet.

The first branches were too high up for them to reach. They might try to burn the tree, but the bark was wet from recent rains, and the wood too green to burn. They wouldn't expect her to stay here, anyway.

No, Kel thought she might be safe now. At least until she passed out from blood loss, or hunger, or thirst, or fell while trying to climb down. It might be possible to climb from tree to tree, but not in her current condition. She was spent, and she felt the pain of the plants below her. They cried out from being used the way they had been. She had asked them to do things so unnatural, things they shouldn't and couldn't do. Kel cried, feeling their pain and confusion.

I'm sorry, she thought. *Thank you, I'm sorry.*

No, she was probably safe her for a little while, at least. And she would stay here and help heal the plants who had saved her life.

She closed her eyes, felt the tears in their trunks, the places the bark had stretched and broken open. Slowly, gently, she eased the wounds closed, pouring all her magic into them. She gave everything she had to the broken trees, and to the vines the men had hacked apart to escape. Kel gave and gave, healing and repairing, until she was completely empty, until she could barely keep herself conscious, and still she kept going. Then she passed out. The tree branch under her shifted, ever so slightly, keeping her from falling.

She fell immediately into a deep sleep, and instantly the dream came back. She was walking along the path, through the white trunks of the birches, now stark and bare of leaves. She came around a bend and there was a figure. It had antlers like a stag, and skin like tree bark. Feathers lined its shoulders and its eyes were black like a moonless night sky, but full of distant stars, too. It reached out one long finger, touched the wound on her leg, and then, very briefly, hesitantly, laid a twig-like fingertip in the center of her chest. Kel felt totally calm and at peace, watching it. It reached up, brushed a sweaty clump of hair from her forehead, and then, quickly as it had come, it withdrew, back into the forest, and Kel slept on, dreamlessly.

∾

"ALL RIGHT."

Finn wasn't sure he'd heard Ronan correctly.

"What?"

Ronan shrugged. "All right. I'll come with you. Reina's crazy anyway."

A furious hope swelled in Finn's chest, and he wanted to hug Ronan, but he stopped himself.

"Yeah, I mean, those goldfish?"

The tension on Ronan's face broke into a fragile smile, and he laughed. "Yeah."

"Was she serious about that?"

"I think so. There used to be more."

They looked at each other for a moment.

"You really want to hug me, don't you?" Ronan said.

"No."

Ronan grinned and hugged him. Finn smiled, despite himself, and hugged him back. Then he pulled away, awkwardly.

"We'd better get going."

"Just let me grab my bag." Ronan grabbed a dusty, beat-up leather satchel from the corner, and together they hurried out the door.

They passed a storage room, and inside Finn saw racks of Reina's wine. Grinning to himself, he ducked in and grabbed a few bottles. Ronan laughed and grabbed one for himself, too.

~

EVERYTHING WAS JUST ABOUT READY. Reina felt the warm glow in her chest which always meant she was close to getting revenge on someone. And not just one person. Today there were so many people to revenge herself upon. There was Arcturus, of course, and all his non-magical minions, but before that there was Jes. Killing her would be a good way to start the day.

Reina swept through the crowded hallways, her soldiers diving left and right to get out of her way. Reina smiled inwardly at this. She had a crossbow slung across her back and a sheaf of bolts in a holder at her waist. In her hand she carried a curved, gleaming blade. Her blade. The merchant who had made it for her called it Cutthroat, and Reina had bought it from him, then tried it out on him. It worked exactly as he'd described, and she'd taken her money back.

Underneath the satisfaction, though, was something uncomfortable, something nagging at her. She didn't want to admit it to herself, but she actually felt a little sad about Jes' betrayal. Jes was the closest thing Reina had had to a friend since… well since before Reina had become Reina. She hated to think that she'd let that weak little idiot get under her skin. Just the fact that Reina was hurting now meant that she'd let herself care too much. But it would be taken care of soon. She would get her revenge and then she would feel better. Then she wouldn't have to worry about this anymore. Revenge always made her feel better.

When Reina came to the cell where Jes was being kept, though, something was wrong. The two guards posted outside were gone. Idiots. She would have a finger from each of them for not following orders. She thought they knew by now that orders from Reina were in no way negotiable or avoidable. They were to be followed, no matter what. Clearly her men needed more examples.

But then she reached the cell door and things got worse. The door was open. The cell was empty. Flames bubbled out of Reina's hands and licked up her arms; she clenched her jaw and her fists and glared about her for someone to hurt, but there was no one. The corridor was empty. She took a deep breath, calmed herself. The flames stayed, but she broke into a militant jog down the hall towards the rest of her army. The traitor may have escaped, but she wasn't going to live for long.

NATE WATCHED Kel's escape with a carefully controlled expression. He could feel Arcturus' eyes on him, even as they both called out orders—Nate of course deferring immediately to Arcturus' authority. Nate cringed inwardly when he saw Kel get hit with the bolt, and his heart nearly stopped when she fell, but the girl caught herself and then kept climbing, and she didn't come back down. Nate hoped she'd be all right.

He turned to Arcturus. "I don't think the girl is much of a threat, sir. She was trying to escape from the other mages when we caught her. Seemed to just want to be off on her own."

Nate realized as he was saying this that it probably just sounded like an excuse to Arcturus, so he changed tacks. "Should I ready the men, sir?"

"Yes. Stealth is key, here, Captain. They don't know we're coming, but as soon as they see us we can expect anything from floods to earthquakes to cave-ins."

Nate nodded. He knew.

"Kill them on sight, Captain. No prisoners." Especially no

prisoners who might mention the blackmail. Not that anyone would believe them anyway, but it might make things awkward.

~

"WHAT WERE you going to do if I said no?" Ronan asked as they hurried down the tunnel.

"Leave without you, I guess," Finn said.

"So, you were just going to let me go off and kill all those people?"

"I thought you said you had better control than that."

Ronan punched him in the shoulder. "I do. That's not the point."

"You left, didn't you?"

They came around a corner and ran into a large group of mages, just milling around apprehensively. Most of them were young, only a few years older than Finn and Ronan, but a few others, like Rafe, were older. The man with the stone ear was there, and several younger mages had bad burns. Clearly, Finn wasn't the only one who had trouble with fire.

Heads jerked up when Finn came around the corner.

"That's him," someone in the crowd whispered. The group fell silent.

Finn stopped and stood there awkwardly as all eyes turned towards him.

Luckily, right at that moment Eraldir wandered around the corner, too, carrying a basket over one arm and leading Sylvia.

"Great job, boy! Good turnout, I'd say." He pulled a piece of pie from the basket at his side and took a bite. He looked at Ronan. "Ah, the famous earth mage. Good to have you along, boy."

Ronan smiled and nodded.

A horrible thought suddenly occurred to Finn. He leaned over to Ronan and whispered, "I told them the school is already set up."

Ronan turned, his eyebrow lifted, stretching the dark ink on his face.

"Please don't say anything?" Finn whispered urgently.

Ronan considered this for a moment.

Finn pressed on. "They wouldn't have come otherwise. We need as many mages as possible, right?"

Ronan looked away, then looked back again. "Seriously, Finn?"

"Um, yes."

"Wow."

"Please?"

"Alright, alright. Fine. I guess."

"Thank you," Finn whispered emphatically.

"You do realize that lying is just another way of forcing people to do what you want, right?" He hissed back.

Finn didn't have an answer for this, but luckily, they were interrupted by Isabelle. She swept up, something bulky tucked under her shirt. She readjusted it, grinning at Finn and Ronan.

"Ready to go?"

"Definitely," Ronan said, giving her a warm smile. She grinned back.

Eraldir ambled up, and Isabelle turned to him. "Where'd you get the pie?" She reached for the basket; Eraldir grumbled and tried to move the basket out of her reach, but she was too quick for him.

"Fine, you can have that one piece, but that's it. To answer your question, I figured Reina would have some around."

"Did you even try to convince her?" Isabelle asked, around a mouthful of pie.

"Course I did!" He set the pie back in the basket, took out

his mug, full of tea, and took a sip. "Can't escape a dictator on an empty stomach, though."

Finn looked over the group. "Where's Noe? Has anyone seen him?"

Blank looks. Crap. That probably meant he had warned Reina. Maybe not, though. Maybe he was just late getting back. Finn hoped that was the case, but his pulse quickened.

"We'd better hurry," Finn said. "Reina might know our plan by now."

Isabelle had finished her pie and was braiding her white hair to keep it back out of her face. She grinned at Finn; a piece of loose hair fell across her face and she tucked it back. Finn's heart skipped a beat. "All right, let's get out of here." She readjusted the bulky thing under her shirt, and it sloshed. Finn decided not to ask.

"All right, who knows the way out?" Finn asked. A few mages raised their hands. "You guys up front with me, then. Isabelle, you and Eraldir take up the back. Ronan, you're with me."

"Who put you in charge?" Isabelle said.

"Yeah," Ronan said. Isabelle turned to smile at him.

Finn tried to ignore the smile. "Me."

"Well, all right, then. If it was you that put you in charge." She rolled her eyes, but took up her place at the back of the group.

Finn shouldered his way to the front. "All right, let's go!"

Behind him were twenty, maybe thirty mages. That was twenty or thirty people he was saving, not to mention the people they might have killed. The furious hope that had swelled in his chest earlier now coursed through his whole body, and he broke into a crazy smile as he ran.

They hadn't run far, though, when the sounds of pursuit came to their ears.

"How much farther?" He gasped to Ronan, who was running easily alongside him, still barefoot.

"Half a mile or so to the closest entrance. It's this side tunnel up ahead."

"Okay, once everyone's inside—"

"Yeah, got it, I'll seal it off."

"Will they just open it back up again, though?"

"Come on, man. I can make it look like there wasn't a tunnel here. Reina's got a terrible memory for these tunnels. I may have been changing them frequently on purpose."

Finn had the urge to hug Ronan again. A sound distracted him, though, and his feeling of elation dimmed. It was the sound of people thundering through the tunnels towards them. He even thought he could hear Reina screaming encouragement to her people.

Glancing around, Finn saw uncertainty on the faces of the mages running around him. How many of them would switch sides if Reina caught up with them? It wasn't like they had much reason to be loyal to him. He should have introduced Eraldir, took a moment to explain again to everyone what they were doing, but if he had then Reina might already have caught them.

"Here," Ronan said, grabbing Finn's arm and skidding to a halt. "In here, in here," he waved the mages into the narrow side tunnel. They bunched up around the small entrance. The sound of pounding feet got closer and closer. Finn expected Reina's army to come around the corner any second now.

The last of the mages filed through, and Ronan and Finn ducked in after them. Ronan lifted his arms, and the ground shook as the tunnel closed behind them.

Silence and darkness. Small fires flickered into life as the fire mages of the group conjured them to illuminate the way. Finn took a slow, deep breath, then held it, listening. If he strained his ears he could just barely hear the army stampeding down the tunnel toward them. He heard them, right on the other side of the wall Ronan had just made. He hoped Ronan had done a good job, that the entrance to this side tunnel wasn't visible anymore. He also hoped that Reina had forgotten exactly where it was.

Finn crouched down, tense, listening. The sound from the other side of the wall increased and increased and then, miraculously, started to fade as the army continued past. She'd missed them.

Finn turned to Ronan, who was picking some dirt from under his fingernails.

"Nice."

Ronan grinned. "I know."

Finn made his way to the front of the group again. "All right everybody. As quiet as you can, now."

They jogged down the tunnel, lit by the light of the fire mages. Long shadows stretched in front of Finn's feet, his own shadow merging with those of the group behind him, a forest of flickering shadow-legs melting into the darkness of the tunnel ahead. His breathing came easier now. They'd made it. They'd escaped Reina. They were almost out of Westwend. And with no death. This was the end of all that, the end of killing, the end of fighting. The mages behind him were just the beginning. They were the seeds of the new world he would create where magic would not be feared. Where mages would be loved and respected.

He was so happy, so lost in this vision, that he didn't hear the shifting feet up ahead.

The mage next to Finn pulled up short, the mages behind plowing into her. Confused, Finn turned to see that the others were looking over her shoulders, past Finn. The rest of the group stopped, some started to back away. Finn whipped around, Ronan standing calmly at his side, to see a row of crossbows pointed at him.

"On your knees! All of you!"

No one got to their knees.

Finn's hands were shaking, so he balled them into fists and stepped forward. He got to his knees. "We don't want to fight. We just want to leave."

A man stepped out of the forest of crossbows, lowering his weapon.

"This is the Westwend guard. I am Captain Nathaniel Jenkins. We have information that a group of mages are planning an attack today. You are all, as of right now, under arrest."

"That's Reina Jeesh, she's behind us. We just want to leave. We don't want to hurt you or anyone." Finn could hear the group shifting angrily behind him. It wasn't true that none of them wanted to hurt anyone. He knew for a fact that Ronan wouldn't mind it. Isabelle wouldn't either.

The captain was looking at Finn closely. "Your name wouldn't happen to be Finn, would it?"

"No." His name wasn't going to be any help at all in avoiding violence.

"I ran into your sister, earlier."

Finn looked up, surprised. He couldn't read Nate's expression.

"She's all right. She escaped us."

Relief and gratitude washed through Finn.

Nate's men behind him said nothing, but their eyes were darting suspiciously from Nate to Finn.

"Get out of our way," a voice from behind Finn barked. Impatient muttering and shuffling broke out behind him.

Finn stood swiftly, turned to those behind him. "Quiet! We're not going to kill anyone." He turned back to Nate. "We just want to leave. Reina's the one you want. She's planning on taking over the city. She's not far behind us. The tunnel's blocked but it wouldn't take you long to dig through it. She's got about a hundred more mages with her."

"Hey, what are you doing, talking to that nothing?" someone said. "We signed up to leave, not to betray our kind. I've got friends back there!"

"Me, too, kid, what do you think you're playing at?"

"Get out of the—"

Fire roared up in a great wall between Finn and Nate. The mages around Finn, who had stepped forward aggressively, stumbled back, shielding their eyes from the blaze. "Stop!" Finn shouted, iron in his voice. "We are not going to fight. We are not going to hurt them if we don't have to."

"Why should we do what you say? Who do you think you are, telling us what to do?" The ground under Finn shook, a crack opened between his feet. Finn didn't move, straddled the crack.

"I'm in charge. I'm the leader here. And I am telling you that this is not how we do things anymore. This violence is just leading to more violence. And I'm the one who started it." The wall of fire raged behind him. Unbeknownst to Finn, the wall was filled with the images of those he had killed, screaming and dying. "We are going to get out of here. We are all going to live, and so are they."

Finn's eyes locked with those of another mage. The man looked angrily back at him for a moment, but then his eyes slid to the side, and his shoulders relaxed. Finn found another set of eyes looking mutinously at him, stared them down, too. One by one he made eye contact, daring anyone to challenge him. No one did. Finn didn't look at Ronan, but out of the corner of his eye he could see him, hands in pockets, a smile on his face.

Finn turned his back on them, dropped the wall of fire, found Nate waiting for him, meeting his eyes.

249

"We've hurt a lot of you," Finn said to Nate. "But also, you've killed some of us, forced us to stop using our powers."

Nate nodded an acknowledgement.

"We just want to leave. We're start—we have a school now. To train ourselves to use our powers well. We won't hurt you."

Finally, one of Nate's men couldn't hold himself back anymore.

"Captain, he's lying. We can't let them go!"

Another joined in. "They'll be back, Captain! If we let them go they'll come back later and slaughter us."

Nate held up a hand. "I have orders, Finn, to kill every mage I find here today."

Finn nodded. "I understand. I understand that."

"I know you wouldn't just let that happen. If we do fight, you'll fight back. We are more than you, and better trained, and despite your powers, our weapons are good. We'd win. You'd all be dead. But probably over half of us would be dead, too."

A voice behind Nate spoke up. "We're ready to die, Captain." Nate acknowledged this with a nod, but raised his silencing hand higher.

"You killed seventeen people, kid, including your parents."

"I know. I did. I'm so sorry. It was an accident."

"That's what your sister said, too."

That knowledge hit Finn like a rock to the chest. Kel knew it was an accident. Tears sprang to his eyes, and he swallowed hard around a thick spot in his throat. Nate watched his face closely.

"We're going to make a bargain, Finn."

"With what terms?"

"We're going to let you and your group pass." Angry

mutterings, both from the mages and the non-mages, followed this.

"You'll go start your school. But, in return, you're going to add some things to your curriculum."

"What?"

"Two things. First, a history lesson of all the atrocities committed by mages against non-mages. Including your own contributions."

"Of course," Finn said.

"Second, after your mages are trained, each one will spend a year traveling between villages, doing acts of service for non-mages, completely for free."

Finn could see the wisdom of this. It would do a lot to repair things. Still, he wasn't going to prostrate mages before non-mages. There was plenty of blame to go around, and both sides could stand to do some atoning.

"The mages will need food, and clothes, and places to stay."

"When they come to Westwend, they'll always have a place in my home. I'll give them whatever they need for as long as they are here. I'll also make it my business to find other homes for them in other cities. Just send them to me first."

"Are you sure you can promise that?"

"No. I may be killed today for letting you go."

"What do I do if you're killed?"

"I'll try to find someone else to keep up my end of the bargain. If I can't, the service requirement can be three months."

Finn turned back to the mages behind him, raised the wall of flame again.

"Raise your hand if you still want to fight these men." Only a few hands went up. "Raise your hand if you can agree to his terms." A slight majority of hands went up.

Finn dropped the wall and turned back to Nate. "We accept your terms."

Nate nodded. "Good. I have no way of forcing you to keep your end of the bargain, but I believe you that you'll see it through. I think you understand what's at stake, and what might happen if you don't make these efforts to repair things between mages and non-mages."

Finn nodded, too. "I understand."

Nate turned to his men. "This is my decision. I will accept the responsibility for this. If you want to run back and warn Arcturus to save yourself from his retribution you may do so now." He waited, but no one left. Nate nodded. Then he stepped aside. His men copied him, lining the walls, making a narrow space in the middle.

Finn stepped forward, into the gauntlet, between the lowered crossbows. He could feel the dislike coming off the guards in waves, knew that it was only loyalty to Nate that kept them from attacking him. When he'd made it to the other side, he turned back, watched as the other mages began to follow him down the tunnel.

THE LAST OF THE MAGES, an old man riding an ancient horse, passed in front of Nate. He winked as he went by, which made Nate uncomfortable because he didn't know what he was winking about. Sometimes old men just did that, though. Nate watched the old man until he turned a corner, and then all that was left of the mages was the echoing of footsteps, fading down the tunnel. Nate's men were watching the mages go, too; one by one they turned back to their captain.

There was a long silence, then Briggs, his second-in-command, spoke up. "Don't know why we're standing around here, Captain. We're supposed to be looking for mages."

The men digested these words.

"Yeah," another said. "There are supposed to be mages around here somewhere, and we haven't found any so far."

"Not getting paid to stand around by ourselves in a tunnel, that's for sure."

Nate smiled, but there was worry in his face. He put a hand on Briggs' shoulder and looked around at the group. "This was my decision, so if you're asked a direct question later, don't lie for me, okay? You look out for yourselves."

"With all due respect, Captain," Briggs said, meeting his eye, "We'll lie about whatever we feel like."

"We're all behind you, Captain."

Nate gave a quick nod of gratitude, embarrassed by the prickling in his eyes. He turned away before they could see.

"All right, let's get on with this, then," Nate said roughly, leading the way.

CHAPTER 19

Finn couldn't quite believe what he'd just done. He'd talked their way past a group of armed soldiers with orders to kill them. Not one person on either side was hurt. His furious hope was quickly solidifying into a sense of real confidence, like this might actually work.

They followed the tunnel along until it took a sharp downwards turn. Ronan placed a hand on the wall, closed his eyes, and, with a rumble that made Isabelle cross her arms over her chest, a side tunnel opened. Afternoon sunlight slanted through it, momentarily blinding them. Rubbing their eyes, they came out onto a narrow ledge on the cliff face. Below them the river rushed through its steep-banked channel.

Ronan made steps leading down to the water's edge, then turned to look at Finn. "Well, fearless leader, what next?"

Finn looked at Eraldir. The old man pushed back one of his sleeves and held his hand out flat, fingers spread.

"Sure thing, boy. Now, diverting or freezing? Freezing is easier, and the ice just floats on top, but it could break, or sometimes it melts partway through, and of course that one time it froze the guy walking across it. Harold was fine eventually; we got him thawed back out. Said it was good for his arthritis, too. Bit of a hassle, though. No, I think diverting this time. Although, there was the time it broke through the barrier and washed away the whole caravan of minstrels..." Eraldir sighed. "I was really looking forward to their performance, too. The townspeople weren't so pleased either. They were a meticulous, hardworking people. I've never seen sharper pitchforks."

"Um, Eraldir?" Finn said.

"Huh?" Eraldir looked up. "Oh, right. Well, let's get going. Everybody stay with me; I'll just divert part of the river at a time." Eraldir clawed and heaved himself back up on Sylvia and waded a few feet into the river. With one liver-spotted hand he gripped the reins; the other he held up over the water again. The surface of the water began to undulate, then all at once the river sprang away from him, leaving a rocky, muddy bottom, surrounded by a roiling wall of water. Eraldir advanced a little further into the water; Sylvia's hooves sank into mud and scrabbled against the wet, slimy rocks.

"Follow me, everyone. This way, this way."

The mages clustered into the small space around Eraldir, a few holding on to Sylvia. Someone grabbed her tail and she made a half-hearted attempt to kick them. They backed off.

Isabelle stepped up to the wall of water, stuck her arm into it, and was immediately knocked sideways by the strength of the current. She started to fall into the wall, where the water was shooting past, instinctively her other hand came up to brace herself, but it just plunged into the water too. She was sliding inexorably into the wall of water, only seconds from being swept away by the current, when Finn grabbed a fistful of her shirt and yanked her back. She fell to the ground, but quickly picked herself back up, wiping her muddy hands on her pants.

Finn was breathing heavily, imagining what had almost happened, seeing Isabelle swept away, dashed against rocks and, minutes later, shooting over the edge of the waterfall, her body breaking against the rocks at the bottom.

"Whoa, strong current!" Isabelle said, grinning at him. She saw how pale he was and punched him on the arm. Then she started to stick her hand back in, more slowly this time, just a finger at a time, but Finn grabbed her arm and pulled it back.

"Isabelle!"

"What?" She lifted her eyebrows.

"Didn't you notice that you just almost died by doing that?"

She laughed. "I probably wouldn't have died. Cool water wall, huh?"

Finn groaned.

"If you fall in again I'm going to let you die so you learn your lesson."

"No, you won't." She smiled.

Finn knew she was right.

Finn looked away, and saw Ronan watching them. Ronan thrust his hands in his pockets and looked away.

The wall started to move. "This way, this way. Keep up, everyone," Eraldir said.

The group pressed together, stumbling along in the small space Eraldir had created. The water closed in around them, rising above their heads on all sides. Their clothes were soaked with spray, and the sound was deafening as the current thundered around them. If Eraldir was giving further instructions, no one could hear.

Shadowy shapes shot by in the dark green, frothy water. A large trout popped out of the wall, fell to the ground, flopping. Thinking of Kel, Finn picked it up, feeling its cold, slimy scales, and tossed it back into the river.

Eraldir continued forward, the mages slipping and crawling along after him, staying as far as they could from the walls. The wall receded in front of them, uncovering a large, shiny black crab. The crab had been scuttling along when the water suddenly disappeared around it. It froze for a moment, then cautiously made itself smaller, crouching down among the rocks next to it and lifting its claws. Slowly, it began to edge sideways. The mages stopped to watch its progress, wary of its pincers. It edged its way over to the wall of water, stuck a few legs in, and then was immediately swept away by the powerful current. The mages continued.

The bank they came to was another steep rock wall, although much shorter than the cliff they had descended from Westwend.

"All right, famous earth mage, your turn," Eraldir said.

Rocky stairs pushed their way out of the cliff face and, relieved, the mages scrambled up and out of the way of the water. Eraldir dismounted Sylvia, and led her up the steps, the water closing back up behind them.

They came over the edge of the cliff and pushed their way into the dense forest that leaned over the edge. Finn asked if there was a naturalist mage who could move the plants back to make a space for them, but they only stared at him, surprised that he would expect them to be able to do that.

So, they crashed through the forest, thorns tearing at their clothing, until they came to a clearing.

Back in Reina's stronghold, Finn had told the mages that he would wait for them in the forest in case they were late, but, having already been chased by one small army into the arms of another small army, Finn wanted to get as far away from Westwend as they could, as quickly as possible. He considered trying to leave a message for the mages, but that could just as easily be found by the guards.

"Eraldir, is there any way we could leave a message that could only be found by mages?"

Eraldir was sitting on the ground, leaning heavily against a tree, grimacing and massaging his chest with one hand.

"Oh, sure, boy. You can always tell regular fire from magical, right?"

Finn hadn't thought about that before, but it was true. Reina's fire had a different quality to it, had a bit of her personality in it. He wondered what his fire felt like to other fire mages.

"It's the same with me, I can always tell water that's been put there by a water mage. I've heard it's the same with the rest of the types, too." He took a long deep breath, and sighed it out.

"Perfect," Finn said. He raised his voice to the group. "I need a wind mage, an earth mage, a..." he trailed off, then turned back to Eraldir. "Um, what types are there?"

"What? I've never told you? That's easy, boy. I thought everyone knew that."

"I mean, there's fire, and earth, naturalist and water, and wind. Is that it?"

"There's thread, too," Eraldir said.

Right. Of course. Like Ronan's mom.

"Thread?" A voice from the back interjected. "That's it? Earth, wind, fire, water, naturalist ... and thread?"

"Yep. Those are the types, far as anyone knows."

"But... thread? That seems random."

Someone else snickered.

"Hey!" Another mage said. "My brother is a thread mage. It's a... it's very useful."

"Oh, I'm sure, I'm sure. Comes in real handy for tying things together," someone else said.

"It's not just that, he can like... make ropes longer and stuff."

"Yeah, totally, I mean, that sounds really useful." The mage snickered again. A couple others giggled, too.

"Um..." Finn wanted to ask Eraldir to explain, but there wasn't time, so he let it go. He turned to the rest of the group. "Okay, so, I need a naturalist mage, and you, Eraldir, Ronan, and Isabelle, and a thread mage. Are there any here?" A few people raised their hands, and Finn picked one of each, avoiding the people who'd laughed at the thread mages. He brought them to one side of the clearing, away from the main group.

"Okay, here's what we're going to do. Each of you make something, something that will last. Make sure it's big enough to stand out."

Finn watched as Ronan made an enormous stone statue of his mother. Isabelle made a swirling current of air that tipped you upside down, held you for a second, and then dropped you on your head if you walked into it. The thread mage pulled colored threads out of her pocket, elongated them, and wove them into a tapestry, which she affixed to a large stone. Finn placed a small flame on top of this stone. Eraldir conjured a pool of water with a geyser in the center that jetted up and tumbled back down. The naturalist mage planted a seed and ever so slowly coaxed a peace lily out of the ground. A single bud formed and blossomed into a pale white flower.

In the center of these six works, Finn had Ronan create a large stone arrow, pointing in the direction they would go.

"As we go," Finn said, "It's your job to leave little markers. They should be indistinguishable from natural objects in the future." He wasn't totally sure how he would do that with fire, there weren't a lot of natural fires just hanging around, but he'd figure that out later. "That way, any mages left behind can follow us." Of course, that would mean Reina could follow them, too. He did just steal part of her army, including the integral part of her plan—Ronan—but... still, that wasn't enough of a reason to give up on her plans. Hopefully. Not to mention, he realized, she already knew where they were headed.

THE MAGES SPENT the rest of the afternoon walking, trailing along behind Eraldir as he ambled his way through the forest. They stayed away from the main roads, in case Arcturus or Reina had decided to follow them after all, but this made it slow-going, fighting their way through brush and detouring around small, rocky cliffs.

For the most part, the group was quiet, focused on making their way as quickly as they could, uncertain what exactly they were doing, where exactly they were going. Even though Westwend had been terrible, at least it had been familiar.

Every so often, Finn placed a small, clear, cold flame in an empty bottle and wedged it the crook of a tree. It would be invisible unless you were a fire mage and knew what you were looking for. Even then you might miss it. When he ran out of bottles he settled for bare patches of rock, making his fires tiny and flickering so that hopefully they wouldn't start forest fires.

He made sure the others were making small markers, too, and imagined future mages, maybe even hundreds of years from now, following the path to the school they were going to build.

It was early evening when they came to a wide river, too wide to cross easily without magic. It bent sharply here, curling around a bare, rocky outcrop. Eraldir stopped Sylvia and slid off into the unprepared arms of several nearby mages.

"Well, this seems like a good place to stop for the night," he said, pulling his tea mug and a packet of herbs out of his pack. "Campfire, Finn?"

Finn nodded, and addressed the group. "If you're tired, you can rest, but if you've got extra energy, you can help me gather wood for campfires."

Finding wood was something the naturalist mages could do easily. Within a few minutes, they had amassed an enormous heap of dry branches, pinecones, and moss. Because there were so many people, Finn started six different fires, although he immediately regretted this decision because the mages split up by type, the five wind mages sitting together, the seven water mages together, and the two thread mages off by themselves with the smallest fire. He'd have to do something to keep them from separating too much. It would be just great if in the process of trying to reunite mages with non-mages he only succeeded in dividing mages up into even smaller subgroups. But tonight, he was too tired to do anything about it.

Gathering an armload of wood for himself, Finn walked to the edge of the camp, where the rock met the water, and lit another fire. He made himself comfortable in front of it, crossing his legs underneath him and placing his hands on his knees, then he closed his eyes.

Taking a deep breath, he felt the pressure that had gathered in his chest. There wasn't anything magical about this pressure; it was the pressure of responsibility. Suddenly there were almost thirty mages depending on him to lead them to safety, to build them a school, to make the world safe for them. He took a deep breath. He was up to it. He was going to do this, but that meant he would have to be a lot better himself. However hard they worked, he would work twice as hard.

Sometime later, he was startled from his meditation by someone sitting down across from him at the fire.

"You did well today," Eraldir said, taking a sip of his tea and smacking his lips. "Talked us out of a tight spot, there."

"Thanks."

Isabelle swept over and sat down, pulled a cake out of her pocket, and stuffed it into her mouth.

"You know, Isabelle, those cakes aren't going to make flying any easier," Eraldir warned.

"Dammit Eraldir, you can't say stuff like that to people," Isabelle said, lifting her chin. "What I choose to eat is my business. I don't complain about that horrible tea you drink. Well, I do, but I don't tell you not to drink it. Or warn you that it'll make you a cranky old man who thinks he knows what's best for other people."

"That tea keeps me alive," Eraldir growled.

"Well, so does this," Isabelle said, cramming another whole pastry into her mouth at once. She chewed for a second. "Technically, anyway." She said this around the mouthful, spraying crumbs. "Mmmm…" She closed her eyes and chewed happily.

"You must have been enormous as a child," Eraldir muttered, but too quietly for Isabelle to hear.

When Isabelle had finished chewing she pulled something out of her pack. It was a bottle of Reina's wine. She uncorked it and took a swig.

"Want some?" She offered it to Finn. "It's not bad."

Finn smiled and pulled out his own bottle. She laughed and lifted hers in a small salute. "Cheers."

"Well, if you're both having wine I guess I may as well." Eraldir pulled out a bottle of Reina's wine, too. They all laughed.

"So, that's what you were hiding under your shirt earlier?" Finn asked Isabelle.

"Part of it." She reached into her pack again and pulled something else out.

It was large, glass jar, with some familiar occupants.

"Are those Reina's fish?" Finn asked, horrified.

Isabelle grinned. "Yep!" She tapped gently on the glass. "Hello, Reginald, hello Ambrose. You guys want some pastry?"

"What are you going to do with them? And, don't feed them pastry, Isabelle, they definitely don't eat pastry."

"I haven't decided yet," Isabelle said, as Reginald tried to attack her finger through the glass. "Mostly I just wanted to take them because she was so possessive of everything. Also, she called me unoriginal. Maybe I'll eat them, get the strength of a thousand goldfish."

Eraldir raised his eyebrows, but took a long sip of his wine, and said nothing.

Finn watched the two orange fish with their enormous eyes and their terrible, tortured pasts. "Haven't they suffered enough?"

"Yeah, you're right," Isabelle said. She stood, pulling the stopper out as she did so and walking over to the edge of the water. Unceremoniously, she tipped the contents into the river.

"Well, that little bit of river's going to be a terrifying place for its previous inhabitants now," Eraldir said. Isabelle laughed.

KEL AWOKE from another strange dream with the last orange rays of sun slanting across the treetops into her eyes. All that was left of the dream was a feeling of wildness, and the smell of moss, damp and loamy. She sat solemnly, her legs wrapped tightly around the branch below her, and watched the sun go down, wondering, in the back of her mind, where Finn was, whether he was all right.

The wind picked up as the sky darkened into evening, and Kel huddled against the trunk for warmth. She considered climbing down to look for shelter, but another part of her was so shaken by what had happened that she didn't want to leave yet. She wanted to stay here, far above everything else, where she felt safe.

After a while she got up the courage to inspect the wound in her leg, but, to her surprise, she found only a large brown mark, like a birthmark only she'd never seen it before. Kel ran her finger across it; the skin felt cold there, hard, like a callous, but also smooth. It reminded her of something in her dream, but she couldn't remember what.

Kel considered just staying up in this tree forever. The crows wouldn't bother her anymore. She could grow plants for food, if there was enough rain. She'd get used to the wind, and no one would bother her. Not her brother, not the guards, and not the man in black. Maybe Smoke would even come to find her here.

But there was a feeling she had from the dream, like someone was looking for her, or trying to tell her something important. She had the sense that the place in her dream was an actual real place, somewhere nearby, and she wanted to find it.

She'd stay here just a little longer, she decided, to finish repairing the damage she'd done to the plants, but then she'd leave. She'd find Smoke, and then together they'd look for the path through the birch trees.

Stars came out, sneaking into the pale violet sky when she wasn't looking. Kel wrapped her arms tightly around herself and just sat, watching the light leave, replaced by the vaulted, infinite blackness strewn with stars. The tree swayed and leaned underneath her, occasionally leaning so far as to make Kel nervous, but this tree, she knew, had been here hundreds of years, lasting through winds much stronger than this.

Slowly, listening to the hum of the forest below her and the whoosh of the wind across the treetops, Kel fell back asleep.

~

FOR THE FIFTH time that morning, Finn had to light himself on fire. He didn't actually burn himself, he just needed enough heat to dry his hair and clothes from the tiny rainstorm that had passed over him.

Annoyed, Finn ran his hands through his still damp hair, trying to put it in some kind of order. A shriek of laughter came from behind him, and he turned to see a young wind mage sprinting past, pursued by a small geyser jetting from a water mage. Behind them, a large rain cloud was dumping water on a cluster of earth and thread mages, following them around wherever they went. The rain cascaded down in sheets, muddying the ground and sizzling where it landed on the flaming head of a fire mage. The girl had apparently lit her own hair on fire to keep herself dry. She saw him looking at her, grinned, and waved. Finn sighed.

Eraldir was the only person who was completely dry. He plodded along with Sylvia, totally unperturbed.

"How are you doing that, Eraldir?" Finn asked.

"Respect, boy."

A wind mage jogging past said cheerfully, "He threatened to drown us," and continued. Finn raised his eyebrows. Eraldir shrugged.

"Like I said. Respect."

At least all this didn't seem to be slowing them down at all. They were still making progress, following the river.

The woman with the grizzled hair came up, pushing her way between Eraldir and Finn.

"Finn, that's your name, right? You're in charge here?"

"Er, yes. That's right," Finn said.

"Well, I want to know why you're letting these idiots," she ducked as a jet of flame shot over their heads, "why you're letting these idiots just run wild. What kind of school is this, anyway? I've been lit on fire three times already, and completely drenched four times."

Finn wanted to point out that at least those two things balanced each other out, but he didn't think she'd appreciate that. Also, he really didn't want to answer her question about what kind of school this was. He hadn't totally figured that out yet. "Er, sorry, but they've been—"

"How much farther is it, anyway?" She squinted up at him.

"Not too far..."

Eraldir met Finn's eye and gave a small shake of his head.

"But, still pretty far... a few..." Eraldir held up three fingers. "Three da—" Eraldir shook his head. "—mon—" Eraldir shook his head again. "Weeks. Three weeks." Eraldir rolled his eyes.

The woman narrowed her eyes and turned to look back over her shoulder at Eraldir, who immediately became very interested in watching the mages on the other side of the camp hurling fire at one another. She turned back to Finn.

"When are we going to start classes? Will we have our own rooms once we get there? What are we going to do for food?"

Finn took a deep breath and put a hand on her shoulder. "What was your name again?"

"Marta."

"Marta. All great questions. Don't worry. Everything's taken care of. We'll be starting classes tonight. Things will calm down; they just need to blow off some steam."

"Blow off—" she started angrily, but he cut her off.

"Here, have a bottle of wine." He pulled one out of his pack and thrust it into her hands. She stared at it, confused, but thrown off track from the angry rant she'd been building up to. Finn wasn't sure what he was going to say next. He'd successfully distracted her, but he didn't think it was going to last. She looked like she was already formulating more reasonable, logical questions that he wouldn't have answers for. Luckily, right at that moment, an enormous bowling ball of a man came hurtling through the air, over the tree-tops, into the middle of their camp.

He was screaming as he sailed through the air, more of a surprised scream than one of fear, and before he hit the ground he somehow managed to slow himself down and turn himself right side up. He landed gracefully in the middle of the camp. Everyone stopped what they were doing and turned to stare. It was Noe.

A bloodcurdling scream followed this, and another figure came hurtling through the air, following the same arc Noe had. She was smaller, a streak of pale yellow, spewing water everywhere. The droplets separated into a fine mist, casting hundreds of tiny rainbows behind her.

Noe turned, lifted his hands towards her, and she slowed, landing gently in his arms. It was Jes, and she was screaming and crying. When she noticed the crowd of people watching her, though, she choked up, wiping her face and looking around, confused.

"You've been following my trail," Isabelle said happily into the silence that had fallen.

That was when Finn realized he really shouldn't have put Isabelle in charge of the wind path.

"Isabelle," he said quietly, coming up to join her. "Did you make a trail marker that catapults people a hundred feet in the air?"

"Yep! Good plan, right? I mean, if they're wind mages they'll be fine. Plus, I don't have to add a direction arrow. Saves them some walking, too, right?"

Just then a squirrel came shooting through the sky. Noe lifted a hand and caught it, too. The animal clawed and bit him and then shot away in a panic.

"Huh," Isabelle said.

"How about you go make it a little smaller… like ten feet maybe? So, if animals, or people who are not wind mages, fall into it they're not going to be shot off to their deaths?"

She shrugged. "Yeah, sure, I guess." She wandered off, back in the direction they'd come.

Finn approached the two newcomers. "Noe, where have you been?"

Noe waved a hand at Jes. "Couldn' leave her there for Reina t' torture."

Jes wiped a tear away from the corner of her eye and sniffed. Finn pursed his lips.

"Okay…" He wanted to trust Noe, but he didn't trust Jes. "Noe, get yourself settled. Jes, come with me." He turned to the group. "Everyone, we're taking a short break. During the break, Eraldir is going to give you your first lesson." He looked at Eraldir, who nodded.

Noe looked like he wanted to argue, so Finn stepped forward, gripped Jes by the elbow, and led her off before Noe could say anything.

"All right, Jes," Finn said when they were alone. He looked her hard in her eyes, which were deep, dark blue, and damp from crying. "Tell me why you were locked up."

She swallowed, but met his eyes. "I was betraying Reina." She looked down, her long, dark lashes hiding her gaze.

"Why?"

She looked away, staring at something for a moment, Finn followed her gaze. She was looking at Ronan. Immediately, she turned back, batted her lashes once at him. "I—I didn't want her to go through with her plan. She was going to kill so many people. She's already killed so many people." She swallowed. "She's my friend, but I had to stop her."

So much of this seemed like a performance to Finn, but... well, it was working. He had no trouble at all believing that someone would want to stop Reina's plans, and that they wouldn't consider talking to her about it to be an option. He did have trouble believing that someone would think of Reina as a friend, but he'd come back to that.

"So... you went to Arcturus?"

She ran a hand through her hair, then dropped it dismissively. "All I knew about him was that he was in charge of the Magical Safety Commission. I'd never actually met him." She shuddered.

"You knew he'd been having mages killed, though, right?"

She nodded.

"You didn't think that he'd have you killed?"

She straightened her shoulders. "I thought he might, but either way he'd be able to stop Reina killing all those non-mages. My parents were non-mages. Most of my..." she choked on a sob... "my friends are non-mages. I was just a cook before I met Reina."

"Didn't you ever try to dissuade her?"

She just looked at him skeptically.

"Okay, right. Right. But, you're... friends?"

She adjusted her ponytail again. "Yes."

He paused, trying to think of the words. All he got out was, "How?"

"I saved her life."

"What?"

"I found her in the woods five years ago. She was dying. She'd been tortured, and there was something...sick...about her magic. It was flaring in and out." Her eyes unfocused as she remembered. "She was covered in blood—hers I think— and burns. Her left leg was broken in several places. I brought her home with me. I was fifteen then."

Part of Finn wished she hadn't, but then he felt bad for thinking that. Even if it was Reina.

"Okay, so you saved her life. Why are you here?"

"Noe rescued me."

"I figured that. I mean, why are you here with us?"

She bit her lip. "I just didn't know where else to go. I can't go back to Westwend."

"How do I know you're not a spy for Arcturus?"

"I don't know. I'm not."

Finn turned away to think. He didn't have any reason to trust her. He was responsible for the safety of the whole group of mages, now, and, if he took a chance on her, he was taking a chance with all their lives. He could send her away, or he could tie her up and keep her as a prisoner, but how long would he have to do that for? If he did that forever he'd never know if he could trust her. Also, she was pretty, and that made it slightly harder to think.

"All right," he said. "You can stay."

She smiled a watery smile. "Oh, thank you, thank you so much." She kissed him on the cheek.

His skin warmed in a blush, but under his embarrassment and the small part of him that felt happy to help her was a strong sense of unease.

When Finn and Jes returned to camp, the place was completely silent. The mages sat in neat rows, with their legs crossed and their eyes closed. In front of all of them, Eraldir lay on his bedroll, napping.

He woke up when Finn tapped him lightly on the shoulder.

"This teaching thing is great, boy," he said, yawning.

Finn decided to wait and let the mages finish their first meditation. It was a relief to have some quiet, and he took the opportunity to reorganize his pack and rinse out some of his clothes in the river. He was just wringing his shirt dry when Isabelle came catapulting up to him in a gust of wind.

"And I'm back. What's up?" She punched him on the shoulder.

"Hey," he smiled at her, but he worried what she'd think about his letting Jes stay. "Nothing—um...did you get rid of the thing?"

She rolled her eyes. "Yes, Mom. I did."

"Okay, good." There was a pause.

"So, you sent Jes back?" Isabelle asked.

Well, she was going to ask eventually. "Not exactly..."

"What do you mean, not exactly?"

"I mean...I'm letting her stay."

"What?"

"She doesn't have anywhere to go."

"Uh...if a Baharran assassin had nowhere else to go would you let them stay, too?"

"I mean... if they weren't going to assassinate anyone..."

"They're an assassin! It's what they do!"

"Yeah. Look. I know. I don't trust her either."

Isabelle threw up her hands in exasperation. "Then don't let her stay!"

Finn ran a hand through his hair, looking away.

Isabelle continued, her rant gaining steam. "How come all of a sudden, you're in charge now, anyway? Eraldir and I found you. We asked you to join us. Not the other way around. If anyone's in charge it's Eraldir. And if he's not in charge then I am."

"Do you want to be in charge?"

"No."

"Why not?"

"I don't want to be a babysitter for a bunch of… babies… who know nothing about their powers."

"Well, I do."

Isabelle threw up her hands, turned, and stormed off.

Finn watched her go, wanting to follow, but knowing it was pointless. Isabelle was probably right, anyway. Letting Jes stay was a mistake. But Finn didn't care. Enough people had died. If there was even a chance that he could save someone, he would.

Over Isabelle's shoulder, he saw the mages getting up from their class, Ronan on the side farthest from him. As he watched, Ronan held out his hand, and something shot up out of the ground into his palm. It glittered as Ronan contemplated it, then he tucked it into his bag.

Apparently, Finn wasn't the only one watching, because a few seconds later Jes approached Ronan, her shoulders bent and her hands tugging nervously at her skirt. Finn was too far away to hear what she said to him, but after only a few seconds Ronan turned away angrily. Jes tried a few more times, and then left, wiping her eyes with the back of her hand.

CHAPTER 20

*R*eina, stalking along with her search party, was furious. Ronan was gone, Jes was gone, and Eraldir and his idiot apprentices were gone, too. They'd taken with them about thirty of her mages, which was enough to make a sizeable dent in her forces. Could she still defeat Arcturus' army? She wasn't sure. What she was sure of was that they'd lost the trail of the escaped mages. Ronan was too good at hiding tunnels. She'd never find them. But, luckily, she didn't have to. She knew where they were going.

Resigned, she halted their progress and brought them back to the hideout. There, they found one of the doors had been welded shut, and a group of mages trapped inside. Once they were freed, they told the story of Finn trying to convince them to leave, and, in front of everyone, Reina presented them each with a bag of gold and a bottle of wine, to reward their loyalty. Clearly, she'd been lax on that front. Well, no more.

Reina sat and thought about what to do. She was in a tricky position. Her forces were compromised, and, at the same moment, she had a whole extra group of people to get revenge on. How could she turn this to her advantage? Because, while she had more enemies now, her enemies also had more enemies. As much as it disappointed her, now was not the time for brute force. No. Now was the time for subterfuge. She sat thinking and planning, until she heard boots marching through the tunnels towards them.

IT TOOK Nate and his men a long time to dig through the wall Ronan had made to seal off and hide the escape tunnel. Once through, they took their time advancing through the tunnels, checking side paths and exploring every branch, to avoid being cut off or surrounded. Nate wasn't going to risk his men's lives any more than he had to.

Eventually, the tunnel widened, the floor becoming smoother and more well-trodden. Nate took the lead, his sword drawn.

Up ahead, a light flickered.

Nate waved for his men to stop. They flattened against the walls, crouching down to avoid being seen. His archers in the back aimed their bows. Slowly they advanced.

A large, iron door stood in their way, closed.

Once his men were in position, Nate gripped the handle and slowly eased the behemoth open. The hinges caught and shrieked as he pulled, and Nate cringed. He ducked back, hiding behind the open door, out of eyesight of anyone looking through the opening. His men waited, swords gleaming in the light, bowstrings tight.

Nothing happened.

Slowly, very slowly, Nate flattened himself to the ground, and peeked his head around the edge of the door.

Inside was a large, empty room, full of boxes and scattered with weaponry. There was no one inside. The tension in Nate's body turned to confusion, and a sick sense that he'd missed something.

~

ARCTURUS FLAVIUS HAD RETIRED to his rooms for the evening. The day had been a disappointment. Luckily, it was one of his mother's days of poor health and so he would not be forced to visit her and recount his failings.

Nothing. They had found nothing in the tunnels. Not a single mage. Something was not quite right about the whole situation, and Arcturus suspected it had something to do with Nate...the up-until-now completely trustworthy Captain Nate. The man who had always been completely honest—to an annoying level even—about everything. That man was now hiding something from Arcturus.

Arcturus sat down at his redwood desk. He pulled out a thick, leather-bound volume, and opened it to an empty page. He sat there, with pen inked but mind empty, for a long while before giving up with a sigh. No, today was not a day to work on his history of Westwend. He put the book away and pulled out an old history of Montvale and retired to his reading chair. His stomach was bothering him; he might have to call down to the kitchens for some tea later.

"Nice place you've got here," a harsh voice cut through the padded silence of his rooms.

Arcturus glanced up, moving slowly to hide his fear and surprise.

"Reina Jeesh," he said. "How pleasant to have a visitor. Would you care for some wine?"

"No, Arcturus, I'm not interested in drinking any of your poisoned wine."

"It's not poisoned."

"Well, it should be. I poison mine."

"How... suspicious...of you."

"So, how did your raids go today?" she asked, her lips curled in a thin, contemptuous smile.

"How did your coup go today?" he countered calmly.

She raised a hand, and the candle next to Arcturus went out. The room was pitch black for a few seconds, and then the sconces around the walls flared to life. Arcturus kept his face expressionless, but inside he boiled with rage and fear. And jealousy. He would love to take Reina apart, to see how she worked. She might be tough enough to remain conscious long enough for him to learn something.

"I have a proposition for you," she said.

"Oh?"

"I know where Finn Vogt is. I know where he is going. He's traveling with Eraldir."

Eraldir. The last mage from before. And Finn, whose murders had set off the wave of fear and hatred Arcturus had been capitalizing on.

"That's interesting," he said, feigning boredom.

"They're organizing the mages. They're starting a school. It's just one step from there to building a mage government. How long do you think Westwend will still be yours if the mages come back to power?"

Arcturus knew his history. He knew that it was only the Fall that had brought about the end of the reign of mages. Only in the last hundred years had non-mages had any power at all. If they really were rebuilding a school, a center of power, it would only be a matter of time before Arcturus and his little empire in Westwend were no more. Before everything was, once again, run by mages. Disgust and fury swelled in him. A world run by people to whom everything came easily, who never had to worry about where their next meal came from, who never had to work a day in their lives.

It had taken him years to build his empire here, starting

business after business, scraping and saving, and it would all be gone. Taken from him by people who deserved nothing of what they had.

"And what, exactly, are you proposing?"

~

THE NEXT MORNING, Eraldir led the group in a few short practice exercises, and then they were on their way. At lunch, Finn sat by himself, watching the others. The wind mages sat with the wind mages, the two thread mages sat off to the side, together and away from the main group, and Jes sat by herself. Finn felt bad for her, but he wasn't going to take the chance of Isabelle coming over and seeing him sitting with her.

Of the two problems—the lack of mage unity and Isabelle being mad at him—there was only one he could currently address, so he might as well deal with that one. Finn stood and lifted his voice so he could be heard around the clearing.

"This afternoon we'll be doing a new exercise," he said. "I'm breaking you into four teams. First prize is the other teams set up your camp and make your dinner. Also, the winners get some of Reina's wine." He held up a bottle, and there were some chuckles.

"Here!" A wind mage said, holding up a familiar-looking bottle. "I'll contribute to the prize."

"Me, too!" A fire mage held up another bottle of Reina's wine.

Finn cracked a smile. "How many of you stole some of Reina's wine?"

About half the hands went up.

"Well, if you want, each team can contribute a bottle or two to the prize," Finn said.

"What's the challenge?" Ronan said, taking a large bite of bread.

Finn had stood before thinking this through. He should really stop putting himself in these positions.

"Er, the challenge… is…"

"What?"

He wanted the thread mages to be valuable. What was thread useful for? Nets? Swinging? Rope bridges?

"Okay… you see that tree there?" Finn pointed to a towering fir tree. "Each team must get every one of their team members up that tree, then, without touching the ground, everybody has to get all the way to that tree," he pointed to another fir about a hundred feet away. "You'll have one hour to make your plans, then you'll get your plans approved by me. Then we'll run the trials. Deviating from your plan will lose you points. Not using all six types of magic will lose you points. You also get points for speed and for style."

"Style? That's totally subjective," someone said.

"Also, how are earth mages supposed to be useful if no one's allowed to touch the ground?" Marta said. "This seems biased towards wind mages."

"Just having a wind mage levitate everyone across—and I think the only one who's even maybe capable of that is Noe —" Noe blushed, and took a bite of the extravagant sandwich he was eating. It looked like he'd scavenged mushrooms and wild onions for it. "Just doing that loses you points because you wouldn't be using all the types of magic."

"I feel like this point system is pretty vague," a wind mage said.

"Okay, fine," Finn said, starting to get annoyed. "Ten points for each different, necessary use of magic. Five points for every different way you use magic that makes things prettier. Fifty points for getting all your team members

278

across. Fifty points for using each type of magic your team has. Minus twenty points for every time one of your team members touches the ground."

"Even if we start over?"

"Even if you start over."

Finn broke them up into four teams of seven, dividing the types of mages as evenly as he could, and separating up the most powerful. There were only two thread mages; he put one on Rafe's team and one on Noe's. Isabelle returned from a tree-climbing expedition in the middle of this, but refused to take part.

When they stood, grouped around him and ready to begin, Finn had another idea. "And, er, you also get ten points for having a team name. And five points if you make some sort of uniform."

Eraldir, sitting off to the side on a log and drinking tea, chuckled.

"You have one hour. Go."

The mages sprinted off, all except Ronan, who ambled after his team, still chewing on a loaf of bread, and Finn went to sit with Eraldir.

"Trying to build some unity, eh? Not a bad idea. Where'd the team name stuff come from?"

Finn shrugged. "I don't know, sometimes the…the kids in my village would play games and they'd wear uniforms and… they always seemed like they were having fun and getting along."

A small explosion issued from one corner of the glade where the teams were preparing. Finn winced. He really hoped no one died from this.

~

"I'M sure you understand why you must come as my prisoner," Arcturus said.

"Because you're too scared of me when I'm not in a cage," Reina replied.

"I know you understand, so I'm not going to bother correcting that."

They stood outside the main gates of Westwend, Reina bound in iron shackles, sitting in an iron cage next to Arcturus, who was resplendent in black and silver. His tiny sapphire coat buttons glinted in the morning sunlight.

As soon as he figured out where they were headed he would kill her, of course. But she must be expecting that. The fact that her whole army was missing was also troubling. It was likely that she was leading him into a trap, giving herself up in order to feed him lies and lull him into a false sense of security before decimating his army. Yes, that was obvious, and it was the reason Arcturus had split his army into three. He kept the largest part of it in Reina's line of sight, hoping to convince her he had kept all his troops in one group, just in case she was getting messages out to her own troops.

He planned to keep Reina close, wait until she slipped up; he would like to know the location of the new mage school—if it existed—so he could destroy it, but his primary purpose was to destroy Reina and her army.

She had even possibly lied about the mage school. But, if she had, it was likely that Finn and Eraldir were with her army. Even if all she was doing was leading him into a trap it was still exactly what Arcturus wanted. He wanted to fight her army and destroy it. This way, he already had her army's general in a cage. It was an easy decision.

"I can still burn you to a crisp whenever I want, Flavius."

"Yes, I am aware of that. Hence the men with the metal spears who will poke you if you do, and the ample buckets of water everywhere."

Small flames licked up Arcturus' shoes. He stepped aside, and they went out. Reina smiled.

"Bring me my wine," she said.

IT WAS SO HANDY, getting other people to do your revenging for you, Reina thought. She wasn't afraid of the men with the spears—two of them were her mages, anyway. She rankled at being in a cage, though. It reminded her of… difficult times… but she'd already had her revenge for those things. She didn't need to think about them anymore. Still, even the appearance of being powerless made her want to torch something. But, if she just waited, she could store all that rage up and use it on Arcturus. In the meantime, she'd use one of her enemies to destroy the other, and then finish off whichever one survived. Just like goldfish.

THE FIRST TEAM TO go immediately burned down the starting tree. Finn wasn't sure how to score that. He went with minus one hundred twenty points because all seven team members touched the ground, but they did use fire, although he wasn't sure if it counted as "necessary" or "pretty." They also got ten points for their team name: "Domination."

Finn picked a new, similarly spaced, pair of trees, and they continued.

Going second was Rafe's team, soberly, but unfortunately no longer correctly named "Team Number Three." They also wore what they had confirmed with Finn counted as uniforms: pieces of vine tied around their upper arms.

To get up the starting tree, the naturalist mage expanded a vine that was already wrapping around the tree. The mages climbed this for two feet, then the water mage made ice steps for two feet, which the fire mage topped—very prettily—with decorative flames. Then Rafe used his earth magic to pull some stones out of the ground, which the wind mage lifted up to them. The fire mage burned some holes in the tree—the naturalist mage averted his eyes—and Rafe inserted the stones into the holes to make steps and the group climbed higher. All the while the thread mage was weaving a pretty design of colored rope to adorn their path.

They inched their way up into the tree, using different types of magic every few feet. When they were as high as they could go, the thread mage created a rope, which the wind mage lifted across to the tree on the other side. The naturalist mage wrapped vines around the ends of the rope, fixing it to the trees on either end. They did this a second time, affixing another rope higher up. Then, one by one, they inched their way across the makeshift bridge, standing on one rope and clinging to the other.

One of the mages slipped. He recovered his footing almost immediately, but the crowd below sucked in its breath. Finn grabbed Noe's arm and whispered in his ear.

"If he falls—you'll catch him?"

"Oh, sure, Finn. Tha's allowed?"

Oh wow. "Yes. Yes, Noe. That's definitely allowed. If you can keep anyone from dying, please do."

The water mage got stuck halfway across. He made the mistake of looking down, then he wrapped his arms around the rope in a death grip, closed his eyes, and refused to move. The crowd below started to heckle him, laughing and describing exactly how far up he was.

Rafe shouted across the gap to the thread mage in the other tree. "Do you have enough left to make another bridge?"

The thread mage shook her head. The water mage groaned and gripped the rope even more tightly.

Rafe held a whispered conference with the two mages left on his tree. One was a wind mage, the other a fire mage. Finn watched their lips move, but couldn't catch what they were saying. The wind mage shook her head emphatically, her eyes darting away from Rafe's in fear. Rafe patted her on the shoulder. The fire mage rolled his eyes, tried to say something, but Rafe shook his head firmly, and the man backed off.

Finally, Rafe said something and the wind mage nodded. She clenched her fists and took a deep breath. Rafe patted her on the back. Then he turned to the bridge.

The wind mage held out a shaking hand, and a gust of wind lifted Rafe's hair. He stepped out onto the rope bridge. It sagged dangerously under his weight, the vines affixing it to the tree strained and groaned. The wind picked up; the wind mage's face focused in fierce concentration, until the air began to lift Rafe slightly. It couldn't hold his weight completely, but it could hold him up enough to hopefully keep the rope bridge from breaking under the weight of the two mages. Rafe nodded at her, and she nodded back.

Slowly, calmly, Rafe inched his way across to the mage. He patted the man firmly on the back. The man cracked an eye open and peered at him in terror. Rafe gestured with one hand, pointing at the tree in front, the tree behind. He smiled a large, calm, smile, his eyes locked on the terrified mage's.

Someone below jeered at the stuck mage. The man, startled, glanced down, saw again how high he was, and clenched his eyes shut again. The fire mage, annoyed at having nothing to do, lit the jeerer's hair on fire. One of the jeerer's teammates put it out before it did any real damage—besides burning off most of his hair—but the man scowled, his head smoking.

Rafe was unperturbed. He just started again. He stood there with the man for a long time, the wind from the wind mage making his short hair whip around. She was losing power now, and her wind was fading in and out. It died every few seconds, coming back in desperate bursts. She called something out to Rafe, but he kept all his focus on the man.

Finally, the man began to move. He kept his eyes closed, and, guided by Rafe, slid his feet along, inch by inch, without looking and without ever letting go of his stranglehold on the upper rope. Rafe spoke to him in a constant stream, shifting the man's focus from the height and the danger.

They reached the other side to cheers and clapping. The fire and wind mages scampered across one at a time, and then they all made their way down in the same slow fashion they had made their way up in. The whole time Rafe had been talking the water mage across, the others had been making little decorative pieces for the climb down, so they ended up racking up another several hundred points. All in all, Finn gave them five hundred and seventy-five points.

"All right, Marta," Finn said, "Your team's up."

"We want to go last."

"Why?"

"We're not ready yet."

"You had your hour to prepare."

"Yes, but then the trees we had originally planned on using were burned down." She shot an annoyed glance at the first team.

"You've already had more time than Rafe's team."

"We still want to go last."

Finn heaved a sigh and looked at Ronan and Jes' team.

"We can go," Ronan said. "We're ready."

"All right, fine," Finn said to Marta, "You can go last."

Ronan stepped up to the start tree, his six teammates

behind him but a little ways back. Hesitant. Finn thought he knew what was coming. More ice steps. That's what had been in their plan.

"Team name?" Finn asked.

"Nope," Ronan said.

Wow, he's really—Finn lost his train of thought as lava spewed out of the ground.

Waves of heat blasted off it, bushes and trees ignited around it. People started screaming and running, but Ronan just stood there, barefoot, backlit by the red-hot, molten rock.

Finn stumbled back a step, but that was it. He was used to heat.

"Ronan! What are you—" he called out, but was interrupted by Jes.

She stepped forward into the heat, a shimmering blue sphere surrounding her. It hissed and steamed. Just like Eraldir had done when Finn had melted the iron, Jes shot a stream of ice and water at the molten rock. Within seconds the glade was full of thick, hot steam, and no one could see anything. Panicked figures darted through the fog. Finn took a deep breath; the steam burned his throat and he coughed. The roaring and spitting of water, instantly vaporizing as it hit molten rock, filled the air. Then the wind picked up. The fog whipped through the trees, and fresh air cooled Finn's damp clothes and skin.

Suddenly, everything was quiet except for the wind. Finn shook himself, tried to gather his wits about him. He needed to collect the mages, make sure nothing was on fire still, and that no one was hurt. Where was Eraldir? Then it started again.

The rushing, and roaring, the fires and the fog. This time it didn't last as long. When the fog had mostly cleared, the mages slowly came out of hiding. They poked their heads out from behind trees and out from holes they'd dug themselves in the ground.

At first, Ronan was just a dim outline, with something huge and hulking behind him. Tendrils of fog blew through the dark, soot-blackened tree trunks.

Finn stepped forward, saw Jes sitting on the ground, massaging her sternum and grimacing.

"You all right?" he asked, putting a hand on her shoulder.

She nodded.

Slowly, the rest of the mages returned and clustered around what Ronan had built. As the fog cleared, the destruction became apparent.

The trees themselves had been mostly burned away as they were encased in molten stone. The stone had hardened around them, piling up eighty feet into the sky. The two trees leaned towards one another, their tips just touching in a staggeringly high arch. The outside edges of the stone trees were cut in right angles. Ronan had made a staircase.

When the smoke and fog had cleared, and the spectators had mostly returned, Ronan and his teammates approached the staircase. With Ronan leading, they climbed the stairs, eighty feet into the air, and descended the other side. They arrived back to complete silence.

"You only used three types of magic," Marta said.

Ronan shrugged. "Yep. Beat that."

"It's only ninety points," Marta said. "You're already losing."

"Darn." He grinned.

No one had anything to say to that.

Suddenly, Ronan's face whitened a little; he bent at the waist and his hand went to his heart. Almost instantly, though, he got the reflex under control, and righted himself.

"Are you okay?" Jes asked, her eyes wide.

Ronan waved a hand dismissively. "Fine." But his face was still pale.

Maybe this competition had been a bad idea. But they were three-quarters of the way through and no one had died yet. They might as well finish it.

They had to find two more trees for the last team, Marta's team. Team "We couldn't think of a team name," according to them, scoring them five—in Finn's opinion not entirely earned—points.

Marta, the water mage, made ice steps that spiraled up around the two trees. The naturalist and wind mages copied Rafe's strategy and made them a vine bridge between to the two trees. The team climbed the first set up steps, and then, for about an hour, the team stayed in the first tree making pretty little decorations. For each different decoration, they made they earned another five points, and they did this until they had confirmed with Finn that they'd racked up over six hundred points. Then they crossed the bridge and descended the other staircase.

Someone booed.

"We win," Marta said. "I don't drink wine. I want pheasant cooked with fresh rosemary for dinner."

A lot of grumbling followed this, partially directed at Finn and his stupid points system, and partially directed at Marta's team for doing what most of them considered cheating. But also, Finn noticed a lot of sidelong, admiring glances in Ronan's direction. Even more disconcertingly, Finn saw that Ronan was ignoring these looks, and instead staring straight at Isabelle.

CHAPTER 21

That night, at dinner, the mages were no longer grouped off by type. Now they were grouped off into the arbitrary teams that Finn had created. Was that improvement? Maybe. At least there were only four groups instead of six now. And the thread mages weren't by themselves. The pile of Reina's wine sat in the winner's camp, waiting for after dinner.

Ronan detached himself from his group of admirers and approached Finn.

"Hey."

"Hey, Ronan."

"What was that, today?"

"Just trying to get the mages to talk to each other."

"I mean, when we left, you said we'd be in this together."

"Oh." Ronan was right, he had said that.

Ronan looked at him. "Did you mean that?"

"Yeah, of course I did."

Ronan placed a hand on Finn's shoulder. "So, you'll run these things by me, first?"

Finn wasn't exactly sure what that meant. "Um, yeah,

sorry." Now that Finn had felt what it meant to be in charge, he didn't exactly want to run things by Ronan. But he would. Ronan was right. They had said they'd do this together.

"Great." Ronan smiled at him and went back to his circle of admirers.

When he'd gone, Finn sighed and ran his hands through his hair. He wasn't completely sure what he'd agreed to. Eraldir came ambling up, sipping his foul-smelling tea.

"Well, that was something, boy." His joints popped in a discordant symphony as he eased himself down next to Finn.

Finn glanced up at Eraldir, noticed how tired he looked. "You doing okay?"

"Fine, boy, fine." But Eraldir wasn't quite meeting his eye. "We've got a small problem, though, possibly."

"What?"

"Well, that Ronan, you saw what he did today. He's overstretching himself. Showing off. You saw him stumble after that display. He's filling himself up with shadow faster than it can bleed out of him."

"Can you address that in tomorrow's class?"

Eraldir stuck a finger in his ear, dug it around for a moment, and then wiped it on the hem of his shirt. "Sure, sure, I can."

"I'll talk to him, too." That would go great. Ronan loved it when Finn warned him about magic.

"Good."

Eraldir took a long sip of his tea and stared into the fire.

Part of what Isabelle had said was still bothering Finn. "Eraldir?"

"Yes, boy?"

"Um, I sort of just…I don't know. Somehow I ended up in charge?"

Eraldir glanced at him out of the corner of his eye. "And?"

Finn wasn't sure what to say.

"You asking for my permission?" Eraldir asked.

"No...I just... Isabelle..."

"Ah, yes. Do you want to be in charge?"

"Yes."

"Good."

They were quiet for a moment. Finn felt like Eraldir was waiting for something. "I'm going to go talk to Ronan," Finn said.

"All right."

Finn stood and went to find Ronan, slightly bemused from his conversation with Eraldir, which, to be fair, wasn't an uncommon occurrence.

He found Ronan at the crowded central campfire, surrounded by a gaggle of mages. The female members of the gaggle, however, were downcast, and Finn could immediately relate. Ronan sat, leaning towards to campfire, elbows on knees and a grin on his face. Next to him, close enough that their knees were almost touching, sat Isabelle.

She grinned and laughed, too, her face illuminated by the firelight.

At least they weren't actually touching. Of course, as soon as he thought that, Isabelle punched Ronan on the shoulder, and a hot sick wave of jealousy punched Finn.

He'd find some other time to talk to Ronan. Meditate. He should meditate. He turned and hurried off into the woods.

Finn leaned against a tree, making sure he was out of sight of the campfire, and took a deep breath. Okay. Calm down. What had he seen? Nothing. Just Isabelle and Ronan talking. It wasn't like they'd been making out or something. But Ronan had sure looked like he wanted to. Finn wasn't sure how Isabelle felt about it. The times she'd kissed him had always come as a complete surprise. Like when she'd found out he'd murdered his family. Well, he had that one over Ronan. He'd murdered Ronan's family, too. *Maybe I should tell her,* he thought wildly, before dismissing himself as an idiot.

No, Isabelle liked him, right? She'd kissed him. Had he ever kissed her, though? He'd wanted to, constantly, and more, but he hadn't. Why? He didn't know how she felt about him. He didn't want to impose. He was scared. Maybe she just didn't know how he felt. Maybe she'd assumed Finn wasn't interested and moved on to Ronan.

The image of her laughing, her white hair glowing orange in the firelight, her brown eyes locked on Ronan's, made his stomach turn over and shrivel up, trying to hide itself. It felt like all his internal organs were rearranging themselves, fighting to hide under the others.

As usual, he had been an idiot. He should have kissed Isabelle, should have told her how he felt about her already. It wasn't too late, yet, though. He could still tell her.

His lungs unclenched as he forced air into them. Across his mind flashed images of Isabelle laughing at him, or her eyebrows raising incredulously as he told her. He shook himself and pushed himself up off the tree. That wasn't necessarily going to happen. He let himself imagine the other possible alternative. Her smiling at him, telling him she loved him, kissing him. He had no idea how she would react, really, but he was going to tell her. Tomorrow.

THE NEXT MORNING, Eraldir gave the group a lesson on shadows. Ronan sat in the back, idly pulling gemstones out of the ground. This would have been an ideal time to talk to Isabelle, but she had blown off into the trees that morning before Finn had gotten up the courage to approach her.

After the lesson, the group packed up and set off. Ronan walked with his group around him. So did Rafe, although his group was smaller, quieter, older, and much less giggly. Finn walked alone, until Jes came to join him.

She looked up at him through her lashes, her large blue eyes thoughtful. "What's the school like?" she asked.

Finn really didn't want to be bothered, and also he didn't know when Isabelle was coming back. She might appear at any minute, and he wanted to be ready.

"It's very... rough," he said.

"What do you mean?"

"It's still in progress. There's a lot left to build. It's hard to explain. You'll see when we get there."

"What's your plan for the school?"

Why was she asking him so many questions? If she didn't want him to think she was a spy she was doing a poor job of it.

"To train mages so they can use their magic safely."

"What—"

"Look, Jes. I kinda need to think right now."

She looked down. "Oh, right. Sorry." She drifted off. Finn considered saying something to her before she walked away —she was just asking questions; she didn't deserve to be snapped at—but she was gone before he could think of something to say. It was just as well. He had too much on his mind.

ISABELLE SWEPT BACK into the group shortly before lunch. Her hair was full of twigs and she was bouncing with enthusiasm. Apparently, it had been a good morning of falling out of trees. Finn saw Ronan starting towards her, but intercepted her first.

"Hey Isabelle," he said, trying to smile, although it felt more like his face was having a spasm. His hands were shaking and apparently a cold sweat was something that actually happened to people. He'd never actually had the experience of being cold with fear and clammy with sweat at the same time before.

"Why is your face that color?" She asked.

"What color?"

"Kind of greenish grey."

Good to know. "No reason. I don't know. Breakfast, maybe?"

The corner of her lips quirked up. Argh, she was so pretty.

"You look like you're going to light something on fire, Finn."

"Sorry. Can I talk to you?" The last words came out of his mouth in a rush of breath.

"Uh, sure? I mean, you're talking to me right now. Sort of."

"Over here?"

He pointed away from the other mages, a few of whom were looking their way curiously. *Please don't let anyone see this.*

"Sure, I guess. I'm hungry, though."

He took a deep breath. "Sorry, just a quick thing."

She picked a leaf out of her hair and flicked it away. "Okay, let's go then."

He led her behind a thick clump of bushes, unfortunately surprising a mage who was squatting over a hole in the ground, his trousers around his ankles and his tunic hitched up. Apparently, they weren't the only ones looking for privacy. Blushing, Finn apologized and found them a new, happily unoccupied clump of bushes.

Isabelle was looking worried now. "Uh, why all the secrecy, Finn?"

He was just going to go for it. "I like you, Isabelle."

She blinked.

He ran a hand through his hair, waiting for her to say something.

"Uh, I like you, too, Finn."

Finn wasn't sure whether she had understood, but, slightly emboldened, he went on. "I—I think you're amazing. I think you're beautiful." She was staring at him now. Recklessly, he reached out and took her hand. Specifics. He should tell her specific things. "I love how free your magic is, I love how strong and brave you are. You never run away from anything."

She had gone quiet, and wasn't meeting his eyes anymore. She looked off, over Finn's left shoulder, her hand shaking slightly in his.

"Um, cool." She pulled her hand away and punched him on the shoulder. "Very funny, Finn."

"I'm not—"

"We'd better go check on Eraldir, make sure he hasn't fallen asleep while drinking his tea and drowned himself."

"He's—"

She had turned and was walking off, completely in the wrong direction.

"Isabelle—"

But she was gone.

Well, at least she hadn't laughed at him.

Finn stuck his hands in his pockets. He took another deep breath. Well, that hadn't been as bad as he'd thought. He actually felt kind of good for having told her. Sure, she was now walking off into the forest, but at least he'd told her. Not the reaction he was hoping for, but really, given what Finn tended to do to the people he loved he couldn't blame her. Seemed understandable. He'd wait and try again later.

. . .

ISABELLE STILL WASN'T BACK that evening when Eraldir started that night's lecture, also on shadows. The mages weren't silent like they had been before, though. Following Ronan's lead, some of them whispered and snickered among themselves. Eraldir soldiered on from his comfortable seat at the front, seemingly oblivious that they weren't paying any attention.

"The worst example of the shadow is of course The Dead Tree. Not many people have seen it. It's from the war after the Fall. Created in the destruction of the last of the mages. Well, not the last of the mages, because I'm still left. But, everyone... everyone else..." Eraldir's eyes were unfocused, and he drifted off, staring blankly into space.

The mages quieted, confused, and stared at him, waiting for him to go on so they could continue ignoring him.

Finn stepped forward. "Eraldir?" The old man didn't answer, his mouth hung slightly open. "Eraldir?!" Finn ran to the old man, placed a hand on his shoulder, bent down, and looked into his eyes.

"Oh, what? What is it boy?" He blinked, looked around him, saw the mages all staring at him. "What are you all doing here?"

"Are you okay?"

"Okay? Course I'm okay, why wouldn't I be?" Eraldir looked around, patting his own knee uncertainly.

A sick sense of unease rose in Finn's stomach. "Here, Eraldir, come on, let's get you some food, or some tea, maybe?" He took Eraldir's thin arms and lifted him gently.

"Oh, sure, food sounds good, sounds like just the thing. We don't have any pie, do we?"

Finn led Eraldir off to the other side of their camp, followed by the silent stares of the mages. He helped Eraldir sit on his bedroll, handed him a slice of cold pie, and started getting his tea things ready. The old man took a bite of pie and stared thoughtfully off into space, chewing, not saying anything at all.

When the tea was ready, Finn handed it to Eraldir, and took a seat next to him.

The tea revived him. He turned to Finn and for the first time his eyes seemed to fully see him.

"Sorry I scared you there, boy."

"What was that? Are you okay?"

Eraldir looked at Finn steadily for a moment. "I don't know; I just sort of lost track of things there for a minute. I wouldn't worry, though. These things happen."

Anxiety constricted Finn's heart. "What do you need? More herbs? Should I get the naturalist mages to grow them fresh for you? Do you need a doctor? Should I go back to Westwend and find one?"

Eraldir chuckled. "That's the spirit, boy. But no. No, I don't think there's anything to be done. This is just how I am. Been getting sick since I was a kid. A few weeks back I couldn't pee for two weeks, like I said. Thought I was done for then, but it cleared up on its own." He shook his head. "Terrible way to go. Just terrible. Like Geraldine, the great Montvan spy. She thought she could last just a little longer pretending to be the new statue in the king's bedchamber."

Finn couldn't think of anything to say. He hadn't quite realized how much he liked and cared for Eraldir already. He was old and sick and falling apart, but that was just the way he was. He couldn't actually die. Another thought struck him then. "Eraldir, is the travel too hard on you? Should we stop?"

"Stop? Course not. Been traveling all my life. Stopping would probably kill me."

Finn didn't want to ask, but it slipped out before he could stop it. "Are you going to make it to the Table?"

"Course I am. Eh, well, probably. Never died before. One of the few things I haven't tried, you know."

"If you, if you... they won't listen to me. Who will teach them?" This was easier to think about than the real fear on Finn's mind. This was a problem. Problems were clear-cut, and could be solved. Finn couldn't acknowledge, even to himself, what he would feel if Eraldir weren't there.

Eraldir coughed a wracking, phlegmy cough.

Finn leaned forward to try to help, but a scream from the other side of camp distracted him. It cut sharply through the air, and went on and on, rising to a fever pitch of panic and terror.

Finn leapt to his feet and sprinted in the direction of the scream. There was a knot of mages standing together around something on the ground. Finn pushed his way to the front as another bloodcurdling scream sliced the air. The mages parted for him, stumbling aside in shock.

There on the ground was one of the wind mages. Her eyes were rolled back in her head and she jerked and frothed at the lips. Finn knelt helplessly at her side, looked in her eyes, seeing only the blank whites. Her jaw was locked tight, and Finn wasn't sure if she was even still breathing. His question was answered when her mouth opened and another agonized scream assaulted Finn's ears. Her hands opened and closed reflexively, scrabbling at the dirt and then clawing at her stomach and throat.

"Eraldir!" Finn cried, leaping up and running over to the man.

Eraldir was trying, unsuccessfully, to heave himself to his feet.

"There's a mage, on the ground—" He described her quickly.

"Poison," Eraldir said. "Here, take the blue flowers and the white berries in my pack." He pointed.

Finn stumbled over to the pack, another scream making his hands shake as he whipped the bag open and dug through it frantically. Blue flowers. White berries. "These?" Eraldir nodded, sinking back onto his bed.

Finn sprinted towards the group. Then he skidded to a stop, turned and called back to Eraldir, "Do I feed them to her?"

"Yes, in a paste. Mix them and try to get them into her mouth. Don't choke her."

Finn's feet pounded the ground; he skidded back into the group of mages, shoving them aside roughly, already crushing the berries and flowers in his hands, dropping about half of them in the process. He knelt by the mage, forced her frothy, and now bloody, lips open, and jammed the paste inside. She jerked a few more times, tried to open her mouth, but Finn held it closed.

"Hey, what do you—" a harsh, panicked voice behind him said, but Finn ignored it.

The mage's body went limp. Finn let go of her mouth, opened one of the eyelids. A brown iris was visible, but unfocused and glassy. The whites of her eyes were a network of bloody red lines. Finn let go of the eyelid in horror, pressed a finger to her neck. Nothing. No heartbeat.

His heart was hammering in his chest, and he felt suddenly faint.

There was complete silence for several seconds.

"Is... Is she dead?" someone said finally.

Finn nodded, wiping the sweat from his clammy face, realized his hands were covered in bloody saliva. He scrubbed them frantically on his pants.

There was a small compression wave and whoosh of wind, and Isabelle careened into the camp, just outside the circle of people.

"Hey, what's with the screaming?"

Finn glanced at her, met her eyes, and gave a small shake of his head, then turned to address the group. "What happened here?" he asked.

"She's dead! That's what happened!"

Finn looked around at the confused, scared faces. He didn't see anything that looked like malice or understanding, until his gaze came to one face in particular. Jes. She was staring at the mage in horror, but there was something else there, too. She met Finn's eyes and then looked away quickly, but before she did, Finn knew. She knew something.

"We're going to bury her here," Finn said. "Ronan," Finn paused, remembering that he'd promised to include Ronan in the decision-making. "What do you think? I think we should bury her, will you make her a gravestone?"

"I think we should do something about the murderer in our midst, first, don't you?" Oh. That was probably a good idea.

"Yeah," Marta said. "Any one of us could be next! There must be spies from Reina here." All eyes turned to Jes.

"We were fine until you came," a naturalist mage said.

"Yeah." A water mage wrapped her cloak tighter about herself. "You show up and suddenly, next thing we know someone's dead."

Jes paled. "I... I don't know anything! I'm not... I'm not a spy."

"She's lying," the water mage said.

"Kill her, before she gets anyone else!" Marta shrieked, to cries of agreement.

A fiery explosion above their heads stopped them.

"Stop." Finn said, and all pretense of including Ronan was gone. "We are not killing someone without evidence." He turned to one of the thread mages. "You. Bring her over there and tie her up." Finn jerked his head to the edge of the forest.

"Why should we listen to you? You're the one who let her in in the first place," Marta said.

"We have. No. Proof." Finn stared down the crowd. He glanced at Ronan, but his friend was just watching thoughtfully. "We'll get to the bottom of this, but we're not just leaping to conclusions and murdering people. Would you want to live in a place where your friends would just kill you if they suspected you of something?".

"She's not our friend."

"No, maybe not. But she's not a murderer. As far as we know." He paused. He had planned to question Jes later, alone, but he was losing his authority. He'd better do something now. He turned to the thread mage, who had started to bind Jes' hands. "Keep her here a moment. Jes. You know something; I can tell. Explain."

Tears leaked out of Jes' eyes. She looked around desperately for a friendly face, but, seeing none, looked down at the ground.

"Jes, talk. Now."

"It's... the..." she sobbed, struggled in her bonds.

Isabelle was in front of her in a second. She slapped her across the face. "No one cares about your crying, Jes. Shut up and tell us what you know."

Jes' face hardened. Snot ran out of her nose towards her mouth, and tears leaked out her eyes. "It's the wine. Reina's wine. She poisons some of it." She looked at the ground.

"You knew this all along!" Marta shouted.

"I forgot! I just forgot! I... I thought you knew, that you wouldn't take the marked bottles."

"Which is it?" Ronan interjected sharply. "You knew, or you forgot?"

Jes looked at him like she'd been stabbed, then she cried harder. "I don't know!"

"I've been drinking her wine, and I'm fine," Isabelle remarked.

"It's only some bottles," Jes wailed. "The ones with the snake on the bottom."

"Which bottle was she drinking?" Finn asked the crowd. Rafe produced the bottle, holding it between his thumb and forefinger, lifted it up, and peered at the bottom. "It's got a snake on it."

"She knew! She knew and she didn't warn us!" Marta cried.

"Okay," Finn said loudly. "Tie her up, bring her over there by Eraldir."

"She doesn't deserve to live!"

Finn rounded on the crowd, his anger boiling over. "We are not a mob. We are not murderers. We are better than that. I am better than that. And you are either better than that or you are leaving. Right now."

There was silence for a few seconds.

Everything hung in the balance. Finn could see it, could see it happening before his eyes. They were thinking about it.

"And who will teach you?" Finn said. Before they could give the obvious answer, Finn continued. "Which of you knows anything about the way magic was before the Fall?"

"And you know so much more than we do?"

"Eraldir does." Except, Eraldir was dying, might die at any moment. "And, yes. I do, too. And the place we're going, it has old magic, from before. We'll have books. We'll have knowledge that it would take a thousand years to learn by experimentation."

They considered this. Their mob mentality hadn't faded enough for real, rational thought to set in. This might be a good thing; hopefully it would be harder for them to see that he was making everything up.

"Well, it seems to me like maybe this was an accident," a considered voice said. All eyes turned to Rafe, standing with his hands tucked into his belt. He took a step forward, looked around at the group, and his eyes were sad. "Let's bury the girl."

The calm power in Rafe's voice swayed them. For the moment, murdering Jes was put aside, and they focused on the dead mage. After they buried her, and the rest of the wine had been poured onto the ground—no one felt like drinking it anymore—and the mages were huddled quietly around their fires, Finn found Rafe sitting by himself.

"Thank you," he said, standing across the fire from Rafe.

Rafe looked up, met his eyes. "I don't like liars, kid."

Finn's mouth went dry.

"I also don't like mobs, or murderers. I happened to agree with what you were saying, and at the moment I don't have anywhere better to go, but I don't like you, and I'm not on your side."

Shame welled up in Finn. Part of him wanted to come clean about the school right then. What would Rafe do? Leave? He wouldn't lie to the others for him.

Rafe looked back into the fire, ignoring Finn, and eventually Finn walked away. He felt like crying, but he had other, more important things to do. Like checking on Eraldir.

The old man was sitting with Isabelle by their fire, drinking more tea.

"Should have known Reina would poison her wine," Eraldir said, shaking his head before turning to the side to cough.

"You okay, Eraldir?" Isabelle asked, not looking at Finn.

"Fine, fine. Had a bit of trouble earlier, but it's nothing."

Isabelle finally looked up and met Finn's eyes. She raised her eyebrows, and Finn shook his head. It was like their conversation earlier had never happened, except that Isabelle looked away more quickly than usual, and her neck and cheeks reddened.

Finn wanted desperately to ask her what she was thinking, but she had already moved away and was unrolling her sleeping blanket.

"'Night," she said, wrapping herself into the blanket and lying with her back to them.

Eraldir raised his eyebrows at Finn, who blushed and changed the subject.

"Do you have the energy to tell me more about magic tonight?" Finn asked.

Eraldir smiled, but let the subject of Isabelle drop. "Sure, boy, course I do. What do you want to know?"

"Everything."

Eraldir's eyes lit up and he readjusted his position. "Well, let's start at the beginning then. What do you know of fish mating habits?"

"Er, not much," Finn said. "But, actually," something occurred to him, "can you tell me why copper sometimes stops magic?"

Eraldir grunted. "It doesn't."

"But, back in some ruins near my village, Ronan and I found what I think was a speaking pool. It didn't work until we got all the copper out of it."

"Ahh. Well. That's different." Eraldir took a long sip of his tea. "Stoke up the fire, there, would you?" The flames had died down, leaving only embers glowing redly in the dark.

Wondering if Eraldir had forgotten his question, Finn piled a few more logs on the embers, and carefully ignited them.

Eraldir leaned forward, pinching his fingers together, and a fine mist sprayed out the ends of them. "See that?"

"You mean the water? Yeah."

"No, boy, not the water." Eraldir readjusted his position,

leaned forward so that the spray of water was between Finn and the fire. Then he held up his other hand. On it, Finn could see a very faint spectrum of colors.

"The rainbow?" Finn asked.

Eraldir ceased spraying water and leaned back, coughing. "Yes, yes, the rainbow." He cleared his throat and took another sip of tea.

"Water, and some other things, split light apart into pieces, into the different colors. Copper is like that, but for magic."

"So, that means the speaking pool—"

"Was using different types of magic that had been joined together, yes. The copper temporarily split them apart, keeping them from working."

Finn sat back, his mind turning over possible implications.

"Now, back to what I was saying about fish," Eraldir said, picking up a stick and poking the logs, sending up sparks.

"Wait," Finn said. "What are the speaking pools anyway?"

Eraldir scratched his beard. "I don't rightly know how they work. The Ael made them. Some combination of water and fire magic. Maybe something else. Never know with them."

"And they let people talk to people in other cities?"

"Oh, yes."

"Can you travel through them?"

Eraldir cleared his throat. "Well, I think you could, but no one did, far as I know."

"Why?"

"Too dangerous. That much magic. I think they tried sending a goat through once, but it came out mangled. Too many feet. And heads. The Ael could control it, keep it stable, but there were only a few of them left and they had better things to do." Eraldir cleared his throat.

"Also, when Ronan and I got the pool working again, there was a… a thing…"

Eraldir lifted an eyebrow.

Finn continued. "A man, sort of, but more like a ghost."

Eraldir's brows knit together. "Hmm."

"Do you know what that could have been?"

"Maybe just some leftover image from the last time it was used."

"It seemed like it was talking to us, though. It looked at me."

"Well, now, that is strange. I wonder…" Eraldir stared into the flames, and the firelight flickered across his face, shadows deepening the creases there.

Finn couldn't help himself. "What?"

"Well, I don't know… maybe it's nothing. Maybe there's a… survivor."

A chill went up Finn's spine.

"The pools, after all, they all connect back up to the City of Mages. We don't know what happened there, and we don't know what's inside. Haven't been able to get near the place since it happened, you know."

"I thought everyone died," Finn said.

"Well, we don't know that, do we? Haven't heard from them in ninety years, seems a safe assumption they're all dead, but we don't know for sure."

Now Finn was torn between wanting to find a speaking pool to try to talk to that thing again, to ask it what it was and what had happened, and wanting to find the remaining speaking pools to destroy them. Because Finn had feeling that whatever it was might have been the thing to cause the Fall in the first place.

∾

SITTING ALONE BY THE FIRE, Rafe examined the scars on his arms. He stretched his hands, feeling the stiffness there. His back, too, and his legs were stiff. He was getting older—nearing forty—but the stiffness was mostly from old injuries —experience. It wasn't exactly true that he had nowhere else to go, but the one place he wanted to be, was a place he was no longer welcome. He closed his eyes, saw a pair of flashing green eyes, could see her short dark hair, and an ache of sadness filled him. But it was better this way.

CHAPTER 22

"Thank you for joining me, Captain," Arcturus said when he heard Nate come in behind him.

"Oh, sorry, sir, it's just me, Gavin. I came to let you know Nate's on his way."

Arcturus sighed. "Thank you, Gavin." He didn't turn around until he heard the man leave.

Arcturus went to the side of the opulent silk tent and rummaged in his bag until he found the small silver mirror he used for trimming his beard. Placing this at the back of the tent, he resumed his position facing away from the door, staring at the large map of what was once Caledonia, his hands clasped behind him.

The tent flap was pushed aside and Nate entered. They made eye contact awkwardly in the mirror. Arcturus sighed again and turned around, giving up on the pretense.

"Thank you for joining me, Captain." He gestured to the small chair. "Would you care for some cheese?"

"No, thank you sir. Jack'll have dinner ready when I'm home and he'll be upset if I'm not hungry. It's his last night here before he heads back to Westwend with William."

"Decided to tag along, did they?"

Nate nodded. His chin was so chiseled, Arcturus thought, with all that manly stubble. And his eyes were like jade. It was annoying. He shouldn't have made someone so good-looking his captain. No one looked twice at Arcturus with Nate around.

Nate was waiting for him to speak. Arcturus let him wait, sitting uncomfortably on the spindly chair while Arcturus stood over him.

"There is something troubling me, Captain." Arcturus watched Nate swallow hard and look down. "You see, I have Reina Jeesh in custody now, but strangely enough her army... well, it seems to have disappeared."

Nate, usually the picture of manly confidence and calm, picked at his knee, still not meeting Arcturus' eyes.

Arcturus popped a piece of cheese into his mouth. "Are you sure you wouldn't care for some cheese? It comes all the way from the Uplands. Finest goat cheese there is. I had three different traders die in the attempt before I was able to find someone who could bring it to me."

Nate took a deep breath. "Sir, as for the bulk of Reina's army, I have no idea. There was, however... a small contingent that I let go."

Arcturus stopped mid-chew. "You what, Captain?"

Nate took another breath, met Arcturus' gaze steadily now. "My men and I entered the tunnels and we came across a group of about thirty mages. They said they didn't agree with Reina. They wanted to leave and start a school and they didn't want to bother us."

"And you believed them?"

"Yes, sir. I believed them."

"So you, you just, what? You let them leave? Without any kind of assurances, or collateral, or..." Arcturus placed a hand flat on his stomach, unable to believe what he was hearing.

"Yes, sir. We were evenly matched. My men probably could have killed them, but most would have died, and all the mages would have died, too. And all they wanted was to leave."

Arcturus was at a complete loss for words. He stared at his captain, openmouthed. Finally, he recovered his wits. "So, what you're saying is that you encountered a group of mages —known killers—and instead of apprehending them you just let them go because... because they said they didn't want to hurt anyone?"

"Yes, sir."

Arcturus had not realized that Nate was an idiot.

"I did make them promise a few things, sir."

"Oh, yes captain? What promises did you require?"

"To include the atrocities committed by mages in their curriculum, and for each mage to spend a year offering free services to non-mages."

"Oh yes. For their... school. Right. And do you have any way of ensuring they keep their promises?"

Nate shook his head. "Only the word of their leader, sir."

"Wonderful."

This was not at all what Arcturus had been expecting. He'd expected betrayal, maybe. Possibly that Nate wanted to kill Arcturus and take over his position. That's why he'd poisoned some of the pieces of cheese. But here Nate was, just owning up to letting their enemies go because they promised to be nice. No, he had clearly overestimated Nate. The man was an idiot, not even worth murdering. Nate's men were loyal to him—very loyal—and that was useful. People didn't tend to be particularly loyal to Arcturus himself, he'd noticed.

Well, he clearly had nothing to fear from Nate. It was obvious the man was telling the truth now. He might kill him for disobeying orders, but for now the man was still useful to him. He took the cheese plate away and set it on a side table.

When Nate had gone off to have dinner with his loving partner and child, Arcturus sat, thinking to himself.

So. More evidence of a mage school; Reina's story might be true after all. Also, part of Reina's army had deserted her. Maybe all of it. That's why she wanted Arcturus to go after them. Interesting.

$\sim$

"...AND that's how I became king of Aprot," Eraldir finished. "At least, until they found out I was the one who had caused the mudslides in the first place."

It was late, and Finn was starting to nod off. Isabelle lay sprawled by the fire, snoring, her white hair splayed danger-ously close the flames. Finn noticed, and gently moved it away with a fingertip. She grunted and rolled over in her sleep.

"I think that's enough for tonight boy. Time for bed."

"Thanks, Eraldir." Finn watched Eraldir as he got stiffly into his bedroll and closed his eyes. There were purple liver spots on the skin of his face and hands, dark shadows illumi-nated by the dying firelight. Finn watched the thin chest rise and fall; he was glad that Eraldir seemed to have recovered himself. Maybe his sickness was just a fluke. Maybe he would live years more. And maybe Ronan would suddenly realize that he should just do whatever Finn said, and Isabelle would realize she liked Finn.

Finn sighed, stood, and stretched, looking up at the moon. The camp was quiet, except for one of the mages' snoring.

Why would they follow him? Right now they followed him because they thought he knew things they didn't. And that was partially true, now. But not as much as they thought it was. Why else? He had to give them a reason.

Walking to the side of the camp, Finn settled himself down to meditate. At the very least, he would practice twice as hard as anyone else here. Maybe that would be worth something.

WHEN KEL HAD AT LAST REPAIRED the damage of her escape from the guards, she set off to look for Smoke. As she travelled, she stopped every few days to plant some berry bushes and nut trees. A group of crows was following her, and she left these as offerings for them.

One morning, she awoke to find a shiny bit of rock in front of her face. A few days after that, a piece of shell. Gifts from the crows.

Thank you, she thought. Then it occurred to her, what she really wanted was seeds. Tentatively, she offered this idea to the birds.

After that, every morning she awoke to find at least one new strange seed, which she would sprout and tend until she discovered what it was. Her pockets were soon overflowing.

After many days of walking, she came to a place where the trees were newer and younger, and the light filtering down through the leaves was still bright and green; here, Kel found Smoke.

At first, she only heard his voice, stronger and clearer in her mind than it had been since she left the nest. Then, as she pushed through a gap between two trees, there he was, running towards her.

The ferret leapt high into the air, then scurried all over

Kel, doing loops around her arms and legs, biting her ears playfully, and messing up her hair. Kel laughed and tried, unsuccessfully, to catch Smoke's tail. She only got Smoke to stop by offering him a nut from her pocket. The ferret quickly gobbled it, allowing Kel a quick pat, and then resumed his zipping around.

Finally, Smoke was hungry, and they went to find some eggs together. Then they climbed trees for a while, until both were too tired to do anything but lie panting on the ground, Smoke curled up on Kel's chest. Kel stroked Smoke absently and stared up at the treetops. The image of that path from her dream came into her mind again.

Smoke? she thought. *There's a place I need to go. Will you come with me?*

Of course, the ferret thought.

～

FINN WAS WALKING along at the back of the group, staring up at the trees and wishing he'd never told Isabelle how he'd felt. She and Ronan were walking along, shoulder to shoulder, just a few steps ahead of him. They were laughing, and occasionally Ronan would touch her on the arm, or brush some hair out of her face. Isabelle was studiously avoiding Finn's gaze. Possibly, Finn thought, that was because he was staring creepily at them.

He started to wrench his gaze away, but then Ronan grabbed Isabelle's hand and pulled her off into the trees. Finn tried not to look as he walked past, but out of the corner of his eye he couldn't help but noticed the entwined arms, and Ronan's hands in Isabelle's hair. Neither of them noticed him.

Awesome. Just great.

312

When they stopped for lunch—a lunch that Finn had absolutely no appetite for—Isabelle sat on Ronan's lap, aggressively making out with him, neither of them touching their food, either.

Finn sat, not eating, not even trying not to look anymore.

"Best not to watch that sort of thing, boy," Eraldir said. Finn hadn't even realized he was there.

Finn jerked his gaze away and tried to focus on Eraldir.

"For one, it looks like it's killing you, and for another, it's generally frowned upon." Eraldir took a large bite of dried meat and chewed with a grimace.

"I know." Finn couldn't help it, he looked back. Other mages were giving Isabelle and Ronan a wide berth, carefully avoiding looking in their direction, except for Marta, who glared disapprovingly at both of them. She met Finn's eye and for once he agreed with her outrage. He wished she'd make a scene, just to get them to stop for a while.

"I gather you told her how you feel?" Eraldir asked, interrupting Finn's thoughts again.

"Yeah," Finn said hollowly.

"Not the way to go with Isabelle, boy."

"It didn't matter, though, she just doesn't feel the same."

"Oh, no boy, I wouldn't say that; not at all. Well, probably."

For the first time, Finn focused his attention on Eraldir. "What?"

Eraldir gestured towards Isabelle with his meat. "I mean, with most people, them making out with someone else, you're right, it's a pretty good sign they don't like you, but Isabelle, maybe not. I mean, who knows, with her it might just be she felt like it, but more likely it's because you told her you love her."

"Um..."

313

"You think Isabelle wants someone to love her? What do you think that means to her?"

Finn thought back over what he knew about Isabelle. She'd travelled alone for a long time, ran away from home, was always running off and coming back whenever she felt like it.

Eraldir continued. "She tell you about her parents?"

"I guess…"

"Her mom left everything to go be with her father, and look what it got her. Drugged herself into oblivion just to avoid having to face that she'd given up everything she was, everything important to her."

"But, I'm not going to—"

"Tell Isabelle where to go?" It had been Finn's idea to go to the Table, after all. "Want her to stay here with you?" Of course Finn would want that.

"I don't want that…"

"But, you want her to only be with you, right?"

"I guess."

Suddenly, Finn understood, and the whole problem shifted. It was like he'd been looking at something, not able to make sense of what it was, and then his eyes had refocused and he'd recognized it, and it was obvious. Isabelle, of all the people he knew, needed freedom the most. There was one thing that bothered him, though.

"What if she really just likes Ronan, though?"

"Well, sure, that is a possibility. I mean, it sure looks like she likes him." Isabelle had thrown a leg over Ronan now, and was straddling him as she kissed him. "Thing is, though, if you love her, what you do is the same either way."

The uncertainty in Finn's chest settled into a solid calm. Eraldir was right. Finn didn't have to figure out what she was feeling. He knew how he felt. He loved her, and if she wanted

314

Ronan she could be with Ronan. But he knew how he felt and he wasn't going to give up that easily.

THE FOREST HERE WAS DARKER, older. Kel stepped softly through the trees, Smoke riding on her shoulder, a warm lump against her neck. The canopy above was so thick that barely any light reached the forest floor, and so the ground between the trunks was bare, except for a litter of dead leaves and twigs, slowly rotting back into the ground.

The woods were silent, too. No birds, only the occasional rustle of leaves from high above. Something told Kel that this was where her dreams were coming from, that she was getting closer, but this was not the light birch forest of her dreams. This was a dark, old place.

Some presence called her forward. It was close, she could feel it.

"Kel." A voice behind her spoke. Kel froze, Smoke trembling against her.

She turned and saw two long, slender arms reaching up out of the ground, the elbows bent and the palms of the hands braced against the earth, as if someone was trying to heave themselves up out of a grave.

A head emerged, pale and insubstantial. The thing, whatever it was, thrust itself out of the ground, but there was no hole beneath it; it was like it was a part of the earth, and was struggling to detach itself.

"Kel," it said again. It was human-shaped, a woman, but her eyes blazed with fire, and her upper body was made of stone. She pulled her legs free at last, and these were like deep underground streams, as if she were wading through water and had become water herself. She stood tall, and her

315

body rearranged itself. Her watery legs swayed and shimmered underneath her.

Only curiosity kept Kel from turning and running. What was this thing, how did it know her name, what did it want, and why had it been stuck there in the ground? Also, was it going to hurt her? The questions got stuck together on the way out, though, and all Kel said was, "Yes?" Her voice came out an octave higher than normal.

The fiery eyes, set in their stone sockets, blazed at her. "You must go back." The voice was like wind in the trees, it echoed through the silence, seeming to come from everywhere at once. Kel shivered, but pulled herself up a little taller.

"Go back where?"

"To your brother."

"Why?"

The thing stepped forward; it lifted its slender stone arms and water rose out of the ground, crystallizing into a smooth sheet of clear ice. At first, Kel could see the creature through the ice, but then it was gone, and instead there were shadows moving behind it. These shadows moved closer, solidified, formed themselves into an image. Her brother. His face cold and emotionless.

The view pulled back, and Kel saw him standing on a dark tower, arms lifted. Around him, at the base of the tower stretched a wide plain, dark with hordes of men, armies, dying in flames. The image shifted, to towns burning and people dying, screaming in agony.

And then it was gone. The sheet of ice disappeared.

"This is who your brother will soon become."

Kel shook her head. "How do you know? He wouldn't do that." But what she had seen called to mind other, similar events.

"There are only two who could prevent this. You are one."

Kel shook her head again. "Why?"

The creature rearranged its shoulders with a slow grinding of stone. "All I know is that you or the other must be there with him. You must leave now."

Kel didn't want to go back. And the presence called to her more strongly than ever. She had to continue, had to find out what it was.

A ripple ran through the creature's legs. "I know he is calling to you. You must ignore it. You must find your brother instead."

"You know what's calling me?" Kel asked.

"Yes. It is evil. You must leave."

But Kel was trusting this creature less and less. "Why? What is it?"

"It is something old and evil, and it will destroy you, Kel."

"What are you? How do you know my name?"

Its eyes dimmed, then flared out. "I was Ruith, builder of cities, oldest of the Ael who remained. The thing that is calling you, I was the one who bound it, and I remain to watch over it."

"Why is it calling to me?"

"It wishes to destroy you." Kel didn't quite believe this either.

"Why?"

"Because of what you are."

"What am I?"

For a moment, the creature didn't answer. Instead, it swelled, pulling itself more fully upright, bracing its watery legs underneath it. "You are its creation. You are the destruction of our people." Flames poured out of its eyes, licked across its bare stone chest and arms. It reached a hand towards Kel, gripped her arm with such strength that Kel felt the bones strain; any more force and they would snap.

Kel cried, but she didn't struggle, for fear that any movement and her wrist would break. "Please," she said. "Let me go."

But the creature began to drag her towards it, reaching out its other hand. "I will not let you go on." As Kel struggled, it flashed across her mind that maybe the creature was lying to her about Finn, just to keep her from going on.

That was when the first crow arrived. It dove out of the sky, scratching and pecking at the stone, then beat its wings and jabbed its beak into the thing's eyes. Its feathers caught fire but it continued to peck. Then more and more crows arrived, in a whirlwind of feathers and beaks and talons, screeching and pulling and tugging at it.

No, Kel thought, *you can't hurt it.* But the crows ignored her.

Kel's arm was still locked in the thing's grasp, her hand going numb, but in her pockets were seeds. The thing was beating its stone arm at the crows, crushing four or five of them at a time. Kel heard their light, fragile bones snap, felt their lungs collapse, their bodies go limp. Kel called to the seed of the vine in her pocket, sent it forth.

The green tendril stretched out, found the thing's arm, twisted itself along and around it, sending roots down into its watery legs. The roots sucked greedily, and the thing stumbled, the vine wrapped tighter, snaking across its chest. The thing tore at the vine with its free hand, ripping parts of it, but each broken part became a new shoot, sending roots into the creature's legs and coiling up around its arms. The thing struggled, but was quickly covered in a mass of vines so heavy it fell to the ground. Its struggles became weaker and weaker, but still it held Kel locked in its grip.

It gave a final heave and was still. The crows retreated to nearby branches to watch. The ground was littered with crushed and broken bodies, mangled black wings sticking up at odd angles. Kel's breathing slowly returned to normal, but she didn't take her eyes off the mound of vines. Finally, when it had been still for several moments, she gave her wrist an experimental tug. The stone had locked around her. She pulled harder, shaking her arm, trying to get it loose, but nothing moved. She was trapped.

CHAPTER 23

*A*fter several hours, the thing still hadn't moved. Curious, Kel began peeling the vines back. She did this slowly, expecting at any moment for the thing to reach out and grab her with its other arm. But when the last of the vines had been cleared away she saw that the creature was no more. All that was left was the arm, thrust up out of the ground, its rock fingers wrapped around Kel's wrist, and a stone face, eyes closed.

Kel traced the stone cheek with a finger, and wondered how much of what the creature had told her was true. She couldn't believe that the thing that called to her in her dreams was evil, but she could, as much as she didn't want to, believe that Finn was in danger of becoming what she had seen. But maybe the stone woman had only told her that to make her turn back.

She turned her attention back to her wrist. The stone was tight around her, so that she could barely even wiggle it without chafing her skin. She picked a rock off the ground and tapped at the stone fingers, then banged, but it didn't so much as chip.

One of the crows hopped over, standing on the face, another perched on the upraised hand, scratched at it with its talons, then cocked a dark eye at Kel.

Thank you for your help, Kel said.

It clicked its beak and flapped away.

Kel tried using the roots of plants to crumble the stone, but it was perfectly smooth, there was no way in for even the tiniest of roots. She banged at the stone with her rock for a while, until the rock she was using broke.

After a while, a bear ambled up, tried to snap off the stone arm at the base, but couldn't budge it. Some moles tried to dig around it, but the stone went deeper into the earth than even they could dig. A weasel offered to chew her hand off at the wrist, but Kel thanked it and said she'd try a few other things first.

All the while, Smoke brought her eggs and worms and beetles and whatever else he could find. Kel munched these and contemplated her predicament.

After a few hours, the crow that had left came back with a piece of iron in its beak. It gave the stone a few experimental taps then dropped it in Kel's lap.

Kel banged at the stone with the iron for a while, but it didn't even make a dent. Undeterred, the crows brought her an arrowhead, a piece of green glass, a sharp fragment of blue pottery, a rough-edged sea rock, and a bone needle. Out of politeness, she tried them all, but none could scratch the rocky fist that held her.

She took a break when evening came, and grew some raspberry bushes from the seeds in her pockets to feed the animals who had been helping her.

That night, the crows, the bear, the weasel, Smoke, the moles, and a few deer kept her company.

∿

THE NEXT MORNING, as Finn was eating breakfast, an idea popped into his head. While the rest of the mages were at their morning class with Eraldir, Finn went to find Isabelle. To his relief, he found her sitting alone, cross-legged, slowly levitating herself fifteen feet up in the air and back down again. Her eyes were squeezed shut in concentration.

Finn waited until she was safely back on the ground before clearing his throat to interrupt her.

"What's up, Finn?" she said, eyes still closed, beginning her slow rise into the air again. Finn had never seen her do something so slow and deliberate before.

"Do you have a minute?"

"Yes." She kept her eyes closed, hovering nine feet above Finn's head for a moment before slowly lowering back down again.

Finn waited, expected her to stop at the bottom and look at him, but she just continued back up again.

"Um, can I talk to you?"

"Yes."

She still didn't look at him.

Okay. So, apparently, she hadn't forgotten what he'd said to her.

"Isabelle, will you come down, open your eyes, look at me, and talk to me?"

She heaved a sigh, but lowered to the ground, stood, and looked at him. Her brown eyes were distant.

"Look. I'm sorry about what I said."

"You're sorry? Why?"

Finn picked at the frayed edge of his sleeve. "I'm sorry I made you uncomfortable. I like you, but it's okay. You can do what you want. I still want to be friends. If you like Ronan—"

Isabelle gave an exasperated grunt and kicked at the ground. Her eyes darted up to meet Finn's and then slipped away again. "No."

"What?"

"Just, no, okay?"

Did that mean no as in, 'Stop talking about this because I'll never like you'? Or, did it mean, 'No, I don't like Ronan'?

"What does that mean?"

"I don't want to talk about it."

"Okay."

He decided to count that as a win and change the subject for now. "Anyway, I had something to ask you."

She narrowed her eyes suspiciously.

"I have another problem," Finn said.

"Does that make me the first problem?"

"No. Well, yes I guess. But... not in a bad way?"

"Hmm."

"Anyway." Finn ran a hand through his hair. "Okay, so... I may have told the mages that we have a school already set up."

Isabelle's jaw dropped. She stared at him for a second, and then she started to laugh. "Seriously?"

"Yeah."

Isabelle laughed harder. "Oh man," she gasped out, "you are screwed."

Finn waited for the hilarity to subside, but it didn't look like it was going to. "Yeah, I know."

"You're lucky no one asked me about the school, you know."

Finn hadn't thought of that. She was right. That was incredibly lucky.

Isabelle took a few deep breaths to calm herself. Then she started thinking it through. "So... you're going to get to the Table and they'll be like 'where's the school'?"

Finn nodded.

"They'll probably leave."

"Yeah."

"Actually, now that their friend is dead, they'll probably kill you."

That hadn't occurred to Finn.

Isabelle laughed. "Man, Finn, you're just not happy unless everyone around you wants to kill you."

"I'd be perfectly happy with no one wanting me dead."

"Well, I guess you're just not very good at it then." But, she was still smiling, a fact which totally overshadowed anything else in Finn's mind.

"So… I have a favor to ask you."

She arched an eyebrow at him. "Oh yeah?"

"Yes. I think you're the only one who could help—"

"Flattery's not going to work, Finn."

"Sorry. It'll make it less likely that the mages will kill me for lying to them?"

"Eh." That hurt.

"Umm… please?"

"Ooh, begging. All right, sure."

"Wait, really?"

She grinned at him. "I was already going to help you, I just wanted to see what you'd try. You know, convincing people of things is part of leadership. I'd assume."

"Yeah, well, thank you."

She punched him on the arm. "Sure thing. So, what is it? Want me to murder someone for you?"

"What? No. Definitely not."

Her eyes lit up. "Jes?"

"No. Absolutely, definitely not."

"Fine. So, what?"

"I need you go to the King's Table, get there ahead of us, and set it up to look like a school."

"What?"

"Er, I need you to go to—"

"No, no, I get that part. Just, what?"

"What do you mean, what?" Finn said.

"I mean, that's your plan? How am I supposed to make it look like we've had a school there?"

"Um... desks? Rooms for students to stay in? A communal eating place? Maybe a library?"

"And it's just going to be empty?" she said.

"I mean, you could put furniture there."

"No, Finn, I mean, what about students? If the school's been there for a while, why aren't there students?"

"Maybe the first class graduated already. We came looking for the second class." This seemed plausible.

"Okay... And, what, you want me to build you some furniture?"

"Maybe you can find some? Eraldir said people used to live there," Finn said.

She considered this, one hand on her hip, the other playing with a loose tendril of hair. "All right, cool."

"You'll do it?"

She looked at him, smiling, her head tilted to the side. "Yeah, no problem."

Hope started to sneak its way into Finn. It was a ridiculous plan, sure, and it was probably going to fail, but it might not. And if it didn't, he would be running the first mage school in a hundred years. Not only that, but for a few weeks he wouldn't have to watch Isabelle and Ronan make out. He grinned.

"Okay... great, just one thing..."

"What?"

"No mountain lions."

She gave him an injured look. "I wouldn't put mountain lions in a school, Finn."

"And no giant wind catapults."

"Fine."

～

ISABELLE HAD WANTED to punch Jes in the face before she left —something about that girl just bugged her—but she'd settled for hiding behind a tree and pulling all the air away from her face a few times. Isabelle laughed, watching Jes freak out when the air was suddenly gone, and then get confused when it suddenly came back again. It only took three times before the girl started to cry, at which point Isabelle figured that was good enough. Isabelle strongly considered stealing Jes' eyelashes so she couldn't use them on Finn while Isabelle was gone, but Finn would probably find out.

She considered saying goodbye to Ronan, but he might take that the wrong way.

Hitching her backpack up onto her back, Isabelle tied her hair back, called some wind, and blasted herself into the sky.

It felt so good, the rush of the air, the shocking speed, the trees shrinking away beneath her, then the slow, inexorable pull of gravity, slowing her until she hung for a moment, just one moment, weightless, and then the exhilarating plunge toward the hard ground. She gathered the air beneath her, compressed it until it had the thickness of bacon fat. It was like plummeting into butter, but without all the grease in your hair.

She wished she could sustain her flight, that it didn't have to be so short-lived, but it was still fun. Even better than climbing trees had been. She didn't need trees for height anymore.

Explosion after explosion, she careened down the mountainside, taking out a few small trees along the way and even startling a bear once. She'd never seen a bear run off in terror before; it was hilarious, and all of a sudden, she had a new hobby.

By evening she had made it to the plains. She tried to light a fire next to the river, but couldn't get it to take. She kept blowing it out. Regular fire was so much weaker than Finn's. After only a few tries she gave up, frustrated and annoyed. And missing Finn. And annoyed that she was missing Finn. And wondering whether Jes was talking to him. She'd better not be.

~

NOT TRUSTING any of the other mages to abide by the decision to not kill Jes, Finn took it upon himself to walk with her the next day. Even though they had ostensibly agreed that the mage's death was an accident, Finn knew that no one liked her. He himself didn't trust her, but he wasn't going to let her die on his watch.

Jes was silent as they walked, her eyes on the ground in front of her.

Finn looked up at the line of mages ahead of them, wending their way through the trees, following Eraldir. At least they weren't grouped off by mage type anymore. And the thread mages seemed to have more friends than they had before. That was good. His team-building game had sort of worked, then. Of course, it had also made Ronan a lot more popular, but that would have happened anyway. And now everyone—not just Isabelle—wanted to murder Jes.

He wondered where Isabelle was. How long would it take her to get to the Table?

~

AFTER BEING BRIEFLY DISTRACTED by her bear-startling game, Isabelle was making good time across the plains. She was following the Blackwater River now, which she'd passed a few times in her earlier travels. She catapulted along, heaving herself hundreds of feet into the air, covering a half mile with every go.

Finally, as she reached the apex of one of her flights, she saw it. There, to the east, was the tip of a tall black tower.

As she made her way towards it, it grew taller and taller. It was perched atop a mesa, which rose out of the flat plains. The mesa's sides were sheer cliffs of red sandstone, and perched atop them were black stone walls. From one end of the mesa rose the tower.

Isabelle thought she would be there by the end of the day, but when darkness fell the mesa didn't look all that much closer. Again, she slept without a fire.

AFTER A FEW DAYS Kel was beginning to think she would have to take the weasel up on its offer. It kept telling her about members of its own family who had chewed their own legs off to escape traps. It made it sound like pretty much no one had all four paws anymore.

Kel contemplated her hand.

No, she couldn't do it. She'd find some other way.

THE NEXT MORNING, Isabelle got up early and continued blasting her way towards the King's Table. She didn't stop to rest or chase animals or even eat. She realized she shouldn't have wasted time earlier. Every hour she wasn't at the Table was another hour she didn't have to make something to convince those mages not to kill Finn. And, as much as she hated to admit it to herself, she really would prefer to keep Finn around.

For hours, the Table drew no closer. She pressed on through the cloudless heat of midday, wishing she had brought more water from the river, hoping there would be water when she reached the Table. Otherwise, they might arrive and find not a school but a shriveled up dead body.

And then, suddenly, she was there: standing at the base of the mesa, craning her neck back trying to see to the top.

The mesa was large, at least half a mile long and a quarter mile wide. At the top of the mesa, she could see stone walls built up around the edges that made it even taller, and at one end a black tower jutted up into the sky.

Now to find a way inside.

She walked along the base of the southern wall, then turned north, walking to let her magic refill itself and dissipate some of the shadow. The sun moved across the sky as she made her way slowly around the base of the enormous fortress.

On the north side, high up in the red rock wall, Isabelle could see platforms, jutting balconies, and windows. That might be a fun way in. The western wall was the highest, and completely bare. In the southern wall, she found a door.

It was enormous, about fifteen feet tall, and maybe ten feet wide. She tugged on it, but it was either locked or the hinges were rusted shut with age. After all, it had been a hundred years since anyone had been here. Probably.

Well, good. A locked door was no problem for Isabelle. She didn't want to use the door anyway. Probably Finn would want her to get it unstuck, though, rather than just making a wind catapult to shoot people inside. That would be a much better way to get into a school, though. Way more fun.

That was enough walking. Isabelle tied her hair back again, rubbed her hands together, and stepped back to examine the wall. She wasn't going to aim for one of the balconies on the north side. That was too easy. Of course, maybe she was wasting time. Damn. Okay, she'd just try a few times and if she couldn't get in this way, on the south side, she'd move around to the easy side.

Levitating or blasting? Isabelle considered this a moment, but the answer was definitely blasting.

Taking a deep breath, she called the wind. She put everything she had into it, pulling every molecule of air around her to her, sucking the breath out of every pair of lungs for a mile around. The air rushed towards her, compressed her, blasted her up into the air. Higher and higher and higher. Her arms were tight at her sides, her hair plastered flat by the oncoming air. She could see the top of the wall above her, aimed for it, but she was losing power already. Starting to slow. She wasn't going to make it. She ran out of momentum and plummeted towards the ground. She was running out of magic, and her air cushion was not as effective as it needed to be. She was still hurtling along when she plowed into the ground. She tucked her head and rolled to keep from breaking anything—Isabelle was well-practiced at falling out of trees—but she still knocked hard against a rock, bruised her legs and back. Something in her left arm twisted painfully, too.

Isabelle lay in the dry dust for a while, panting and taking stock of her injuries. Nothing too bad. She started to get up, but her back twinged and a hot bolt of pain shot through her arm. She swayed, a little dizzy from the pain, but after a few more deep breaths it retreated to a manageable level.

She surveyed the wall. She had gotten close that time, but she'd used everything she had. What else could she do? Suddenly, she grinned. She had it.

She was so excited to try out her idea that she forgot to take stock of how much power she had left. Holding her arms tight by her sides she again called the wind to her. All of it. The animals in the plains around her who had just gotten their breath back felt a rush of terror as again all the air was sucked away from them. Birds fell out of the sky where the wind beneath them was suddenly gone. And Isabelle was rocketing into the air. This time, though, she wasn't just pushing herself upwards, she was emptying the sky above her.

Before when she had launched herself into the sky she had felt the wind in her hair, the breeze against her face. She loved that part of it; it was a rush; it made you feel the speed. This time, though, she moved it all out of the way, and around her was a cone of stillness and silence. It wasn't like flying at all. She couldn't breathe, she couldn't hear anything, but she was rising faster than she ever had before.

The top edge of the mesa loomed close, but again Isabelle was starting to run out of magic. And then she realized that she didn't have enough for the way down.

She was running out of magic, not just running out of upward momentum or air to cannon herself forward. She wasn't going to be able to make a cushion to catch herself.

Isabelle dismissed the thought immediately. She'd better just make it, then. All or nothing. She angled towards the lip of the wall, feeling like she was moving in slow motion. She reached out her arm as far as it would go, but it caught the air current around her; it felt like when she had stuck her arm into the river current and it had tugged her aside, but there was no Finn to pull her back now, and the drag was slowing her. She yanked her arm back into the airless void around her.

The edge came closer, but she was moving so slowly now. She wasn't sure if she was going to make it. Using the last ounce of her magic she pulled more air around herself, lifted herself an inch higher. Her arm shot out and her fingers grasped the stone edge of the wall.

Her magic was gone, the air rushed away from her, and sound returned. Her eardrums popped painfully. She was holding on with one hand, scrabbling with the other and her feet to try to find purchase on the wall, but she slipped, and dangled by one arm, and then, because she was Isabelle and therefore curious and easily distracted, even from death, she looked down. Whoa. Better not. Maybe she could just hang here until her magic returned, she thought. But it wasn't coming back. She had used more than she had ever used before, and instead of feeling the magic bubbling back up inside her she felt a heavy darkness that was settling into her guts, weighing her down. And it wanted out of her, too, she could feel it. She knew that she shouldn't let it out. This was the shadow, stronger than she'd ever felt it before. It would do something destructive, something even she was afraid of.

Dangling from the edge, her fingers slipping off the dusty surface, Isabelle struggled to contain the shadow. One finger slipped off the edge and she lost her focus. Then, two things happened simultaneously. The first was that Isabelle got a huge jolt of adrenaline, and used it to whip her injured arm up high enough to grab the ledge, too. She should have felt searing pain, probably—she felt something tear—but all she could feel was the desire to live. The second thing was that all the air left. Isabelle felt relief, a lightness, and then panic, because she couldn't breathe. The shadow was gone, it had poured out of her and driven all the air away from this place. How far had the air gone?

No time to think. She had to get to the top of the wall. Her feet scrabbled against the wall, and with every last bit of strength she had she managed to heave herself up and get her stomach over the edge. She wanted to lay there, panting, but there was no air to pant. She was suffocating, her muscles screaming in protest, needing oxygen.

Scraping her stomach along the edge, kicking with her

feet, and tearing her clothes, Isabelle heaved herself over the wall, falling five feet to a stone battlement on the other side. She crawled desperately, looking for air, and about ten feet away she finally found it. There, she collapsed, gasping.

For a while she just lay there breathing. Man, air was great. Then the pain hit her. It felt like she'd torn every muscle she had. Her arms were the worst, but there wasn't anything she could do about them now, so she stood, swaying from the pain, and walked back to the edge, crossing back into the quiet, airless void.

She found a rock to stand on and peeked over. Wow that was high. Sweet. That had to count as flying, right? This would be a good place to jump off of, actually, once her magic came back.

Running out of air again, Isabelle turned from the wall and limped off to see what this place was like. Further down the wall, in a darkened doorway, a pair of eyes watched her go.

CHAPTER 24

*K*el's wrist was thick with calluses and brown with dried blood. Her knees ached and stung, her back was knotted, and she could no longer feel her arm. In her free hand, she held the sharp fragment of blue pottery. She ran her thumb along the edge, feeling it slice along her skin. Then she put it down, picked up the arrowhead. Not sharp enough either.

Can you bring me a knife? Kel asked. Two crows flew away.

ONE OF REINA'S SCOUTS, a fire mage named Cin, snuck back into Westwend that afternoon. She was Reina's favorite spy, because she could light fires that no one else could see. So far, Reina had only used her for sneaking around and watching people in the dark, but she also liked the idea of a fire that could consume a building without anyone understanding what was happening.

Cin entered through the main gate because the guards were spread too thinly now. There was only one man posted there, and he was busy talking to some traveling merchants.

One merchant's eyes followed Cin as she snuck past, behind the guard's back. But Cin winked a green eye at him and he smiled foolishly enough that she knew he wouldn't say anything. Then, Cin found a dark corner and waited until night. Her time.

As she waited, her mind drifted unpleasantly back to her last conversation with *him*. Resentment boiled within her.

I'm too old for you. She heard him say again. Like she was a child. And now he'd just left. Gone off without telling her anything. Without even asking if she would have come with him. Angrily, she pushed her thoughts away, focused on what she had to do for Reina.

IT WAS A SMALL KNIFE, light but sharp, only a few inches long, with a dark wood handle lashed tight with leather. Kel took a deep breath, wrapped her fingers around the handle, and moved it towards her wrist.

You have to break the bones, the weasel said.

Smoke snapped his teeth at the weasel. *Don't do it Kel, we'll find a way to get you out.*

It's been a week, nothing breaks this stone.

What about Finn? If it's magic, maybe he can break it?

Finn is too far away. That wasn't true; Kel had enough food and water to stay alive here as long as it took, but she didn't want Finn to come back, didn't know if he would. He had other things to do, and even if he didn't, she didn't think he, or anyone, would be able to break the stone.

Kel decided to cut first, then break the bones when she got there. She wasn't sure she'd have the nerve to cut into her own body, and if she didn't she'd rather find out before she'd broken her wrist. She lifted the knife, held it against the already bloody skin of the back side of her wrist. She felt the little bones there, underneath the skin. They felt loose, maybe she could just pry them apart with the knife.

Kel's mind recoiled in horror. She turned and heaved onto the ground the gooey, acidic mess of a partially digested egg. Shaking, she wiped her face with the back of her good hand, the knife flashing in front of her eyes. Panic started to overtake her. Her hand would be gone forever. For the rest of her life she would only have one hand. She wiggled the fingers, and could just barely still feel the motion. That part of her would be gone. She dropped the knife and started to cry. Smoke curled himself around her neck, stroking her face with his paws.

It's okay, we'll find another way.

But Kel didn't think they would.

~

HAVING BARELY SLEPT at all the previous night, Finn was having trouble staying awake to eat his dinner. The light was fading from the sky and with it his eyes were beginning to close of their own accord.

"You know, I was in a love triangle once," Eraldir said. "Well, it was more of an octagon, really. I loved two women, but the first one, well, she was in love with a bandit who was in love with a princess who was in love with a simple farm girl who loved only herself. But the farm girl was also loved by a traveling soldier who had sworn to avenge his brother's murder, and he was loved by the other woman I loved. Didn't end well."

"Ah," said Finn, giving up on his food and laying down on his bedroll.

"Come to think of it, that's only seven. Maybe I'm

thinking of a different time. Right, right, no the octagon was —" A great, wracking cough choked off the last of his words. He bent double, dropping his tea mug, the spilled tea spreading and soaking into the ground.

Finn was up and by the man's side immediately. But, there was nothing he could do as Eraldir hacked and gasped for air. He placed a hand on the man's back, but feeling the wheeze and rattle in the man's chest as he coughed was more than Finn could take. He reached for Eraldir's pack.

"What do you need? Herbs? Berries?" He started taking things out and holding them out to Eraldir. Eraldir shook his head, coughing into his hand.

Eventually, the coughing subsided. Eraldir wiped his hand on a cloth, and Finn saw blood. For a while they just sat in silence, staring into the fire. Then Eraldir took a long, rattling breath, and looked sharply at Finn.

"There's something I need to tell you." The words set off another bout of coughing, but this one was shorter than the last. "Not... without tea... though."

Finn set about making tea for the old man; he made it carefully, exactly the way Eraldir did.

Eraldir blew on the liquid to cool it and then took an experimental sip. He sighed.

"Eh, I won't miss this stuff. Terrible. Been drinking it for almost ninety years now. That's too long to drink something that tastes so bad. Met a midget once who liked it. He was a good man."

Finn waited for the inevitable story, but Eraldir didn't continue. Instead, he shook himself, and looked sharply at Finn. "There's a Teacher left."

"What?"

"One of the old ones. The Ael."

"Oh, right, really?"

Eraldir cracked his back. "Back when I was a boy. The old

City of Mages. It was led by seven of them, although one was only half Ael. Most of the Ael were gone, as I think I mentioned. But these were left, and they were the ones who taught us about magic."

Eraldir stared into the fire a while, then continued. "Far as I knew, they were all killed in the Fall, too. And all their knowledge was lost and the City of Mages was closed to us and almost all the mages died, and the ones that didn't die then died in the wars soon after. Back when I was a boy, just a young lad of thirty or so, I went looking for the old Teachers. I couldn't believe they were dead, and I'd heard stories that maybe one was left. And there was. And I found her."

"What? Did she tell you what happened? Can she get us back into the old City?"

"Hold on there, boy, not so fast. Don't you suppose there might be a reason why she's the only one left?"

Oh.

"I don't know, but I have my suspicions. I think she may have had something to do with the Fall in the first place. I asked her about it once. I was a little drunk, I confess. She'd had a fair amount to drink, too, but I don't think her kind can get drunk. I think maybe she was trying to get information out of me, actually, because she was the one who brought it up in the first place. Kept asking me about what I'd seen when I'd been up near the boundary of the City of Mages. Couldn't tell her much."

"What did she say about it? When you asked her, what did she tell you about the Fall?"

"She said she didn't know what happened, either." Eraldir took a long sip of tea. "But she was lying."

"You're sure?" Finn asked.

"Yes, boy, course I'm sure. I thought you knew by now what an excellent judge of people I am." He cocked an enormous eyebrow at Finn, who smiled. "Anyway, she knows things, that's for sure. She just doesn't tell you all she knows, and she's got some motive I can't figure out. She was the one who told me to come find your sister."

Finn sat back, stunned. "What?" A creepy sense of being watched snuck up his spine. How had she known about Finn and Kel, and what did she want with Kel?

"Yeah. Said there was a mage down there needed my help. Said she needed to get out of the forest."

Finn's insides clenched in fear. "Is she in danger in the forest?" If Kel got hurt... Nothing mattered. Yes, he cared about the mages and about starting a school and making amends for what he'd done, but in that moment Finn realized that nothing was as important to him as his sister. And he'd left her. The old familiar self-hatred roared back to life inside him.

"Slow down there, boy. Like I said, she has her own reasons for wanting that girl out of the forest and I don't know what they are but I can tell you for sure that it's not because it's in her best interest. That's why I didn't mind too much when she headed back off on her own. Figured she'd learned what she needed to from me. No, it's something else."

Finn couldn't help himself. "What?"

"I just told you. I'm not keeping information from you for dramatic effect. I don't know why she wants your sister out of the forest."

"How do I find her?" Finn wanted to question her himself. Part of him wanted to go find her right now and not leave until she answered his questions.

"You don't."

"How do you find her?"

"She calls to me, sometimes."

"How?"

"In dreams. She sends me dreams, and I follow them and I find her and she gives me advice. Sometimes I follow it, sometimes I don't. Been doing that for almost seventy years now. Gotta tell you, it hurts being friends with an immortal that long. I started out younger than her. I was the handsome young adventurer. Now I'm an old man, but she still gets to be the wise one." He shook his head.

"Is there any way for me to find her?"

"Not that I know of."

Finn digested this. Maybe she knew something that would help him get into the old City and get books and artifacts, things that would lend legitimacy to his school. He doubted it. But at least it might be something to try.

He stared thoughtfully into the darkness around them.

"What, exactly, did she say about Kel?"

Eraldir was staring into the fire. At first Finn thought he was thinking, but when it had been several seconds and Eraldir still hadn't responded, Finn tried again.

"Eraldir?"

The old man didn't seem to have heard him.

Finn placed a hand on the man's skinny shoulder. "Hey, Eraldir? You okay?"

Eraldir blinked. "I think the octagon was over in Montvale, because I remember meeting up with Rose in a tea emporium. Excellent tea in Montvale. Surprised Isabelle's never mentioned it. It may have been an octagon, but for me there was only Rose..." he sighed.

"Eraldir?"

The man turned to look at Finn, but it was like he wasn't quite seeing him. "She never loved me, but I never needed her to." He turned back to the fire. Finn felt desperately alone. He sat there, next to the old man, for a long while, unsure of what to do. Knowing, deep down, that there was nothing he could do.

Eventually, Eraldir turned and clapped Finn on the back.

"Well, Finn, we'd better get to bed. Can't stay up telling stories the whole night."

Finn knew he could tell Eraldir what had happened, that he'd spaced out again, but he didn't. "Night, Eraldir. Sleep well."

A moment of confusion passed across Eraldir's face, but then he shook himself, and turned towards his bed. "You, too, boy."

CHAPTER 25

inn's boots slipped as he climbed the rain-slicked side of the boulder. He bent down and used his hands to pull himself up, scraping a knee as he did so. He made it to the top, though, and was rewarded with exactly what he was hoping for. To the south the ground sloped down, and from his vantage point he could see over the tops of the trees. Only a few miles away they began to thin out, and not far beyond that they stopped completely, giving way to the brown vastness of the plains. He scanned the horizon, looking for the Table, but it was too far away. He imagined Isabelle somewhere out there, hoped she was all right.

The boulder shook under his feet, and he turned to see Ronan hop up next to him, having made himself a set of stairs up the boulder's side.

"Morning," Ronan said, stretching and yawning. "Nice view."

Finn yawned, too. He should probably stop staying up so late listening to Eraldir.

"Hey," Ronan said, "Have you seen Isabelle?"

Finn couldn't tell whether he felt more guilty for sending Isabelle away or more annoyed that Ronan was asking him about her, when he clearly knew how Finn felt about her. Well, it didn't matter anyway, because Finn knew she didn't like Ronan. Maybe. He still wasn't totally clear on what Isabelle had meant by 'No.' Still, for right now, he was going to go with it meaning "No, I don't like Ronan at all. I am in love with you, Finn." Right. Ronan had asked him a question, though. Had he seen Isabelle?

"No." It was technically true.

"Should we look for her?"

"No, she goes off by herself all the time."

"Look, I'm sorry, Finn," Ronan said.

"About what?"

"I know you like her. I shouldn't have..."

"It's okay."

"No, I'm sorry. I just. I really like her."

"That's okay. I get it." And he did. And it didn't matter what Ronan said. What they had was a passing thing.

"Finn..."

Finn turned and smiled a rueful smile at Ronan. "It's really okay, Ronan. Isabelle can do what she wants."

Ronan scratched the back of his neck and considered this. "Okay, well... thanks."

"Plus, I killed your parents."

Shock passed over Ronan's face, then he laughed incredulously. "Too soon, Finn."

"Yeah, sorry."

"Also, my dad's still alive. Far as I know."

"Not for long."

Ronan lifted an eyebrow.

"Just kidding."

"Still too soon."

"Yeah."

Neither of them knew what to say for several moments. They turned and stared out at the view.

"Anyway…" Ronan said. "I noticed you're including me in the leadership now, like you said. That's great."

"Oh, sure, of course. I meant what I said."

"Good. Because I've been thinking."

Finn's stomach tensed. "Yeah?"

"Eraldir's classes are all well and good, but we need to add in some other material."

"Like what?"

"Battle magic."

Finn grimaced. "I don't know, Ronan."

"Come on, Finn. There's no way we're going to create a country without having to fight at all. At the very least we'll need the ability to fight back."

Finn knew Ronan was right, but he didn't want to go in that direction. The whole point of this was to avoid violence.

"Okay. But, the focus of the training should be on fighting to control, rather than to kill."

"There are people out there who want us dead. I'd rather it be them than us."

"I see what you're saying, but we're so much more powerful than non-mages."

"They have weapons."

"Yeah, and so do we. We should be able to convince them without killing."

"Sometimes you can't."

"Who's going to teach it?"

"Me and Rafe."

Unease, bordering on dread, floated up like a cloud in Finn's mind. But it was only a class. It wasn't like he was agreeing to build an army and attack people. It was the first step in a direction he didn't want to go, though. But he'd agreed to share leadership with Ronan, and this was a pretty small concession to make.

"All right," Finn said finally.

Ronan smiled and clapped him on the back. "Great. First class is this afternoon. Rafe's going over the basic attacks, and how to incorporate magic. You coming?"

"No, thanks."

After Ronan had left, though, Finn wondered if he was making a mistake. If he didn't attend the class he would be the only one of the mages who wasn't learning how to fight. Probably not the best position for him to be in. And learning how to fight didn't necessarily mean he ever had to use it. Maybe it was just yet another way he could learn more control. That thought changed his mind. He would go to Ronan's class.

THIS PLACE IS INCREDIBLY CREEPY.

Isabelle was underground, never her preferred place to be. It turned out that the fortress extended down into the mesa itself. There were walls built on top, encircling the edges, and the black tower at the west end, but most of the structure was underground. It was a warren of dim tunnels lit by dusty lamps. The fires that lit the glass globes were clearly magical. Some had gone out, and in places the tunnels were completely dark. Isabelle stayed out of these. But even the lit tunnels were close and creepy. Isabelle hated feeling the weight of the earth on top of her, hated the claustrophobic sensation that she was trapped.

She sent a blast of wind rocketing down the tunnel in front of her, just to make herself feel better. It kicked up dust, blasted the grime off the lamps, and made the place a little cheerier. Instantly, though, Isabelle felt the ache of being

345

almost out of magic, and the heaviness of the shadow creeping back up inside her.

She found her way out of the tunnels and into a large, open courtyard on top of the mesa. The great black tower shot upwards at the far end. Walking to its base, she stared up its smooth black sides. Then she grinned. That would be a great place to jump off, too. Also, a great place for a wind catapult. Something that lifted you up to the top of the tower. She giggled and moved to start making it, but then remembered Finn's instructions, and her lack of magic. She sighed and dropped her hands.

Hearing a footstep behind her, Isabelle spun around, but there was nothing. Just an empty, dead garden, and ancient, crumbling statues. She looked at her arms and saw goosebumps, then shook herself and rubbed them away.

Stupid. It'd been too long since she'd been alone, that was all. She could take care of herself.

Maybe she could just make the school up here in the daylight. People liked being outside. It snowed like crazy here in the winter, though. Piles and piles of it. She'd crossed just the north part of the plains in winter once with Eraldir and it hadn't been fun. No, it'd probably have to be an indoor school.

Isabelle took a deep breath, squared her shoulders, and entered the tunnels again.

CAPTAIN NATE CAUGHT the trail of the mages down in the thick forests of the lowlands. The mages were no more than a few days ahead of them and were heading for the plains. Nate reported the signs to Arcturus himself, following Arcturus' strict instructions to tell no one else.

Arcturus smiled a thin smile and ordered Reina brought to his tent.

SIX TERRIFYING HOURS LATER, Isabelle succeeded in finding her way to the main entrance door she'd seen from the outside. It had been locked from the inside, which Isabelle found strange. She considered leaving it locked, but who was going to come in anyway? The first step in having a school was being able to get inside it, Isabelle reasoned, so she left it open.

Then she gathered armloads of rocks and marked the way from the entrance up to the main courtyard where the tower was. It probably wasn't the shortest route—it took almost an hour to get there from the entrance—but Finn would just have to make up some reason for that.

Okay, now what? Isabelle tried to think back to her own school days, but all she remembered was how to thwart each of the tutors her father had hired. She'd succeeded in making three of them cry.

What else did this place need? Places to sleep, places to eat, and some sort of classroom. Maybe something official-looking. Ugh. That meant more exploring.

Isabelle lost track of time down in the tunnels. The light never changed, and the air was so still. It was like being dead. Finn better appreciate this, she thought.

REINA WAS LEANING against the bars of her cage when Nate found her. Broken shards of glass littered the edges where she'd shattered wine bottles against the bars. Her eyes were closed and she didn't open them when Nate arrived.

"So, you've found the mage trail," she said.

"Arcturus would like a word with you, ma'am," Nate said.

"So polite. And naïve. He doesn't want a word, he wants to kill me."

"I don't know about that."

Reina got slowly to her feet and placed her arms behind her so that Nate could shackle them. He shackled her feet, too.

Then he brought Reina to Arcturus, but rather than leave her there, he stood outside the tent, listening through the thin fabric. A couple of his men gave him questioning looks, but he waved them off.

DUSTING, Isabelle thought with contempt, directing another gust of air through a tunnel. This was not what her powers were for. She thought of her mother's maids. The whole contingent of them. They must have had thirty maids, and of course they were always being fired for some reason or another. Or quitting. She smiled, but then remembered some of her father's lectures about it, and the smile faded.

She found a large, fancy hall that had once been a dining room—there were even some tables left, although many of them had been turned over, and there were broken dishes and bones scattered on the floor. No human skeletons, though, that Isabelle could see. She righted the tables, torna-doed the refuse into another room, and then dusted the whole thing. Not bad. That could be a dining room. There were kitchens off to the side, too, and the sound of water running through underground streams.

In the kitchen, she found a sink built into the wall, with a lever above it, and, when she pulled the lever, water shot out of it. Clean water, and cold. Water mages, it must be. Maybe earth mages, too, that had built this. And it had all been here a hundred years or more and it still worked. Unbelievable. Isabelle had never made anything that had lasted longer than a few weeks. She thought the trail markers she'd made might last longer, but a hundred years? How did the old mages make things so permanent?

The water tasted great, too. Sure, maybe it wasn't a good idea to drink it. She was thirsty, though; what else was she going to do?

Handily, there were already halls and halls of bedrooms. More than the mages could ever need. There were army barracks, fancy apartments for rich people, and servants' quarters. Isabelle found some plain rooms near the dining hall and cleaned those out. They were full of abandoned possessions. Clothes and jewelry and books and letters and diaries. Isabelle just gathered them all up and dumped them in other, farther rooms. She did find a silver hairpin she liked and stuck it in her braid.

THAT NIGHT ISABELLE HAD A STRANGE, vivid dream. She was in the Table, out in the main courtyard with the tower. There was a door in the south wall, and it called to her, looming towards her.

She approached, pushed the door open with her hand, and started down a long, bare tunnel. She felt a terrible sense of urgency, and began to run, the tunnel spiraling down into the heart of the mesa. She felt something up ahead, around the next turn, but just before she got there, she awoke.

The next morning, Isabelle ate the last of the food out of her pack, sitting on the bed, heedless of the crumbs she was scattering over it, and tried to recall every part of the dream. She wondered if the place she had seen was real. Well, only one way to find out. Finn probably wouldn't be here for another week or so, so she had time to take a break from school-making. It was pretty much done anyway, a little empty and nothing fancy, but Isabelle thought it mostly worked.

She climbed out a door into the main courtyard, and found herself in full, bright, blinding sunshine. Apparently, it was closer to midday or even early afternoon; she hadn't been able to tell down in the darkness. Isabelle blinked in the sun for a while, then looked for the door.

The door was not as obvious as it had been in the dream, and it wasn't calling out to her. It was just an ordinary door like all the others, but it was the one from the dream. Just as she had earlier, she went to it and tried to push it open. Stuck. Or locked.

Isabelle first tried kicking it, then pushing as hard as she could, then sending rocks hurtling towards it from across the courtyard. Finally, one of these cracked the wood. She sent a few more careening into it—the noise of the door splintering was deafening—and the destroyed door gave way, breaking off its hinges and crashing in a heap inside.

Isabelle dusted off her hands, stepped over the ruined door, and looked curiously inside. Again, it was just like in her dream. A long, bare tunnel that sloped downwards, curving. She'd only taken a few steps down this tunnel, however, when a gust of wind knocked her off her feet. She landed hard on the stone floor, her sprained arm shrieking in pain, but she immediately rolled to the side, onto her back, and looked behind her. A small, pale girl stood there, arms raised.

"Flavius," Reina said.

"Good afternoon, Reina."

"Heard you found the trail of the mages."

Arcturus covered his frustration that she'd heard already. "Indeed. You were telling the truth, it seems. Much to my surprise." Unless they were now following the trail of Reina's men and it was a trap.

"So, you've brought me here to kill me, since you think you don't need me anymore."

"Actually, I have a somewhat different offer."

Reina uncrossed her arms in surprise.

"As you know, for a long time I've been curious about magic. Where it comes from. That sort of thing. I've made some...forays into understanding. However, my... researches have been hindered in that the mages I've... worked with... have been somewhat fragile. You, on the other hand..." His eyes lit up. "You are quite tough."

"What's your offer?"

"Help me with my research and I'll let you live. If you hold up your end of the bargain by being strong enough to live through it."

"Tempting, Flavius. Tempting. You do know how to make a girl an offer. I think you're forgetting that you still don't know where they're going."

Arcturus looked at her, disappointed. "Ah, Reina, you really shouldn't start your drinking so early in the morning. I can quite obviously just follow them."

"Insult my wine preferences again and I'll light your balls on fire." Flames flickered around Reina's fingertips. She crossed her arms, still smoking slightly. "This place they're going. I guarantee you you've never been there. I know what's there. I know how to get in. Also, you know I'll fight on your side. For a while, at least. All those mages... You need me."

Arcturus smiled. Ah, that was better. He'd hated to think he could defeat her so easily.

351

Outside, Nate turned away from the thin fabric of the tent walls, his brow furrowed.

∾

AN INTERNAL STRUGGLE showed in the girl's face. Her cracked lips moved, her eyes locked on Isabelle's.

At last, she forced out a single word. "Run."

Isabelle immediately conjured a gust of air to buffet the girl back, but the girl raised one hand higher and Isabelle's wind was diverted. The girl clenched a skinny fist, and the air around Isabelle constricted, holding her motionless.

A red light flashed through the girl's eyes, and ropes sprang up around Isabelle.

Her magic is ripe. Take her.

The disembodied voice pounded into Isabelle's mind, but she didn't think the words were meant for her.

The girl cringed, shook her head, then looked at Isabelle with terror and despair. She turned, and Isabelle was drawn forward, carried by a current of air and held fast by the ropes.

She struggled, tried to blow the girl back a few times, but it made no difference. So, for the moment, Isabelle gave up, and simply watched her captor.

The girl walked barefoot in front of her, and Isabelle noticed that her feet were raw and left flecks of blood on the ground where she'd stepped. She was older than she'd looked initially, too. She was so skinny, and her hair hung lank, tangled and uncut down her back. She wore a shapeless grey dress, and nothing else. All these made her look younger, childlike, but now that Isabelle looked more closely she guessed they were close in age, which made sense if she was doing magic, except she had already done both wind and thread magic, something Isabelle hadn't thought possible.

352

The girl floated Isabelle across the courtyard, and down through a small wooden door into a narrow tunnel. Immediately, the thick smell of rotting flesh assaulted Isabelle's senses.

There were no lights here, but Isabelle could feel the walls pressing close around her. Panic rose in her chest and she struggled instinctively, but it made no difference, it only made her breathe in more of the thick, putrid air.

A tiny flame flared in the darkness ahead, illuminating the palm of the girl who held it. Her shadow loomed large on the wall. They were passing doors, now, and Isabelle didn't want to look, but she couldn't help herself. The smell was worse now, choking her.

Reluctantly, she moved just her eyes, looking to the side through an open doorway. There she saw a grey foot, its toes black and rotting. When, unable to tear her eyes away, she followed it up, she saw it was connected to a stick-thin, emaciated leg. Past that was a bare chest, the skin stretched tightly over jutting ribs. The chest expanded ever so slightly, and the wheeze of a breath reached Isabelle's ears. That skinny, decomposing corpse was still alive. And there, past it, were more and more. Every room they passed was filled with bodies, some barely alive, some dead and rotting. The living piled on top of the dead.

Revulsion and terror rose in Isabelle and she jerked her arms and legs against her bonds; shockwave after shockwave of air thundered out from her. The girl stumbled slightly at the first one, but then continued her slow walk, pulling Isabelle after her. Nothing Isabelle did made any difference. For the first time in Isabelle's life, as far as she could remember, she felt herself start to cry in frustration.

"What the hell are you doing?" Isabelle yelled, her voice choking on the fetid air.

The girl didn't answer, only led her past room after room,

finally stopping in front of a barred door. It looked like a prison cell, and this one was, mercifully, empty. Although, Isabelle noted, this was the only room with a door of any kind. The others didn't even need bars to keep them here.

The door grated open, the rusted hinges scraping and groaning, and Isabelle was pushed inside. Her bonds dropped away and the air loosened around her, and Isabelle immediately threw herself at the door, but it clanged shut, the bolt crashing home. Heat flared and the hinges and bolt melted, fusing together. Isabelle grabbed the bars, jerked them as hard as she could, ignoring the searing pain in her sprained arm as she did so. She pushed herself back, lifted a foot, and booted the lock as hard as she could. Immediately, she regretted it. The door was iron, and it didn't even budge as Isabelle kicked it.

Isabelle shrieked in pain and despair. Then, gasping the rancid air, she saw the girl was still there, standing just outside the cell door, staring at her through the bars.

Her eyes were wide, pale and bloodshot, with heavy circles under them. Her cheeks were sunken and shadowed. She looked long and hard into Isabelle's eyes, opened her mouth, then closed it again. Then she turned and left, taking the last of the light with her.

Isabelle screamed after her, kicking the walls, banging them with her fists, scratching and the floor, clawing her way up the walls until she could scrape at the ceiling with her nails, heedlessly tearing them, but nothing helped. There was no way out.

THE BATTLE CLASSES quickly became the most popular activity of the day. There was at least one injury every class, but so far no one had been seriously hurt. Everyone was back to breathing normally, with most of their blood back inside their bodies, by the end of class. Usually. Or a couple of minutes after, at the very latest. Ronan and Rafe were now, if possible, even more popular.

The mages had left the last of the trees behind them a day or two ago, and now they trekked across bare, rolling plains, following the river south. The Blackwater. Finn stared and stared at the horizon, so far in every direction. He'd never been out of the forests before. Never been out of the shadows of the Iron Mountains.

Far to the south he could see the dark rising crags of the Uplands, a mountain range he'd heard of, but never seen.

In the afternoon the wind picked up, blowing in from the east. It carried with it a great cloud of sandy red dust that within a few hours had reduced visibility to only a few miles in every direction.

Noe and the other wind mages blew as much of the dust away from them as they could, and the group travelled in a huddle, a small pocket of semi-dust-free air in a thick haze.

"Where's all this dust coming from, Eraldir?" Finn asked.

Eraldir was looking off towards the horizon. "The wastelands to the east," he said absently. Finn waited to see if he would say anything else, but he didn't. No long story about running away from villagers or meeting strange travelers or getting horribly injured.

"Ever been there?" Finn prompted.

"No, no..." Eraldir trailed off, shaking his head.

Finn couldn't believe there was a place Eraldir hadn't been, and this new, quiet Eraldir who stared thoughtfully at the horizon scared Finn down to his core.

Finn wished they would get to the Table sooner, wished he could make Eraldir more comfortable, and hoped that when they got to the Table it was livable. They just had to make it another week.

～

THE KNIFE TORMENTED KEL. The crows were taking it in shifts to scratch and peck at the stone, and hours of listening to talons scraping impervious rock was driving Kel crazy.

The bear sat with his nose almost resting on her hand, occasionally snuffling as a thought passed through his mind.

What if you just break some of the paw bones? it wondered to Kel.

Why?

Then it might fit through.

Kel shook herself, and pressed herself up to a seat. She'd been lying on the ground, her left arm sticking up in the air, clenched in the grasp of the stone. She grit her teeth.

Do it.

The bear shuffled back a few steps. *Oh, no, I didn't mean—*

Please. You're strong enough.

The bear squinted its eyes shut, and they disappeared into a mass of rough hair.

Are you sure? the bear asked.

Yes. Do it!

She put some force behind the thought, felt guilty for doing it, but she couldn't stay trapped here any longer. She might not be dying, but whatever was waiting for her here in these woods was fading away.

The bear reached up with its two enormous paws, placing its palms on either side of her tiny hand. In one swift movement, it crushed them together.

Kel heard the sound rather than felt it. There was a sickening crack, and a few snaps and pops, and Kel felt a horrific emptiness in her stomach, then a white-hot pain seared through her, sparks of it exploding in her vision. She blinked them away and found herself lying on the ground again, her whole body screaming in pain, the animals clustered around her.

Kel choked on a sob, and pulled herself dizzily to her feet. Her hand, still wedged firmly in the stone hand, was a searing mass of pain. She tugged at it, and it sent bolts of agony through her. She groaned and pulled harder, but her hand wouldn't budge. The stone fingers were either too tightly wrapped around her, or the grip they held was magical.

Help me.

The bear wrapped its paws around her and yanked. Smoke and the weasel pushed at her injured hand, trying to stuff the mash of bones and flesh through the opening. They pulled even when Kel passed out again.

She swam back into consciousness through the pain; the animals had finally given up their pulling and pushing, and Kel lay in a cold, shaky sweat. Her whole body was trembling, but she stared at her hand, still locked firmly, and she knew what she had to do. The shaking stopped, and all feeling dropped out of her. It was like she was watching herself from very far away. Some part of her mind had taken over, some essential, business-like part of her mind was just going to do what needed to be done, and there weren't any more feelings or physical sensations to get in the way. Kel took up the knife.

With only a small shake in her hand, and with Smoke's help, she sliced strips from the end of her dress. She lay these by the side of the stone face. Then she gripped the knife so hard her fingers turned white, raised it high, and chopped it down as fast and as hard as she could.

The flesh sliced easily, her knife only stopping when it chipped the bone underneath. Blood began to ooze out as she lifted the knife again, hacked it down on the bones. They did separate after all. She braced her feet on the stone arm, pulling herself as far back as she could, stretching the remaining bones and tendons and skin, and hacked again and again, until at last, with a wet, gristly sound, she wrenched the last of her wrist apart and she fell back. Free.

Blood was spurting out of her in multiple thick streams, so she quickly took the wool and pressed it to the wound. With the crows' help, she wrapped the stump in the remaining strips, and tied the ends tightly, cutting off the blood supply. The blood soaked the makeshift bandage and began to drip in heavy droplets onto the ground. Kel lifted her arm above her head, as she'd seen her mother do with small nicks and cuts while she was cooking, but her whole body was shaking again now, and Kel swayed. The pain and the reality of what she'd just done hit her in a sickening wave, but at least it was over.

She glanced over to see the bear holding Smoke and the weasel, all three staring at her in horror. She was covered in blood, as was the ground around her. She must look horrible. She sensed an attitude of cold approval from the crows, though.

A powerful tremor shook through her muscles, and she almost fell, but instead she placed her good hand on the soaked bandages. She suddenly knew what she could do. Closing her eyes, she forced herself to reach into the wound, to feel the broken pieces of herself, the veins like torn roots, the skin like bark. Under her attention, the veins sealed themselves off, pulled back into the wound, and the skin grew like bark over the top. There were tinier creatures there, so tiny she'd never noticed them before, but her body told her it was afraid of those tiny animals. She killed them, millions upon millions; she snuffed out their lives and closed her skin back over them. The pain was coming from other roots, like the veins, but searing angrily. She calmed these roots, pulled them back into positions where they were comfortable.

The pain was gone now; only the blood and the shaking were left. Her whole body shook as she pulled the sodden bandages off to see a clean, smooth stump where her hand had been.

She looked back again to see the animals still staring at her, their eyes wide and round.

Let's go.

Without a backwards glance at the stone creature, or her mangled hand, Kel turned and walked into the forest, in the direction of the presence that had called to her in her dreams.

～

EVENTUALLY, Isabelle's strength gave out. She lay torn and bleeding in the dark. Then the noises came. Slight rustlings and moans, the wheeze and rattle of breath of those barely alive. The sounds tormented her. As soon as she could move, she searched her cell again, this time more calmly, but still she found nothing. The walls were smooth, the iron door welded shut.

She went to check the ceiling. She called the air to lift her, but it wouldn't come. She didn't have the sense of depletion, either. It wasn't that she had used too much; it was just gone. Her magic was gone. Her body went numb, and she sat down heavily on the ground. Shaking, she pressed the palm of her hand to her breast bone, feeling for the lightness, the freedom that had been there since she had turned sixteen and discovered what she was.

It was gone.

. . .

ISABELLE DIDN'T KNOW how long she had lain in the darkness, alternating between despair and plotting. Despair was not a normal feeling for her. She'd never felt it before, and she despised herself for feeling it now. But the longer she lay there, the harder it was to keep pulling herself back. It was made all the more difficult by the fact that there wasn't much to plot. Unless she could convince some of the corpses to help her, but she'd tried calling out to them, and they'd given no response.

Isabelle lay on the ground, gripping her white hair in her fists. She released her grip and started piling it over her face, trying to hide under it. Her hair was a gross, dirty mess, though, and she brushed it back away, blowing the last few strands away with her breath. This almost made her start crying, which she definitely wasn't going to do. She kicked the wall as hard as she could, and the anger burned away her fear.

She was completely trapped. For some reason, this reminded her of Finn. She couldn't remember why she'd been so annoyed when he'd told her he liked her. Maybe, if she ever got out of here, she'd tell Finn the truth. Well, she probably wouldn't go that far, but she might stop making out with Ronan.

Suddenly, in the darkness, there came a noise. This was a purposeful noise, the scrape of a foot along the ground, and a pebble rattling away from it. Isabelle froze, listening intently, straining her eyes. A few more steps, light and quiet, but there.

Light and heat flared brilliantly, and Isabelle threw her arm over her face to protect her eyes. Almost immediately, there was darkness again, except for the soft red glow of molten iron. Isabelle pushed her exhausted body up and stood, squinting into the darkness. The door was open, and there, on the other side of the red glow, was the girl.

"Run," came the whisper. The girl's eyes were closed. Isabelle wanted to ask her name, wanted to ask what was going on, but she'd had enough of this place. She ran, tripping and stumbling into the walls as she went, feeling the bodies and some other presence around her. She heard the girl start to chase her, and pushed her legs harder, crashing into the door, yanking it open, and finding herself at last in fresh night air.

If she could have, she would have blasted her way off this mesa immediately, but she couldn't. There was, though, the smallest tingle of magic there inside her again. It wasn't gone completely. She slammed the door shut behind her, hearing the girl stumbling and running after her. Isabelle sprinted across the courtyard, picking a door, any door, and throwing herself through it. Then she ran, desperately, through the dark tunnels, until somehow, she found her way down to the main entrance. Sobbing with relief, she pushed the doors open, then kept running, as far and as fast and as long as she could, until she collapsed with exhaustion a few miles away.

"Build a school, Isabelle," she muttered to herself. Finn was an asshole.

CHAPTER 26

*W*alking along at the back of the group, Finn watched Ronan as he strode confidently ahead, chatting with the other mages. It was strange to think how much had changed since they were kids. He remembered when Ronan first became a mage.

RONAN HAD BEEN ACTING STRANGELY since his sixteenth birthday. He'd avoided their usual study sessions in the library, and had even skipped class several times. Finn was worried about him, but he was also worried about what it meant, and he wasn't sure he wanted to know. Otherwise he would have sought Ronan out sooner.

He didn't have to, though. Ronan found him.

It was a cloudy day in early autumn. Still warm, but with the hint that summer was ending. Finn had taken a book and walked alone out of town, up to the ruins of the old city. As always, the signs of magic there—the weird, ever-burning lamps, perfectly smooth stone walls, and the ever-present sound of water moving unseen underground and through walls—made Finn uneasy, but he was drawn by the sense of the past. The remnants of the grandeur of the old country.

He climbed one of the towers and sat at the top, leaning against a wall in a warm space protected from the wind, and lost himself in his book. He didn't notice the sound of footsteps until Ronan was standing there, barefoot, in front of him.

Finn looked up, and was shocked to see how pale Ronan was. His eyes darted nervously from side to side, and there were dark shadows in the hollows of his face.

"Ronan, what—what happened?"

Ronan shivered, and the ground shook underneath them. Finn braced himself against the wall, his stomach giving a panicked swoop as he waited to see if the tower would topple. It held.

"What… are you… what did you do?"

"Nothing." Ronan's voice broke. The ground shook again. "I—I can't control it."

Finn stood, dropping the book, not even noticing that it landed splayed on the ground, its fragile pages smashed against the ground. He gripped Ronan's upper arms. "You did it, you're a mage?"

Ronan closed his eyes, swallowed, and nodded.

Anger flared through Finn, but he pushed it back down. "It's okay, we'll get rid of it. I'll help you."

"I can't get rid of it, Finn."

"I'll help. It's okay."

Ronan groaned. "No, Finn, I just need to control it."

Finn swallowed. The tower shook and the floor cracked underneath them. The tower began to list off to one side.

"Okay, okay, I'll help you. I promise. We'll figure this out." He'd told his friend so many times that magic was dangerous, that it couldn't be controlled. But Ronan hadn't listened. Finn wondered briefly how he'd done it, but he didn't have time. The tower shook again. "Let's get down on the ground, okay?"

Ronan nodded and Finn helped him down the steps.

They collapsed together against a wall at the base.

"I can't go home like this," Ronan groaned. His body shook, and his skin felt feverish under Finn's touch.

"It's okay. You can stay here. I'll bring you food."

Ronan opened his eyes, his face was pale and there was a thin sheen of sweat on his skin. "Thank you, Finn." Ronan tried to say something more, but his body shook again, and he cried out in pain.

Powerless to help, Finn watched, desperately trying to think of what to do. He gripped his friend's hand. "I'm here. I'll help."

He sat there as the sun slowly went down, holding Ronan's hand as he and the earth around them shook violently. Ronan's jaw clenched so hard that Finn thought his teeth would break. He sat there all through the night, until the sky lightened to a soft grey and the birds began to sing and Ronan finally fell into an uneasy sleep.

Then Finn left to get food and supplies.

For almost a week, Ronan lay sick in the ruins. Finn brought him food and water. He stole books on magic out of the library, and sat near his friend, reading, looking for anything that might help. Ronan was delirious, his awareness coming in and out. He didn't seem to remember that Finn had been there, was surprised every time Finn showed up with more food and supplies.

One evening, Finn left Ronan in a fairly good state, and went home so that his parents wouldn't worry. He heard voices inside, stopped at the door of his home to listen.

"...reports of a mage hereabouts. The council is sending the watch out to look for them."

"Well, good. I hope they find whoever it is. That has to be stopped."

Finn's body went cold. He turned around and ran back the way he had come as fast as he could, but when he got the ruins it was too late. They were already taking him away.

Months passed before Finn saw Ronan again. When he finally did, Ronan was even thinner and more sickly white, and had the black moon tattoo on his face. Finn tried to talk to him, but Ronan, thinking it was Finn who had turned him in, avoided him. For his part, Finn, angry at Ronan for choosing magic and still afraid of it, finally stopped trying to explain the truth to Ronan.

A FULL MOON glowed redly in the black sky above. No stars were visible through the dust. Finn sat by the fire, alone except for the sleeping form of Eraldir. He poked a bone needle through the strap of his pack, which had started to tear loose, and tugged it out the other side, drawing the coarse cotton thread through, stitching it tight.

The other campfires were surrounded by huddles of mages, talking and laughing, but Finn didn't feel like joining them. Out of the corner of his eye he could see Ronan sitting in the middle of the largest group, gesturing emphatically about something, to nods of agreement.

Finn was glad Ronan was there, glad that they were friends again, but there was an uneasy tension in the pit of his stomach. Ronan was more popular, if you could even compare someone who had a fanatic following to someone who was openly disliked. Ronan was also starting to talk more and more about what they would do when they got to the Table. Writing new laws, recruiting more mages. To hear him talk, you'd think Caledonia would be reformed within a few months. And the rest of the mages were excited about this.

Finn could understand their excitement. They'd been oppressed, hunted, living in hiding, and Ronan was offering them power. But the cost Ronan was willing to pay was too high. Ronan was willing to trade one form of oppression for another. Finn had to make them listen, somehow. He would figure out a way to convince them, but so far, he had been unsuccessful. No matter how much time he spent practicing and meditating they still didn't seem to respect him. That had been a stupid plan, anyway.

Finn remembered Rafe looking at him, after he had kept the mages from killing Jes. *I don't like liars.* Who did, really? Was that it? Could they tell he was lying to them?

They also were not too enthusiastic about his commitment to safety. Did he even deserve to be leading them? He was judging Ronan for trying to force people to respect mages, but here Finn was trying to trick them into following him by lying to them. If he won that way, he wouldn't be any better than Ronan or Reina or Arcturus. He remembered Ronan telling him that lying was just another way to control people. As usual, he was starting to realize that Ronan was right.

The needle jabbed into Finn's thumb and he shook his hand, clenching his fist and wiping the blood on his pants. He set his pack down, stowed the needle carefully in its leather pouch, and looked over towards where Ronan and most of the mages sat talking. He knew what he had to do, and that knowledge filled him with a reckless excitement. Yes, this was the right thing to do, but it was also completely stupid.

Finn waited for the bleeding to stop, then stood and crossed to the other campfire.

The mages went silent, turning to look at him as he

approached. Ronan was in the middle of some rant about non-mages, and he stopped, too, as Finn stepped into the circle of light around their campfire.

"Hey," Finn said into the silence.

"Hey, Finn," Ronan said.

"Mind if I interrupt?"

"Oh, sure, join us, pull up a chair." Ronan gestured next to him, and some rocks pulled themselves out of the ground, tumbling upwards into a pile, making a rough seat.

"Thanks," Finn said, but remained standing.

They were all staring at him. This was a terrible idea. He should have thought more about what he would say. As usual.

"I lied about the school."

There was silence, a lot of blinking, and some raised eyebrows and opened mouths. Okay, well, the worst part was over. Finn barreled onwards.

"I'm sorry I lied. We haven't made the school yet. It's true that Eraldir has been teaching Isabelle and I, but I've never actually been to the Table. You are the first group of students."

"I knew it!" shrieked Marta. Hearing the commotion, the other mages from the other campfires were coming over to join them.

Finn continued. "I sent Isabelle ahead to set it up." He caught Ronan's eye. "She's there now." Ronan was staring at him, bemused.

"You sent *her*?" Someone said. "It'll be a death trap!"

Finn didn't completely disagree, but he didn't want to say that.

"The place isn't what's important, though," Finn said.

No one was listening to him anymore.

"What's even there?"

"I don't know." Man, honesty felt great. On the other hand, everything was falling apart.

"How do we know you're telling the truth now?"

"What would I possibly gain from telling you this?"

"We should just leave," someone said.

"Let's go back to Westwend," Marta said.

"Reina'll kill us for deserting."

Ronan leapt up onto a boulder that spontaneously rumbled out of the ground. "Hey, hey, look, we don't have to go back. This doesn't change anything."

"Of course it does. We can't trust him. Maybe he poisoned the wine."

"Yeah, he's the one who's been protecting her." The mage gestured with contempt to Jes, who stood on the edges of the circle, trying to make herself small.

"They're both probably Reina's spies. This is all some trick she's played on us. A test! And we failed, and now she's going to kill us."

"No," Ronan said. "Look, I've known Finn my whole life. He's not a spy, he's just being an idiot." He shot an annoyed look at Finn.

"Isn't he the one who killed a whole village?"

Finn wanted to correct them, but he figured it wouldn't help things if he said, 'only half' right then.

"Yes, he did," Ronan said. "It was an accident, though."

"How do you know, were you there?"

"No."

"All this is his fault, then! All the mages they've executed! He brought this down on us!"

"Exactly!" Finn projected his voice as forcefully as he could, but it came out desperate to his ears. "That's why I want us to stop the violence against non-mages! So they'll stop fighting us! We need to put things back together."

"Then why don't you just turn yourself in?"

"Yeah, why don't you?"

"Because…"

"Why don't we turn him in ourselves? That would get them off our backs, right?"

There were some murmurs of assent around the crowd. Finn really didn't like the direction this was going.

"No," Ronan said. "Finn's a mage, like us. We're not turning on one of our own."

"He's lied to us! All this is his fault!"

"Yes, but part of his idea is good, and it's gotten us out from under Reina, which is a good thing, right?"

Ronan looked around the group. "You're right, maybe we can't trust him, but we're not turning him in. The idea to go to the Table was a good one. Let's just do that."

"What about him, though?"

Ronan eyed the group, his bare feet planted firmly on the rock. Finn saw just the tiniest flicker of indecision on Ronan's usually confident face, as it dawned on him just how angry the mages were at Finn, and just how much they wanted to kill him. It wasn't surprising to Finn. He waited to see how Ronan would get him out of this.

"We'll leave him here," Ronan said.

Finn suddenly felt everything he'd worked for slip out from under him. Ronan wasn't meeting his eyes.

"We can't do that, he'll go straight to Reina!"

Finn rounded on Marta. "I'm not working for Reina!"

She eyed him coldly.

Finn looked around at the other mages, looked them in the eyes one at a time. Mostly, what he saw there was dislike. Rafe, though, smiled a small, sad smile, and gave him a brief nod. Weirdly, Finn felt a swell of pride at that. He'd won Rafe's respect at least. That was worth something.

He could see that he'd lost, though. He took a deep breath.

"You can leave if you want. I won't go to Reina. Or Arcturus, or anyone. I'm sorry I lied."

"I'm good with leaving," someone said, to general agreement.

"All right," Ronan said. "Everyone pack up." The group moved to follow.

"What about her?" Marta said, pointing to Jes.

"I'll stay with Finn," she said. Great. That wasn't suspicious.

"Good," Marta said. "Leave the murdering spy with the traitor."

As the group moved off, collecting their things, Ronan approached Finn.

"Well, thanks for not letting them kill me," Finn said.

"Of course."

"Sorry, Ronan."

"So, you did know where Isabelle was?"

"Yeah. I lied about that, too."

Ronan shook his head. "I don't remember you lying this much back when we were kids."

"Maybe I was better at it then."

"Were you?"

"No." Why was he lying now? He knew the answer immediately. Because now there was something he wanted. And he hadn't thought he was strong enough to get it with the truth.

"Look, maybe wait a while, then meet us there? Maybe once things cool down..."

"Yeah, maybe. Um, Ronan, I made a promise, to get us out of Westwend, about mages being better to non-mages."

"I remember."

"Will you keep that promise for me?"

Ronan's face tightened. "I'll do what's best for mages."

"Please, Ronan. Fighting the non-mages is just going to lead to more death on both sides."

"I'm not going to make mages grovel, Finn. These people have had enough of that. They will never treat us well unless we stand up and make them."

"You're wrong, Ronan."

Ronan rolled his eyes. "I just kept you from getting killed, or at least turned over to Reina, you know that, right? Which of us is turning out more successful at things? Can't you consider that I'm right about this?"

It was true that so far Ronan had been right about everything. But Finn wouldn't accept that he was right about this. "Non-mages have a point, too. They were oppressed for so much longer than we were, Ronan."

"That doesn't make it right."

"Exactly."

Ronan looked at Finn sadly. "Bye, Finn."

Finn swallowed hard. "Bye, Ronan."

Finn watched as Ronan turned and joined the group of mages. He picked up his bag and the group filed out of the camp, leaving five empty campfires burning down to coals.

Keeping his head held as high as he could, Finn crossed the darkness back to his own fire, and sat with his back to the retreating mages. Jes joined him.

She was looking at him. He wished she would just leave him alone.

He wasn't going to give up. It sounded idiotic even to himself, but he wasn't giving up. No. Those mages were going to respect him and be students at his school in the King's Table. Finn was going to stop them from murdering non-mages and then he'd stop non-mages from murdering mages. Sure, he had absolutely no idea how that was going to happen, and things, admittedly, looked bleak, but this was what he was going to do.

"How come you told them you lied?" Jes asked.

Finn looked up, annoyed to be distracted from his

attempt to convince himself he wasn't a failure. "I didn't want to be lying anymore," Finn said.

"Yeah, but, I mean, it was kind of the worst possible time, right?"

Finn reflected on this. "Yes."

"And you'd already sent Isabelle to make it look like there was a school there."

"Yeah." It'd been a split-second decision, and those were not his strong suit. "I guess I just realized I didn't want to lie anymore."

"What are we going to do now?"

"I don't know yet."

"Is there somewhere else we can go?"

"I don't know."

"Do you know how to find food out here, without the naturalist mages?"

"No."

"Are there any towns around here?"

"I don't know."

Jes bit her lower lip. "Are we going to die?"

"What? No."

Finn controlled his annoyance and looked up at her. Her blue eyes welled up. She blinked away her tears and looked off into the darkness.

THE NEXT MORNING, as always, Finn awoke early, but he didn't practice or meditate. He just sat staring into the ashes of the campfire, thinking, as the red dust settled over everything. Jes avoided him, puttering nervously around their camp, organizing their food supplies and taking stock of how long they would last.

After a while, Finn noticed that the sun was high in the sky, and he was still just sitting there. He stood, stretching the stiffness from his body, and then he noticed that Eraldir was still asleep. Well, at least the old man had gotten some rest. Finn didn't want to wake him, but he didn't want to let the mages get too far ahead before following.

Finn bent down by Eraldir's bed, placed a hand on the man's shoulder and shook it gently.

"Eraldir?"

The man didn't move. He'd have to try the pie thing.

"Eraldir? There's pie. Wake up." Finn shook Eraldir's shoulder more firmly. The man still didn't stir, or even mumble in his sleep. A horrible sick feeling crept into Finn's heart. He bent down, put his ear right next to Eraldir's lips. Finn held his breath, listening. Nothing. Panic was rising in Finn's chest now. With a shaking hand, he pressed a finger against the loose skin of Eraldir's neck, feeling for a pulse. Nothing.

Nothing.

Numbness overcame Finn. He sat back on his heels, unable to cry or speak or do anything. Eraldir couldn't be...

Again, Finn shook Eraldir by the shoulders. He placed both hands on either side of his head, opened Eraldir's eyelids, but his eyes were glassy and empty, unfocused. No. No, he couldn't be. It didn't make any sense. It must be a trick, or something. How could he be...

Finn stared at the man's face, expecting any moment for the eyes to snap open and for Eraldir to sit up and start grumbling about how he had to pee, and then launch into some insane story.

"Finn?" Jes had come up behind him. Finn wished she would go away. He didn't know how to explain, didn't want to say it, didn't want to make it real.

"Oh, oh no, Finn," Jes' voice trembled. "Is he..."

Finn couldn't bring himself to say anything. Couldn't even nod. But she knew the answer anyway.

"Oh, oh no," Jes started to sob, loudly, and suddenly Finn's numbness was replaced by anger. She hadn't even known him. What was she crying about? Finn stood, rounding on her.

"Shut up!" He snarled, and Jes, terrified, closed her eyes and sobbed louder. Finn kept yelling. "Stop it! Why are you even crying?! You didn't know him! Shut UP!" The camp around them burst into flames. This startled Finn, shook him out of his rage. Jes was in the midst of the fire, and Finn ran to her, tried to grab her to pull her out, but she screamed and ran.

Finn ran, too, out of their burning camp. He tried to turn back, to get Eraldir's body, but the heat was too intense now. The grass around them was burning. Everything was burning, and there was no one, no Eraldir, to put it out.

Desperately, Finn stood and watched everything be destroyed. He watched the fire catch the dry grass and ignite it, watched the flames rage away from him, consuming everything in their path. Birds took to the sky in droves, avoiding the columns of smoke. A few hundred feet away Finn could see Jes crouched on the ground, a dome of water around her. Her arms were wrapped around her legs and her face was pressed into her knees. She looked terrified, vulnerable. Finn wanted to comfort her, to apologize, but he didn't. She would just run away from him again.

The fire had consumed everything. All their supplies, everything was ashes. Finn found Eraldir's partially burned body. This wasn't the funeral he wanted for him. It wasn't the funeral Eraldir deserved. Finn sat in the ash and the smoke, sat next to the body of the man who'd saved him, and cried.

With no wind mages to keep it at bay, the red dust returned, blowing into Finn's eyes, hanging in the air, and settling over everything, a layer of red over the black ash.

Finn periodically brushed it off Eraldir's body. The skin was weirdly cool to the touch, now.

The sun climbed through the red dust, to the peak of the sky, and then slowly descended into the west. When evening came, the last rays of light glowed only dimly through the red haze. It was like everything was in a red fog.

Finn sat, his head in his hands. He kept waiting for Eraldir to sit up and say something like "Dead? What? Course I wasn't dead. Always pretend to be dead when the rest of the group abandons you, that's what I've learned." But every time he looked up, the cold, burned body just lay there.

Suddenly there were a thousand things Finn wished he could have said. He'd just taken it for granted that Eraldir would be there. They were going to the Table together. They would start the school. Eraldir would teach, just like he'd taught Finn.

Finn flashed back to their first meeting, how Eraldir had guessed what Finn had done. He'd hinted at it, but he hadn't judged him for it. At that point, Finn had thought his life was over, that he'd live in the woods, alone, forever, that no one could ever love or accept him after what he'd done. But Eraldir hadn't seen a monster. He'd seen someone who needed to be trained, and that was it. And now he was gone.

He wished, more than anything, that he could make Eraldir a cup of tea and tell him that he was grateful.

Sobs shook him, tears poured down his cheeks. He wiped his nose on his sleeve, like a kid, leaving snot and tears.

He had to do something. He looked around the burned camp, and there was nothing. No water. No herbs for tea left. Only ash and the red dust.

There was one thing he had, though.

Control. Eraldir had taught him control. It wasn't perfect, obviously, but it was at least there.

Finn stood, swayed a little, then walked up a small rise

near the camp. There, he knelt on the ground. Slowly, using all his focus and concentration, Finn created a pure, white flame. It lifted, taller and taller, into the sky.

Finn sat back on his heels, looked up at the shining white wall of heat. It was perfect, but it wasn't quite right. It wasn't Eraldir. He sat thinking for a long time, and eventually his mind wandered off. He found himself thinking about when he'd rescued Jes, how Eraldir had tried to convince Finn not to look for her, and then had gone off himself to rescue her. He smiled, remembering Eraldir's annoyance that Finn hadn't listened to him. Something flickered in front of his vision. He looked up, into the pure white column, and saw a dash of color. There, in a bright, shimmering blue, was Eraldir, walking down the hall towards Finn, and Finn melting the door, and both of them stepping across the threshold to see Jes.

A sense of peace and rightness settled into Finn, and he knew what was missing. Standing, he reached out to the white column, closed his eyes, and, with a smile, remembered Eraldir's story about the traveling sea nuns. When he opened his eyes, there it was, in sparkling pink, the story playing out in the flames.

He closed his eyes again, and there was Geraldine, the famous spy, and the time Eraldir had hidden in the tree from the Baharrans, and all the many times Eraldir had been on fire, or chased with pitchforks, or narrowly escaped death from a ruthless dictator. And there were pies, all the pies Eraldir had ever described to Finn.

Fondness and gratitude towards the old man poured out of Finn and into the flames. When at last he'd finished, he knelt in front of it, and watched the stories play as the sky grew dark around him and night swept over the land. At some point, he fell asleep, in the warm light of everything this man had meant to him.

CHAPTER 27

*W*hen Finn awoke, the sun was already high in the sky. He stumbled down to the campsite. Jes was back, sitting like a traumatized rabbit on a stone by the remains of their campfire.

"Do you have any food?" she asked.

Finn stared at her for a moment. His eyes felt puffy; they burned when he blinked, either from the smoke or the dust or the crying. Probably all three, actually. "No," he croaked. "Why don't you try to find us something?" It came out harsher than he had intended. Jes' eyes went wide and she hurried away timidly. Great. He just kept making things worse.

Finn took a deep breath, coughed out the dust, and looked at the body. He had to do something about the body. He wished Isabelle were here, it didn't seem right to bury him without her. Although, thinking about it, he'd probably do better with cremation. The body. He hated thinking about Eraldir like that.

He walked back up the rise and sat in front of the monument he'd made the night before. It was just as bright in the light of day.

What now, Eraldir? What do I do now? But the stories didn't answer.

He had no reason to go on, now. The mages wouldn't listen to him, so he had no students. Eraldir was gone, so he had no teacher, and no one to advise him, no one to put out his fires, or fix his mistakes. But Ronan was going to lead the mages into war. Finn desperately wanted to keep that from happening, and he knew Eraldir would have wanted him to stop it, too. He'd always agreed with Finn that the non-mages had reasons for being afraid and angry. They'd dealt with it poorly, but they didn't deserve to die, or at the very least killing them wouldn't make anything better.

He looked around for Jes, but she was gone. Oh, right. He'd sent her off to look for food.

Of course, he could just give up. It would be easy, now, to just leave. But where would he go? To look for Kel in the forest? His sister didn't need him, and was probably better off without him. Most people were probably better off without him. Or, they would have been better off if he hadn't existed at all. Now, with all the trouble he'd created with non-mages, everyone was a lot worse off.

I can't do this without you, Eraldir. What if I just keep making everything worse? Finn bowed his head. He didn't cry, his tears were spent. There was only despair.

FOR A WHILE, Finn just sat there staring at the ground. He was just thinking that maybe he should go look for Jes when the dust hanging in the air in front of him shuddered. A second later, in a huge gust of wind, Isabelle rocketed into the camp.

378

She skidded to a halt in the soft ash and burned debris, her white hair whipping around her.

"Man, Finn, I leave you alone for like a week and..." Her eyes fell on Eraldir's body and she froze, her face going whiter than usual. She took a step towards Eraldir, then stopped, whirled around, walked a few steps away, then turned back again. Her eyes darted towards Finn, and he saw that they glistened with tears; Finn found answering tears rising in his own eyes.

She swallowed, trying to keep her voice even, but her words came out choked, and a tear ran down her cheek. "How did he..."

Finn stood, walked over to her and hesitantly put his arms around her. She felt stiff and tense against him. "In his sleep."

Isabelle pulled out of Finn's arms, walked a few feet away, rubbing her hands across her face. Finally, she turned and approached the body, knelt in front of it. She picked up one of Eraldir's blackened hands and rubbed her thumb across one of the nails, wiping the soot from it.

"I hope he was dreaming of pie," she whispered. Her shoulders shook a little. Finn waited, aching to comfort her, but not wanting to intrude.

They stayed like that for a long time.

Eventually, the white flame on the hill caught Isabelle's eye. She stood, looked back at Finn.

"What's that?"

He took her hand and led her up the hill. To his surprise, she let him.

Finn watched her upturned face as she examined his work, the colors reflected on her skin. She saw something she remembered, and laughed.

She turned to him. "I like it." She paused, and then squeezed his hand. "You missed some, though." She let go of his hand, and reached out. Tiny, delicate tendrils of air mixed with the flames, moving them, dancing through the heat. Little, curling breezes formed out more stories, some Finn had never heard.

"What's that one?" he asked, pointing.

She laughed. "That's how he and I met."

A tiny, dancing, wind figure was trying to pitch a tent. She wasn't making any progress, and she quickly grew frustrated and blasted the entire thing into the nearby lake. Behind her, a tall, bent figure was watching, shaking with laughter. He pulled the tent out of the lake, showed her how to assemble it, then unassembled it and made her do it, much to her annoyance. After he finished, though, and started to walk off, she followed him, leaving the tent behind. He kept gesturing for her to go back, tried to avoid her, but she followed him, through forests, over lakes, up and down mountains.

Isabelle's eyes filled with tears, but she was smiling. "He stopped trying to get rid of me eventually. Decided he actually liked teaching, I think, although he never admitted it."

Finn smiled. "He told me he liked it. Mostly because it involved a lot of napping, though."

Her smile broadened.

THEY STOOD FOR A LONG TIME, Isabelle adding stories, and Finn watching. After a while, she turned to Finn. He nodded, and they walked down to the camp. Isabelle lifted Eraldir with a breeze, ever so gently; Finn folded the man's hands on his chest. With Finn walking in front and Isabelle bringing up the rear, they slowly carried Eraldir up the hill and laid him before the monument.

They both bowed their heads, and Finn called up more hot, white flames, which consumed the body. The fire rose high into the air, and, where it touched the monument, the flames turned gold, and more figures poured into the white pillar. Now, amidst the colors and the wind, were bright threads of gold: Eraldir as a young man with a bright-eyed young woman whose smile lit up her entire face. Eraldir, walking through an impossibly grand city, trekking through deserts, clinging to the edges of mountaintops.

The flames died down, and Finn saw that where the body had been was now a perfectly round pool of water. The pillar of white fire reflected off its calm surface.

CHAPTER 28

*K*el walked, and the walking felt so good, so awkward and strange. Her muscles were stiff and weak from inactivity and blood loss, but Kel felt strong. For the first time in weeks, she thought to check on Finn.

Kel reached out with her mind, through the millions of lives and minds around her, searching for a familiar voice. It didn't take long to find.

Girl, I thought I told you to leave me alone.

Sylvia sounded more disgruntled than usual.

What's wrong?

What's wrong? Besides being mentally accosted by a nosy child? Besides having to walk all over the place, carrying that old... that old... She whickered in distress.

Where are you? Is everything okay? Are you with Finn?

Finn. You mean the one who's always lighting things on fire. Oh, I just barely escaped him.

What?

Sylvia didn't answer her, though. Instead, she drifted off into her own thoughts. *He wasn't so heavy. I didn't mind carrying him, really.*

And then Kel knew what had happened. She stopped walking and looked up at the sky through the dry leaves above her. She pulled out an aloe leaf she'd found to replace the one Eraldir had given her. She wished she had the original, but at least this was in some ways a connection to the old man. Kel wondered how he'd died. It wasn't unexpected, but in other ways it was. Kel never expected anyone to die.

She hadn't liked Eraldir right away. The old man had made her uncomfortable, and he'd made them leave the forest. But Kel had seen what Eraldir had done for Finn. She hated to think what would have happened to Finn without Eraldir.

Eraldir had also always been willing to water Kel's plants. Partially because they provided fresh herbs for his tea and food, but also Kel had thought Eraldir had shared a little bit of Kel's love for growing things. Maybe because they had kept him alive so long.

Finn must be feeling terrible right now.

Kel planted the aloe leaf in the ground, gently sprouted it and helped it grow until was large and healthy. Then, with a small bow to the plant, Kel cut one of its leaves and tucked it into her bag. Then she hurried on, reaching out again with her mind.

I'm sorry, Sylvia.

Yes, well.

Are you okay? What happened?

Again, she didn't answer, but Kel saw into her mind, saw the memories she was thinking about. How she'd wandered away from camp after sensing her master had left her. How she'd meandered through the dry grass, not tempted by any of it, not even sure where she was, until she'd smelled smoke. Then, the running. The terror. The fleeing animals, and the flames right behind. She'd narrowly avoided death.

It was possible that the fire was natural, but Kel didn't think that was likely.

Kel could feel that Sylvia was many miles south and a few miles east of her. She thought of a green meadow she'd passed not long ago, where she'd seen some deer grazing. She impressed the image into Sylvia's mind, along with the path to find it. She asked the deer, too, to watch over her. They agreed.

Kel let Sylvia's thoughts slip away from her. There was a change happening in the horse's mind. The words were fading. She might never go back to being a completely normal horse, but the human-like consciousness was already beginning to recede.

Kel closed her eyes and said a prayer for Sylvia, and another for Eraldir, wishing her peace and safety and wishing him well, wherever he was now.

KEL CONTINUED to walk in whichever direction felt right.

After a while, the deer started to hang back, following only hesitantly. Kel turned back, saw it watching her with wide eyes.

Are you okay? Kel asked.

I'd rather not go this way.

Why?

But the deer wouldn't answer, it only bounded away.

The bear went a little farther, but after only a few minutes more he became nervous, too.

It's all right, I can go on by myself. Kel said.

Are you sure? I don't think you should go there alone.

Why? What's there?

Something bad.

It's okay. I'll be okay by myself. You can go.

Reluctantly, the bear ambled off.

The weasel laughed at the deer and the bear, and continued on. A few moments later, though, it cocked its head to the side, its body stiffening.

I just remembered. I have to... there's food...and the tree might be... but I need to go.

Smoke snorted into Kel's neck, and they continued alone.

They came to a line where the trees abruptly changed. Behind her were ancient, gnarled, thick-trunked firs and cedars, and in front was a grove of young alders. Here the light streamed down, and the forest floor had responded by sending up a profusion of wide-leaved bushes and grass. Kel pushed her way into the sunny, crowded patch. The trail was gone, but she sensed she was close, and wound her way through the alder trunks, breathing deeply of the smell of sunshine on leaves.

In the middle of the clearing was an enormous stump. It was twice as tall as Kel, and bore thick, ugly scars and burns, as if it had been blasted by lightning.

Kel placed her hand on the trunk, and a vision swam before her. A man holding a woman, his arms wrapped around her, her head buried in his shoulder.

The vision faded, but Kel could feel a warmth in the trunk, something alive moved inside it.

Kel lifted her left arm, placed the new skin of her wrist onto the trunk, too. A bit of dried blood rubbed off, and where it touched it, the trunk began to shimmer.

Kel stepped back, and watched the ripples expand into waves; then the bark split apart, like a wave breaking on the shore. A crack opened in the middle, Kel caught a glimpse of darkness, with a few distant pinpricks of light, and then a pair of antlers thrust their way out.

The antlers were attached to the head of a creature with dark red skin, smooth like the bark of a madrone tree. He looked almost human, but on his shoulders were long black feathers. Kel stumbled backwards as he stepped out of the chasm, which closed behind him. He looked at her with large, black eyes, like empty voids except, in those voids, in between what felt like infinite space, were millions of tiny white stars.

The creature stared at her, blinked its infinite eyes with red, bark-like eyelids, then smiled a sharp smile and reached a hand with long twig-like fingers towards her. Kel flinched, stumbling back, and the hand was immediately withdrawn. The creature blinked, then began to shimmer, becoming transparent and then fading completely before her eyes, replaced by a man with smooth, reddish skin, and long brown hair. His eyes had become a deep, warm brown, although they still held a trace of the infinite voids they'd been before, and hinted at the twinkling of distant stars.

The man wore a brown linen tunic of the highest quality, and a belt of finely worked leather. He looked like a wealthy merchant or a noble. He placed a hand flat on his chest and gave a short bow. His eyes never left her face.

"Forgive me. My name is Faraern."

"I'm Kel." A wave of exhaustion hit her and, feeling too tired to stand anymore, she took a few steps back and sat down on a stone, hugging her knees to herself.

"Forgive me, Kel," Faraern said. "I needed some of your strength for the transformation."

Kel's heart was beating uncomfortably hard, but she'd wondered what was here for too long to run away now.

"Are you hungry?" he asked.

Kel shook her head. "Who are you? Why have you been calling to me?"

Faraern's fingers twitched. "Did your mother not come with you? Did she not explain?"

"She died." Kel's eyes pricked, but she didn't cry.

Faraern sat down hard on the ground a few feet from Kel.

When he looked up, his strange eyes were red-rimmed. "I can't believe it. How did it happen?"

"Our house caught on fire." Something about Faraern was unsettling to Kel. She didn't trust the creature who'd tried to kill her, but there still might be something to its warning, and she'd wait before she gave Faraern all the information she had.

Faraern started to reach out towards Kel, but caught himself, pulling his hand back. Instead, he rubbed his upper arm with the palm of his hand, then put his hands flat on the ground. He looked away, then back at Kel.

"I'm sorry, Kel. Did she... did she ever tell you about me?"

"No."

Faraern sucked in a breath and let it out heavily. "I see." His eyes searched her face for a moment. "Well. I suppose you've noticed some... abilities."

Kel nodded.

"That would be because I am your father." He let out another rush of breath.

Something shifted in Kel's heart, a piece of her understanding of herself that had never quite fit. Whatever else this creature might be, that part at least felt like the truth.

"I've been trapped here since just before you were born. I'm so sorry you've had to grow up without me, never knowing what you were. It must have been terrible." He swallowed hard, his eyes heavy with sadness.

"It was fine," Kel said, then leaned forward and patted him on the knee. Faraern looked at her hand, and smiled. His gaze strayed to her other hand, and his eyes widened. Too quickly for Kel to react, he reached out and gently caught and held the bloody stump of Kel's wrist.

"What happened to you?!" His eyes were locked on the stump, examining the new skin Kel had grown there.

"There was a... thing... in the woods back there. She tried to stop me."

A darkness passed across Faraern's face, and his voice was tight. "What kind of thing?"

"Kind of like a person but made of stone, and her legs were water."

Faraern's eyes were black pools with pricks of light deep in their centers. "Where?"

Kel pointed with her good hand. "Back there, but she's gone now."

Faraern's teeth were lengthening, and his nails sharpened into claws. He gently released Kel's wrist. "I will be right back."

He turned, without waiting for a response, and bounded off with a snarl. Briefly, Kel remembered Finn leaving her in the woods, saying he would be right back and then returning days later.

But Faraern was barely gone a minute before he had bounded back into the clearing. The anger was gone, replaced by a new distance, something calculating.

"You killed her."

"I didn't mean to," Kel said.

Faraern watched her, not coming any closer. "No, you were right to do so."

Kel was skeptical. "Who was she?"

"Ruith. My sister. She trapped me here."

"Why?"

"Because she knew I would protect my children, and she wanted them dead."

Kel's eyes widened. "There are others like me? Why would she...?" Kel trailed off, unable to finish the thought.

"Yes, there is one other. Your half-brother. My son, Morthil. She nearly succeeded in destroying him. He is trapped now, dying. As for why she wanted to kill you... that is simply because she hates what you are. We should leave this place." Faraern glanced around at the brightly lit clearing. "It may not be safe here."

Kel still wasn't sure whether she trusted him, and she had so many more questions, but so far what he'd said made sense. And Ruith had attacked her. A wave of exhaustion hit her as wings sprouted from Faraern's back.

"This way, daughter," he said, flapping into the air and then perching on a branch as if waiting for her to follow.

Kel looked around, unsure what he wanted her to do.

"Oh, I'm sorry. Of course." Faraern flapped back down. "I was close to death when Ruith trapped me here. But I needed to live for you and Morthil. To keep myself alive, I used the link between you and me; I took just a little of your strength, when I needed it, to keep me here. A side effect of that, I think, is that you haven't had your full strength. I'll break the link for a moment to allow you to change."

Kel wasn't sure how she felt hearing that this creature— her father—had been connected to her her whole life, using her energy, without her knowing. She supposed he would have died otherwise, and it didn't sound like he could have asked, but Kel still wasn't comfortable.

Faraern closed his eyes and steepled his fingers. A thread of energy deep in Kel's chest was suddenly cut; a tiny current Kel had never even noticed before suddenly ceased to flow, and Kel felt a rush of power and wholeness. The strain she'd felt a moment before was gone, and suddenly Kel felt like she could run a thousand miles if she wanted to. And she did want to.

Without even thinking, she took off at a dead run through the woods; sunlight and shadow flashed across her eyes and she breathed a deep lungful of bright cedar and pine-scented air, smelling in it the wind and the last rain, the dampness of the soil beneath her feet. She could hear the trickle of an underground stream a half mile away, and feel the birds darting through the treetops above her. Her heart roared up with joy and she wanted to join them. No sooner had she thought that than wings sprouted from the space between her shoulders, her feet curled into talons, and she leapt into the air, climbing into the sky, laughing as she darted through tree branches, higher and higher until she broke out through the canopy into the endless bright blue sky. She laughed again and stretched her wings, catching an updraft and wheeling in a long, lazy circle before gathering her wings in and plummeting towards the ground. She pulled up and paused, beating her wings in long, slow, comfortable beats to hold herself hovering in midair.

She heard wings flapping behind her, and turned to see Faraern—his red skin translucent now and his movements heavier than before—coming to join her.

He smiled, and in his face was warmth and pride.

"Impressive."

Kel realized Smoke was trembling in terror in her pocket. *Sorry, Smoke. I'll be more careful.*

He didn't answer, but she patted him a few times and the shaking reduced.

The strain of keeping himself up was starting to show on Faraern's face. "Come, let us see if my home is still here," he said.

Kel didn't want to go. She could see a lake nearby, and she wanted to dive into it and see what it felt like to have gills, but she could see Faraern was struggling, so she agreed, following him as he winged heavily across the treetops.

FARAERN'S HOME was a glittering tree house, perched between several cedar trees. It had a large cedar porch that went all the way around it, and in the exterior walls were large windows set in dark wood frames. Inside were fruit trees, and a floor made of stone. A stone fireplace sat in the middle, surrounded by comfortable couches and armchairs. Staircases led up to higher levels, and down halls there were more rooms, all with large windows and most with glass roofs open to the sky.

Dust lay over everything, and on a table there sat a single plate with the moldy remains of a meal, a mug, and a half-finished letter.

Faraern scooped the letter off the table and tucked it into a pocket of his tunic. Then he waved his hand and the dishes disappeared.

"Should have cleaned before I left," he said.

Kel walked over to the fireplace and ran a finger along one of the rocks.

"You must be tired," Faraern said. "I'll show you to your room."

Kel didn't say anything, just marveled at the richness of everything as Faraern led her up some wooden steps and down a hallway to a small bedroom with windows on two sides and a large skylight. There was a small white crib with a soft pink quilt on it. Kel barely had a chance to take it in before Faraern waved his hand again and the crib was replaced with a small bed with a white frame and the same pink quilt.

"I'll let you get settled. Do you need anything?" he asked. She shook her head, and he left her alone, closing the door behind her.

She stood for a while at the window, looking out over the treetops. In her heart, she could feel the little thread now, the little draw of energy. Sometimes it tugged harder, and then it would let up as Faraern finished whatever he was doing. Kel planned on going back down and questioning Faraern more, but she lay down on the bed for just a moment and, despite the newness and strangeness of her situation, fell immediately asleep.

KEL AWOKE to Faraern's knock at her door, and when she came down to join him she found an elaborate meal spread out on a large, oak table. He sat, smiling at her while she ate, touching nothing himself, but sipping on a glass of water.

There were three different kinds of juice in silver pitchers, and Kel poured some of all three into the same cup and took a sip of the resulting mixture. Delicious. She eyed Faraern over the rim of her cup, wondering if he would chastise her for only having juice for breakfast.

"How is it?" He asked.

"Good."

He reached for the pitchers, poured a little of each into his water glass, and tasted it. "Mmm. You're right, much better."

Kel thought it would taste terrible with all that water in there, but she didn't say anything. Instead, she sliced a small piece of cheese off a block and nibbled the edge of it.

"How old is my brother?"

"You're seven?"

Kel nodded.

Faraern tapped his chin thoughtfully. "He would be around five hundred and sixty-five, then."

Kel dropped the piece of cheese. That was older than Eraldir.

Faraern laughed.

"But," Kel said. "Why isn't he dead already?"

"You and he are special, Kel."

"Special?"

"Yes. You see, I am one of the Ael."

The Ael. Her mother had told her so many stories of

them; they were powerful spirits roaming the land, and the stories always involved them tricking mortals into doing their bidding. "The Ael are real?"

He smiled. "Yes."

She narrowed her eyes.

He laughed. "What have you heard of us?"

Kel started listing them on her fingers. "The Twelve White Ravens, Vorana and the Man of the Mountain Wind, The Dancing Stone, Elyon and the Grey-Eyed Man, Nan and the Laughing Boy—"

Faraern lifted his hands, palms up, and gestured for her to stop. "Okay, okay; I see. Yes. Understand, though, those were all written by non-mages, hundreds of years ago, who never had much interaction with us. And the stories have changed a lot over time."

"Did they really happen?"

"I don't think any of them are literally true. They may be based on the truth. When there were more of us."

"Where are the others?"

"They're all gone."

"What happened to them?"

"They faded. We lived here for thousands of years, long before humans were here, but eventually we fade back into the energy of the world."

"Except you."

"Yes. I think I am the last, now."

"Am I an Ael, too?"

"No, Kel. You are something special. You and Morthil."

"What?"

"Well, you see, we Ael are very powerful in some ways. We are formed straight from the magical energy of the world, and we can connect with it and become it and transform it however we wish. But, because we are more energy than substance, we eventually fade back into that energy."

"And you like tricking people?"

"Well, we were here for thousands of years before humans even arrived. After that we mostly kept to ourselves." Faraern had a faraway look in his eyes. The corner of his mouth turned up in a smile. "Humans were so strange to us, once we noticed their presence. Always industriously building things that crumbled back down a few hundred years later. But then I noticed that they had something we lacked."

"What?" Kel had completely forgotten about her juice now.

Faraern looked startled. "There were starting to be fewer and fewer of us. We were all fading back, and not many of us were returning to the physical world. That would never happen to a human. Of course, humans die, but they are so solid, so physical, for the time they are alive."

Kel thought she heard envy and longing in his voice. Faraern looked down at the food, and picked up a nut, examining it. "I wish I could enjoy this as much as you do."

He sighed, then continued. "But humans die, and most lack any aptitude for magic. I would never choose to be a human. But I thought that maybe I could figure out a way to bring human qualities to the Ael. So, I had Morthil, who is half-human."

"Who was his mom?"

"A human woman. Her name was Lyla."

"She's dead?"

"Yes. She lived much longer than most, though. She was over a hundred when she died."

"Why didn't you have more kids?"

"Raising Morthil was a lot harder than I was prepared for."

"Why?"

Faraern took a long, slow breath in. "You have a lot of questions."

Kel thought she had a pretty normal amount of questions, given the situation.

"Morthil was the first, and only, one of his kind. And the other Ael did not take kindly to him."

That sounded lonely to Kel. Also, she wondered if all the other Ael would hate her, too.

"I taught him what I could, helped him learn his powers, and kept him as safe as I could from the rest of the Ael. There were a few that were interested in what I was doing, and eventually came over to my side to help. Ruith was one, initially."

"She was helping you?"

"Yes. But then Morthil, whose very existence the others found disturbing, did something they found unforgiveable."

"What?"

"He gave humans magic."

"There weren't always mages?"

"No, Kel. Around four hundred years ago, Morthil gave humans magic."

"Why were people so mad?"

"Because to do it he had to split magic into pieces. As it is, humans are barely strong enough for the fragments he gave them. It was a disaster at first. Those who became mages were overcome by the magic that entered them. They had no control over it. They killed others and themselves. Ruith and I and the others first tried to undo what Morthil had done, but we couldn't. So, instead we created the City of Mages. Any humans that were taken over by magic when they turned sixteen, we brought them to the city to protect them and those around them. Then, Morthil surprised us again by teaching them how to use it." There was pride in Faraern's voice.

395

"He taught them to control it, and, once we saw it could be done, the rest of us began to help. There is a part of magic that they could never control, though."

"What?"

"When Morthil broke magic apart, he split it into six pieces: fire, water, earth, wind, naturalist, and thread."

"Why thread?"

"Lyla was a weaver."

"Oh."

"Those were the six he intended, but there was a seventh. The shadow."

Kel reached for a cookie. "What's that?"

"It's a part of magic that underlies all magic, and humans couldn't ever control it. Everything they tried to do, shadow was created. It collected in themselves, twisting their magic and affecting the works they tried to make. Or, if too much collected, or if they overreached themselves, it would slip out of them, creating unintended consequences and destruction. No matter how hard we tried, we couldn't teach the mages to control the shadow. The best we could do was teach them to be aware of it. The more aware of it they were, the more quickly it dissipated, the more they could hold without it affecting them, and the less it twisted their magic without them knowing."

She realized that Finn had had to deal with all of this without anyone to teach him. Until Eraldir. She understood then. He'd had to leave. He'd had to leave her. She took another cookie.

"We did our best to help them. We tried to control the shadow, to contain it. Ruith and I and our brother Elyon created three stones. They could hold shadow, collect it from the mages around them. We gave these to the most powerful mages, who needed them the most."

Kel wondered if she could find one of these stones and

give it to Finn. She reached for a third cookie, glancing at Faraern out of the corner of her eye to see if he would say anything.

"You're immortal, Kel, you can eat as many cookies as you want and it won't hurt you."

A surge of vindication went through Kel, and she wished her mother could have heard that. Then she wished her mother were there, just to tell her not to eat more. She put the cookie down. The idea that she was immortal didn't mean much to her, as her own death had never seemed real to her, anyway.

Faraern stopped his story. "Are you all right?"

Kel nodded, but she suddenly wanted to be somewhere else.

"This must be a lot for you to take in. Let's stop for now."

"Okay."

"Would you like a bath? A change of clothes? The clothes in the trunk in your room should all fit you, and there are several baths here, if you'd like," he said.

Bathing hadn't occurred to Kel. She didn't think she really needed one, but her dress was a little stiff from the blood. Her mind flashed back to that lake she'd seen, though; she'd have to get Faraern to stop using her magic so she could fly over there. "Actually, there's a lake over there," she pointed, "and I'd like to..."

Faraern smiled indulgently. "Yes, of course we can go," he said.

Kel hadn't meant for them both to go, but she supposed that would be all right. Faraern was slow, though, and she'd have to wait for him.

Kel went to look out the window while Faraern cleaned the breakfast dishes. Looking out across the wide expanse of treetops, Kel could see the sparkle of the lake in the distance. Watching it, thinking of what it would feel like to dive in, she quickly forgot her loneliness and the heaviness of the knowledge of what magic was.

Within a few minutes, the plates of food were gone and Faraern had transformed into a hawk.

Then Faraern cut the thread and Kel, joy beginning to course through her, became a sparrow, then a butterfly, then an eagle.

Neither of them could open the door like that, though, so Kel transformed back to her usual form, opened the door, and they both darted out into the sky.

When Kel got tired of turning into new kinds of birds, she gave herself thousands of tiny pairs of bug wings all over her body, which still weren't enough to hold her up, and she careened towards the treetops before smoothly transitioning into a bee and then an owl.

She could hear Faraern laughing behind her. "You're quite good at that," he said.

"Really?"

"Yes. You're a natural."

She'd had to be, she thought, but didn't say it.

They landed near the lake, or, in Kel's case, in the lake. She dove straight into it, still as an eagle, and startled a school of minnows, immediately shifting to mimic them, which confused them even more.

When she'd had her fill of swimming, she climbed out, becoming human again, still wearing her bloodstained blue wool dress, and found Faraern sitting at the shore, watching her.

She sat next to him and looked out over the smooth surface of the lake, the wind rippling it in patches.

"I'm really sorry, Kel. I know this is a lot to take in, and you've had to do so much on your own. I would have been there if I could."

Having a father that she'd never known had existed was

so strange. She couldn't tell if she was mad that he hadn't been there, or sad that she hadn't known him before. She still didn't know if she could trust him or believe him. She had gotten used to the idea that she would be alone. She'd wanted Finn to love her and take care of her and stay with her, but she'd given up on that because it was clear that Finn had his own things to do. She missed Finn, and she missed having someone to care about her. It felt like Faraern cared about her.

Kel had so many more questions, but she didn't know where to start, and was still overwhelmed from the answers she'd been given that morning, so she just watched him out of the corner of her eye as he looked out across the water with her.

WHEN THEY ARRIVED at Faraern's home that evening, Faraern lit a fire and prepared dinner. Kel was starving, and ate as much as she could of the lavish meal Faraern provided. Again, he ate nothing.

"Don't you get hungry?" she asked him, the question just popping out.

"Ael don't need to eat."

They were silent for a while.

"Are there any others like me, besides…"

"Morthil? No." He paused. "Speaking of that, Kel… your brother… I can feel him, he is trapped, and dying. He doesn't have long. I… I would rescue him alone if I could, but…"

Even though she knew he was five hundred years old, Kel imagined a boy—like Finn but more like herself—trapped in a cave, lonely and dying. "I'll help you."

A smile of relief lit Faraern's face. "Thank you, Kel."

"Where is he?"

"In the City of Mages. It's high in the Iron Mountains.

Miles and miles from here. But we can fly there. It's sealed, but you can get us in. Morthil is trapped there, only barely keeping himself alive by using the energy of the old speaking pools."

There was an uneasy feeling in the pit of Kel's stomach, but she didn't have a concrete reason to distrust Faraern.

"Okay."

"Wonderful. We'll leave first thing in the morning." Her father smiled. "Before that, I have something for you."

He stood, and went to a small bookcase at the side of the room, pulling a box off it. He rubbed his palm across it, wiping dust from it, and handed it to Kel. There was tree inlaid in silver on the lid. She opened it, and inside was a simple necklace, the same silver tree hanging on a leather cord.

"This was your mother's. I gave it to her and she left it here for safekeeping. Would you like it?"

Kel took the necklace out and held it up. Her mother had worn this. Her mother had been here. Suddenly the tree house felt less foreign. Had her mother sat on these chairs? Watched the fire in this fireplace? All before Kel was born. Kel slipped the necklace around her neck and did the clasp.

"Thank you."

"And, this was... I got this for you, when she told me." Faraern pulled another box from his pocket, and inside was a little silver bracelet with turquoise stones. It sparkled when Kel took it. It felt too fragile to wear, like she wouldn't be able to move if she had it on for fear of breaking it, but she marveled at how the stones caught the light of the fire.

"You don't have to wear it. If you don't like it. I just wanted you to have it."

"Okay. Thank you," Kel said, still examining the bracelet. She slipped it into her pocket and looked up at Faraern.

"I want to go to bed now."

"Of course, it's getting late." Faraern bowed. "I'll be here if you need anything."

Despite the strangeness, Kel realized she believed him that'd he'd be here, which was something she hadn't felt in a long time. And there was something small and broken in Kel's heart that desperately needed that, even if there was something not quite right about Faraern.

ONCE SHE WAS ALONE in her room, she sat cross-legged on her bed, looking out the window at the silhouetted treetops outside. Smoke curled up on her knee.

What do you think of this place, Smoke?

I don't like it.

Why?

Smoke poked his cold, wet nose into her hand, and didn't reply for several minutes. *I don't know.*

Kel could understand that, and part of her felt the same, but she liked the idea of having a family again. And tomorrow they were going to go rescue her brother.

Kel wondered how Finn was doing, and decided to check on him. Faraern was using her power, so she couldn't transform, but she could still reach out into the minds of animals. She curled up under the quilt, closed her eyes, and let her mind expand, reeling out into the expanse of life around her. It was so much easier now, especially because she'd spent all day being one type of animal after another, she understood their minds more deeply now, found it easier to inhabit them and anchor herself to them.

She found a small field mouse, up late and scurrying through the burned grass, looking for something to eat. She asked its permission and then joined it, making her way towards a bright pillar glowing in the middle of the burned patch.

As she approached, she noticed two figures sitting at its base. They sat shoulder-to-shoulder, their hands almost touching, looking up at the bright white pillar. Now that she was closer, she could see colors and patterns shifting in the light—little figures moving and gesturing.

Finn murmured something, and Isabelle laughed, then sighed, and leaned her head on Finn's shoulder.

Kel watched them for a few moments, but she felt like she was intruding on something she wasn't meant to be a part of, and Finn didn't seem to be needing her, so she released the mouse back to its scavenging, and let herself fall back into her own body, curled up in bed. She wiped the tears from her cheeks and fell into a sound sleep.

THE NEXT MORNING, when Kel made her way down the steps into the main room of the house, Faraern was sitting on a cushion, looking out the windows at the sunrise, waiting for her. He smiled, pushed himself up, and began pulling dishes out of cupboards and putting them on the kitchen table before Kel.

"Good morning. What would you like for breakfast?"

Kel shrugged; she wasn't hungry, but he kept putting more food on the table until eventually she picked at some fruit to appease him.

"How did you sleep?" Faraern asked.

"Okay," Kel said, smiling at him.

"Do you need anything before we go?"

"No." Kel wondered if she should take Smoke with her. It might be dangerous, and as a bird she might not be able to carry him. The thought of leaving him sent a tremor of loneliness through her, but she wanted him to be safe.

I'm coming. The thought from Smoke came through loud

and decisive. Kel hadn't realized she was broadcasting her thoughts.

I don't want you to get hurt.

I'm coming.

Kel could make him stay, and part of her thought she should, but she really did want Smoke to come. *Okay. Thanks.*

After breakfast, Kel went to collect Smoke from her room. She left the silver bracelet in a drawer of the little desk there. It was too fragile to take with her, but she wore her mother's necklace. Faraern smiled when he saw, lifting a packed bag to his shoulder, and transforming. Kel transformed, too, and they set off into the cloudy sky.

CHAPTER 29

*A*rcturus sat alone on the high, windy parapet of his secret castle on the coast. He reclined easily, picking at a bowl of olives, but the olives were tasteless. He tossed a half-eaten piece over the edge, watched it sail down towards the black rocks below, then turned to the spread laid out around him. There were cakes and pastries, every kind of fruit and exotic animal imaginable, even a selection of wines. He tried one after the other, but they were ashes in his mouth. He would be halfway through chewing something and would completely forget about it. Despair crept into him, with a sharp edge of panic.

Suddenly, a knife was at his throat. The blade nicked his smooth skin, and Arcturus felt the sting, and a trickle of blood. He gripped the knife arm with both hands, but only for misdirection while he stomped his attacker's foot. The assailant grunted, and the grip around Arcturus' neck loosened just enough that he was able to shake free and jump away.

Reina laughed.

She slipped the knife back into a pocket of her small,

tight, ruby-encrusted, white dress. Her red hair was loose about her shoulders and her feet were bare.

Arcturus took a step to the right, pressed his foot down upon a wooden lever. A series of crossbow bolts zipped across the balcony, cutting through the air towards Reina. She laughed again, diving out of the way, pulling another silver knife from somewhere near her ankle and hurling it at Arcturus. It embedded in the wooden medallion he happened to be wearing directly over his heart. He could feel the impact of it, and the vibration it sent through his chest. He laughed and stepped towards her.

She stood up and grinned, picked a stray grape up off the table and popped it into her mouth.

"Too slow, Arcty," she said.

He pulled the knife out of the medallion and dropped it to the ground with a clatter. He took another step towards her, reached out and took her hand. She leaned in, laid her head on his shoulder. He wrapped his arms around her, and in that moment, he felt completely and utterly at peace. With one hand, he gently lifted her chin up as he bent down to kiss her.

Arcturus awoke with a feeling of blissful peace, his arms wrapped tightly around his pillow. It took a long time for the dream to fade, for the images that it had created to be replaced by reality. When reality did return, Arcturus was left with loneliness and confusion. He pushed the pillow away, moving it back to its proper place. Then he glanced around quickly, making sure no one had seen. But luckily, as usual, there was no one in his tent.

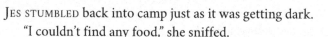

JES STUMBLED back into camp just as it was getting dark.

"I couldn't find any food," she sniffed.

"Guess we'll have to eat each other," Isabelle said, baring her teeth at Jes in a terrifying grin.

"I—I know you're joking," Jes said, but her voice shook.

Finn pursed his lips at Isabelle and turned to Jes. "Jes, I'm sorry. I'm really sorry. We're not going to eat you."

Isabelle rolled her eyes at Finn. "We might eat her."

"No, we definitely won't."

Isabelle punched him on the shoulder. "There's the Finn I know. Always demanding people be all nice to each other."

Finn smiled, despite himself.

"Okay," he said. "Let's get some sleep. First thing tomorrow we're going after the mages."

"But..." Jes said.

"Jes, you don't have to come with us. I'm not giving up, though."

"But... none of them want to listen to you... none of them even like you, and he's dead." She tried to point to Eraldir, then noticed the body was gone. She looked around, disturbed.

"Hey," Isabelle said. "Be polite. Finn might not want to eat you but that doesn't mean he can stop me."

Jes shut her mouth and wrapped her arms around her knees.

Finn was happy Isabelle was back.

THEY SPENT several silent hours around the campfire, during which time Jes, after a great deal of struggle, made herself a spindly bow and sharpened a stick into an arrow. She fell asleep clutching both to her chest.

After Jes fell asleep, Finn and Isabelle sat up talking.

"So," Isabelle asked, "Where is everyone? They leave once Eraldir was gone?"

"Um, no. Before, actually."

"Why?"

"Um. Because I told them I lied to them."

"What?! Why would you do that?"

"I realized I was going about this the wrong way. The whole point was that I was trying to be honorable." He laughed hollowly.

She sighed in exasperation. "So, I just went all that way—nearly killed myself—to set up a school so that they wouldn't know you lied and while I was gone you just went and told them anyway?"

"Pretty much. Sorry."

"Good. You should be sorry! That's ridiculous, Finn!"

"I know." He rested his chin in his hand.

"Well, it's probably for the best anyway. There's something bad there."

Finn lifted his head. "What?"

"Yeah. Turns out it's not as empty as Eraldir thought." She told him what had happened at the Table. She spoke lightly, but Finn saw a tremor in her hands. He gripped one of them tightly.

"I'm so sorry, Isabelle."

"Yeah, well, I'm fine." She extracted her hand and began to pick at a tangle in her hair. Finn wanted to say more, but decided not to push it.

"So, whatever this thing is, it's still there?"

"Yep."

"So, Ronan and the others are all going to end up…" he trailed off, not wanting to bring back the image of those living corpses, lying in the darkness.

"Probably."

Finn waited to see if she was worried about Ronan at all, but she didn't say anything else. He was torn between being happy that she didn't seem too concerned about Ronan and disturbed for the same reason. That was how he usually felt about Isabelle, though. He should probably think more about that at some point. Luckily, right now there were more important things to deal with.

"Well, now we definitely have to go after them," Finn said, scratching his beard.

"Or, you know, start a school someplace else," Isabelle countered. "If they're all dead they won't interfere." Finn was pretty sure she was joking.

"No, we definitely have to go after them," he said. Isabelle shook her head in amusement. Then she shuddered.

"Whatever it was, it said the creepiest thing."

"What?"

"It said my magic was 'ripe.'" Isabelle grimaced.

Finn's jaw dropped open as a memory struck him. Isabelle glanced at him.

"What?" she said.

"When Ronan and I were younger, we were exploring the ruins of one of the old mage cities, and we opened a seal on the speaking pool. There was… something there. It used the same word." Finn's eyes were wide. "I'm sure the King's Table had a speaking pool, too; why wouldn't it?"

"I didn't see anything like that."

"But, you also didn't see whoever it was that was talking, right?"

"No, but—"

"So, what if there's something living in the pools, trapped there? That would make sense; it would need someone else to do its bidding, if it couldn't get out."

"Were there a bunch of bodies in these ruins you hung out in?"

"No, but the communication link was broken. We fixed it, and the thing appeared, so we broke it again and it was gone." Finn turned to face Isabelle. "You didn't see anything at all? Like, a guy with a burned face and red eyes?"

"No. Well, the girl had red eyes."

"Well, that's interesting. If it's the same thing, I know how to get rid of it."

Isabelle's brows knitted together. "Um, so, just because the girl who attacked me had red eyes and I heard a disembodied voice use the word 'ripe', you think you know what the thing is and how to kill it?"

"And because I know the King's Table had a speaking pool."

"I thought you said you only thought it did."

Finn shrugged. "At least I have something to go on."

"Yeah, or, more likely, you plan on that and then it's something else and it kills you immediately."

Finn figured it was a bad sign if Isabelle was advising him to be more careful.

Finn glanced up then and noticed a hawk perched on a rock just on the other side of the campfire. It was still, its head cocked to the side, one large eye examining him. Finn stared back at it for a few seconds, then it blinked and flapped away.

There was a bird watching him.

Suddenly, Finn found himself laughing. Isabelle turned to stare at him, but Finn couldn't stop. The people he was trying to save had left, his mentor had died, he'd burned up all his possessions, traumatized the one follower he had left, and then, on top of all that, the place he had planned to take all those people had some murderous super-mage and a bunch of dead bodies in it. Yeah. That made sense. That seemed about right.

When at last his laughter died down, he took a couple of deep breaths. The heaviness was gone. It didn't matter anymore. What he was trying to do was impossible and there were an infinite number of insurmountable obstacles. That made it easier to try, in some ways. It couldn't get any worse, at least. He turned to Isabelle.

"Do you think I should give up? Go be a farmer maybe?"

"No."

"Good, me neither."

～

KEL PICKED herself up off the forest floor and flexed her talon. Hand. It was yellowish and slightly scaly, though, now that she looked at it. She hadn't intended to transform, but it must have happened on its own while she was with the mind of the hawk.

"Very good," Faraern said. "You went far that time."

They'd stopped for the afternoon so that Faraern could rest and he'd suggested that she practice reaching out into the minds of faraway animals.

Kel nodded. She was thinking about what she'd heard.

"Do you know about a place called the King's Table?" she asked.

Faraern shifted and looked away. "It's the old capital."

"Do you know what's in it now?"

"I haven't been there in three hundred years."

"But do you know what's there? Do you know why there are rooms of dying people?"

"That's enough questions for now, Kel. I need to recover my strength, and you need to practice."

"You know, don't you."

Faraern lifted his hands in annoyance. "No. I don't know why there are dying people there. I don't know why there are people there at all." He lay back against a rock and placed a hand over his eyes. "There may have been people left there after the wars."

"The wars?"

Faraern sighed and massaged his temples. "After the Fall.

Most of the human mages were killed in the Fall, but there were a few left—advisors and council members at the Table."

"Where were you?"

"I was traveling."

"Where?"

Faraern sighed and waved a hand. "Many places, Kel."

"Why did all the mages die?"

"Ruith killed them."

"Why?"

"So that she could kill Morthil."

"Why did she want to kill Morthil? And, why did she need to kill the mages to kill Morthil?"

Faraern sighed and sat back up. "Kel. I'm sorry, I know you want to know about things, and I'll tell you everything, but it's hard for me to talk about, and I'm tired. I need to save my strength so we can rescue your brother. I'll explain everything after we get him, okay?"

When Kel didn't respond, Faraern moved over to her and put an arm around her, pulling her into a gentle hug. "I'm sorry, Kel. I know this is all new to you and you want to know everything. I know you don't quite trust me, yet. It's okay. I haven't been there for you. But I will be. I'm going to be here, and tell you everything, and help you learn everything you need to know about yourself. Don't worry."

He did look very tired, and Kel could understand not wanting to talk about things. There were things she didn't want to talk about, either. Deep in the pit of her stomach, though, there was a loose, shifting feeling, like she was trying to find stable ground but it kept crumbling underneath her. Faraern's arm around her, though, was strong and gentle and there was sense of safety there. She believed him when he said he would be there for her. It made her realize that she'd never quite believed Finn when he said he would take care of her, even if she knew he really wanted to.

Still, Faraern had said that Morthil was keeping himself alive in the magic of the speaking pools. Finn had seen something come out of one of those, something burned and threatening, and he thought that might be what was at the Table, too. And he was going to try to fight it. Maybe Faraern was telling the truth, and they were just going to rescue her brother. Or maybe he wasn't and Morthil was what Finn thought he was, in which case he'd need her help. So, either way, Kel was going to the City of Mages to save her brother.

"Okay," Kel said, looking up at Faraern's warm brown eyes.

"Thank you." Faraern squeezed her shoulder and then moved away, stretching back out on the dry ground and returning to his nap.

CHAPTER 30

*T*he dream wouldn't go away. Arcturus was having it almost every night, now. And every morning he awoke with a feeling a contentment and his arms wrapped around his pillow. He'd taken to sleeping without a pillow, but then he'd just bunch up the blankets and cuddle those. It was ridiculous. The more he tried to ignore the dreams, the more he thought about them.

He'd been avoiding Reina since the dreams had started. Luckily, she was in a cage, so that was easily done. Arcturus was never one to sit idly by and wait for things to happen, though. Something had to be done.

Luckily, that day, while trying to distract himself by perusing his historical maps of old Caledonia, he stumbled upon the perfect excuse to take action.

REINA COULDN'T TAKE it anymore. It had been almost a week since she had been let out of her cage, and, when she wasn't in a drunken stupor, she was, sometimes literally, climbing the walls. Before, they'd been letting her out periodically to stretch her legs, but no more. Something must have changed. Maybe they'd discovered her mages in Arcturus' army. That seemed unlikely, though. She was careful.

She had decided she just couldn't take being cooped up anymore and was about to instruct her men to release her when the dutiful Captain Nate showed up and unlocked the bars for her.

"You know," she said, hobbling out past him, her legs and back stiff and aching, "just because you're not actually punching someone doesn't mean you're not torturing them."

He looked down. "I'm sorry, ma'am. I was given orders to keep you locked up. I don't know the reason."

"Just because you're given orders doesn't mean it's not you doing to the torturing."

Nate took her arm and helped her towards Arcturus' tent. "I agree, ma'am."

"Stop calling me that."

"All right."

He held the tent flap aside for her and she stumbled in.

She must have been a lot drunker than she'd thought, because she was seeing things. For one, most of the room had been cleared, and only a single table stood in the center. A small table. With two chairs, and a single, lit, candle, in the middle. Two fine plates, two crystal wine glasses, two sets of silverware, and at the side of the tent was another long table, heaped with food. A soldier sat in the corner of the room, attempting to play some sort of stringed instrument.

Reina blinked a few times.

"Flavius," she said, but she couldn't quite manage the usual cold, condescension. Instead, it just came out confused.

"Good evening, Reina," Arcturus said. "Care for some food?"

"How much of it is poisoned?"

414

"None."

"I'm fine, thanks."

They stood there, staring at each other. Arcturus fiddled with his fingers. Reina had never seen him fiddle with anything. The man in the corner stumbled through a few more notes. It sounded terrible, though. Arcturus rounded on him.

"Gavin, I thought you said you could play," he growled.

"Oh, well, sir, I..."

"You may leave."

"I... sorry sir... I—"

"Now."

The man paled, lifted the side of the tent, and rolled under it, dragging his instrument with him.

Arcturus blew out the candle and lit the usual lamps. Then he picked up a pastry and sat in one of the chairs. He crossed an arm over his chest, took a bite of the pastry, chewed, swallowed, and then spoke.

"I know where the mages are headed."

So that's what this was about. Inwardly, she heaved a sigh of relief.

"Oh yeah?"

"Yes."

"Where?"

"The King's Table."

She tried to hide it, but she knew her face gave it away.

Arcturus continued. "It should have been obvious from the start, of course. The old seat of power."

She crossed her arms over her chest and stepped her leather boots a little wider. "You still need me."

Something passed across his face, but she couldn't tell what it was.

She continued. "I know the Table. I've been there. There

415

are secret ways in, ways that I can guarantee they don't know about."

"What if I decide I don't need that? Maybe I'll just kill you now." He took a delicate bite of pastry, chewed, and swallowed.

Her lip curled with contempt. "You can try."

"I believe I would succeed."

"Only because you're an arrogant weakling."

"And you are an overconfident drunkard."

Arcturus set the pastry down on the immaculate plate. "You may prove useful still. I will allow you to live a little longer." He called out for Nate, who entered immediately. Arcturus made a gesture, and Reina was led away, back to her cage.

AFTER REINA HAD LEFT, Arcturus called Gavin back to clean up the tent, while he himself went for a stroll. He avoided the rowdy, smoky fires of the men, heading instead for the large stacks of supplies. At the far end of these, he found a place to sit and look up at the stars. Not something he was accustomed to. But there was something burning in his heart now, a craving he had never experienced. Tonight had gone poorly, at first. He'd tried the usual things, but of course the usual things hadn't worked with her. For a moment, he'd been afraid he'd messed things up completely, but they'd gotten back to normal by the end.

What could he possibly do to win her heart? The answer occurred to him almost immediately. He could defeat the mages. Even better, he would give her Finn to kill. Then, of course, he would defeat her army. She'd likely get some punches in, too, in the meantime, but after he had bested her, once he had won, and she had nothing left, then she would love him.

THEY CAMPED that evening under a rocky outcrop. Faraern lit a small fire for Kel, but then he wrapped himself in a blanket and fell immediately asleep. The wind whistled around the edges of the outcrop, and hushed through the branches of the few pines that could cling to the rocks this high, and Kel felt a deep loneliness and unease. She wondered what it would be like when they got to the City of Mages, and she wondered if Finn was doing all right.

She wasn't tired, and Smoke had gone off hunting, so instead of sleeping, she moved closer to the fire, crossing her legs and closing her eyes, and reached off, looking for Finn. Without Sylvia nearby, he was harder to find, but there were bats swooping through the night and she flitted from one to another, making her way across the plains, looking for him.

Eventually, she found him. She'd have to find an animal more likely to get his attention than a tiny bat, though.

ISABELLE GIGGLED and elbowed Finn in the ribs.

"How long should we let her keep trying?"

Finn poked at the fire with a stick. His stomach growled. "Aren't you hungry? I'm starving."

Isabelle tossed her hair. "Look how hard she's trying!" As they watched, Jes crouched down behind a clump of bushes, then leapt up, firing an arrow at something they couldn't see. She dropped the bow in the process. Isabelle collapsed in another fit of giggles.

"She's a water mage, though," Isabelle said, "I don't know

why she's not just drowning the first squirrel she sees. That's what Eraldir always did."

There was a brief silence.

"If she doesn't catch anything in, like, the next hour, I'll get us something," Isabelle said.

The grass next to them rustled. Finn heard Isabelle gasp, and looked up to see, across the fire from them, an enormous grey wolf. Its paws were mud-spattered and its coat shaggy, and it stared at them with bright, yellow eyes. It lifted a paw, held it for a moment, then dropped it.

It looked deep into Finn's eyes and blinked twice. Then it lifted its paw again twice.

"Kel?" Finn said.

Isabelle let out a rush of breath. "Man, I wondered for a second whether Eraldir had reincarnated."

"Don't you reincarnate as a baby, though?" Finn said, unable to help himself, even though there was a giant wolf staring at them.

"Reincarnation isn't real, Finn."

"Yeah, but, I mean, you can't reincarnate as an old thing. The whole point is that you're born again."

"If the whole thing is imaginary, does it matter?"

"I guess not."

Isabelle rolled her eyes. "Come on, Finn, I can tell you don't mean that."

"Yeah, well—"

The wolf yelped in pain, and they both turned to see an arrow protruding out of its neck. Growling, it spun around, its claws tearing grooves in the dirt. Behind it, a look of surprise on her face, was Jes.

The wolf bared its fangs and leapt for her throat. Her surprise changed to terror, and she dropped the bow, stumbling backwards, raising her hands to protect herself. It was almost on her when a crack like a blacksmith's hammer on hot iron rang out, and the wolf froze. Jes picked herself up off the ground and looked at it in surprise.

"Oh my," she said softly. She reached out and tapped on the wolf. It was frozen solid.

"Finally occurred to you to use your magic?" Isabelle said.

Jes nodded without speaking. She stroked the fur and the wolf sagged, collapsing dead on the ground, blood leaking from its nose and eyes.

"Also, you just killed Finn's sister," Isabelle said.

Finn rationalized away the fear that swelled up. No. That wasn't really Kel. She was just speaking through the wolf. The arrow wouldn't have hurt her.

"What?" Jes said, a look of horror on her pale face. "Oh, oh no, oh I'm so sorry," she stumbled backwards, her face going green.

"It's okay, Jes," Finn said, sounding more sure than he felt. "That wasn't Kel."

"Let's eat," Isabelle said, gesturing to the wolf. "You can thaw it out, right?"

Finn didn't know how he felt about eating the wolf that not long ago had been his sister, but he was starving and decided just to try not to think about it.

THE ARROW STUNG when it hit her, and the wolf reacted before Kel could, taking control. It had been willing to let her share its body, but it wasn't willing to die without a fight. It snarled in rage as she struggled to keep it from attacking. It whirled around and lunged for the woman who'd shot it. Kel wasn't going to be able to keep it from ripping her throat out. She didn't want to be around to feel that, but she couldn't leave the wolf; she had to at least try to help it get away, and keep it from killing the woman. But the woman wasn't as defenseless as she'd appeared.

With a horrible crack, the body of the wolf, Kel's body now, froze solid. Blood no longer pumped; muscles exploded in pain. The wolf died instantly, and Kel felt herself pulled along with it, dragged down by some dark current. She fought it; this wasn't her body, she wasn't ready to die, but like a nightmare in which she knew she was dreaming, she still couldn't stop it or wake herself up. She felt herself getting heavy, her vision of the world fading to black, her sense of self dissolving into nothingness.

Kel knew she was dying. She didn't want to die. She still had a body, but whatever force was pulling at her didn't know or care. It only knew that there was death. That the body had died and the soul must be pulled down.

Grey light appeared, illuminating shadowy figures. She felt the soul of the wolf beside her, dissolving into the ether of this dark place.

A grey figure materialized in front of her. A woman. Not her mother, but familiar. Blazing eyes, strong shoulders. The lips of the woman moved, trying to say something, asking something, but Kel couldn't hear her.

Something jerked at Kel from behind, and she turned to see Faraern, his face a mask of fury and terror. Kel felt herself pulled against the current, back from the cold dark of death. She turned back, and saw rage in the face of the woman, before she vanished.

With a gasp, Kel was suddenly back in her own body, collapsed by the fire, Faraern kneeling at her side.

"What were you thinking?" He snarled.

"I didn't mean to!" Her body was ice-cold, and her legs and arms tingled. She shivered.

Faraern staggered back, wiping sweat from his face and taking deep breaths.

"You were dead! What were you doing attaching that strongly to an animal?"

"I—I didn't know."

Faraern's eyes were black voids again, but he quickly turned away from her, taking more deep breaths. When he turned back, his eyes were warm and brown again. "I'm sorry, Kel. You almost died. I almost lost you. If I hadn't—" He closed his eyes, and she could see how drawn and pale his face was. "Please, don't do that again."

Her heart fluttered unevenly in her chest. "Okay."

Faraern looked at her evenly for a few moments, then turned away. "All right. Go to bed."

"Okay."

Shaken, Kel watched as Faraern fell into an exhausted sleep. It had clearly taken energy he didn't have to spare to pull her back.

Kel chewed a fingernail and stared into the fire. She took the silver tree pendant from around her neck and examined it as the light and shadow flashed across its bright surface. She was glad to be alive, but part of her wanted to just go back to the forest, alone. She wondered if she could break the link with Faraern, and what would happen if she did.

RONAN WAVED the other mages back as he strode up to the doors in the otherwise bare cliff face. His heart roared with a fierce joy, and part of him hoped the doors would be locked or stuck and he'd have to rip them off their hinges. He felt like he could split the cliff in half if he wanted to. And he wanted to. Just to see if he could. But he already knew the answer to that. Of course he could.

He pulled the door, it stuck for a moment and then swung smoothly outwards. Disappointing. Well, there would be other things. The mages entered, locking the doors behind them.

Ronan beckoned a fire mage to come to the front and light the way for them, but there was no need; the tunnels were already lit with ancient mage light. The blood in Ronan's veins began to race. The old mages. The rulers of the world. The ones who'd understood their powers and used them to the fullest extent. His pace quickened, and he sped up the tunnel, the other mages hurrying to keep up, the stone floor chilly beneath his feet.

A trail of stones was laid out. That must have been Isabelle. Where was she? Still here somewhere? He hoped so.

They came out into the stone courtyard at the top of the mesa. The top of the Table had once been an elaborate garden, running the entire length and width of the mesa. Stone paths wound through raised beds that now held dead trees and dried-out stalks of plants and bushes. Stone culverts, now dry, ran along the ground and connected to each raised bed. A statue of a man holding a book tucked under his arm stood near them, and past him a dry fountain held a few scattered leaves and the skeletons of several large fish. Around the far edges rose the stone battlements, and at the westernmost end the black tower stabbed into the sky.

The sky above them was cloudy, the undersides of the clouds were lit with the pink and orange light of sunset. Everything, including the faces of the other mages, was glowing with warm, orange light, and the chipped statues in the courtyard cast long shadows.

Ronan wanted to explore, but there was a strange, unsettling feeling here, and he found himself glad when Rafe suggested they find someplace to spend the night and wait to explore until morning. They found the large room that Isabelle had set up to be a dining room, barricaded themselves inside, set up a watch, and fell into an exhausted sleep.

THAT NIGHT, Rafe had a dream. He was in the courtyard, walking, examining the faces of the statues, one-by-one. He came to the far end, and there he found a door. It seemed to grow larger in front of his eyes, to swell and block all else from his vision, and he felt an intense curiosity about it. A girl materialized in front of him, between him and the door, staring straight at him, refusing to move aside.

Rafe looked down and saw that in his right hand he held a dagger. He felt the urge to lift it, to drive it into her heart so that she would no longer block his way. But even in the dream Rafe knew he didn't want that. He had no reason to hurt the girl. Still, the urge to kill her raged inside him, like a powerful itch, driving him mad. He had to get past her, had to go through that door.

His arm started to raise on its own. There was something very wrong about this. He didn't want to kill her. He had no reason to kill her. Through sheer force of will, Rafe forced his arm back down, dropping the knife; it clattered to the ground at her feet.

Her eyes glowed red, and she reached out her pale arms, placing one hand on either side of his head. Rafe knew what was coming, but couldn't move. All he could do was stand there, frozen, as she gripped his head with incredible strength and wrenched his head to the side, breaking his neck.

THE NEXT MORNING, Ronan sent out search parties to collect weapons or anything else of value they could find. Rafe went with one of the groups, rubbing the sleep out of his eyes and stretching the stiffness out of his back.

423

He wasn't the only one who had slept poorly. The others were silent, lost in their own thoughts, and jumpy. One of the younger wind mages approached Rafe nervously.

She walked along next to him in silence, trailing slightly behind, until Rafe asked her if she wanted something.

"There's something weird about this place," she whispered.

Rafe had been thinking the same thing, but he didn't want to worry her.

"No one's been here in a long time," he said. "Makes sense."

"Yeah..." He could tell she wasn't comforted by this.

"Maybe we should go someplace else." He agreed with this, but currently Ronan was the leader of their group, and Rafe knew the importance of having clear leadership. He wasn't going to be the one to undercut Ronan, even if he didn't think much of him.

They had just entered what appeared to be an old armory. It was mostly empty, but a few swords and bows remained in their spots on the walls.

"We don't have to stay here. If you'd rather leave you should let Ronan know."

She fell into a worried silence.

Rafe wondered if he himself should just leave on his own. Go back, find Cin and apologize. He was feeling less and less enthusiastic about being here, but he couldn't shake the feeling that something bad was going to happen, couldn't leave them now. He wondered what Cin would say to that.

WHEN THEY GOT BACK to their barricaded dining room, Rafe approached Ronan.

"Hey Ronan," Rafe said, sticking his hands into his belt

and leaning against the wall next to him. Ronan was eating a piece of bread, watching the weapon collections pile up.

"Rafe."

"So, what's the plan, here?"

"The plan is to figure out what all is here, set this up as our stronghold, train, then go out and conquer the major cities so the rest will fall in line."

Rafe scratched the stubble on his chin. "All right. Well, some of the people around here would like to discuss that."

Ronan's blue eyes met Rafe's evenly. "I know, Rafe. I was planning to talk to everyone after lunch."

"Well, great, then."

"Yes."

Rafe pushed himself back upright, and walked casually off, his hands still stuck in his belt.

Ronan wasn't much of an improvement over Finn. At least Finn told them things, even if they were mostly lies.

THAT NIGHT the two mages who were on guard duty caught Marta as she was trying to sneak over the barrier. She was clutching a large, rusty cleaver. At first, she was disoriented, and didn't know who they were, until they shook her and said her name several times. Then her eyes focused and she woke up out of whatever trance or sleepwalking state she'd been in. *So, I'm not the only one,* Rafe thought.

"HOW FAR FROM the Table do you think we are, Isabelle?"

"How far are *you* from the Table, you mean? I could be there in like an hour."

"Yes, how far are we from the Table, by walking."

She tossed her hair. "I have no idea."

425

Finn rolled his eyes. "Great, thanks."

She laughed. "Okay, maybe like the day after tomorrow."

"Can you fly us there?"

She glanced at Jes. Finn could see that she didn't want to admit she might not be able to do it.

"We could split up," Finn said.

"I want to come with you," Jes said.

Isabelle glared at her. "I can't lift all three of us."

Finn couldn't tell if she was being honest or just saying that out of spite. "Do you think you could catapult two people? Me and you?

Isabelle looked Finn up and down. "Yeah, you're small enough. I could lift you."

Finn had a moment of trepidation. He'd seen how Isabelle travelled, and it didn't look like something he ever wanted to try. Still, Ronan might already be at the Table. The monster might already have them.

"Jes, I'm sorry, can you follow along behind us? We'll leave most of the food with you. You'll be okay. It's not far."

"No, I don't…"

"You'll be okay. Please? We have to get to the Table as fast as possible."

Jes swallowed. "Okay." She looked at the ground.

"Thanks," Finn said.

"Quit crying all the time," Isabelle said cheerfully.

Jes narrowed her eyes.

"Isabelle!" Finn said.

Isabelle shrugged, and turned to walk away from the group, sending out a few test breezes.

"It's all right," Jes said.

"Okay, um, thanks. See you soon?"

Jes nodded.

"Do you need anything before we go?"

She shook her head.

"Okay. Well, bye, then." Finn walked over to stand next to Isabelle, glancing over his shoulder a few times to see if Jes was crying—she wasn't—and trying to ignore the nervousness that was threatening to turn into terror. "Okay, so, how does this—" With a great roar of wind, he was suddenly fifty feet above the ground, flinging through the air, his arms and legs windmilling wildly. Nope, his arms were not wings. He had no control at all over this. It occurred to him, as he reached the peak of his trajectory, that he was screaming. Then he started the fall back down, and the ground came rushing up towards him, faster and faster. That's when the real screaming started.

THREE HOURS LATER, Isabelle's magic was spent, and Finn was lying in a sweaty, shaking heap on the ground at her feet, trying not to cry too much, or at least to not sound quite so much like a terrified three-year-old when he did. Sobbing could still be manly, right? It didn't matter, because he didn't have a choice, anyway. Nope, sobbing uncontrollably was apparently the only thing his body wanted to do right now. Except also it wanted to throw up.

When Finn's stomach was completely empty, he heaved himself to his feet. Then he fell over. So, he heaved himself up to his hands and knees and crawled over to where Isabelle was sitting, munching on an apple.

She eyed him. "Stay over there if you're going to throw up more."

Finn wiped a hand across his sweaty, tear-stained face. "I'm fine. Fine." He paused. "What a horrible way to travel."

She grinned and took a bite of the apple. "Isn't it the best? Terrifying."

"That third jump, there. Was I as close to dying as it felt like?"

She thought back. "The third one? Oh, yeah. I tried to take us both up at the same time and I forgot to put up the slowing cushion for you." She shrugged. "I remembered in time though."

"Great. I would say let's walk the rest of the way, except I don't think I can walk anymore."

"Poor Finn."

"Hey, do I make fun of your fear of earthquakes?"

Her eyes narrowed. "That's a totally rational fear."

"So is plummeting to your death!"

"Fair point. I'm sorry." She tossed the apple core away. "Ready to keep going?"

Finn flopped onto his back and lay there, staring at the sky. "Just a couple of minutes. Until I'm sure I won't be spewing vomit as I go."

"Gross."

RIDING HIS DAPPLE-GREY STEED, Arcturus barely noticed where he was going. In his mind, he was replaying the conversation he'd had with Reina the previous evening. Despite the failure of the first dinner, he'd taken to inviting her to eat with him every evening. Mostly, they insulted and threatened one another, but Arcturus felt he was making progress. Everything about the world felt fresh and interesting today.

Suddenly, Arcturus' wandering attention was caught by something strange. It was a man. Hurtling through the air. He seemed to have been propelled about a hundred feet up, and was in freefall. He looked ridiculous, with his arms and legs flailing in terror.

Watching this spectacle for a few minutes, Arcturus realized that there were two of them. They must be mages. The second figure had long white hair, and was hurtling through the air in a graceful, controlled manner quite unlike that of her companion. Arcturus realized he was looking at a wind mage, carrying a man with her. They were going in the same direction Arcturus was.

Hmm. Mages. Heading towards the Table. But only two. What could that mean? Arcturus was still following the trail of the main group, so he knew they were ahead of him. Why were these two so far behind? Perhaps one of them had been injured or sick and had been left behind.

The second thing Arcturus realized was that if he could see them, they could certainly see his army. Once they reached the other mages they would warn them. Of course, they might already know Arcturus was coming. Reina probably had spies. But if she didn't, or if she for some reason hadn't managed to get word to the mages ahead, or if she was telling the truth that she wanted them dead, they might not know that Arcturus was on his way, in which case he would lose the element of surprise if those two mages got there first.

Well, he wouldn't let that happen.

That evening, as soon as it was dark, instead of allowing his men to rest and eat, he instructed them to continue, under the cover of darkness, at twice the speed. At this rate, they would reach the Table late morning the next day.

THAT NIGHT, Finn started a small campfire between two hills. They sat in front of the fire, chewing on leftover wolf meat, and for a while Finn forgot that the next day they would be at the Table and he'd have to figure out what to say to Ronan and the mages. He and Isabelle talked and laughed until they both fell asleep and the fire spread to the surrounding grass and they woke up in the midst of a small brush fire, which Isabelle tried to put out using her wind, which of course just made it worse.

It started to rain, though, and the flames went out. Finn wondered if somehow Eraldir had had something to do with it, but he didn't want to say that to Isabelle.

"Thanks, Eraldir!" she said, her face upturned, the water sprinkling into her open mouth. She grinned at Finn. "Remember when you lit all those crows on fire?"

He smiled. "Yep."

"That was great."

"Sort of... in a terrifying, not-in-control-of-my-powers, accidentally-killing-people kind of way."

"Well, yeah."

They set the campfire back up, making sure to clear everything flammable well back from it, and Isabelle quickly fell back asleep. Finn, though, couldn't seem to relax. All his thoughts and worries about the next day came crowding back into his mind, and so, instead of sleeping, he stayed up, and sat staring into the fire, thinking about what he was going to do.

～

For a while after Isabelle and Finn left, Jes sat crying.

She was still sitting there, crying, when a horse came up to her. It put its nose in her face and blew a whuffling breath into her mouth. Jes coughed and looked up.

"Kel?" she asked, having followed the course of Isabelle and Finn's conversation the night before. The horse nodded. Jes' eyes welled with more tears.

"You're here to help me?" The horse rubbed its face on

her shoulder, which Jes took to be a yes. It tossed its head towards its back, indicating that she should get on.

Jes was usually terrified of horses, but as this one was also a person she didn't mind as much; she climbed awkwardly up and gripped its shaggy mane tightly.

KEL CROUCHED on a rock in the middle of a bare slope on the edge of a mountain. Rain spattered down around her, and a family of pikas was cuddled into her lap, keeping her warm. She knew the city lay just over the edge of the next ridge; Faraern had left her here for a few moments to scout ahead, and she'd taken the opportunity to check in on Finn one last time. She'd seen him leave Jes behind, and decided she could help. So, she sent her mind out to guide Jes' horse to the Table.

Part of Kel was there, with the warmth of the pikas in her lap, and the rain cold on her shoulders, and part of her was down on the plains, placing one hoof in front of the other. After a few minutes, though, she asked the horse if it could continue without her. It agreed, and Kel left it, knowing Faraern would be back any moment.

JES RODE in silence for a while, but it was weird just riding and not talking, so she tried to start up a conversation.

"Thanks for doing this, Kel." The horse whickered, which Jes took to be an answer.

"Everyone's usually so mean to me," Jes said. "It's just crying. I can't help it if I cry all the time. Everyone hates me, and all I wanted was to stop Reina killing everyone."

Jes lapsed into a moody silence.

"Do you like Isabelle?" she asked.

The horse shook its mane in a noncommittal way.

"I agree. She's terrible. I don't know what Finn sees in her. He doesn't even like me. He thinks I'm annoying. She never cries. She's all strong and stoic and insane and he thinks she's the greatest thing ever."

A fly landed on the horse's back and it flicked it away with its tail.

"I'm glad you understand," she said. "No one likes me anymore. Ronan used to love me. Or, I thought he did. Course, soon as everyone thought I was a traitor he just stopped talking to me." She sniffed again, and her eyes welled with tears. "He's nothing compared to Finn, though." She sighed wistfully. "What does he see in her? Ronan liked protecting me; he didn't mind that I cried all the time. Up until he threw me to the wolves." She sniffed. "Oh, sorry, not that wolves are bad." She waited a moment, then continued.

"Finn's not like that, though. Finn likes girls like Isabelle, who never cry and who just fearlessly rush in and do things..." her voice trailed off into a thoughtful silence.

Off and on throughout the rest of the day, Jes continued talking to the horse. It was the best company Jes had had in a long time.

THE NEXT MORNING, Finn considered having breakfast, but ultimately decided there was no point. He stood around, shaking his arms and legs and taking deep breaths to keep himself from sprinting away in panic or starting his crying early, while Isabelle gorged herself on their food supplies.

"Don't worry," she said, "I'll eat your breakfast, too. Someone has to do it."

He was a nervous wreck by the time she finished eating,

and again, she shot him into the air before he was expecting it.

This time was a little better than yesterday, though. He was maybe getting used to this. His stomach heaved a little, but there was nothing to throw up, so it had to give up. *Ha. Take that, stomach.*

Just then, Finn caught sight of the Table. It cast a long, dark shadow over the plains, and there, partly in that shadow, was an army.

Finn tried to catch Isabelle's attention as they plummeted to the earth, but she was too focused to hear him. Not on keeping Finn alive, but on reaching out for a bird that had unwittingly flown too near her. Isabelle was soaring through the air, giggling and reaching for its tail feathers, but it flapped its wings frantically and narrowly evaded her.

When they landed, Finn didn't even have time to get a word out before Isabelle had catapulted him back into the air again. It was comforting to know that she wasn't even listening to him as she was tossing him through the air.

ARCTURUS WAS tired from the long night of travel, but the push had been worth it. They'd arrived at the Table ahead of the two flying mages, at least as far as he could tell. The main group of mages appeared to be already inside, which was unfortunate, but couldn't be helped now.

Arcturus scanned the horizon, looking for the place he'd seen the mages last. There they were. On the move, and heading straight for the Table.

You're too late, though.

He heard Nate coming up behind him.

"Excellent, Captain, I have a question for you."

And this time, because today everything was going his

way, it was Nate behind him, and he did sound exactly as disconcerted as Arcturus had hoped he would.

"Yes, sir?" Nate came to stand by Arcturus, surveying the horizon.

Arcturus pointed. "Do you recognize them?"

Now Arcturus turned to watch Nate's face. Because Arcturus knew who these mages were now; he recognized the pair from the inn. The white-haired wind mage and her murderous, black-haired friend.

Without hesitating, Nate identified them. "That looks like Finn Vogt, sir."

"That's what I thought, too." Arcturus smiled a thin smile. Then he turned back towards the camp. It was time to give Reina a present.

"Bring the prisoner to me, Captain."

"Ah, Reina, thank you for joining me." Arcturus could barely contain his excitement. Earlier, he had wanted to have Finn publicly executed—and it would have done a great deal to add to Arcturus' popularity—but now, surprisingly, that mattered little to him.

"Any time, Flavius," Reina said, sounding bored.

"I suppose you see that we have arrived at the Table."

"And now you want me to tell you how to get inside."

"Yes, but first there's—"

"See, the thing is, I don't actually feel like doing that."

Reina's words hung in the air between them.

"And why is that?" Arcturus asked finally.

"That just makes it too easy on you." She smiled. "Oh, I think you'll find your way in, but it won't be through any help of mine. I am going to leave now and go take care of my business with Finn Vogt."

How ironic. Exactly what he had been planning to offer her.

"If you're not going to assist me, I have no reason to let you live." He had every reason to let her live, though. Or, a single, very important reason. But he couldn't let her know that.

"Don't worry, Flavius, I have a reason for you."

He raised an eyebrow.

"About a month ago, I poisoned you."

Arcturus laughed. "That's ridiculous."

She shrugged. "You were killing my mages. In what I suspect were slow, and painful ways." She paused, staring him down. "So, I had Jes slip some poison into your food."

"I have a food taster."

"Then, when he dies, you'll know you have about a day to live."

"I don't believe you, Reina. It's too convenient."

"Stomach trouble? Constipation?"

Arcturus went white.

"It's okay, Arcty, there's an antidote. Not that you deserve it."

"Give me the antidote, then, and I'll let you live."

"That's not how this is going to work."

"Maybe I'll just kill you, then, and take my chances. I know all the best herbalists."

"You could do that. But, I doubt even the best will be able to find out what I gave you. And making the antidote... well, if you make the antidote for the wrong poison it could kill you right away."

"All right, then. Where is the antidote?"

"Not so fast. If you let me go, I'll take Nate to it. He's a nice boy, I think we can trust him to do the honorable thing."

Arcturus was so pleased by her ruthlessness that he could

barely contain his glee. All this time! He'd been poisoned this whole time!

He kept his voice calm and even as he replied. "Very well, then. I suppose I'll allow you to go after Finn."

Nate popped his head back in as soon as Arcturus called, and, if Arcturus hadn't been so distracted by his conversation with Reina, he would have noticed the dark, pensive expression on the man's face, but he was and he didn't. "Captain. Ms. Jeesh here will be taking her leave of us now. She is to give you a vial before you release her. Walk her away from the camp, but make sure you have the vial in your hand before you let her go. If she doesn't give you anything, then bring her back here."

"Yes, sir."

Arcturus watched her walk out of the tent. He wasn't worried about the poison. Arcturus really did know all the best herbalists, and, despite what Reina said, he was reasonably confident that one of them could undo what she had done. No, all Arcturus needed now was to kill the rest of Reina's mages.

NATE TOOK hold of Reina's elbow, and led her back outside, into the cool air of the cloudy morning.

"Where to?" he asked.

She rolled her eyes and started walking. They made their way through the rows of tents, past the guards sharpening their weapons and checking the fletching on their arrows, through the drifting smoke of campfires. They passed one of the soldiers who had been guarding her; she gave him a tiny nod and then bumped up against him as she passed. He slipped a vial into her pocket without Nate seeing.

Reina led Nate out of the camp and into the shadow of

the Table. The air was colder there. When they were out of earshot of the camp, Reina turned back, reached into her pocket, and pulled out the vial.

"Why are you working for that murderous old spider?" Reina asked casually, as Nate took the vial from her and started to unlock her shackles.

Nate stopped what he was doing. He took a long, deep breath, and looked into her eyes. "What makes you say that?" he asked.

"Man, it's a good thing you're pretty, because you're too naïve to live, otherwise. Makes sense why Arcty likes keeping you around."

"Trusting the good in people doesn't make me naïve," he said.

"It does if there isn't any good there to trust, kid."

"What reason do you have to think he's evil?" But, in his heart, Nate didn't need proof, didn't need to hear an answer. He didn't think Arcturus was evil, didn't think anyone was evil, but he knew there were things his boss did that Nate wouldn't agree with.

"All those mages you captured, were they executed right away?"

"No, they were all questioned and tried."

"And those trials, did they seem fair to you?"

No.

She continued. "And, were there any of those mages that just… disappeared?"

There was a wall in Nate's mind. The wall was the idea that maybe they'd escaped, or Nate had forgotten, miscounted. Or even that Arcturus had let them go.

Reina was shaking her head. "I'll let you think about it." She reached down, took the keys out of Nate's shaking hands, and finished unshackling herself.

437

CHAPTER 31

"Our magic won't work past here," Faraern said, alighting on the rocky ground and folding his wings behind him.

Kel landed, and, when Faraern had cut the thread that connected them, she transformed. As her talons shifted back into fingers, she tucked Smoke into his favorite pocket.

"Why not?" Kel asked.

"Because when Ruith killed the mages, she used their magic against them. She forced them to use their powers, causing shadow to build up until it exploded out of them. Hundreds of mages at once. There is very little air, water, or life in the city now. The shadow became so bad, and of all the forms of magic at once, that magic itself has left here."

Rain spattered down on the rocks around them, soaking Kel's hair and dress. She shivered, looking up the steep incline they still had to climb.

"It's just over the edge of this ridge," Faraern said. "Are you ready?"

Kel nodded, giving Smoke a pat.

They'd only walked a few steps, though, when Smoke began to shudder and claw his way out of her pocket. He shot out, scurrying back the way they'd come. After a few feet, he collapsed on the ground. Kel rushed over and knelt by his side. His heart was skittering in his chest.

Smoke, are you all right?

I think so.

Faraern had come up behind her. "You can't bring him any farther. Nothing lives in this valley."

Kel wasn't going to leave Smoke unless she knew he was all right.

I'm okay, Kel. I'll wait here for you.

She ran a hand along his body, and didn't feel anything wrong or out of place. *Okay.*

Kel wished she could leave him with food, but she wasn't able to make anything grow.

It's all right. I'll find something.

Reluctantly, Kel left Smoke and she and Faraern continued.

Kel wasn't used to the slowness of walking; she had gotten used to judging distances by how long it would take her to fly them. For a long while, the ridgeline seemed only a short way above them, but over an hour passed before they reached it.

The rain continued to pour down, the sky grey and the wind buffeting, and there were no trees to shelter them. The clouds were too thick for them to see very far, but Kel had the sense of open space; without the heavy grey mist blowing past, they might have been able to see for miles. They were so high, she wondered if they could have seen the King's Table from here.

Finally, they crested the ridge, and looked down the rocky slope to the other side.

Kel had never seen a landscape so barren.

There were no animal voices here, no skittering beetles or birds soaring overhead, and there was no deep presence of trees or bushes or even moss here. There was only the heavy silence of death and emptiness. Kel had thought Westwend was lonely, but this made Westwend seem like a garden of life.

Smoke hung in the air, rising to meet the grey clouds above, and an eerie reddish glow lit the fog in the distance.

A smooth slate road wound along the base of the ridge line; at one end, it turned and stretched across a bare field of choppy black rock, itself broken apart in places, and ended at an impossibly high black wall. This wall was taller than anything Kel had ever seen, and all that was visible past it was smoke, and the red glow.

"There it is," Faraern said, his face hard. "It wasn't always like this. This is what Ruith did."

They caught their breath at the ridgeline for a moment, then began to pick their way down, heading for the road.

"This whole valley was full of flowers and fruit trees and gardens."

Kel tried to picture it, but it was difficult to imagine that this place had ever held life.

They made camp that night in the boulder field, although it wasn't much of a camp because they weren't able to light a fire. But they slept fitfully for a few hours before the sun rose in a grey, orange sunrise. Then they pressed on.

As they approached, the wall appeared taller and taller, and Kel started to feel something on the other side of it, a sense of death and pain.

"Ruith built this wall to keep the mages in while she killed them."

Kel shuddered.

"If you were human, you would already be dead," Faraern commented.

Kel reached out and touched the wall. It was cold and smooth against her palm, but more than that, there was a sensation of deep pain there. "How do we get inside?" she asked.

"I don't know."

Kel stroked her hand along the wall. "What?"

"It is closed to me. I've tried to get in before, but I can't. Either I'm not strong enough, or Ruith did something so that I can't. I'm hoping you can."

Kel wasn't sure if she could open the wall. It wasn't a tree or an animal; she couldn't just ask it to open, and she'd never done any other kind of magic. She looked at Faraern.

"Magic is fragmented now, Kel, which is why you've only been doing one type of magic. But it's just the one you have the most affinity for. Before Morthil split magic apart, I could work with any aspect of it, and so could he. Now, it's harder, but you should be able to work with other types."

Kel had never wanted to build anything, or burn anything, or work with air. She'd wanted water for her plants, but it had never come when she'd asked. She wasn't sure she could do what Faraern said.

Faraern placed a hand on her shoulder. "It's okay, daughter. Take your time." He clasped his hands behind his back and walked a few steps away, staring thoughtfully up at the sky.

Kel sat cross-legged on the stony ground and placed her palm on the wall. She leaned forward, resting her forehead on its cold surface.

I don't think I can do this, Smoke.

Smoke's voice came through as a faint whisper.

Good. I don't think that wall should be opened.

Kel reached into her pockets, took out some seeds, only

441

to realize that they were dead now. Sadness surged through her for the little plants who hadn't been able to run away like Smoke had. She wished she'd thought to leave them, too.

She leaned forward against the wall again, closing her eyes. There was pain in the wall, and fear. There had been so many deaths contained within it. She could see flashes of mages throwing themselves against it as their magic exploded out of them, turning to stone themselves, or bursting into flames, or crumbling into dust as all the water left their bodies. Tears trickled down Kel's cheeks as she watched this. She wanted to make it better, wanted to come inside and help heal whatever horrible things had happened within it.

As she thought this, the wall shifted under her forehead, and a stone door appeared, its edges glowing a faint turquoise. Kel stared at it for a moment, then stood; reaching out with the palm of her hand, she leaned her weight against it and pushed it open.

"Excellent, Kel." Faraern said behind her. "Let me go first in case there is danger."

Kel watched as Faraern stepped through the door. The wall had wanted her to enter, not Faraern. *I'm sorry,* she thought. There was no response.

Faraern stepped back through. "There is no air on the other side. I don't need to breathe, but you do. Stay here while I find a pocket of air for you."

She waited several minutes, then she stepped through the door. It was as Faraern had said. Airless, and utterly silent because of it. But Kel held her breath for a moment, dumb-struck by the devastation around her.

Towers a hundred feet high were crumbling towards the ground, their windows blasted out, leaving shards of colored glass littering the ground. One tower had tipped over and fallen against another, dragging with it a tangle of thick cables with bright boats hanging on them.

Some of the city remained intact. Pure marble columns and multi-storied limestone homes had been blackened by the fires that had raged through. And everywhere were bodies. Magical flames still burned, and smoke drifted over everything. This place had not recovered from the disaster, nor even fallen into comfortable ruin. It was as though the destruction had only been wrought moments ago.

The bodies that littered the ground had been preserved by the lack of air. Their faces were twisted in expressions of anguish and terror. To her left, a group had been turned to stone while running; their stone cloaks billowed out behind them, their hands clenched in fists. One was glancing over his shoulder, terror in his face. Past them, a wall of flame burned, its black smoke rising into the sky.

She didn't hear Faraern as he sprinted towards her, only noticed him when he grabbed her shoulder and started dragging her through the streets. She realized she was running out of air, started to struggle against him, needing to get back to the door, back outside where she could breathe, but he dragged her on, his grip digging into her shoulder. Faraern pulled her up a shattered street, past a pile of still-burning corpses—only their skeletons were left now—then he pulled her into an alleyway and stopped.

Kel fell to her knees, coughing, and hearing herself cough. There was air here. She gasped and choked, unable to look up, focused only on breathing.

"I'm sorry about that," Faraern said. "Are you all right?"

Kel coughed again, but nodded. She felt tears running down her face. "Ruith did this?" And her brother had been trapped in this place for ninety years. Her heart ached at the thought.

Faraern's face was grim. "Yes."

"Where is Morthil?"

"In the center of the city, where the speaking pool is."

FINN GAVE up trying to get Isabelle's attention as she blasted him through the air, and instead focused on examining the army camp. A couple hundred soldiers, maybe. Lots of tents and horses. He didn't see anything that looked magical, but it was hard to tell.

At last, the hellish ordeal was over and they landed about a quarter of a mile from the Table. The ground here was flat, so they were totally exposed. Finn expected to see soldiers running towards them any second.

"Well," Isabelle said, "looks like we're not the only ones here."

"Yeah."

She turned to him. "So, what's the plan?"

"First, we need to find out who's over there, whether it's Reina, or Arcturus, or what. Then, get inside. How did you get in before?"

"Blasted up the side." She grinned. "But I also unlocked the main door. It might still be unlocked."

Finn pursed his lips. "Unless Ronan locked it. Which he probably did. Let's try it anyway." He really, really, didn't want to experience any more of Isabelle's preferred method of travel.

Isabelle's eyes darted away for a second, looking up at the high edifice. She bit her lip, looked like she wanted to say something, but instead just looked away, retying her braid.

"What is it?"

"Nothing. It's fine. If the door's locked I'll blast us up."

"Are you sure? What's wrong?"

"Nothing. Let's go."

She jogged off towards the camp. Finn really, really wished they had some cover. Any cover. A tree, a hill, a bush, but there was nothing at all between them and the camp. It was only luck that kept them from being seen.

They stopped a few hundred feet away, and crouched down in the grass to watch the camp and wait for a good opportunity to approach the door. About an hour had passed when they saw two figures exit the camp. Two familiar figures. It was Reina, in shackles, followed by Nate. So, this was Arcturus' army, and they apparently had Reina prisoner. Finn couldn't say he felt bad about that. As they watched, though, Nate bent down and started undoing Reina's shackles.

"Apparently, you're not the only mage Nate is nobly setting free," Isabelle said.

"Does he just let everyone go?" Finn asked, as Nate handed Reina back her sword.

They ducked down as Nate turned back to the camp.

A trumpet sounded. Then another. Men and women started emerging from their tents, pulling on armor and latching on weapons. Arcturus himself emerged from a large, red and blue tent.

"Well, too late, time to go," Isabelle said. She jumped up and started running for the door in the base of the mesa.

"Isabelle!" Finn hissed, but she didn't stop so he jumped up and ran after her, not at all sure that they should be sticking with their plan now that the army was mobilizing.

REINA HEARD A SHOUT, and when she looked, to her astonishment, there was the white-haired wind mage who'd stolen her wine, and, right behind her was the idiot who'd stolen her mages and delayed her plans. She drew her sword.

445

~

FINN SAW Isabelle reach the door and yank on the iron ring that served as its handle. It didn't budge. She tugged it a few more times, some white hair coming loose from her braid, but it didn't move. Finn slammed into the door behind her, grabbed the ring, and jerked on it, too. Nothing.

"Perfect timing," said a voice behind them. Finn and Isabelle spun around to see Reina, flames flickering up and down her arms and along the sharp edge of her sword.

"Where's your army, Reina?" Isabelle mocked. Finn really wished she wouldn't antagonize her.

"It's where it needs to be," Reina said, smiling a thin, sharp smile. "Now, I think I remember saying that if you took any more of my wine I would cut off one of your fingers and I'd make him choose which one. So, Finn, which'll it be? Pointer finger? Ring? Thumb?"

"Reina," Finn said, "I'm really sorry we messed up your plans."

"You did that on purpose, kid. Don't take it back now. You'll look cowardly in front of your lady friend here."

Over Reina's shoulder, Finn could see the soldiers finishing their preparations, lining up in straight, efficient lines, preparing to attack the Table. Any minute now they'd start towards them and there'd be nothing to stop them killing Finn and Isabelle. Isabelle seemed to be thinking the same thing. She turned to Finn.

"Look, Finn. You're a huge idiot, but good luck, okay? Start a good school."

"What?"

Isabelle didn't say anything, she just grabbed the back of his head, pulled his face towards hers, and kissed him. Then, grinning, she stepped back, taking three quick, deep breaths. Finn, confused, opened his mouth to say something, but all the air had gone, he couldn't breathe. Beneath his feet he felt an intense compression wave lift him up into the air, but everything around him was silence. Half a second later, Isabelle and Reina were tiny figures far, far below him, and he was fast approaching the top edge of the mesa. His progress was slowing quickly, though. He wasn't going to make it. He stretched out both his arms, making himself as long as possible. He felt one last burst from below, and he jolted a few inches higher. His fingers scrabbled on the wall, a foot below the edge. The wall here was perfectly smooth, nothing to grab hold of. He flailed his hands against the stone.

In desperation, Finn shot a bolt of fire at the wall, blasting a groove into it. Without thinking he shoved his fingers inside the groove. They caught, and held, his weight swinging down, flattening against the wall, but the heat seared his fingers. He screamed in pain, but held on.

Another bolt of fire carved a shelf for his feet to stand on. He pulled his fingers out of the hot groove, and some of his flesh stayed behind, burned off and stuck to the rock. He swayed in dizziness from the pain, stuck his fingers in his mouth to cool them, and tasted blood and soot and a horrible cooked-meat flavor.

Taking a few gasping breaths, Finn looked around, expecting to see Isabelle shooting up past him. But she wasn't there. He looked back down, and what he saw made his heart stop.

Isabelle and Reina were circling one another, Reina in a low crouch, her sword held high, Isabelle standing straight as an arrow, her arms loose at her sides and her hair, most of which had escaped from the loose braid at her back, blowing in the wind.

No, Isabelle. Run away. But he knew she wouldn't.

He tried to yell down to her, but she either didn't hear or

chose to ignore him. She must be out of magic now, or nearly so, and Reina still had all hers and a sword on top of that. Run, Isabelle, he thought. It was her only chance. Even that, though, wasn't likely to work. Behind Reina, the army was marching towards the two circling mages. Finn could see Arcturus and Nate riding out in front.

And then, Isabelle charged. Finn didn't understand what he was looking at. It looked like she was… hugging Reina. The two of them fell to the ground, Isabelle's arms and legs wrapped around Reina's torso. A few fires flickered, but extinguished immediately. Reina got her sword arm free; she lifted the blade and hacked downwards into Isabelle's back. Isabelle didn't even flinch. It looked like she'd bitten Reina, though, because Reina screamed. Or, Finn thought she'd screamed. He couldn't hear anything. Now Reina was struggling, gasping, bringing her sword down on Isabelle again and again and again.

Finn was too far away to aim accurately with fire. He wanted to let go of the wall, to leap off, to push himself downwards as fast as he could go. Gravity alone wouldn't bring him to the ground fast enough. He had to stop what was happening, but he couldn't. He could only watch.

And then, Reina collapsed. The sword dropped out of her hand, and she and Isabelle lay, entwined and unmoving, in a heap on the ground. Finn waited to see if Isabelle would get up. She had to get up. She couldn't have just…

Finn screamed Isabelle's name, but it came out as a strangled gasp. She didn't move. And then the soldiers reached her. They pulled the two of them apart, and Finn watched as they dragged Isabelle and Reina away, both limp.

Finn fought back the panic that threatened to overwhelm him. Maybe Isabelle was still alive. Either way, he was clinging to the side of a cliff, and Isabelle had just… gone through a lot of pain but probably not actually been killed…

to get him up here. Apparently, she'd meant what she'd said about believing in him.

Isabelle was alive. He had to believe that. And, because she was alive, she would need rescuing from the army that had captured her. That meant Finn had to get inside. He grit his teeth, and, burning hand and footholds into the wall, slowly, he began to climb.

WHEN FINN REACHED the top of the battlement, he took a deep breath, and found that there was no air to breathe. He panicked, and, luckily, in his panic he started to run, because he immediately encountered air again.

Finn stopped for a moment, hands on knees, gasping to catch his breath. When his breathing had slowed, he looked around and for the first time realized where he was. The King's Table. The capital of old Caledonia. This was where the council had been, and the libraries and the scribes. He'd dreamed of this place, had read every book there was about it in his town's library.

The ancient, crumbling architecture dwarfed anything he'd ever seen before. He stood on the top of the wall that encircled the whole mesa. To his right was a guard tower, a square, solid building of red sandstone, with carved trees ornamenting the sides. He could see that the roof had been glass, but it had shattered.

In front of him, a staircase descended to the courtyard in the center of the mesa. He could see across its full mile-long length to the black tower at the other end. There were at least a hundred statues of men and women throughout— these were the original formers of Caledonia, Finn knew. The men and women who had been its early leaders, who had negotiated the treaties incorporating the Uplands, the

Macai, and all the villages and towns of the Iron Mountains —all those who had magic—into the realm.

Here, all the food needed by the inhabitants of the Table had been grown. Plenty of luxuries had been imported, of course, but with water and naturalist mages they had been totally self-sufficient, able to withstand any length of siege with ease.

For a moment, he forgot what he was doing, that Isabelle was... in danger... and that he needed to find the mages. He recovered himself, though, and, looking around one last time, jogged down the staircase.

FINN KEPT ROUNDING corners only to be stopped dead in his tracks by the sight of something familiar. The statue of an old woman, with a book across her lap. Serina the Wise, who had brokered peace with the Uplands four hundred years ago. The infamous tea room where a Montvan assassin had been poisoned by his own apprentice. It was hitting Finn over and over that the history he'd spent his whole life reading about was real, had happened, and here. But he'd have time to explore later. Hopefully. With Isabelle. Who was definitely still alive.

Right now, he had to find the mages and warn them about the monster and the army at their gates. He came across passages that were free of the thick dust that coated almost everything else, and he followed these, jogging up and down flights of steps and turning sharp corners, until he heard voices.

Light shone from an arched, jade doorway, and, without pausing, Finn bolted inside.

There, in the center of a cavernous hall, stood Ronan, feet planted wide on a mahogany table, the mages standing clustered around him. He was saying something, but stopped when he saw Finn. They locked eyes from across the room.

Out of breath from running, Finn stepped towards them.

"What are you doing here, Finn?" Ronan's voice cut through the silence.

"I came to warn you."

Ronan crossed his arms over his chest. "Well, thanks. We already know about Arcturus, though."

"That's not what I'm here to warn you about." That had been one of the things, but he wanted to sound like he had the upper hand.

"Okay. What, then?"

Finn searched the eyes of the mages, looking to see whether anyone was really listening. They were watching him, at least.

"This place is dangerous." He told them about the trapped mages and the monster who siphoned energy from them.

The mages looked at one another, and there were a few uncertain mutterings.

"Really, Finn?" Ronan looked torn.

"Yes."

"Kind of convenient, isn't it? You're not just trying to distract us so we won't go to war?"

Finn could understand how Ronan would think that. "No, really."

Ronan looked skeptical. "All right. Well, look. We've got Arcturus to deal with. After that, we'll look into this."

Finn could see there was no way they would believe him. Well, he hadn't expected them to, but he'd had to try.

"Get out of the way, Finn," someone said.

Finn stepped away from the door.

Ronan hopped off the table, and the mages parted to make way for him. There was a silver sword belted around his waist, and he picked up a longbow from where it leaned against the wall. Not that he even needed weapons, Finn thought.

The energy in the group picked up, and the crowd surged around him. Rafe nodded to Finn as he left, and some understanding passed between them. Rafe, at least, would not ignore the danger here.

When they'd gone, Finn found his real objective. Ronan's bag.

FINN CROSSED THE COURTYARD, weaving through the crumbling statues, and found the door that Isabelle had described. Finn swallowed hard. He hoped Isabelle was okay. There was a pretty high chance that he wasn't going to live through this, though, so either way he probably wasn't going to see her again.

He was about to step through the door, when a brittle voice called out behind him.

"Stop." He turned to see a skinny girl with lank hair and red eyes. She swayed on her bare feet.

"Tell your master I would like to speak with him," Finn said gently.

Her forehead creased, and her eyelids fluttered. She opened her mouth, and a deep voice echoed out of her.

"Hello, again, little mage. You've come a long way."

"I want to speak with you in person."

The red eyes examined him. "And why is that?"

"I think I can give you something you want."

"Oh, you do." There was a pause, during which the glowing eyes slid unhurriedly down Finn's body and back up again. "Yes. Perhaps you can. Come, then."

The girl dropped, shaking, to her knees. Finn wanted to stop and help her, but he didn't know what he could do. So instead he turned and walked through the doorway.

~

STANDING NEXT TO FINN, watching Reina approach, Isabelle had a really hilarious idea. She knew she had just barely enough magic to get Finn to the top of the wall, so she couldn't get them both over. She could have blasted them both a short ways away and they could have run for it, but, for some reason that surprised even herself, Isabelle wanted Finn to get over that wall. She knew he had no plan, and that the mages had no reason to listen to him, and that he was way too tactless to be diplomatic with the mages and too weak to do anything about the girl with the blazing eyes, but at some point, his relentlessness had won her over. Yes, he was an idiot, but he just cared so much. It was cute.

She still thought he was being ridiculously naïve with all this "let's not fight" business, and "I can understand where the non-mages are coming from" crap, and he was clearly drowning in guilt and self-criticism, which was totally stupid, but... well, for some reason Isabelle really wanted him to get what he wanted. It was a new, and kind of annoying, experience for Isabelle.

Her plan, though, was so great it made up for all the weird feelings crap. Because she knew what would happen when she ran out of magic, and Reina didn't. Sure, she could have told Finn about the balconies around back, and yes, they could have tried to get in that way from the beginning, but this way was going to be much more fun.

Isabelle kissed Finn goodbye, but it was kind of a disappointing kiss, because he was too surprised to realize what was happening and so just stood there, tense and still, until she finally stepped away and shot him off into the sky. Luckily, he didn't throw up this time.

She took a last deep breath, felt the shadow straining

453

inside her, and turned to face Reina. She grinned a sharp-toothed grin. Reina was also smiling.

"Very touching. I'll just kill him later, though. One at a time just makes it easier for me."

Isabelle didn't say anything, just leapt for Reina and wrapped her in a bear-hug. At the same time, the shadow exploded out of her. Everything became silent, airless.

Reina was struggling like mad in Isabelle's grip. Perfect. She was wasting the last of her breath. Isabelle smiled and gripped harder, keeping her mind calm, her heartbeat slow and steady.

Flames flared up, but quickly winked out. There was no oxygen to sustain them. Finn could make fire that burned without air, a couple of the others could, too, but Reina's magic was weaker, fickle. Isabelle suppressed a chuckle. She wasn't going to waste the last of her breath on laughing, despite how hilarious it was.

Then, things stopped going quite as perfectly as planned. Reina got her sword arm free and sliced into Isabelle's back. That hurt, but the bones stopped the sword from getting at anything important like organs. In a moment, Isabelle knew, Reina would be dead. All Isabelle had to do was keep holding on, not waste any air, and Reina would die.

Reina flailed with the sword, cutting into Isabelle's back again and again. Now Isabelle was having trouble remaining conscious. She was used to pain, had broken every bone in her body at least once, and been attacked by more wild animals than was seemly for a young lady, but this was worse. She could feel the sword cutting through muscles, and it was hard to keep holding on. Her body was being sliced apart. Isabelle clung to consciousness, through the searing pain and the terror of being cut apart, and slowly, Reina began to weaken. Her struggles became more desperate. She dropped the sword and beat her fists against Isabelle's head and stuck them into the wounds in her back, ripping and tearing whatever she found there, her fingers slipping in the blood, but her sharp nails finding purchase.

And then even that stopped. Her silent struggles became weaker and weaker, and then she passed out. Isabelle held on a little longer, waiting, making sure it wasn't a trick. But it couldn't be a trick, because Isabelle's own lungs burned with the desperation to take a breath, and her vision was starting to go dark. She had meant to let go now, to crawl to the edge and back out into the air, once Reina had suffocated, but she couldn't. Her muscles wouldn't obey. She tried to move her arms, but they were stuck under Reina's body. Her mouth opened of its own accord and her lungs tried to suck in fresh air, but there was none to breathe, and instead the vacuum outside only sucked more air from her lungs. Her mouth opened and closed, desperately. Then her vision went dark.

ARCTURUS HEARD the commotion before he saw it. Soldiers running and shouting. Something about mages.

Striding out of his tent, he caught sight of Nate sprinting towards the fortress. Following the man's path, there ahead, Arcturus saw something that made his heart stop. Reina. Lying on the ground, her sword dropped from her hand, the white-haired wind mage collapsed on top of her. Both of them dead. A terrible grief pummeled through him, the loss of the only thing that really mattered. She couldn't be dead, not his best enemy. She couldn't possibly have been defeated by that maniacal child.

Arcturus stood, numb, as the soldiers pulled the two women apart, dragged them out of the circle.

"This one's alive!" One of the soldiers shouted, and for a moment hope rose in Arcturus' heart, only to be dashed again immediately when he saw it was the one who held the white-haired girl.

"Take her to the cage, then," Arcturus said. "The rest of you, carry her," he pointed to Reina, "to my tent. Fetch the doctors."

"Which one?"

"Did I say doctor? Fetch all of them."

The soldiers looked at one another, but they did as he said.

The world swirled around Arcturus as he stood alone; he knelt on the ground to steady himself. Nothing seemed real; was this another dream? He looked up at the Table. He'd come here to kill mages, and suddenly he found it didn't matter to him. But it had mattered to her. She had wanted revenge, and she hadn't been able to get it. That was what he could live for now. He would get her revenge for her, on all the people who had wronged her. It occurred to him that that included himself. He pulled the small glass vial out of his pocket and looked down at it, so small in his large hand. Slowly, he worked the cork stopper out of the vial, and poured the contents out onto the ground. There, Reina, that's one act of revenge. The rest of my time left is for you.

ISABELLE FLAILED, pulling her arms and legs in any direction she could, no longer knowing where she was, or if she was still trapped with Reina, but then she felt a hand on her shoulder. Two hands, grabbing her roughly and dragging her through the dirt.

And then, around her was the precious, luxurious, thickness of air, breathable air, and she gasped it into her lungs. It was the best feeling of her entire life, breathing those breaths. She lay on the ground where she had been dumped, breathing delicious air. She was victorious.

She heard a voice nearby saying something, something about taking her to a cage. Another voice protesting that her wounds needed to be tended to. The first voice dissented, commanded, and she was again dragged off.

The pain was gone now; she was in a delirious state. She'd almost died a couple of times before, so the feeling was familiar to her, but this was by far the best it had ever been. She enjoyed it fully, not paying any attention to what was happening or where she was going, just relishing the fact that she was alive.

Someone dressed her wounds. Someone tried to talk to her, but Isabelle just giggled, and they gave up. She was left alone to breathe the wonderful, perfect air.

FINN STEPPED into the mouth of the tunnel, and the air immediately grew colder. The stone passageway sloped gently downwards, curling like the body of a snake, deep underground. It wasn't long before the only light came from the magical sconces holding their ancient, steady flames. No side tunnels branched off from this main passage. He passed a few empty alcoves, but they were the only interruptions in the smooth walls.

He was beginning to wonder if the tunnel continued forever, if he was trapped in some sort of magical loop—maybe this was a trick of the monster's—when the tunnel ended at a door.

The door was made of wood, inlaid with iron, attached to the frame by iron hinges. Above the door was a stone arch, carved with symbols. The language was old, one he'd seen in places around Old Cromwic, and in books. A language which he knew now was not a human one.

Fear pried cold fingers into his heart, finding cracks in his courage. He might be wrong about what lay behind this door.

Finn placed his hand flat on the door and pressed. Slowly, it swung open.

Inside was a large stone cavern. The floor was flat, but the walls and roof were one smooth, grey dome, about three times Finn's height. On the walls were flickers of light, like reflections off the surface of water. As Finn took a single, echoing step into the cavern, he saw the small, round pool recessed into the very center of the stone floor. Ghostly light emanated from it. This speaking pool was in much better shape than the one in Old Cromwic.

That's when he noticed the bones. He'd thought they were just clutter, like the clutter that filled every other place in the Table. But no. This room was full of human skeletons.

Finn tried to conjure some light, a small fireball he could hold in his hand, but his magic wouldn't work. His legs were shaking now, and the self-preservation part of his subconscious was demanding that he run away, but he ignored it, and approached the pool of water.

He hadn't expected this to be quite so terrifying. Now, standing amidst piles of skeletons, Finn was rethinking his assumption.

He'd taken a few more steps and was fumbling with the lump of metal in his pocket, when the door behind him slammed shut, and red light flared up out of the water, momentarily blinding him.

The fiery image of a man stood before him. He was much clearer, more solid, but he was the same man Finn had seen with Ronan all those years ago. He was almost twice as tall as Finn, and his hair was black and long, his eyes blood-red with poisonous black pupils. His nails were long and sharp, and he wore ornate red robes over sallow, partially burned, wasted skin that hung in loose folds from his face.

Finn swallowed. He should have thrown the copper in immediately.

"Well, well, little fire mage." The figure laughed, and the sound echoed painfully loudly in the dark chamber. Finn didn't flinch.

"My name is Finn."

The laughter stopped. The creature's eyes flashed with anger, and suddenly Finn's blood was scalding him from the inside. He collapsed, writhing in pain on the ground. It seemed to go on forever, moment after moment of more pain than Finn had ever endured. He felt his sanity slipping away from him. And then it stopped.

"And mine is Morthil. You be careful, little mage," he hissed. He drew himself up and eyed Finn. "What brings you to my domain?"

Finn pushed himself back up to standing. A wave of dizziness washed over him. He'd dropped the copper. His eyes scanned the room until he found it, lying on the floor near Morthil's feet. All he had to do was kick it into the water and the connection would be broken. Hopefully. The other pool had already been functioning poorly. This one seemed in perfect condition. And clearly Morthil could stop him. Finn would have to distract him.

It occurred to Finn that he might be able to learn some things from Morthil before he broke the pool. There was a lot he wanted to know about the Fall, about magic. And Morthil knew the answers. He cleared his throat.

"I'll answer your questions if you answer mine."

The room went dark and silent. Finn could neither see nor hear anything. Something slithered across his foot. Something long and sinuous wrapped itself up Finn's leg. He could feel its smooth body constricting. But Finn held strong. He closed his eyes, even though there was nothing to see, and he shut his mind against the snake. Ignored it as it wrapped its way around his torso, then his neck. Ignored it as it squeezed, tighter and tighter, wresting the breath out of his body. Finn let himself go limp. Accepted death, if that was what was coming.

With a roar of annoyance, Morthil reappeared. The snake was gone. Finn could see and hear again. He met Morthil's eyes.

"I am going to kill you, little fire mage," Morthil whispered. "And before I do, I am going to hurt you. I will hurt you for longer than you think possible."

Finn's legs were shaking. It was probably noticeable. But in case it wasn't he'd try to pretend to be brave. "You can torture me, and I'll probably tell you things. But if you do, I promise that I will also lie to you."

Morthil's face was expressionless. Finn continued.

"I will lie, and you won't know if anything I've told you is true. Like I said, I have things to offer you. I know things. I know where the others like you are, I know what has been happening these last hundred years that you've been trapped here. I might even know something that could get you out. But you won't know."

"I can tell if you're lying," Morthil hissed, but there was uncertainty in his red eyes.

"Maybe you can," Finn said, "But there's another option. Tell me things, and I'll tell you the truth." At this point, Finn was just stalling, trying to figure out his next move, and his mind would be a lot clearer if Morthil stopped torturing him.

Morthil's eyes glowed with heat, reminding Finn of lava, which he'd seen more than enough of lately. "Very well. But if you bore me, or lie to me, or refuse to answer, I will hurt you."

"I understand. You asked why I'm here. I'm here for information." It was true, in a way.

"About?"

"Magic. Your turn. Where are you?"

Morthil turned away, long-nailed hands clasped behind his back. "I am in the City of Mages, trapped with the bodies of my dead siblings. Ruith's doing. I am drawing power from my speaking pools. The magic I laid down in these pools keeps me alive. I would have died without them, and I cannot leave them."

Finn watched Morthil's back carefully, but it gave no signs as to whether he was lying or telling the truth. Finn edged towards the copper, but he had gone only a few steps when Morthil turned back.

"Now. Tell me who you are."

"I'm a fire mage, from a small town. Which I accidentally burned down, killing most of the people there." The guilt and shame was clear in his voice, but the corners of Morthil's eyes crinkled in mirth. Finn ignored this and asked his question. "How did you come to be trapped?"

"My aunt betrayed me. Why are you here?"

That wasn't a full answer, but Finn decided not to push it. "I'm here to start a school for mages. Why did your aunt betray you?"

"Because she's a treacherous weakling. If you knew what I was, why did you come here?"

Finn carried on with his lie. "I need books. Information. No one knows much about magic anymore. It was all lost in the Fall, when you were trapped."

Before Finn could get another question out, Morthil spoke quietly. "I can offer you that, and more, little fire mage. "I can give you books, all the books written by my uncle,

Elyon. And more than that, I can give you the shadow stone, which Ruith created to hold the shadows that overwhelm and control you, limiting you from greater magics. All I ask in return is to be free."

Despite his better judgement, Finn's heart swelled in excitement, but he managed to hold himself back. He didn't trust Morthil, doubted that his story could be believed.

"If I were to free you, how would I do that?" he asked.

"You would give me your body," Morthil said, his eyes locked hungrily on Finn's. "My body is broken, trapped here. You, I can see now, are strong enough to hold me. None of the others have been." He gestured to the skeletons.

Unconsciously, Finn took a step back, unable to look away.

Morthil looked away and picked casually at his nails. "Or someone else's. Someone strong enough. And willing. A body must be given willingly."

There was no way Finn would ask someone else to do that.

"There has to be some other way. Why can't you use your body?"

Morthil gestured to his wasted skin. "I am not what I once was. This body would only last a few days outside of the magic of the pools."

Finn tried to think. He couldn't give Morthil his body, and he wouldn't ask anyone else to, either. "Isn't there some other way to help you escape?" Not that he intended to release Morthil, but maybe he could trick him into giving him the books and the shadow stone.

Morthil ignored the question, just continued to eye Finn's body hungrily. "Of course, you will have things you need to accomplish. So, perhaps we could make a bargain for time. I've been here a hundred years, I can be patient. What if you agree to give me your body in a year?"

"There has to be something else I can offer you," Finn said.

"There is not." Morthil's image burned in anger. Pain flickered through Finn, but quickly stopped.

"I can't agree to that," Finn said.

"Then you are just like all the others, and I will torture you here until you die, and no one will hear your screams."

Finn lunged for the copper. He struck it with his hand, knocking it straight for the pool. It slid across the stone floor, spinning as it went. It hit the edge of the water, began to tip over, but then it stopped, hanging in the air, suspended by a ghostly red light.

Morthil bent down and picked it up. He held it up to his ruined face. Then he laughed. "This was your plan?" His laughter echoed louder and louder. Finn winced.

"Last chance, little mage, will you consider my offer?" Morthil tossed the copper behind him. It clattered against the bones.

Finn swallowed. He'd prefer to keep living. He really didn't relish the idea of spending the rest of his life being slowly tortured to death, and if he gave Morthil his body, at least he could live a little longer, and he would also have the books and the stone. But then he'd be responsible for releasing Morthil into the world. Morthil, who used humans for his own ends.

Finn's skin prickled. He thought of Isabelle, and the look on her face when she'd described being trapped in the dungeon here, the magic sucked out of her.

"I won't agree to your terms," Finn said. The last echoes of his voice faded away.

"Very well. Someone will eventually." Morthil stretched out a hand, its pointed nails reaching casually for Finn's eye. Finn tried to jerk back, but found himself held in place. Pain was blossoming across his body; one of his fingernails wrenched itself off his hand and floated to the ground.

Finn shut his eyes. His eyelids still worked, at least. He felt cold fingers grasp clumsily at his eyelashes, tearing a few out before forcing his eyelids back open. Now Finn could see Morthil's other hand coming closer, the sharp nails like spikes ready to spear his eyeball and pluck it out.

"Don't worry, I'll leave you one. I always eat one eye first and the other eye last."

Finn jerked and struggled, sweat pouring off his body, his muscles shaking with panic, but nothing made a difference, and the fingernails kept coming closer.

"Wishing you could change your mind?" Morthil asked, pausing just long enough to tap the exposed surface of Finn's eye with the end of one dark nail.

Yes. Definitely, yes. He hoped Morthil didn't give him the option, because he would probably take it. "No," he gasped out. He knew it was the last no he could make himself say.

"Very well." Morthil laid a fingertip on the white of Finn's eye and stroked. The rough pad of his finger scraped, scratching and pulling Finn's vision down. Briefly, the images from his eyes were confused, mismatched. Morthil laughed.

THE BODY of a woman lay on the marble steps to the white, domed building. Her bones had contorted as her skin had dried around her; her jaw was twisted and her eyes were shrivelled berries in the centers of their sockets.

Kel stared at her until Faraern took her by the hand and tugged her forward without speaking.

They entered through a golden door between two white columns, and crossed an empty marble entrance hall, their footfalls echoing in the silence. Kel wondered if Finn had already reached the Table. Maybe she was too late.

They passed through another golden door, and descended a wide marble staircase. Warm, golden lights illuminated their way. Kel's fingertips tingled.

"There's magic here," she said.

"Yes. It's coming through the speaking pool."

At the end of the hall was a jade door set in a granite façade. There were strange symbols carved above it. Faraern placed his thin fingers on the door, and it swung open to reveal a dim cavern with a high, domed ceiling. In the center of the room, a small pool of turquoise water shone with white light.

Kel glanced at Faraern as he approached the water. She could run, now, but she wasn't going to leave Finn to face Morthil and Faraern alone. And a tiny part of her deep down wanted to believe what Faraern had told her. Because, so far, he had been true to his word. He'd never left her for more than a few minutes, he'd rescued her from death, and he had waited almost a hundred years for her to come and help him rescue his son, her brother. No one since her mother had taken care of her like that.

Kel felt a tug, just below her heart, as Faraern knelt over the pool, reaching out towards it.

"Morthil?" he said, his voice shaking.

The water only shimmered.

The tug in Kel's heart increased as Faraern directed more magic into the pool. He gripped the edges and leaned over, his smooth face only inches from the water.

"Morthil!"

Faraern gasped and leaned back; a translucent figure lifted out of the pool, an image projected into the air.

He had been burned, horribly, and Kel's eyes widened in pity to at the dark pits and scars and dead, blackened tissue.

He had long, black nails, and Kel noticed something red dripping from one of them.

The red eyes flicked to Kel and examined her. She tried to smile, but faltered, and when his eyes flicked back to Faraern her muscles went weak.

"I'd assumed you'd faded," Morthil said.

"I managed to keep myself alive," Faraern said, and Morthil's eyes examined Kel again.

"What took you so long?"

"Ruith sealed the City."

A flicker of annoyance passed over Morthil's face.

"She's gone, now," Faraern said. "Kel killed her." He turned and smiled at Kel, who stood at the edge, watching them.

"Is that so? And who is this Kel?" Morthil smiled a thin smile and his eyes bored into hers.

"Your sister."

Morthil's lips quirked up in amusement. "So that's how you stayed alive."

Faraern glanced at Kel. "That's not the only reason... I loved your mother, Kel. I love you."

But those words rang hollow, as Kel had known all along. He kept her around to keep himself alive. She should have known that from the beginning, but she hadn't wanted to let herself see it. She'd wanted a family too badly.

"You should have brought me a body," Morthil said, his eyes still locked on Kel.

"She can heal you," Faraern said.

Morthil looked down at himself in contempt. "This?"

"I won't," Kel said.

"She's more powerful than she looks," Faraern said. "Despite how young she is. This place drains me; even with Kel's magic I'm barely hanging on. Let's go."

Kel considered running again, but she knew that, if Finn

hadn't already encountered Morthil, he would soon. She didn't have a reason to kill Morthil, though, except a deep distrust.

"Very well," Morthil said, and suddenly Kel's decision was made for her.

Faraern lifted his hands and the tiny thread of energy between him and Kel became a torrent. Power slammed out of her, and she collapsed. Pain seared across her face and arms, as she felt his burns as her own. His body was broken, death flowed in his veins, and Kel felt the energy pour out of her, filling him.

She sank into a fuzzy grey world. Her sense of time slowed, and she lost awareness both of Morthil and of her own body. She sank further and further, all sounds and images fading.

A face coalesced out of the darkness. A woman, with burning eyes, the woman she'd seen before, when she'd followed the wolf's spirit into the land of death. Kel wondered if that meant she'd died.

"You must stop what you are doing," the woman said, lifting a shadowy hand, and Kel realized it was Ruith.

"You tried to warn me," Kel said. Her mind was hazy, but a vague annoyance crept into her. She wasn't choosing to die.

"You cannot let him out. Stop," Ruith said.

"I'm not doing it on purpose! Why didn't you tell me?"

"I tried to stop you."

"No, you told me I had to go save Finn, and that Faraern was evil, but then you tried to kill me."

"I couldn't let you release him."

"If you'd explained, I wouldn't have! Instead, you just tried to make me!"

Ruith looked at her for a moment. "You're his child. I assumed you—"

467

"I didn't know anything about him! I still don't! Tell me what's going on!"

Ruith's shadowy mouth opened and then closed.

"All right. You're right. I will explain. Faraern is my brother, and from the time we were born, he was never happy. He was terrified of dying, even from the beginning. I tried to help. We talked about it so many times, but it didn't do any good."

Ruith passed a shadowy hand across her face.

"To keep himself alive, he sought the physicality of humans, had a son with one of them. And it worked. He used his son's energy to keep himself alive while the rest of us faded. His son resented his own lack of power, he hated the Ael who hated him, who thought him an abomination. He split magic into pieces, and gave it to humans so that he would have his own followers to draw power from. He also taught them to use it. We didn't know that he only wanted to draw power from them. We helped him teach them; we'd never cared much for humans, but we pitied them because the magic overtook and destroyed them. So, some of us helped. Until one day I found the rooms where he kept them. The mages he drew power from. There were secret caverns under this city, filled with bodies."

Ruith shuddered.

"I told the others, the last of us. Faraern would never let Morthil be killed, because it would mean his own death, so we waited until he left, and then we attacked. But he had so many mages under his control that we couldn't match his power." A great sadness filled her eyes. "So, we killed them. All of them." Ruith was unable to speak for several long moments. Kel felt herself losing focus, beginning to forget herself.

Ruith continued. "We weren't able to kill Morthil, though. Even with all that. He was still too powerful. We destroyed his body, but he killed all of us but me, and hid himself in the speaking pools he had built. I had barely any strength left, but I sealed the City of Mages, hoping that Morthil would never be able to escape.

"My greatest fear was that Faraern would come to release his son. I wasn't strong enough to stop him anymore. Luckily, the seal I had placed over the city was strong enough. I knew Morthil's shadow could travel through the pools to the other fortresses that had them, but I hoped he would be too weak to go far, and that his power would stay confined to the city. I began sealing off the other exits with copper. It took me years. I would fade, meld into a tree or a stream, and only pull myself out years later. And I had to keep an eye on Faraern.

"He tricked your mother into falling in love with him, and I realized he planned to make another child, and to use their energy to free Morthil. I helped your mother escape, and together we trapped him in the forest. I had hoped he had faded, but I stayed, watching, waiting for you to come. I thought you would be another Morthil, sharing your father's dreams of power. I thought if I told you the truth you would free him and Morthil all the more quickly."

"I would have understood. If you'd told me."

"I see that. I'm sorry. For both of us." Ruith hesitated. "Seeing you, I wonder if perhaps Faraern wasn't right all along. Perhaps you are what was meant to be, stronger than both of our people alone."

The image of Ruith swam in front of Kel, and Kel tried to focus on Ruith's words, but kept forgetting where she was. She wanted to sleep.

The torture had stopped. Finn's broken body seared in pain, but new pain was no longer being added. That was fine with Finn. He lay there, knowing the pain would begin again soon, and there wasn't anything he could do about it.

Somewhere, Kel was crying. That couldn't be, though. She was gone, in the forest. Maybe Morthil had gotten tired of torturing Finn's body, and had moved on to torturing his mind. But then Finn heard another voice, a man's voice echoing in the cavern, and Morthil's reply.

Finn rubbed the dried blood from his remaining eye until it opened, and he saw that he was alone in the cavern. The voices echoed out of the pool, and Finn dragged his broken body over to it and looked in. Through the water, he could see another room, like the one he was in, and Morthil, his back towards Finn, and another man, and behind him, Kel. Collapsed on the ground, crying, her eyes closed and her body twitching. Her skin was deathly pale.

Finn launched himself into the pool.

Instead of hitting water, as he expected, or being mangled, as Eraldir had said might happen, he slammed into the floor of the other room. Faraern and Morthil turned in surprise, but Finn was too quick, he threw himself, screaming Kel's name, at Faraern, and fire exploded out of him. Faraern stumbled back, lifting his hands to shield himself, beating the flames back.

A wave of energy slammed into Finn, throwing him to the ground. His head cracked against the floor and he lost consciousness.

Someone called Kel's name. No, they screamed it. Finn screamed it. Suddenly, the torrent of energy that had been pouring out of Kel stopped, reduced to a tiny thread, and she could see Ruith again.

"Help me," Kel said. "I have to get out of here."

Ruith nodded. She closed her eyes and darted at Kel. Kel felt the spirit slam into her; a jolt of power went through her body, and she thrust herself upwards, swimming through the darkness, up towards the light and the sense of her body.

She could feel her hands, then her feet. She reached out, felt the thread, the drain of power. Gently, she pinched the invisible current of energy between the tips of her fingers, and disconnected it. It vanished, and immediately, she felt a rush of power, her own power. Her eyes snapped open.

She climbed to her feet, her hands curling into claws, her teeth sharpening. Finn lay bleeding and unconscious on the floor; behind him, eyes wide with terror, was Faraern.

He lifted his hands in supplication, "Please, Kel," he said stumbling back. "I love you, don't kill me, don't let me die."

His hands were already gone, and his arms and legs were translucent.

She was on him before he could say another word, her jaws locked around his throat. She gave a quick, sharp shake, and his body went limp. She dropped him to the ground, and turned to Morthil.

"Impressive, little sister."

Kel moved between Morthil and Finn. Reaching out with her mind, she found Finn's erratic pulse, and felt the broken and missing parts of his body. She directed her magic there, asked his body to heal, and had the sickening realization that he was missing an eye. She couldn't fix that.

"Leave. My brother. Alone."

Behind her, she heard Finn stir.

Finn swam back into consciousness, his body a throbbing mess of pain. A girl stood in front of him, facing away. Her feet were the heavy paws of a mountain lion, gripping the floor with sharp claws; green lichen sprouted across half her face and down the left side of her body, her left arm shone iridescent green with scales and her right was covered with glossy feathers. It was Kel.

471

"You're going to leave us alone, Morthil." Kel's voice rang out, loud and clear.

"You think so, little sister?"

Kel glanced over her shoulder and her eyes met Finn's. Then, she smiled.

Morthil lunged for her. The ground shook. Fire and light sprayed out of him, aimed straight at Kel, but a shining green shield sprang up between them, absorbing and deflecting the heat and light, leaving only a calm green glow.

A vine twisted its way up Morthil's foot, but he pinched his fingers together and the vine withered and died. Kel flinched.

Finn pulled himself up and ran forward, hurling a fireball straight at Morthil. It disintegrated around him.

Morthil grunted with the effort of bearing down on Kel's shield. The cracks spidered out through it, widening, and the edges began to fade.

"Run, Finn," Kel said. "Close the connection. I'll keep him here."

"I'm not leaving you, Kel."

"She's right, little fire mage," Morthil hissed. "Either you close it and I kill her, or you don't and I kill her and then kill you."

"Kel," Finn said, "Don't give up, I'm not letting him get you."

Her eyes locked on his, her voice calm. "Go, Finn."

Finn searched desperately for something he could do. He screamed in frustration and directed fireball after fireball at Morthil.

The shield shattered, and Morthil grabbed Kel by the hair. He yanked her head around. His free hand wrapped around Kel's small throat.

"Stop!"

Morthil paused. Claws sprouted out of Kel's hand and she

ripped them across Morthil's throat. The torn flesh hung loose and ragged, swaying in the currents of air from Morthil's lungs, but no blood poured out.

"Sorry little sister," he gasped, his voice a whispery rattle. "Thanks to you, it's not that easy to kill me anymore."

"Stop!" Finn cried again. "I'll do it! I'll give you what you want!"

"Finn, don't!"

Morthil turned his red eyes on Finn. Sweat poured down Finn's body, and his voice shook. "I'll do it. You can have my body."

Morthil smiled a cold smile at Finn.

Finn knew he was making the wrong decision. He refused to meet Kel's eyes; instead, he stepped forward, towards Morthil. "Give me Kel. And ten years. And the books and the stone."

Morthil laughed. "You're in no position to bargain, little fire mage."

Finn swallowed, and clenched his sweaty palms. "That's my only offer. Kill her, kill me. See how long it is until someone else comes."

Morthil shrugged. "Very well. It matters not to me."

"How do we make the bargain?"

Morthil stepped forward. "We will use an oath stone." Morthil held out his hand, and a red stone, translucent like a glowing drop of blood, appeared in his palm.

"How do I know it does what you say?"

"You don't."

"And there's no way for me to know."

"True."

"All right," Finn said. Maybe there would be a way to get out of it later.

Morthil clicked his teeth. "Wonderful."

473

Finn swallowed around the hard lump in his throat. "Yes. I'm ready."

Morthil reached out, his shadowy hand becoming solid. He handed the stone to Finn, then wrapped his long fingers around Finn's hand.

Morthil began to speak, calmly and precisely listing out his side of the agreement. When he finished, he nodded to Finn, who did the same, careful only to say that his body would be Morthil's. Not necessarily his living body. Or his completely-in-one-piece body.

The stone glowed hot in Finn's hand, burning his palm. The fire spread through Finn's veins, through his entire body. He felt the binding there, felt the deep knowledge that his body belonged not entirely to himself anymore. Regret flashed through him, the terrible certainty that he'd made the wrong choice, but Finn shoved it down, ignored it.

And then Morthil stepped away, a grin of triumph on his face. Finn opened his hand and saw it was empty. The stone was gone. Morthil stepped aside, and bowed to Kel and then Finn.

"Now, I've fulfilled my end of the bargain. You have ten years, then this—" he reached out towards Finn's body, "is mine. As a reminder, I think I'll take part of it with me." He reached out, and Finn found himself rooted to the spot as Morthil grasped the smallest finger of Finn's left hand. Heat seared through it and Morthil gave the finger a great wrench. The joint snapped and the flesh around it tore. Heat burned through it, and Morthil stepped away, holding the finger up, examining it, and smiling widely.

"I'll keep the pool stable for a few more minutes, so you can travel through it."

"Generous of you."

"Just protecting my investment." Morthil smiled. "See you in ten years, Finn," he said, and then disappeared.

They were alone in the dark chamber.

Sweating and shaking with pain, Finn ignored his mutilated hand and wrapped his arms around Kel, holding her tightly for a long time. "Are you okay?"

"I'm fine, Finn; you shouldn't have done that."

"It's okay, I have a plan."

She started. "Oh, okay, what?"

"Er, I'll tell you later. Let's go."

They passed through the pool together, back to the Table. There, on the stone floor, amid the bones, were books. Stacks and stacks of books. On top of one of the stacks rested a large blue stone on a silver chain.

"Are you okay for a second? I have something I need to do," Finn said.

"I'm okay," she said. She took a deep breath and closed her eyes, and Finn suddenly got the sense that she was somewhere else.

Finn fished around in the bones until he found the copper. He bent over the pool, holding the copper out over the smooth surface of the water. He opened his hand and the copper plunked into the water. He watched it sink for a few seconds, throwing off sparks. The surface of the water shuddered and the light went out. Deep below them, something rumbled, and the ground shook. Good enough, for now. He'd come back with more copper later. Make sure he had disabled it fully. Finn lit a flame, careful to keep it far from the books.

Curiously, he picked up the blue stone. It vibrated slightly in his hand. With his uninjured hand, he placed the chain around his neck, and tucked the stone beneath his shirt. He didn't notice anything particularly different. He was about to try some magic when Kel opened her eyes again.

She saw the darkened, broken speaking pool. "Good," was all she said.

475

She went to the door and pulled it open. Faint screams and cries, and the clash of weapons drifted down to them, jolting Finn back to reality.

"Kel, Arcturus' army is here. I have to go; are you okay?"

Kel gave him a look. "I'm coming, too, Finn."

Of course she was. Joy and gratitude flooded him, but before he could tell her that, a bloodcurdling shriek rent the air. Together, Finn and Kel sprinted out into the tunnel and up towards the light.

CHAPTER 32

$\mathcal{A}$s Finn sprinted up the tunnel with Kel, every jolt sent fresh pain through his hand. He held the arm tight against his body, which helped, but not much. He kept tripping, misjudging distances now that he only had one eye.

Before he got to the entrance, he tested his magic again to make sure it really was back. That was when he discovered just how well the shadow stone worked.

The fire burst out of him in a glorious, unconstrained rush. The usual cost, the heaviness, was gone. There was no drain on his magic anymore, nothing to hold it back. He stumbled into the wall, surprised, and a little afraid, but the fire was perfectly in his control. As soon as he wanted it to stop, it stopped. He reached out to the lights on the wall, balled his hand into a fist, and the flames winked out, crushed into nothingness.

Joy, and the heady rush of power lifted Finn up, the pain in his hand completely forgotten, his bargain with Morthil completely forgotten. Easily, without even trying, he lit the flames in the wall sconces again. And then he turned and continued running after Kel.

The bright midday light blinded him as they sprinted out through the bashed-in door into the rocky garden. Everything was in chaos. The crying came from his left, in the shadow of the wall, where emaciated people in grey, tattered clothes were dragging themselves out of an open doorway. Some lay flat on their backs, blinking up at the sun, mouths hanging open.

The screams came from his right. Shouting, the clash of metal, the rush of wind, the hiss of water meeting fire. The ground shook, stones cracking apart.

The mages were huddled together up on the south ramparts. They had barricaded the stairs with ice and rock walls, and were sending bolts of fire down into the attacking army below. There were about a hundred soldiers in defensive positions around the stone garden, attacking the mages' fortification, and firing hails of arrows into their midst. Most —but not all—of the arrows were deflected by wind or burned by fire. But too many had found their marks. Marta lay dead, as did one of the naturalist mages. Rafe had an arrow sticking out of his shoulder but was still returning fire with arrows of his own.

The ground shook in a continuous earthquake. They were apparently too high up for Ronan to call lava, but rocks hurled themselves at the attacking soldiers. Thirty or forty soldiers lay dead, scattered around the stone courtyard, but they vastly outnumbered the mages, and more were pouring into the courtyard every second.

Finn didn't hesitate. He sprinted into the fray, sending up hissing fireballs which exploded, showering sparks down on everyone. He skidded to a stop right in the middle of the chaos. Reaching out with his magic, he found every sword, every bow, every arrow. The swords he heated until their owners dropped them in pain. The bows and arrows he ignited into slow, small fires, that gave their carriers time to drop them, too, before they were incinerated.

Then he raised a wall of bright white flames around the mages.

The soldiers screamed, and turned to run. The mages yelled in anger—Finn could hear Ronan bellow in rage and felt the ground shake harder.

"Stop!" Finn yelled, and to his surprise his voiced boomed out like thunder above the fray. Everyone stopped. He turned to the nearest soldier. A man whose face was white with fear. "Where is Captain Nate?"

The man stumbled backwards mutely. Finn turned to another, encircling both soldiers with another wall of fire so they couldn't run.

"I am not going to hurt you. You are going to leave here unharmed. Where is Captain Nate?"

"D—down on the field," a woman stuttered.

"Good, thank you. Return to your camp now. Go."

He dropped the wall—which had cost him nothing to maintain—and immediately every soldier turned and ran. They fought with each other for the doors, shoving each other out of the way. When they had gone, Finn dropped the wall of white fire around the mages. They froze, staring at him. The water mages had already replaced the weapons Finn had burned with swords and cudgels of ice. Finn melted them, and they went up in puffs of steam.

The mages stared at Finn in fear and awe, but he didn't have time to talk. Without saying anything, Finn turned and followed the soldiers down through the tunnels, out into the field. He ran as quickly as he could, panting; the adrenaline was masking his pain now, and he felt great. Invincible.

They poured out through a small side door, camouflaged in the rock, and the soldiers sprinted across the field towards the rest of the army, which was occupied with battering down the main door.

When the soldiers there saw Finn chasing their comrades towards them, they stopped what they were doing, and opened fire on Finn. Arrows streaked towards him, but he incinerated them before they could touch him. The soldiers started shooting rocks from slings, but he melted those, too, so thoroughly that they burned up and dissipated into hot gasses.

The soldiers drew their swords, stumbling back a few paces as Finn shot fire into the air, lighting up the space around him, making himself a flaming juggernaut hurtling towards them. He skidded to a halt when he was about fifteen feet away. Dropping all his fire, he stood there in front of them. He raised his hands in surrender. They took this as a threatening gesture, though, and some started to back away. Others turned and ran. So, instead Finn put his hands behind his back, and dropped to his knees on the hard ground.

"Where is Captain Nate?" he called out, his voice ringing clearly across the empty space between him and the few hundred, terrified, soldiers.

At that moment, something out in the tall grass caught his eye. It was Jes, crouched on the ground, watching him. She'd arrived.

Out of the fearful, whispering soldiers, Nate stepped out. His sword hung, sheathed, at his side. His green eyes were bright but hard, like agates, and his chin was messy with several days' worth of stubble. He strode up to Finn, stopping only a few feet away.

"Neither of us wants this war, Nate," Finn said.

"True."

"I can stop this from my side, can you?"

"A lot of us are dead. Maybe too many."

Finn nodded. "I'm sorry. I wasn't quick enough. You know this isn't right, though. You know this is Arcturus' war, not yours, not mine. And not your men's. Are you going to let them all die?"

"Part of what makes my men loyal is that they see my loyalty to my own superiors."

"I don't think that's what it is. I think you're just a good guy."

Nate almost smiled. He took a breath. "You're sure you've got your side under control?"

"Yes, absolutely."

"Let's try this again, then." Nate started to turn away.

Just as he did so, though, Finn heard a shout behind him. It was Ronan. The mages had followed Finn down. Finn turned, saw Ronan raise his hands, Finn started to his feet, but it was too late, he was too slow. The ground was rumbling, cracking open beneath their feet. Finn was just far enough to the side that the crack missed him, but it cut directly between Nate's legs. Almost as if it were happening in slow motion, Finn saw Nate start to fall, saw molten rock bubbling up beneath him.

Just at the last second, though, Nate landed, not on the lava, but on an ice bridge. The ice blossomed beneath him, just a foot below the surface of the ground, catching and holding him, keeping him safe from the heat of the magma beneath him.

Finn turned and saw Jes, standing, her arms raised. She'd run forward, was only about twenty feet from him now. She smiled shyly at Finn, a look of pride in her eyes. Finn smiled back.

The fissure beneath Nate splintered, sending off cracks in all directions, one crack heading in Jes' direction. The ground near her split open, lava geysering out, spraying chunks of molten rock into the air. Jes screamed as the

481

searing liquid struck her, too quickly for her to react; then the lava poured up and over her. A split second later her screams were choked off, and she was gone. All that remained was a shifting pile of molten rock.

Finn didn't have time to react. More screams were coming from behind him. He turned to see Ronan clutching his arm, yelling in pain. His arm had been turned to stone. He'd stretched his magic too far and some of the shadow had slipped out.

Grimly, Finn pulled himself to his feet. He gripped Nate's arm, lifted him up from the quickly-disintegrating ice bridge and onto firm ground. Then Finn stepped in front of Nate, placing himself between him and Ronan. Ronan looked up from his arm in pain and anger, and stepped forward, lifting his remaining hand towards Nate. The ground shook. Sweat poured down Ronan's face. It was clearly costing him dearly to keep using his magic, but he was beyond caring. He stepped forward and the ground cracked under his feet, shattering and splitting open again and again, red flecks shooting up out of the cracks. Mages and soldiers alike screamed and ran, but Finn stepped forward grimly.

"You think you can make them accept us?" Ronan screamed. "You think you can convince them we're not dangerous?"

"No," Finn said quietly. "No. I know we're dangerous."

"It's us or them, Finn! They'll never leave us alone!"

The ground broke under Finn's feet and he dodged to the side, narrowly avoiding the molten rock that sprayed out of it. He rolled, coming to his feet again.

"Do you know what they did to me, what they did to my mom, too? Because we were 'unrepentant'? They tried to torture us into giving up what we are. What she was." The ground cracked again, and lava oozed out of it. "They deserve whatever they get, Finn."

The ground under Finn bubbled and strained, molten rock pouring towards him from all sides. Ronan was on his knees now, his face a sickly grey with red splotches. He was drenched in sweat, and his good arm was wrapped around his body, trying to hold in the shadow that must be nearly overpowering him now. His control slipped, just for an instant, and two mages and four soldiers turned to stone as they ran. The other mages screamed and ran faster. Ronan was the most powerful mage Finn had ever seen, and the amount of shadow he was holding in now looked like it could kill everyone for miles. Finn had to stop it.

"Ronan!" He called out, but Ronan ignored him.

Finn knew the stone could stop the shadow Ronan was creating, but if he let it go he'd be letting go of his own power, too. If he didn't do something, though, everyone here was going to die.

Finn reached out into the lava around him, found the heat, the fire that burned within it, and, using all his strength, he sucked it out. The rock cooled, cracking and flaking as it did, making a cool, hard path.

Finn sprinted along this path, straight for Ronan, leaping over pools and flows of lava. He reached inside his shirt, tearing the shadow stone from around his neck, pulling the chain up over his head. Skidding to a halt directly in front of Ronan, he pressed the jewel to Ronan's chest. Surprised, Ronan stumbled back, raising his stone arm defensively. Finn felt the blue jewel grow hot in his hands as it pulled the shadow from Ronan. Ronan's eyes went wide in relief. He grabbed the stone reflexively, then stumbled backwards, pulling it from Finn's grasp.

"What is this?" he said in wonder, taking a deep, cleansing breath.

"It's—" Finn gasped. "A shadow stone."

Ronan contemplated it, held it up to the light. "So, this is why you're so powerful all of a sudden." He grinned. "Well, thanks, Finn." He slipped the chain around his neck.

In that moment, Finn saw the future. He saw Ronan raise his hands again—one stone, one flesh—he saw that Ronan would kill Nate, and the rest of the soldiers. Then, no longer limited by even the shadow, Ronan would decimate the rest of the non-mage forces in the rest of the cities. He would kill or enslave all the non-mages he could find.

"Crap, Ronan."

"What?"

"I've just realized you're right. You're right about every-thing. All of it."

Ronan was still looking at the stone. "About time." Finn's words sunk in a little further, and Ronan looked at him "Wait, what do you mean by that?"

"I'm not totally sure. But, I'm sorry Ronan. I want you to know, it wasn't me. When you became a mage. I didn't tell anyone."

The blood drained out of Ronan's face as he realized what was coming.

There was no other way. Finn lifted his hands. Ronan lifted his, too, but he was a fraction of second slower.

This fire was the hottest Finn had ever made. Hotter than the fire that had melted the iron door. Hotter than the fire that had killed his parents and destroyed his town. Instantly, Ronan was a pillar of fire. His screams choked off as the fire consumed him, and within seconds only ash remained. Ash, a blackened stone arm, and a blue jewel in a puddle of molten silver.

The ground shook in several violent aftershocks, and a few surges of liquid rock boiled from the cracks in the ground, but finally everything was still.

Finn fell to his knees, gasping, pain exploding in his right cheek. He lifted his hand to his face, only to jerk it away because it was too hot to touch. Tears streamed down his face, sizzling as they ran across the burn.

And then there was silence, the mages and soldiers had stopped running, and all eyes were on Finn. Ash and smoke drifted across the cracked ground. Part of Finn suddenly wished intensely that this weren't real, that he could go back in time, just a few minutes, and choose differently. But he couldn't. Ronan was gone forever. Even if he could go back, though, he knew he would make the same choice, and that thought filled him with grief.

Finn turned his head, saw Nate coming up behind him.

His throat was dry, his mouth filled with ash, but Finn managed to get a few words out. "You all right?" he rasped.

"Yeah, you?"

"Yeah. I'm fine."

"You sure? You don't look fine."

Finn looked down to see that the whole right side of his torso had been burned. His shirt was gone, and his skin was a raw, bloody mess under blackened flakes. He wasn't feeling any pain. He was shaking, though. Light-headed, too. The last thing Finn saw before he passed out was Nate's worried face.

CHAPTER 33

*R*eina opened her eyes and found, to her surprise, that, not only was she still alive, but she was also in Arcturus' tent. The man had been acting weird, lately, and Reina didn't feel like sticking around to see what else he had planned. Especially now that she'd used her back-up, the poison. No, the war she'd wanted had been started; she could hear it raging outside. She'd prefer to stick around and see how it went, make sure everyone she wanted dead was dead —especially Finn—but her body felt weak. That little idiot had nearly killed her. Well, at least Reina felt reasonably confident that the girl was dead. That was probably enough of a revenge on Finn anyway.

No, now seemed like a good time for Reina to go. Just one small thing to do first.

NATE RAN for Finn as the mage collapsed, picking the boy up in his arms. He carried him, through the cooling lava fields, towards the camp. Soldiers backed away as Nate passed, but he shook his head.

"I need the healer," he said firmly. He had to say it three times before the disbelieving soldiers followed his orders and brought the man to him.

"Just what do you think you're doing, Captain?" Arcturus' voice was like ice.

Nate spun around. "This boy needs the help of a healer, Arcturus."

"That boy is a criminal. A murderer. He will be executed immediately."

Nate swallowed. He looked around at the gathered crowd. "No, sir."

Arcturus' voice was so quiet it was barely a whisper, but it cut clearly through the silence. "What was that, Captain?"

Nate placed a hand on the pommel of his sword. "This boy just risked his life to stop those mages from killing us, sir."

"I believe what I saw was him convincing you to surrender."

"No, he—"

"Arrest this man," Arcturus said. "Briggs, congratulations on your promotion, you are my new second in command. It comes with a substantial pay raise."

Briggs looked uncertainly at Nate, who shook his head. Nate lifted his voice, so that it rose above the mutterings that had broken out. He lifted his hands for silence.

"All right, everyone, calm down. Briggs, as much as I'd love for you to get a promotion, what's happening here is that I'm taking temporary command."

"I think not," Arcturus sneered.

"I've discovered some information about Arcturus. He has been having contact with mages, which has provoked this war. He's been torturing them."

"And this traitor here has been letting them run wild. He let them escape."

"No, sir," Briggs said. "We let them escape."

Arcturus turned to him in surprise.

Briggs continued, "And I don't want your damn promotion. If I want a promotion I'll ask the captain."

There were nods and a few chuckles. Arcturus looked around, his eyes wild.

"This is insubordination. You won't be paid."

"We'll deal with the consequences after your trial," Nate said, and Arcturus' face went grey.

"If you let that mage live, you'll regret it," Arcturus said.

There were some uneasy looks, but no one protested as Arcturus was led away to replace Isabelle in the iron cage.

WHEN FINN OPENED HIS EYES, he was lying on something soft. He was wearing white pants and a shirt, with a bandage wrapped around his head, covering the missing eye. Only a thin linen sheet lay across him. When he moved, the cloth rasped against his skin like someone was grinding sand into his wounds. He groaned and closed his eye.

"You're alive!" came a familiar voice. His eye snapped open, and he whipped his head around, ignoring the pain, searching for the source of the voice.

There. In the bed next to his, her white hair still stained red with blood, was Isabelle. She grinned at him.

He blinked. "You're... you're..."

"Isabelle. Jeez. How hard did you hit your head? That's basically the only part of you that still looks normal. Except for the bandage. And the tattoo. Cool, by the way, although you're copying Ronan."

Finn glanced in a mirror and saw that he now had the crescent moon tattoo. That was the burn he'd felt when he'd killed Ronan. He wondered if it was the shadow, or his own subconscious, that had done it. But he didn't care right now, because Isabelle was alive.

"No... I mean... I thought you were dead. I saw Reina kill you."

"What? No. You saw me kill Reina, obviously."

"But... you were just lying there and she was hacking at you..." Finn tried to make a hacking motion with his arm, but regretted it instantly, and had to lie still for a second while the dizziness from the pain passed.

"Oh, yeah," Isabelle grinned. "I suffocated her." She told him about how the shadow had emptied that area of breathable air.

Finn stared at her. "So... your plan was to take all the air away and hope she suffocated first?"

"Yep!"

"But... but what if you'd suffocated first? What if..."

Isabelle shrugged. "Worked, didn't it?"

Finn opened and shut his mouth. He opened and shut it again.

Then, despite the pain, despite the dizziness, he pushed himself up to a seat, remembering too late that some of his fingers were broken, and one was missing. Although, looking down, the hand appeared to be well-wrapped in bandages now. He stumbled over to where Isabelle lay, wearing some of the same loose cotton clothes. He leaned in, cupping her face with his broken and burned fingers, and kissed her long and hard.

When at last he pulled back he found there were tears in his eye, but he didn't wipe them away. She looked embarrassed by the display of emotion, but also pleased.

"You're alive!" He hugged her again, and his whole body screamed in pain. But it was totally worth it.

After a long time, it finally occurred to Finn to wonder where they were.

"Hospital tent," Isabelle said.

"Arcturus' hospital tent?" Finn asked, suddenly looking around and realizing that maybe they were prisoners. He didn't see any guards.

Isabelle smiled. "Nate's hospital tent."

"What happened?"

Isabelle filled him in.

"Have you seen Kel?"

"Yeah, she's been by a few times to check on you."

Finn sighed in relief. Then he remembered that Jes was dead. She'd saved Nate, meaning she'd saved Finn's life, too. Finn wished he'd been more patient with her. *Thank you, Jes,* he thought.

"That was weird," Isabelle said.

"What?"

"You like, looked up at the ceiling and mumbled something. What were you thinking?"

"Nothing." He didn't want her mad at him for thinking about Jes.

"No, you were definitely thinking something. It was about Jes, wasn't it?" She narrowed her eyes.

Finn sighed. "She's dead. She saved Nate and then Ronan killed her. I was wishing I'd been nicer to her."

"You were nice to her. She was annoying."

"Still."

"Back with the guilt already?"

"A little, I guess." He looked up at her. "I realized you were right about something, though."

"Not surprising. Glad you realized it."

"You don't even know what I'm talking about."

"Doesn't matter."

He laughed. "Well, all this time, I wanted to prove that I wasn't dangerous. That mages weren't dangerous. And you kept telling me that was stupid. You were right."

"Awesome. Glad you see that. Want to go make a fire tornado?" She started to struggle out of her bed.

He laughed again. "No! I don't want to go make a fire tornado, Isabelle. I mean, I was partly right, too. But I was too afraid of it, and I hated myself for it."

"Yeah, that was dumb. You should kiss me some more."

He smiled and gave up trying to explain what he'd learned in those moments fighting Ronan and Morthil. Morthil. The bargain. Oh crap. He'd made that deal when he thought Isabelle might be dead, when he'd thought nothing was as important as making a new Academy and averting a war between the mages and non-mages.

Now, suddenly, things didn't look so bleak anymore. Isabelle was alive. Nate was in charge of the army. Kel was here. And now Finn only had ten years.

Isabelle was looking at him, probably wondering what he was thinking again. Well, ten years was a long time. He'd figure something out. After all, this whole thing had seemed completely impossible when he'd first started, and now it had all worked out. Mostly.

He smiled and kissed Isabelle again, but she pulled back. "What were you thinking?"

He hesitated only a second before answering. "There was a stone with me. Did someone take it?"

Her brown eyes were suspicious. "Yeah. It's under your pillow."

"Why?"

"Nate said it seemed important for it to be near you."

Finn felt around under his pillow with his good hand, and felt a rough lump of metal. He pulled it out. There was the blue stone, now stuck in a messy blob of silver, the remains of the chain it had hung from. He slipped it into his pocket. Isabelle looked curious, and suspicious, so Finn explained. He told her everything about Morthil, including that he'd agreed to give him his body.

"Cool," Isabelle said. "Guess we'll have to kill him first."

CHAPTER 34

*B*ribing the guard was a simple matter. Arcturus did still have means, after all, and not all men were as honorable as the captain, thank goodness. He simply told the man where to find one of his many contingency stashes, and the man slipped him the key and took a short break.

There were soldiers all around, though. He was in the middle of the camp, and any second someone was going to notice him and wonder why he was no longer in his cage. But Arcturus knew how to slip below the attentions of the crowd; it was a rusty skill of his, from the period of his life he would prefer to forget, but useful.

He strode purposefully through the camp, as if he were meant to be there, as if he had business to attend to. Only a few people even glanced his way. Those that did looked confused, but then, assuming he'd been let out without their being told, just went back to what they were doing.

When Arcturus made it to his tent, he breathed a sigh of relief. Relief changed to confusion. His tent had been ransacked, and Reina was gone.

Had they simply moved her? He didn't think so, and Nate would never have let the men disrespect his things this way. No, this was a parting shot. From her. She was alive.

Joy and hope erupted back through him. He was going after her. He would find her, after which he didn't know what he would do. She still hated him, obviously, but that could be remedied. Yes, that could be remedied. First, though, he would kill the black-haired fire mage who had wronged her.

Arcturus realized he was grinning, and that a tear was running down his cheek. He wiped it away. What should he take with him? He found a sack and began filling it with supplies: a spare shirt, knives, one of the bottles of Reina's wine she had insisted on bringing along. He opened the crate where he kept his food, and stopped. His body grew cold and a sick fear gripped his stomach.

"No. Please no." Arcturus whispered. The thief had stolen most of his food, including the poisoned cheese.

There was only a small amount of dried meat and fruit at the bottom of the crate. He shoved this into his bag, cinched it tight, and ducked out of the tent.

He walked quickly this time; he couldn't focus, all he could think about was Reina. He had to get to her before she ate that cheese, and he didn't even know which way she had gone.

Another soldier tried to stop him as he left, but Arcturus pressed a few coins into the woman's hand, and she let him leave. He stole a horse, and, taking a guess, urged it into a smooth canter towards the mountains in the north.

ARCTURUS RODE FOR DAYS. He rode in great sweeping circles to the north, east and west of the camp. The ground became slightly hilly to the north, but it was at least clear of trees and he could see for miles in every direction. At night, he slept on the ground, taking better care of the horse than of himself. Before he passed out from exhaustion, he sat in the dark, squinting towards to horizon in all directions. Looking for the light of fire.

Finally, one night, he saw it.

The horse was brushed and clean already, and almost as tired as he was, but he saddled it back up, and swung his stiff, sore, body onto its back. He was starting to shake from cold, and could feel his body protesting. He let the horse walk slowly towards the light, which, to his joy, was in fact a campfire.

There was no one there, though.

He slid off the horse, stumbling, and limped into the fire-light. There was a blanket. His blanket. He took a deep, joyful breath, but before he could let it out, a knife was around his throat.

"Flavius."

Arcturus nearly cried from joy. Ignoring the knife, he turned around, finding himself pleasantly in her arms, her bright gold eyes and red hair only inches away from him.

"Are you all right?" he asked. He couldn't help himself; he placed a hand on the small of her back, the other lifted towards her cheek.

She lifted an eyebrow, and stepped back. "That's a new one."

"I don't understand."

"Usually when I knife someone they fight back."

Arcturus realized he didn't know what to say. He'd been galloping around the country for almost a week looking for her. He'd forgotten how she felt about him. To give himself time, he turned away, sat down next to her campfire and stared into it.

"Sure, by all means, just make yourself at home," Reina

said. "What are you doing here? You realize that without your men I'm just going to kill you, of course?"

Arcturus looked up at her. "Of course."

"So, why are you here?"

He couldn't tell her the real reason. Not yet. "I wish to continue our partnership. I have encountered... difficulties."

"You want my help?"

"I am not without considerable resources."

Reina considered this. "What do have in mind?"

"Revenge."

She moved to sit across the fire from him. He continued.

"But, first... there is the matter of... the slight matter... I don't suppose you have another vial of the antidote?"

She raised both eyebrows and picked at her teeth. "Why?"

"Well... I... I lost it."

"Careless of you."

"Yes, well."

"Eh, it was just water."

"Is there no antidote, then?"

"I never poisoned you." She threw a stick into the fire.

"What? What about my... my symptoms?"

"A person who eats as much cheese as you do... of course you'd have trouble. Not that I blame you. It's good cheese."

Arcturus went white. "Reina, you haven't eaten any of my cheese, have you?"

"Don't be so possessive. I stole it, it's mine."

"It's poisoned. I poisoned it. Don't eat it."

Her head snapped up, her eyes narrowed. "Don't go trying to play my own tricks on me, Arcty."

"I assure you, I am not. I poisoned it. I was planning to remove the captain. I wish I had done so. For many reasons, now."

"What did you poison it with?"

"An extraction of Amanita."

She leapt up, running her hands through her hair. She picked up a pack and started pushing things into it, then she dropped it and moved for the horse.

"I'm taking your horse," she snapped.

Arcturus felt sick. "If you've... there's no antidote... there's—"

Reina was muttering to herself as she climbed up into the saddle. "Flaxseed tea, or nettle... a strong purgative maybe... and a bloodletting."

"Ash? To absorb it?" Arcturus scraped a handful frantically out of the fire, ignoring the heat as it burned his fingers.

"It's too late for that, I ate it yesterday."

"All of it?" He asked, feeling faint with panic.

Something shifted in her face, and she slid out of the saddle. A silver knife appeared in her hand.

"You came to watch me die, didn't you?" She advanced on him.

"No, no, I—I came to save you."

"You came for the antidote you lost."

"No, Reina." Arcturus stumbled backwards, the ash falling from his hands.

She sliced at him with the knife. It cut him across the chest, catching on the silver buttons, popping one off.

"Reina, please, I—I poured the antidote out."

She rolled her eyes and then sliced at him again. She grit her teeth and strained, and his shirt caught fire, but only a small patch of it. Arcturus patted it out, but was barely looking at it, his eyes were locked on Reina.

"So, you poured it out because you thought it was poison. Then you had second thoughts and came after me."

"No."

"What, then?"

He stumbled back over the fire, kicking the logs apart. Her blanket caught fire.

"I'm sorry. Please."

"What?"

She sliced at him again, cutting him deeply through the shoulder, he lifted his hand to deflect it, and the knife scored deeply through his palm. He looked at it in horror, and she took the opportunity to drive the knife into his chest. He gasped and stumbled backwards again, tripping and falling to the ground. Blood was soaking through his shirt, and he thought he could hear air bubbling up through the hole. He coughed, and choked on blood.

She stood over him as he gasped and clutched at his chest.

He looked desperately up at her. "I... I thought you had died."

"What?"

"I poured it out," he coughed and gasped. "because I thought you had died. I... I love you." He had to look away, found he could barely breathe.

Her long fingers were gripped tightly around the knife's handle. She knelt, and looked at him.

"I'm... sorry... Reina..."

He reached up and tucked a piece of hair back behind her scarred ear. She pulled back, still clutching the knife.

"I wanted... to give you your revenge... on me." He gave a wheezy, hopeless chuckle. "I guess I have." His face was going white.

It wasn't long before Arcturus was beyond talking. Reina sat quietly next to him until at last his breathing stilled. Then she unsaddled the horse, put the fire back together, sat down next to it, and waited for the poison to take her.

CHAPTER 35

*A*s soon as Finn had recovered enough strength, he went to see Nate. He had planned on thanking him, and saying goodbye, but when he entered the captain's tent, he found Nate looking pale and serious.

"The mages have taken Westwend," he said. "The mayor is dead, as are the last of the guards that were stationed there."

Finn stopped.

"I'm sorry, Nate."

Nate looked up. "What's the situation here? Didn't look like the rest of the mages were too friendly with you anymore."

"Oh, nope. Last I heard, they hate me. But, I think they'll come around."

Nate raised an eyebrow.

"That's what I was coming to see you about. I appreciate the hospitality, but I need to go."

"And Westwend? I don't have enough men to take it back. Not without losing most of them and destroying the city in the process."

"Leave that to me, Nate. I'll figure something out." Optimism was great. Apparently, it worked, too. "At the very least you can stay here."

"Right."

Finn smiled. "Yeah, I know, I know." Then Finn grew serious for a moment. "Thank you, Nate. I mean it. Without you…"

"Just keep up your side of the bargain. Don't make me look like the naïve idiot some people think I am."

"Well, you're definitely naïve."

"Yeah, yeah. Go tell a bunch of older and wiser mages that they have to do what you say now."

Finn grinned and ducked out of the tent.

ISABELLE HAD INSISTED on going back to the Table with Finn, but every time she moved more than a foot or two her wounds reopened and she started to bleed profusely. She tried to convince Finn that this wasn't as big of a deal as it looked, but he secretly asked the nurse to give her some double-strength, sleep-inducing tea and slipped out of the room once she'd fallen asleep. He'd be back before she woke up. Hopefully.

The main gate was locked again, but he melted it into a puddle. Then he sucked the heat out of it and walked across the threshold.

He took a circuitous route up through the Table. Now that there wasn't the imminent threat of death he took some time to appreciate where he was, the glory of the ancient magic and architecture. This reminded him more of Ronan, though. They should have explored this together.

Eventually, he found the mages in the dining room again, thoroughly barricaded and arguing loudly.

"That's why we should just go back to Westwend!"

"You're an idiot! You want to go back there?!"

"And, what, you want to stay here? Who knows what else is here!"

Finn knocked loudly on the wall of furniture that blocked the door.

"Hello?" Finn called out.

The mages went silent. At last, someone approached. It was Rafe.

"You're back, eh?" Finn could swear he saw a twinkle in Rafe's eye. "You just don't give up, do you?"

"Nope!" Finn smiled. "Sorry I lied before. You were right. But, now, I actually do have stuff to offer."

"Oh?"

Finn explained about Morthil, the books, and the shadow stone.

"That explains the extra powers," Rafe said drily.

Someone leaned over Rafe's shoulder. "Hi, Finn!" It was Noe.

Finn smiled at him. "Hey, Noe."

Then he turned back to Rafe. "Can I come in?"

Rafe stared at him for a while, considering. Then he pulled a few chairs and a table out of the way.

Finn strode into the room, and the mages backed up a few steps. Their eyes flicked uncertainly between him and Rafe. Rafe stuck his hands in his pockets and waited, watching Finn.

"So, first off, I'm sorry I lied to you about there already being a school set up. I promise I won't ever lie to you again."

Some of the mages rolled their eyes. The more mature just crossed their arms.

"Anyone who wants to go, can. But. You should know that I have books. All the old books on magic from the old Academy. I'll be using them to start up a new school here. Eraldir —" he choked up for a moment, but struggled through.

"Eraldir is dead. So, all we have are the books and what I learned from him before he died. Which isn't much."

"Did you kill him, too?"

"What? Eraldir? No. Of course not."

"You killed Ronan."

"Yes."

"You going to kill us, too, if we don't agree with you?"

"No. I'll kill you if it's the only thing I can do to keep you killing a whole bunch of other people."

"What happened to the whole 'we're not going to hurt anyone' thing?"

"I was wrong. Partly." He paused for this to sink in, meeting the eyes of each mage until they looked away. "As for non-mages, we will be kind to them even if they are not kind to us. If you can't accept that, leave now."

There was a shuffling of feet, and people looked at each other. They whispered among themselves, and looked at Rafe, trying to figure out what he was thinking.

"How'd you defeat... Morthil?" Noe asked.

"I bargained with him."

"What'd you offer him in return?"

"That's my business."

They looked uneasy. Finn just waited.

"What if we just kill you and take the books?" This sounded more like a philosophical question than a threat.

Finn shrugged. "You can try."

One of the naturalist mages looked at Rafe. "What do you think?"

Rafe cracked his knuckles. "I think his heart's in the right place."

"I'll stay," Noe said. Finn smiled at him.

"I guess I will, too," said one of the water mages.

After that, everyone decided to stay. And just like that,

Finn was the leader of the first school of magic the old empire of Caledonia had seen in almost a hundred years.

LATER THAT DAY, Finn approached Rafe and Noe, and asked them if they would accompany Nate back to Westwend to negotiate with the remains of Reina's army. They agreed, and Finn took them down to introduce them to Nate.

Isabelle had awoken by then and was furious with Finn for leaving without her. She levitated herself out of her bed and floated along behind him, repeating everything he said and dripping blood all over the camp until he gave up trying to accomplish anything and apologized loudly and profusely in front of the whole camp. When that didn't work he lit her shirt on fire. She laughed, extinguished it with the blanket she was carrying, and went back to bed.

WHEN ISABELLE WAS WELL ENOUGH, they moved her up into one of the rooms at the Table. She still could barely walk, but she insisted on levitating herself the whole way, rather than being carried. Finn was just barely able to convince her not to blast her way up. Then Nate and his army, carrying their dead to be buried in Westwend's cemeteries, set off with Rafe and Noe for the long journey home.

CHAPTER 36

he dreams had stopped, and now there was only darkness. Darkness in front of her eyes, darkness behind her eyes. Grief filled the spaces where the dreams had been, where the whispers had been. For two days, she had lain in darkness.

But then she began to wonder.

She wondered what was outside the walls.

And then she realized she could go there, now. Morthil was gone, and her mind was an echoing, empty place now.

On the third day, she found her way up through the tunnels, to the large main tunnel. She'd crossed it a few times, never paid it much attention. But now she walked straight down its wide halls, to the melted-out door. It hadn't been melted the last time she'd seen it.

The light was blinding as she stepped across the hard puddle of iron. She lifted her pale arm to shield her eyes from the sun. Above her was a cloudy grey sky, so much wider than she'd ever seen it before. The emptiness and height took her breath away.

She'd never looked past the walls of the fortress before.

Hadn't even wondered what was out there. But now she stood, barefoot in the dirt, her arms dropped to her sides, her fingers tingling with excitement. The plains stretched for miles and miles, too far to be comprehended, meeting with the sky in a flat line that swam close and then far away. She blinked. Then she smiled a wide smile. She was going to find a tree. Slowly, she began to walk. Then, she began to run.

CHAPTER 37

"Ein!" Rafe called across the moat. "I know you're there! I know Reina put you in charge!"

"Traitor!" A sharp, high voice shot back.

"Come listen to what I have to say!"

"Why don't you get your new army to make us?" She taunted.

Rafe sighed. He looked at Nate. "I'm no good at this negotiating thing."

"You're doing fine. Better than I would, anyway."

"Only because I'm a mage."

"Yeah, well, still." Nate thought a moment. "Tell her Reina's dead."

Rafe turned back to the wall. "Look, Reina's dead. Things have changed."

"If Reina's dead, then I'm in charge. And I say, if you want this city, take it!"

"We will if we have to. But we don't want to. We have a proposition for you!"

"Oh yeah?"

"Yeah!"

"Well, I'm not that kind of girl!"

Rafe groaned in annoyance. Some of the soldiers giggled, which wasn't something Rafe had ever heard soldiers do before.

"Look, how about just you and me talk somewhere?" Rafe called out.

"You, me, and your new friends?" She shouted back.

"No! Just you and me!"

"No deal. I'll talk to you. But we'll do it where both our armies can see. I'll lower the bridge, and you meet me out on it. On one condition."

"What?"

"I won't take the chance that you're armed. So, you come out naked."

Rafe rubbed his temples with his hand. The soldiers giggled harder. "Fine! Sure! Whatever you want."

"All right, deal!"

The drawbridge began to lower. Rafe turned to glower pointedly at the soldiers who were staring at him, until they turned around. Then he dropped his weapons, pulled off his clothes, and strode out onto the bridge. He had some very pronounced tan lines.

There was unconstrained laughter now from both sides of the bridge. Cin strode out, well-armed and completely clothed. She carried a crossbow in one hand and a dagger in the other.

Rafe eyed her. She eyed him back. "Not a good look for you," she said.

Rafe stretched his arms wide, and did a slow turn. The laughter turned into cheers.

When he completed his turn, he met Cin's eyes seriously.

"I'm sorry, Cin."

Her face hardened.

"You were right," Rafe said.

507

"I thought I was 'too young' for you," she countered bitterly.

"No. I'm too old for you." He gestured to himself. "As you can see."

She ignored this, looked him in the eye. "You left. Without even saying anything. Without even asking if I wanted to come with you."

His heart stopped. "Would you have come with me?"

She glared at him. "Of course I would have."

His heart started again, skipping several beats. "I'm sorry. I was wrong. I thought if I left you'd find someone else you'd be happier with."

"I'd definitely be happier with someone who didn't leave without telling me."

"Fair enough." The soldiers on either side of the bridge had gone quiet now, all straining to hear. Tension filled the air. "I'm sorry, Cin."

Her glare became fiercer. "Well, me too. I'm sorry I called you old. I didn't think you would leave. Idiot."

Rafe's face broke into a wide grin. "I promise I won't do that again."

"Good." A reluctant smile crept across her face, and her whole demeanor softened.

He wanted to lean forward, sweep her into his arms, and kiss her, but this was, after all, a diplomatic negotiation. He drew himself up a little taller.

"So, on to less important matters, then?" He asked, still grinning.

"Sure. You said Reina's dead?"

"Far as we know."

"Guess I'm in charge of a city, then."

"Yeah, about that… we're hoping you'll give it back."

"Why should I?"

"Because things have changed."

"How so?"

"Well, for starters, that other guy, the naïve one, Nate, is in charge now."

Her eyebrows lifted even higher. "How did that happen?"

"Long story. Anyway, he doesn't want a fight. He will, if it comes to that, and he has a good chance of winning because he's got Noe and me on his side."

Her face went cold and stony.

"But," he continued. "There's something better than West-wend for us, now."

"What? The exiled mage camps at Lake Iori?"

"No." He told her about the school. Tried to make it sound slightly more official and legitimate than it was, then caught himself. He understood why Finn had lied, now. It did sound pretty ridiculous. "So, we can fight, destroy everything here, probably kill most of us, or we can all go to the new Academy. Work on things."

She stared off into space for a while. "How do I know this isn't a trick?"

"Well, I would have brought the proof, but someone made me come out here naked."

She laughed. "All right. Tell Nate to pull his soldiers away —at least a mile—and we'll leave."

"Right away," Rafe said, taking a low bow, to groans and gales of laughter from the soldiers behind him.

Rafe turned and ambled slowly back to the other side, grinning.

NATE and the soldiers camped out that night a mile and a half from the city, giving Cin and her mage soldiers plenty of time to vacate it before coming back the next day. Rafe and

Noe said goodbye to Nate, wishing him well. He asked them to remind Finn of his promise.

The non-mages who were still alive in Westwend were terrified, and it took days before they would even come out of their homes. When they did, and found that it was safe, Nate led the process of rebuilding the town and burying the dead.

Nate was quickly elected mayor, and one of his first acts was presiding over the trial of Arcturus Flavius. Even though Arcturus had fled, Nate insisted on a trial.

Arcturus' many businesses were searched, and his secret room for torturing mages was found. Nate himself questioned Arcturus' mother, who insisted she knew nothing about any of what her son did.

"He was always a good-for-nothing," she spat.

The more Nate learned, the more revolted, but also pitying he felt. He hoped that, wherever Arcturus was, he was happier than he had been here. Nate knew that he was probably alone in that opinion.

CHAPTER 38

$\mathcal{K}$el perched on the battlements, watching the army break camp. She had healed as many of the mages and non-mages as she could, had spent the whole battle preventing as many deaths as possible. She readjusted her shoulders, her feathers ruffling in the breeze. Finn was down there somewhere, she knew. She'd watched him kill Ronan, and wondered how he felt about it.

She wasn't going to say goodbye.

She stretched her wings, and launched smoothly, her talons scraping the stone. Her power was effortless now, and she could flit through the minds of the animals around her without fear of losing herself. Faraern was gone, and Kel felt fully herself, in a way she never had before. The forest still called to her, but less insistently. It was just a place she wanted to be.

As she winged north over the empty plains, heading towards the mountains, and Smoke, she thought about how much she'd wanted a family, how much she'd wanted Finn to stay with her, and then Faraern. Finn had wanted to, even if he hadn't been very good at it. He'd sacrificed the rest of his life to save her. She wished he hadn't, and she hoped his plan —whatever it was—would work, but she wasn't convinced he even had a plan. Whatever it took, she would find some way to help him.

Faraern had been everything she'd wanted. He'd never left her side, he'd saved her, been totally devoted to her, but only because he needed her to survive, too. She wondered if that was how it always was. Between the two, she realized she'd choose Finn.

That evening, as the sky faded to greys and blues, Kel alighted in a stand of pine trees on a rocky outcrop. The wind hushed through their needles as Kel transformed back into her human form. Under the trees was a thick carpet of needles, protected from the wind by the granite around them. She sat, crossed her legs, and examined the stump of her wrist, stroking it softly.

The light faded from the sky, leaving a white line on the horizon to the west. The temperature dropped, but Kel didn't call any animals to keep her company; she wanted to be alone.

From her pocket she took a wisteria seed. Wincing, she pressed the seed into the new skin of the stump, and asked it to sprout. Little roots poked their way out, feeling their way into the tiny streams of blood running through her veins. They sipped the liquid from her, and a green shoot pressed its way out. Kel went slowly, taking her time, waiting for the pain to abate, letting the roots of her arm get comfortable with the roots of the plant. Then she sprouted another seed and another, until there were five in all, which she extended, sending out little branching tendrils to connect them to one another, until she had what looked like a hand, with four fingers and a thumb.

Kel squeezed it experimentally; it didn't behave like a

normal hand, but the vine fingers did twitch a little, and she thought that, with time and practice, she would be able to use it. Like Eraldir had told her, most things got better with practice.

Exhausted, she curled up on her side, cradling her new hand to her chest, and fell into a deep sleep.

The next morning, she went to find Smoke, and together they headed back to the King's Table.

FINN SAT ALONE in the old stone garden. The sky above him was a soft lavender fading to indigo. A single star had emerged. He looked up at it, wondering where his sister was; she'd been gone almost a week, now.

A shadow passed across the star.

Something large swooped down out of the sky. It was an owl, heavy and amber-eyed, with a sharp beak that it clicked at Finn as it landed. It had a ferret clenched gently in its talons. The beak shortened, the feathers pulled back and became skin and clothes, and the talons straightened and softened into bare feet. The ferret scurried up into a pocket of the blue dress.

Kel stood there, disheveled, twigs and leaves stuck in her messy brown hair. She smiled, and Finn's chest loosened.

"Hey, Finn."

"Hey, Kel." She crossed the space between them and wrapped her arms around him in a hug. She didn't say anything for a long time. Then she pulled away and sat next to him, resting her elbows on her knees.

"Where'd you go?" he asked.

She waved her hand absently. "Around. It's hard to describe."

Finn could imagine.

Finn looked at his sister; she looked different, and it wasn't just that she had recently been an owl. He couldn't quite put his finger on it, though. That's when he noticed she was missing a hand, although there was what looked like a topiary on her wrist instead.

"Kel, your hand!" He reached out for her wrist. She jerked it away too quickly, but held it up so he could see.

Finn spluttered. "What happened?"

"I had to cut it off."

"You what?"

"I cut it off with a knife."

The knife detail did not seem important. "But why?"

"I was trapped."

"And the only solution was to cut off your hand? You should have called me!"

She glanced at him, then looked away. "Sorry."

"No, don't be sorry, I just, I... I'm sorry."

She turned and met his eyes. "It's not your fault. I went there on purpose."

"I'm sorry, Kel. I dragged you on this whole thing. This is my fault. If I hadn't..." he still couldn't say it.

"You had to. And I found out what I was, too."

"You would have found out anyway, though. You'd probably have gone for a walk, picked some flowers, then suddenly realized you had magic powers and spent the rest of your life making more flower gardens. With both your hands. And both... yeah."

"Maybe."

They were quiet for a while.

"I'm sorry, Kel."

"It's okay, Finn."

"What are you going to do now?"

"Stay here with you, I think."

"Really?" Finn felt a smile spreading across his face.

She smiled. "Yeah. This place needs trees."

"That's great!" He paused. "Also, I hadn't figured out yet how we were going to get food without you."

"That's easy."

"For you."

She leaned against him and he put an arm around her shoulders.

"Oh, I'm immortal," Kel said.

"What?"

"Yeah." She told him about Faraern.

"So that's what you meant when you said Morthil was your brother. I thought that was weird. I'd totally forgotten about it, though."

"That's okay."

"So, you're basically a god. Half-god. No, half-Ael. The Ael aren't gods."

She rolled her eyes.

"Just because you're immortal doesn't mean I'm not still your older brother."

She smiled.

"That makes so much more sense..." Finn said thoughtfully. "I thought I'd traumatized you into being a mage."

"You didn't."

"I guess I just automatically assumed it was my fault."

Kel patted him on the knee.

"I need to stop doing that."

"Yeah."

She threaded her arm around his back.

A breeze played against their faces, and Finn shivered.

"Do you want to go inside?" Kel asked.

"You go ahead, I have one thing I need to do first."

After she'd gone, Finn found his way up to the ramparts at the easternmost end of the Table. There was a crumbling lookout tower here, and he climbed the worn stone steps to the top. The wind was stronger out of the protection of the walls, and Finn squinted against it as he looked out over the plains. He imagined the mages in years to come who would walk across that ground, heading here. Maybe they would be like him, scared and not in control of themselves. They might have killed, or run away from home, or been exiled.

Finn sat, wrapped his arms around his knees, and looked out across the darkness. Had he done the right thing by killing Ronan? He wished he hadn't, he wished he'd been able to convince Ronan to be careful, to forgive the non-mages. By killing him, he'd gone against everything he believed about not hurting or controlling other people. He supposed that meant he didn't really believe that anymore. He wanted to, though.

What he did feel was grief, and an aching empty space in his heart at the knowledge that his best friend was gone.

Closing his eyes and taking a deep, centering breath, he focused on the source of magic in his chest. It was a familiar place now, and he felt calm, completely in control, as he began to work.

The pillar of flame stretched up into the sky, higher and higher as Finn worked. It was like what he'd made for Eraldir, but more chaotic, a beacon of many-colored, dancing arcs of light and heat. The colors shifted, bathing the tower in reds and greens and blues. Finn lifted a hand and the pillar curved smoothly, widening in the middle. A crescent moon.

Finn guessed it would be visible all the way to the foothills of the Iron Mountains in the north, and as far as the Uplands in the south. Anyone traveling across the plains would see it every night once the sun went down, and it would guide their journey, whether they were a new mage heading to the Table to be trained, or a traveler crossing on their way to someplace else.

Finn's heart swelled with excitement, and again he wished Ronan were here to see this. Then, he turned and headed back down the stairs, down to find Kel, the mages, and Isabelle, and start the work of building the school, and of building peace.

ACKNOWLEDGMENTS

It takes a lot of time to read an entire early draft of a novel, and I am incredibly grateful to the people who were willing to read it and give me their feedback. Jenny Mapes, thank you so much for asking over and over when you could read it; you helped give me the courage to show it to people. Robb Effinger and Josie Naylor, you guys are awesome; thank you for the thoughts on characters and pacing, and for the encouragement, and for giving me permission to keep the manatee in. Jenny Ingersoll, thank you so much for the giant packet of handwritten notes, and the expert plot analysis, and for loving Kel. Piper, thank you for being so enthusiastic; you helped me think I could actually do this. Guy Srinivasan, expert GM, thank you for taking the time to make whole Google doc's worth of notes; they gave me a whole new perspective on reader experience, plot, and character. Jaimie Mancham-Case, thank you for your endless encouragement and your help with publishing.

Thank you to my parents for taking me on the many camping and hiking adventures that provided the soul of the book for me. The working title of this book was "Finn and Kel go Camping".

Also, thank you to Akiko Kinney, without whom I would understand a lot less, and might never have been able to write anything at all.

Special thanks to Claire St. Hilaire, who read draft after draft and helped me see all the places where the world building could be more detailed, the dialogue more realistic, and the prose smoother. She is an amazing writer and her books are available on Amazon.

I owe a truly enormous amount of gratitude to Nick Feldman, who read draft after draft of this book and talked me through the problems I was having with plot and characters. He is also an amazing writer and his books are also available on Amazon.

Lastly, thank you to my husband Sean McCarthy, for believing in me. And for the enormous amount of thoughtful, well-researched editing.

NOTE FROM THE AUTHOR

For more, visit www.SarahMcCarthy.ninja

New releases are always $0.99 for the first three days. If you would like a single email notification when a new book is published, you can sign up here.

If you have a moment, please write me a review on Amazon. I greatly appreciate honest reviews. Thanks!

Made in the USA
Las Vegas, NV
08 February 2021

17442870R00308